THE REDO

WINSLOW BROTHERS BOOK FOUR

max monroe

New York Times & USA Today Bestselling Author

Editing by Silently Correcting Your Grammar

Formatting by Champagne Book Design

Cover Design by Peter Alderweireld

Cover Photo by Wander Aguiar Photography

Cover Model: Andrew Biernat

AUTHOR'S NOTE

The Redo is a full-length romantic comedy stand-alone novel in the ***Winslow Brothers Collection***. This book is full of fun-loving laughs, but it's also got loads of heart and steam.

Fun fact: This is one of our longest books to date! As the final book in the Winslow Brothers Collection, it took a lot of words to say all the things we needed to say. But we feel strongly about each and every one of those words, and we can't wait for you to experience it.

Sit back, buckle up, and get ready for *The Redo* to take you on a ride worthy of Universal Studios.

Also, due to the hilarious and addictive nature of this book's content, the following things are *not* recommended: *reading in public places, reading in bed next to a light-sleeping spouse and/or pet and/or child, reading on a date, reading on your wedding day, reading during the birth of your child, reading while eating and/or drinking, reading at work, reading this book to your boss, and/or reading while operating heavy machinery. Also, if suffering from bladder incontinence due to age/pregnancy/childbirth/etc., we recommend wearing sanitary products and/or reading while sitting directly on a toilet.* It might seem like a long list of places not to read, but we assure you, if you do it in the right setting, it'll be worth it.

Happy Reading!

All our love,

Max & Monroe

DEDICATION

To July 17th—a date we've become so irrationally obsessed with, we made our release on a Sunday instead of a Saturday, just to use it: Thanks for being weird with us.

To Paper Mate felt pens: Thanks for bankrupting us with the lure of your pretty colors.

To blue-light glasses: Thanks for hiding the dark circles under our eyes while we were on this deadline.

To Remy, Flynn, Jude, and Ty: You guys are bastards. But we love you.

To our Readers: Thank you for reading.

INTRO

Remy

It's official. I'm not losing my mind; the fucker is already gone—hydrated, packed, and halfway across the universe on its journey to another dimension.

I stare up at a big neon sign. It blinks obnoxiously with the words "Fortune Teller," and it takes everything inside me to keep the pucker out of my asshole.

A year ago, I stood in this very spot, my three brothers dragging me here after we'd hit up a strip club and eaten Taco fucking Bell. Jude had said it was something fun to do as part of my big bachelor party bash, and I was just a blissfully happy, completely naïve bastard who had no idea his life was about to be flipped upside down. At twenty-nine years old and only a week away from getting married, I was ready to settle down and commit myself to Charlotte for the rest of my life.

I thought I had the world by the ass. Hell, I thought I'd won the game of life.

But I was wrong. I didn't know shit.

Apparently, though, she *knew.* She knew all of it.

Now, I'm thirty, and as is evidenced by the fact that I'm back here again, I'm still a dumb fuck.

I shake my head and look at the sign again, this time noting the small wooden plaque that sits below the neon letters and reads *Miss Cleo's Prophecies.*

Am I really doing this? Have I really been reduced to a man who seeks out a fortune-teller because she just so happened to predict the demise of his relationship?

At this stage in my pathetic existence, what do I have to lose?

You already lost the girl. Why not lose your sanity too?

On a sigh, I reach out and grip the door handle, swinging it open on a whoosh of air that blows across my face. The familiar smell of incense and stale dust assaults my nostrils.

Moody, dramatic lighting still makes it difficult to see all the knickknacks lining the walls, and those ancient-looking burgundy curtains are still here, tied back by gold-tinted ropes.

The place hasn't changed a lick.

I blink several times, urging my vision to adjust to the low light, but before it can, a female voice fills my ears from somewhere behind a closed curtain on the opposite end of the room.

"Remington Winslow. I knew you'd come back."

Instantly, I'm on edge. Creeped out. No way this woman should know my name without seeing my face and, beyond that, recognize me this quickly after a year of time has passed.

I look around the room, seeking out the security cameras that must be hidden somewhere with fucking facial recognition. The corners of the ceiling are empty, and I don't see any of those beady little boob cams anywhere either. *They must be outside the entrance door.*

Silent, I stand there, rooted to my spot in the center of the room and wait for the woman of the hour to show her face. I refuse to move deeper into her lair without locking her in my sights first. Of course, she takes her sweet-ass time, the lingering faux-loneliness of my wait putting me even more on edge until she finally appears.

The curl of her red-tipped finger is the first of her I see, followed quickly by the twinkle of her bright-green eyes as they meet mine. A hint of an annoying-as-fuck smile crests one corner of her mouth.

Yep, she's the same know-it-all, pain in the ass too. Her dark hair is pulled back beneath the same velvet hood, and her mysteriously youthful skin still doesn't match her age. If anything, she looks younger than she did a year ago.

I don't know whether it's plastic surgery or fortune-teller voodoo, but I know she's at least a decade older than she looks. I don't know how I know that, but I do, and that's probably her fault too.

She sits down in her chair that presides over a small table covered by a black silk cloth. A set of Tarot cards is stacked in the corner, but I get the sense they're just for show. Last time I was here, she didn't use them on my brothers or me. And the layer of dust that sits atop them whispers a tattle about their infrequent use.

"Please, sit down," she instructs and gestures with one hand toward the empty seat across from her. And for some shitfucked, insane reason, I *do*.

"It's good to see you. I had a feeling you'd come alone this time."

I shrug. Only a masochist would bring my brothers back to this place a second time.

"Today's events aren't a bachelor party."

The last thing I needed was my brothers thinking I've officially lost my mind. Lord knows I've been an insufferable hermit ever since Charlotte decided she didn't want to marry me...*on our fucking wedding day*.

A cloud passes over Cleo's eyes, dulling the brightness of their green momentarily. "I'm sorry about that, my dear. It truly broke my heart reading those events in you."

I shake my head and look down to the table. I don't need this crazy chick's pity.

"How are Jude, Ty, and Flynn?" she asks in my silence. Unstoppable sarcasm locks and loads itself on my tongue.

"Shouldn't you already know the answer to that?" I retort. "I mean, you are the all-seeing fortune-teller, right?"

"Still a skeptic, I see." She grins like the joke is entirely on me. "Still, you're here."

She's got you there, bro.

"Go on," she continues. "Ask me the burning questions that've been on your mind, my child."

My child. Give me a break.

"Who says I have burning questions?"

"Your presence…and your broken heart."

I don't know why those last three words feel like a punch to the gut, but they do—a steel-toed boot straight into my abdomen.

You'd think, a year after being left at the altar, time would've helped heal those wounds. I mean, that *is* the saying, right? Time heals everything? Well, I know from experience that saying is utter bullshit. Time hasn't done anything but make me more of a bastard.

"A man's strength isn't measured by his ability to hide his emotions," she says quietly. "It's measured by his ability to *face* his emotions."

I scoff at her motivational-poster words. "What are you trying to say, *Oh wise fortune-teller?*"

She's not put off by my attitude. Her face stays neutral, and her words keep flowing. "You don't have to put on a show for me, Remington. I'm not your mom or your brothers or your sister. I know it's in your nature to play the strong male role, and it stems from being the oldest and the years of having to pick up the pieces after your father left your family, but you don't have to pretend to be okay when you're not okay with me."

My father? *Pfft.* He's inconsequential. A man who doesn't even deserve to be thought about. Frankly, a man who can leave his wife and five young kids doesn't deserve much of anything.

"I'm not pretending shit."

She quirks a brow, and I sigh, staring down at my hands that currently rest on the table.

Coming here was the worst idea you've ever had.

"I would disagree."

I look up and meet her eyes again. "Excuse me?"

"This visit can only be a bad idea if you leave before getting the answers to the questions that brought you here."

A chill runs up my spine, and all of a sudden, I'm afraid this woman can hear every single thought inside my head. Yes, that's crazy, but that doesn't mean it's not happening.

"Your thoughts are sacred, my dear. I only listen when I need to."

Like fuck. Right now, she's listening to every goddamn one.

The corner of her mouth hitches, and I know instantly that she's heard that one too. Obviously, for as long as I'm here, she's going to be eavesdropping on every single thought I have. *And even though you fucking hate it, you came here for a reason. So, get to asking before she hears something you really don't want her to, you bastard.*

"How?" I blurt out. "How did you know?"

"How did I know that you weren't going to get married?"

"Yeah, Cleo. That would be the big question that brought me here." I snort in annoyance. I mean, fuck, it's pretty obvious that's the biggest question rolling through my mind. How did a random fortune-teller know I wasn't going to get married before I did?

"Because fate whispers her plans into the universe, and my ears are always listening."

I want to roll my eyes at her kooky explanation.

"I know the devastation is still there," she adds. "And I know you're still trying to understand why. But one day, you'll realize that marriage wasn't meant to be. The universe has other plans for you."

All I can do is stare at her. *Is she saying I'm going to be alone forever?*

I always thought I'd be the kind of man who would settle down with someone, the kind of man who would plant roots and have a family. Not some never-to-be-married, lone-wolf, fifty-year-old sleazy bachelor.

"No, darling. *That* marriage wasn't meant to be. The rest of your fortune is much brighter," she states, and I search her eyes.

"What do you mean, *the rest*?"

"I mean, my dear Remington, I had more to tell you before you left. Though, Flynn did stay back to hear it."

"He did?" I question, outright shocked by that revelation. "He hasn't said a word about that shit to me. And it's been a year, so I'm pretty sure he's had an opportunity."

"While I do agree that family shouldn't keep things from one another, I think in these circumstances, it makes sense that he hasn't told you."

I raise one eyebrow at her. "And why would that make sense? It's about me, I should fucking know."

"Oh, darling, you've been too closed off. Too angry." She raises a hand and gestures toward me. Even now, I'm practically vibrating.

I wish I could say she's wrong, but for the past year, I've been a real unbearable asshole. But her being right, of course, only pisses me off more.

"Okay, fine. I'll bite, Miss Cleo. What's the rest of my *supposed* fortune?" I ask, disbelief and sarcasm still dripping from every word. "Am I going to move off-grid? Become some kind of loner from society? Or are you going to tell me I'm months away from winning the lottery and everything will start coming up roses?"

Cleo doesn't balk at my words or my tone. For some reason, she seems immune to both, reaching out to take my hand and smiling softly when I pull it away. "Yes, you have experienced the great heartbreak I predicted, but there will be a chance for happiness for you. A redo, so to speak. But only if you learn to open your heart."

"You're serious?" A wolflike laugh jumps from my throat. "*That's* the rest of my *oh so great* fortune? I'm just supposed to open my heart and all will be well?"

After Charlotte leaving me on our actual wedding day, when all our friends and family were there, waiting to watch us say "I do," opening my heart to anyone sounds like the worst fucking idea in existence.

She nods with a patronizing tilt of her head. "It's understandable that you're not ready now, but one day, someone will walk back into your life, and it will have the power to change everything. Only you will be able to determine if it's worth it to open yourself up again."

"Someone, who?"

"Someone whom you still hold close in your heart."

I narrow my eyes. "For a woman who can apparently read my mind and predict my goddamn future, you sure like to say a lot of vague shit."

"Oh, my child," she says with a knowing smile. The kind of smile that makes goose bumps roll up my arms. "I can't tell all of fate's secrets. Otherwise, I risk altering your true path."

I stare down at my forearms and hands, my skin still prickling with visible uncertainty. All this effort, all this time spent here listening to her bullshit, and I'm supposed to figure it out on my own? Just wait for opportunity to come a-knockin' on my evil ogre door?

What a waste.

"So…that's it, then? That's all you're going to tell me?"

"It's all I can say, Remington," she comments and surprises me by attempting yet again to place a gentle hand over mine. "You just need time. Lots of time. But it will be okay. That, I can tell you with certitude."

I glance down at her bright-red, inch-long nails on top of my olive skin and wonder how I've been reduced to a man who is taking advice from a fucking psychic in a velvet robe.

Probably because said fortune-teller was right about Charlotte.

Even thinking her name stings like a bitch. When I care about someone, when I love someone, I'm an all-in kind of guy. I don't hold back. I don't play games. And I certainly don't mince words or feelings.

I gave my everything to that relationship—bet everything on it going all the way. And all I got was a knife to the back.

Is that the way it went, dude? Or was it your ultimatum that forced the knife into her hand?

I shake off the unwelcome introspection. Those kinds of thoughts can fuck right off.

I let out a deep exhale. "I have to ask you one more thing."

"Of course."

"How is…Charlotte?" I start out bitter and cynical, but I don't miss that my voice is practically a whisper by the end of my question. Neither does Cleo, unfortunately.

Charlotte might be the woman who tore my heart out of my chest, but anger and spite don't erase their emotional counterparts. This is the woman I was in love with—the woman I planned to marry; I want her to be okay. And since I've had no contact with her since the wedding-that-didn't-happen, I have no idea if she is.

"I'm not sure if I've ever met a man with a bigger heart than yours, Remington. Always taking care of other people. Always putting other people's needs before your own. It's a noble quality. One I hope you don't let disappear because of the hardships life throws your way."

Miss Cleo's smile is soft and compassionate, and I loathe it with every fiber of my being. As a kid, right after my father left, I saw that smile often. From friends, acquaintances, teachers. I never ever wanted to be the grown man on this side of a smile like that. I should know by now, though, some plans just don't work out. *Some really fucking don't,* my mind adds bitterly.

"And Charlotte is doing okay. She's finding her way."

Although I have no idea if this woman can *really* know how Charlotte is doing, my chest still eases with relief from her words.

"So…she's safe? In California?"

That's where she got the job offer that altered our entire course. She wanted us to go, and I didn't want to move to the West Coast when my entire family was on the East. She couldn't understand where I was coming from and, ultimately, chose the job over me.

Because you made *her* choose. I shake my head to clear it again. *Whose fucking side are you on?* I ask my brain before shutting it off completely.

Miss Cleo nods. "Very much so."

There's a part of me that wants to ask more questions about Charlotte. That wants to dig deeper and try to figure out what she's feeling and thinking and if she's as miserable as me, but I know that's not going to help anything.

I have to focus on my future now—my version of it. Not Cleo's love-drunk, hippie-dippie, second-chance shit. Truthfully, who even knows if this woman really has psychic abilities. I mean, sure, she got my whole left-at-the-altar situation right, but that was *one* thing. She also said all three of my brothers were going to find love, and I've yet to see a single one of them settle down. Quite the opposite, in fact. Jude appears to be on a mission to fuck every woman in New York.

I need to focus on me and my work and my clients and building my business. The biggest favor I could do for myself at this point is to get piss-in-a-golden-toilet rich and drown my sorrows in big-ass piles of money.

"Are you still taking on investment clients?" Cleo asks suddenly, breaking me out of my thoughts and, frankly, sending my balls a little farther into my body.

I meet her eyes with a furrowed brow. "Excuse me?"

Damn. Maybe she really can hear everything I'm thinking.

"Investment clients, my dear," she repeats with a wink. "I have some money I'd like to invest, and I think you're just the man to do it for me."

"But you're a fucking fortune-teller," I blurt out on a shocked laugh. "I appreciate the confidence in my skill, but wouldn't yours be more of a sure thing?"

"Oh, Remington, my moral compass doesn't allow me to predict things revolving around money, and I would like to stop renting and purchase my own building while there's value in it."

"Why?"

"Why what?"

"Why won't your moral compass let you fuck with money? It sure as hell doesn't stop you from screwing around with other shit."

"Haven't you heard, my dear? Money is the root of all evil, and I only like to utilize my abilities for good."

"Like telling me I was going to be left at the altar a week before my wedding?" I snap back. "That felt like a good thing to you?"

"I don't *make* things happen, sweet Remington. I only convey the message. And fate isn't done with you yet, I promise."

I sigh, and she jumps from her seat excitedly. "I'll get you a check."

Pretty sure this will be the first time in my investment and day-trading career that I'll be investing a *psychic's* money. Hell, this might be the first time in the history of the stock market something like this has occurred. I have a hard time believing Warren Buffett takes on kooky, Tarot-card-reading clients under his hedge fund.

I pause and run a hand through my dark hair. "Fine. But if you're going to be vague, so am I. When it comes to your investments, you'll just have to watch and wait for the results."

"Oh, Remington, my dear." Cleo just smiles that stupid, all-knowing smile of hers. "I look forward to the friendship that will blossom between us."

Friendship? I'm sorry…*what?*

I can't exactly picture grabbing a beer with this woman on the weekends, let alone sitting around and gabbing while she makes scrambled eggs out of my brain.

"I'll get the check," she says again before my mind can quiet enough to come up with a coherent response, and she heads toward her secret back room. "And consider today's reading on the house."

And then, she's gone, through the dark curtains and out of sight, leaving me sitting there, a fully executed check on the table in front of me as if by magic, wondering, *what in the hell just happened, and why do I get the feeling it's not over?*

ONE

Fourteen Years Later...

Saturday, July 20th

Remy

I step through the exit doors of JFK airport, and sweat starts to dot my brow before I can even wave down a taxi.

Late July is notorious for being hot as fuck in New York, and the constant influx of traffic and tourists doesn't help the matter. We all might as well be ants under a magnifying glass while the neighborhood bully, Scumbucket Billy, tries to incinerate us.

With one sharp whistle from my lips and a wave of my right hand, I make eye contact with a cabbie with a beard, a backward cap, and a goatee that would've been the epitome of fashion in the early nineties.

He comes to a skidding stop at the curb, and I don't waste any time shuffling through the crowd of people and suitcases on the sidewalk and hopping inside the back seat. I toss my leather backpack, the only luggage I brought with me to LA, into the spot beside me.

"Where to?"

"Greenwich Village," I answer and then elucidate by giving him the address to my brother Ty's apartment building.

He nods, taps the meter on the dashboard, and hits the gas without a second thought. In true New York cabbie style, we're careening into the airport traffic in balls-to-the-wall, offensive-driver fashion. He swerves between cars, ignores the honks of other drivers, and I pull my phone out of my pocket to check for any missed notifications while I was on my flight back from the West Coast.

Most people would probably be too focused on whether they were about to get killed by a taxi driver, but when you've been a New Yorker your whole life, erratic driving doesn't make you blink an eye.

Besides texts from an anxious—and annoying—Ty, I find an unexpected message in my inbox.

C: *Love is in the air.*

I smirk to myself and type out a response.

Me: *And so is a 12% return on your investment this quarter. PS: You know the rules, Cleo. No love bullshit.*

That's right. I invest money for a fucking psychic. For fourteen years and counting, to be exact.

Frankly, I don't know what it is about the woman, but I've grown to find her strangely likable over the years. Like an eccentric, wacky aunt I can't get away from.

In my defense, though, from the very start, I set the ground rules of our weird pseudofriendship, or whatever you want to call it. It only revolved around one task—predictions about my love life are off the table. She might be batting a thousand so far with her prophecies for my brothers, but that doesn't mean I want to buy into all that nonsense. These days, occasional dates and one-night stands when I'm feeling froggy are about as close as I get to a relationship. It's easier that way. Less risk. Less complications. Less fucking nonsense. Exactly the way I prefer it.

My siblings, though? They've thrown caution to the love-filled wind. That's right, all three of my brothers *and* my baby sister are officially off the market.

First Winnie, second Jude, then Flynn, and now, Ty is the last bastard to bite the dust. I know this because I have a diamond ring in my backpack to prove it—the *engagement* ring he begged me to pick up while I was in LA meeting with a few clients.

C: *PS: You're my favorite Winslow brother.*

THE REDO | 13

Me: That's not a hard thing to achieve with brothers like mine.

Being the oldest of three boys and one girl, I've grown accustomed to being the most responsible out of our wild brood. Plus, all my brothers are assholes.

Well, besides Flynn.

But Jude and Ty? Definitely assholes. Lovable assholes, but assholes all the same.

C: One day, I'd like to see you all together again. It would make my day.

Me: Pretty sure you just saw Ty not that long ago. And Jude, too.

Those idiots ended up seeking out the mysterious Miss Cleo when they realized they'd fallen on their fucking asses in love, just like she predicted on the night of my bachelor party nearly a decade and a half ago.

Of course, they didn't tell me shit about it. Even after all these years, they still tiptoe around the subject that is the Remy and Charlotte wedding-that-never-happened like it's cracked glass.

In their minds, it's the period of time that is never to be talked about.

Sure, for the first couple years after Charlotte left me high and dry, I wanted it that way.

But now? It's become a secret, amusing pastime of mine to watch them skirt around their words whenever topics like love and marriage are brought up when I'm around.

If only they knew the truth—that I've been in contact with the infamous Miss Cleo for that same decade and a half. Shit, they'd lose their minds if they found out I've been handling her investments ever since I sought her out, one year after my failed wedding.

My phone pings with a new text, and while my cabbie runs a red light, I look down at the screen.

C: Be sure to give Ty my congratulations.

Hence her initial but cryptic love-is-in-the-air text. *I guess she was following the rules after all.*

And I can't not laugh at the idea of me following through with her insane request. Ty might be a fit, forty-year-old man, but if I even mentioned the name Miss Cleo to him, he'd be at risk for a damn stroke.

Me: Since I'd much rather attend my brother's wedding than his funeral, I'll keep that information to myself. And…can't you send it to him telepathically or some shit? I mean, you ARE the psychic.

C: Oh, Remington, you always do amuse me.

Once I'm about ten minutes away from Ty's building, I switch out of my text convo with Cleo and pull up the one with my anxious-as-hell brother.

At least twenty texts sit unanswered from him. All of them variations of "Where the fuck are you?"

Me: I'm on my way.

His response back is instant, like he's just sitting there with his phone in his hands.

Ty: You got the goods?

Me: No, Ty. I'm just coming over to have afternoon tea.

Ty: At least tell me this, you bastard, are said goods being carefully handled and protected during transport?

Me: Yes.

Ty: By yes, do you mean that you are guaranteeing that you are not going to lose, drop, or ruin the very expensive goods on your way here?

Me: For fuck's sake, Ty. Relax. I'll be there soon.

It's safe to say, I'll be glad when this engagement ring is out of my possession and the last Winslow brother who wants to get married says "I do."

Then I can finally put all this love shit in the rearview mirror.

TWO

Maria

I swallow thickly against a wave of nausea brought on by the combination of ninety-degree heat, six-inch heels, and a pregnant stomach the size of a Volkswagen Beetle, and finish typing out a text message to my assistant as I walk inside the building of my next showing.

Me: I need you to contact the mortgage broker for Mrs. Clemmons and see where they're at with the financing for the Greenwich Village property. I'm at the property now, and if the inside is just as good as the outside of the building, they're going to have to make an offer today if they really want it.

I assess my surroundings with scrutinizing eyes and, still, only see good things.

Doorman? Check.

Marble floors and modern updates in the spacious lobby? Check.

Yep. They'll definitely need to put in an offer if they want a chance. The New York real estate market is booming, and the buyers currently outnumber the sellers by a landslide.

When I reach the elevator, I hit the call button and tap the tip of my heel against the marble floor as I wait for it to arrive. A distraction in the form of a text message pulls my eyes away from watching the little screen above the elevator entry doors that showcases the cart's ascent and descent floor by floor.

Claudia: Ugh. Can't you do it? I hate contacting mortgage brokers.

My assistant is a real gem. And by gem, I mean the worst assistant on the face of the planet. She spends more time Instagramming and TikToking with her friend Leslie than NASA spends on rocket launches, I swear.

Pregnancy hormones make the urge to throw my phone across the lobby strong, but I go with a less violent reaction and type out another text with irritated, harsh fingers.

Me: Claudia, for the love of God, just contact the mortgage broker for me.

Claudia: Can I do it after I eat lunch?

I swear on everything, my assistant might be the reason I go into labor early. Or, you know, end up on that show *Snapped* because I've strangled her.

Me: CLAUDIA.

Claudia: Okay, fine. Fine. I'll call them now. I think pregnancy is making you moody.

First rule of life? Never tell a pregnant woman she's moody.

Second rule of life? Never hire Claudia.

You'd think the owner of The Baros Group, a successful, high-profile real estate firm in New York, would have a competent, hardworking assistant. Sadly, that is not the case. Two years ago, I hired Claudia at my sister's urging, and she's been a thorn in my side ever since.

A still-employed thorn-in-my-side, that is, because apparently, I'm a masochist.

Claudia: Where can I find the number for the mortgage broker?

Lord help me. Seriously. *Help. Me.*

As I start to type out a response, the elevator dings its arrival, and the doors whoosh audibly with their opening. My fingers run across the screen quickly, and I don't even bother looking up before stepping inside—and bumping right into another human.

He grunts as he catches my momentum by the tops of my arms, and I nearly jump into another dimension.

"Oh my gosh!" I cry, embarrassed by my rudeness. "I'm so sorry. I wasn't paying attention at all." Honestly, I'm still kind of not as I finish typing a message to my worthless assistant, but once I hit send, I tuck my phone into my purse, ready to give him my full attention.

Or, at least, as much as my mortification will allow.

I cringe and look up into crystalline-blue eyes then, just as a smile is curling onto the handsome stranger's face. But it only takes a millisecond for me to realize he isn't a stranger at all. Truth be told, he's as little a stranger as a man can be—my first real love and the man I gave my virginity to when I was sixteen years old. It seems like a lifetime ago and just yesterday all at once, but the memory of his gentle hands coaxing my nervous hips up to meet his is the kind of thing you don't forget. No matter how many years have gone by.

"Maria?" he asks, his smile deepening further, if you can believe it.

Me, though? I'm nearly speechless. Because I haven't seen my high school sweetheart Remington Winslow in two fucking decades.

And yes, trust me, if you got an eyeful of everything that Remy is now, you'd know it absolutely deserves the use of the f-word. Same strong jaw, same intense eyes, same full lips and dark hair—somehow, he looks as good as I remember. Maybe even better.

Goodness, he's aged well.

"Remy." His name passes over my tongue and has the power to bring back so many memories of the past.

"Holy shit," he says, his beaming smile still in place. "I can hardly believe it's you. Quick, run into me again so I can decide if you're real."

Nausea and annoying assistant all but forgotten, I smile so big it hurts. "I *also* can't believe it's you. After all this time. What are you doing here?"

His laugh is soft and gooey like caramel. "My brother lives in the building."

"Jude?" I ask, taking a shot in the dark with one of three names I know to be his brothers'. Jude and Ty were younger—cute little shits, though—and Flynn, who was the same age as me, always had a mysterious hotness about him. But for me, it was always Remy. The moon rose and the sun set and the stars aligned when I looked into his eyes. I was young, sure, but if Remy hadn't graduated and gone off to college before me, I'm pretty sure I would have found a way to keep him forever.

He chuckles with a shake of his head. "Ty, actually."

"Rats," I say with an overly dramatic snap of my fingers. "So close."

He chuckles again, his eyes falling to my rounded stomach and flaring. "So… wow…you're pregnant," he murmurs, the statement rocking me to my core. I know I am. I *know*. And yet, still, having Remington Winslow point it out to me in a random New York elevator feels like an out-of-body experience.

My hand travels to my belly button reflexively, and blind panic seizes at least eighty percent of my organs. For a minute, I almost forgot my reality—I *am* pregnant. Almost full-term and just a couple of weeks away from my official due date, in fact.

"Uh…well…"

His eyes meet mine, and it's the same look I've seen from other people who have noticed my current miracle-of-life state. Curiosity makes the blue of his eyes lighter, and his silent questions are most likely ones I have no idea how to answer out loud.

Holy mackerel, how do I even begin to explain this…*complicated* situation?

Oh, well, you see, Remy, I am pregnant, but the baby's not mine genetically. My sister was having a hard time getting pregnant, and I agreed to be her surrogate. Her gestational carrier, to be specific. It felt like a brilliant idea at the time, getting to help my sister's baby dreams come true, and then, once this little bambino was born, I'd get to play the role of fun aunt. And it was all going to plan…for about three months into this pregnancy. Isabella and Oliver were over-the-moon excited. Truthfully, we were all excited. Until, you know, six months ago when my sister and brother-in-law died in a helicopter crash. Now, I'm challenged with raising this baby alone without a fucking, fucking clue what I'm doing. And most days, I feel like I'm one breath away from a nervous breakdown.

Yeah. Great small talk.

"Yeah… Your eyes are not playing tricks on you. I am pregnant," I eventually say, choosing to keep the details of my situation out of the conversation, while trying hard to keep the sound of despair out of my voice. The intricacies of my pregnant state are a little too complex for pleasant chitchat.

The elevator lets out a high-pitched squeal, and that's when both of us realize we've been too busy staring at each other to push the buttons for our floors.

Remy grins. "What floor do you need?"

"Twenty-second."

He presses the button for me and then taps the one for the twenty-fourth floor too.

The cart jolts as it begins its ascent, and Remy's eyes glance down at my rounded belly again.

"Congratulations, by the way," he says with a tender smile that slices through my shield and grazes against the recesses of my pain.

"Thanks." I lick my lips and look to the ground to gather myself, but when the elevator jolts erratically, I'm knocked off-balance and right back into Remy's body.

And seconds later, everything turns to pitch-black darkness.

I scream a little—I can't help it—and he immediately squeezes the flesh of my arms to reassure me. "It's okay. I think we just lost power for a bit. Should come back on soon."

Claustrophobia isn't an affliction I struggle with on a regular basis, but something about being trapped in utter darkness with the guy I once thought was my soul mate while pregnant with my sister's baby and on the brink of throwing up is really triggering a flare-up. *Go figure.*

But the light never comes, and the continued darkness inside this far-too-small elevator cart urges a wave of nausea to grab ahold of my body like a vise.

I try to breathe deeply, but before I know what's happening, I'm heaving, and Remy is lowering me down to the floor and gently pushing my head between my legs. "It's okay, Maria. Just breathe," he coaches calmly, falling to his ass beside me and rubbing a reassuring hand up and down my back.

I nod, trying to put him at ease, but before I know it, I'm heaving again. *I swear, if I throw up in this elevator, just kill me now. Seriously, God. Just yeet me into the universe because I'll never make it back from that.*

My hair is lifted off my neck then, and a breeze of cool air blows across my damp, overheated skin. Remy shifts slightly beside me, and then I feel the air again, tickling over the tiny hairs at the back of my neck. It's not exactly the refreshing feel of air conditioning, but compared to the suffocating summer heat and darkness, it feels like an ice bath.

"Thank you," I murmur carefully, not wanting to tempt vomit fate by opening my mouth for too long.

"Of course," Remy whispers and leans closer to me once more to softly *blow across my neck.*

Holy hell in a handbasket, how didn't I realize that's where the cool air was coming from?

Panicked, I scoot away a little, but my rounded belly makes me have to reach back and squeeze his knee for stability. *Please, let that be his knee.*

Instantly, I remove my hand just as quickly as I put it there. "Uh…thank you so much, Remy, but I'm feeling better now." *I think.*

"Are you sure?" he asks with concern, and I spin around to put my back to the wall on the opposite side of the elevator and face him.

An emergency light flickers at the top of the car—a little delayed, but I'll take it—and I can just make out the crease between Remy's eyebrows. Confident he'll see it now, I nod. "I'm okay. Really."

"Good," he says with a small smile and pulls his phone out of his pocket. He taps the screen, and it comes to life, illuminating his handsome face. "Looks like I still have service. I'm going to call Ty."

Phone to his ear, he waits while the faint sounds of ringing come from the receiver.

"Fucking answer, you bastard," he mutters three rings deep, and I want to grin over the memories of the familiar banter that always occurred between him and his brothers.

And when he rolls his eyes heavenward, I can assume that Ty finally answered.

"What's up?" Remy asks into the receiver on a harsh laugh. "Well, I'm stuck in your building's fucking elevator."

He pauses and furrows his brow at whatever his brother says.

"And Lloyd would be…?"

Ten seconds later, he pulls the phone away from his ear and looks at the screen. "Did he really just hang up on me?" he grumbles on a sigh and meets my eyes.

"Everything okay?"

His responding laugh is softer this time. "Well, if you were wondering if Ty is still a pain in my ass, I can tell you with certainty that he is. Though, he is calling the maintenance guy."

"Okay. Okay. That's good, right? It's at least something?"

"Yeah." He grins at me as he shoves his phone back into the pocket of his jeans. "And…I guess that means we can use this time to catch up, huh?"

Time to catch up—time to explain—time to look at Remington Winslow and remember just how in love I was with him twenty years ago.

Oh boy. I'm not sure I'm prepared for that…

"But first, I guess I should see if this elevator's phone works," he says, standing to his feet. "Maybe I can get in touch with the fire department or something."

"That sounds like a really good plan," I answer, silently hopeful that it will take enough time to let me dodge the kind of conversation that would make it hard to avoid my truth.

The last thing I want to do is pull Remy into the complicated mess I call my life.

What the hell, New York? Couldn't you have chosen a better time to throw a summer blackout my way?

THREE

Remy

After speaking with Ty briefly to explain the situation, I'm not confident he's doing anything more than talking to the building maintenance man, and I'm even less assured that he's doing it in a hurry. In fact, he sounded *incredibly* preoccupied… In the way that tends to make all the blood leave a man's brain altogether. *Ahem.*

Luckily, the elevator emergency equipment is in good working order—not often the case in New York—and I've managed to get in touch with the fire department myself.

"It's another summer blackout," the dispatcher's voice bounces from the red emergency phone receiver held close to my ear. "Pretty sure the ninety-degree heat and everyone using their air conditioners like goddamn fiends is to blame. How many are in the elevator, sir?"

"There are two of us," I answer. "From what I can tell, I think we've stopped between the fourth and fifth floors."

I glance to Maria to see her shifting uncomfortably. I can't even imagine how hot she must be right now with as pregnant as she is.

"Are you both okay?"

"Yes. But the other passenger is pregnant, and it's starting to get pretty warm in here. We're going to need to get some water soon, at the very least."

Now, I'm regretting finishing off that bottle of water and granola bar I had stashed in my backpack on the plane. Maria certainly could've used it right now.

"Understood," the dispatcher responds, and the faint sounds of fingers over a keyboard fill my ears. "Just hold tight, and we'll get you out of there as quick as we can. Half of Manhattan is blacked out right now, though, so prepare yourself to settle in for a bit."

Great. I'm not sure I should repeat that part out loud.

"Okay, thanks."

I hang up the phone and turn to an eager-for-good-news Maria. Her face nearly makes me laugh, it's so comedically desperate.

I try to break it to her gently. "The good news is, they know we're in here, and they're coming to help."

Her eyebrows immediately draw together with skepticism. "And the bad news?"

I shrug calmly. "This isn't the only building with elevators with similar issues."

"Ha-ha-ha," she laughs, a firm edge of hysteria creeping in as she spins to the corner of the elevator and tries to gather herself. "Did they…did they happen to mention where we are on the list?"

I wince. "I'm afraid not."

"Well, great. That's great."

"It's going to be fine, Maria. I promise. We have each other to shoot the shit with, and for my part, I'm pretty sure I could have ended up in an elevator with a lot worse choices."

She almost smiles at the compliment and then seems to remember the situation all over again.

"I'm supposed to meet a client upstairs in five minutes."

Ah, I see. *That's* why she's here, in Ty's apartment complex. For real estate purposes.

A while back, I'd heard through the grapevine that Maria and her sister Isabella had started a real estate firm. And it's possible that I've kind of kept an eye on The Baros Group's success over the years. It was no surprise to me that they've grown to be an incredibly prosperous firm in New York. Maria always was a go-getter.

"If they're in the building, they know the power is off," I attempt to reassure her. "I'm sure they'll understand."

"Uh, *no*." She scoffs. "Not this client. This client only understands that time is money."

I grin. "Do they actually use that phrase with you? Time is money?"

"Only once a day."

"How obnoxious."

"Oh, Remy. You have no idea. I work with some of the most insufferable people in the city. Mrs. Clemmons is just the tip of the iceberg."

"Patricia Clemmons?" I ask, my interest piqued.

"Yes…" Her eyes narrow in surprise. "How did you know?"

"I've done some investments for her and her husband. She called my assistant a half-wit for calling before nine a.m. one day."

"Oh my God, yes! *Ten to four, Maria*," she mocks in a voice that is spot-on Patricia. "*Anyone with class knows those are the only acceptable hours if you have any human decency.*"

"Oh man, I hope she buys a place in this building and makes Ty's life a living hell." I laugh, and Maria feigns a pout.

"Poor Ty."

"Nah. Poor Ty's doing just fine with his life. That's why I'm here, actually. I'm delivering the ring he's waiting on to propose."

"*What?* Ty Winslow is proposing?" she squeals excitedly. "As in, he's going to get married?"

"Yep." I nod slowly. "Hard to believe, but he found someone who can tolerate his ass. I'm sure he's hysterical right now, waiting for me."

"That's crazy. Almost unbelievable," she responds with a shake of her head. "Oh hey, did you happen to park in the garage?"

The abrupt change in conversation makes me furrow my brow. Of all the things to ask me about, she's wondering about the garage of this random building?

"Uh…no, but I had the cab driver drop me off there because traffic by the main entrance was crazy. I'd only gone up one floor in this elevator when you got on at street level."

"How are the spaces? Big or compact only?"

"Wait…" I feel my mouth curve slightly as I look at her with a tilt of my head. "Are you…using me for realty questions right now?"

"Mrs. Clemmons!" she snaps, as though that's the only explanation I need. And truth be told, it is. That woman is basically a caricature of a human.

"*Maria*," I say her name with feigned disappointment. "I'm wounded."

"You're not wounded." She scoffs. "You're perfect."

Her cheeks turn bright red immediately, and her head bows toward the floor as everything inside me lights up. *Maria freaking Baros.* I cannot believe I've gone this many years without thinking about how amazingly earnest she always was—especially when she didn't want to be. Her nerves always made the words just fall right out of her mouth. *Fuck. I always loved that about her.*

The urge to ease her embarrassment is too strong to deny. "Oh boy, perfect? Me?" I laugh and flash a wink in her direction. "Can I get you to sign a sworn affidavit to present to my family, stating your exact words?"

Awkwardness gone, she meets my eyes with a grin and quips back, "Oh, Rem, you and I both know your family wouldn't accept that affidavit. If Jude and Ty are still the same as they used to be, they love busting your balls way too much." She quirks an amused brow. "But surely your wife wouldn't need an affidavit to know how amazing you are."

Her statement makes me realize just how long it's been since we've spoken. "If I had a wife, I'd hope that would be the case."

"Wait…what do you mean?" she questions and searches my eyes. "You and Charlotte got divorced?"

Well, fuck. After this long, it's hard to believe that anyone doesn't know what happened that day.

"Actually, Charlotte and I never got married."

"But the last time we talked…you were, like, a week away from your wedding…"

"Yep. She left me at the altar."

Her eyes go wide in shock. "You're kidding me!"

"No, babe. I can assure you I'm not," I remark with a laugh.

"Goodness, I'm so sorry, Remy. That's horrible."

"It's fine," I tell her and truly mean it. "It just wasn't meant to be, you know? I'm at peace with that." I shrug. "Plus, it was like a million years ago."

"Oh God, don't say that," she responds on a snort. "You're making me feel old. Surely it was just last year that we spoke."

In reality, it was about fifteen years ago that Maria reached out to me unexpectedly via text message. The exchange was sweet and friendly and made me remember how much I'd always still care about her. But it was nothing more than that. Seeing her now makes me wonder how…how I ever thought it was a good idea to walk away from her, honestly.

"Sorry to break the news to you, but it was a long-ass time ago when you sent me that text message. Hell, I don't even have the same number anymore."

"Gah. Me either." She groans. "Are we really in our forties now?"

I nod. "We really are. Though, I'm the only one of us who looks it."

"You're right," she says with a playful roll of her eyes. "You're practically an old man compared to me."

"Older by only two years," I state and point one teasing index finger toward her. "And careful, Ri, or else you're going to start sounding like my family."

She giggles. "Are they still as rambunctious as they used to be?"

"No." I shake my head on a laugh. "I can assure you they are much, much worse."

She snorts, and the sound is so sweet, I find myself spouting some more Winslow family updates.

"Flynn has a wife and twins. Jude is married, and Ty, as I mentioned, is on his way over the cliff. And Winnie—well, as I'm sure you remember—is the only sane one out of all of us. She's married to Wes Lancaster and has a brilliant daughter, Lexi, who keeps us all in check."

"Wes Lancaster? As in, the billionaire owner of the New York Mavericks?"

"The one and only." I nod, and Maria's face turns soft with nostalgia.

"I always loved watching you play football."

I laugh at the irony. Eighty percent of the reason I even played was getting to look over at Maria cheering for me.

"Winnie hated it," she adds with a knowing grin. "Only two reasons she was there were you and the snacks."

"I know," I agree, thinking fondly of all the times my baby sister was sitting in the bleachers, cheering me on at my games with a bored expression on her face. "She eats, sleeps, and breathes it now. Her position as team physician is how she met Wes, the man who is so smitten with my sister he honestly thinks he got the better end of the deal. Which he did, of course. Not many people better than Winnie," I answer with a doting smile. Winnie might be a grown woman now, but she'll always be my baby sister to me.

"Holy shit. Winnie is a successful doctor and scored an actual billionaire. I should've known that little, adorable, talkative social butterfly would go on to do big things."

It's hard to believe, but Winnie was only six years old when Maria and I first met in high school.

"She always was a chatty little thing, wasn't she?"

"And determined." Maria grins. "She had a way of getting exactly what she wanted."

Truth be told, that six-year-old chatterbox was a big reason Maria and I met in the first place.

"Speaking of sisters, how is Isabella? And your mom?"

Back in the day, both Carmen and Isabella were like family to me. I spent a lot of time with both of them. Isabella was only a few years older than my sister, and Maria and I would often let them tag along when we'd go to the movies or to Central Park.

"Well…uh…" She pauses and digs her teeth into her bottom lip. "My mom has been gone for a long time now. She died of a brain aneurysm when I was thirty."

The unexpected news pulls at my heartstrings. And it makes me sad that I had no idea. That I didn't get to attend her funeral or offer any kind of support to Maria.

I can't imagine losing my mother now, much less when I was thirty. Wendy Winslow is the pillar of our family. She's everything to me.

"Damn, Maria. I'm so sorry. I always loved your mom."

"Me too." Her smile is sad, and her face softens in a way that seems overly irreverent. In a way that makes me a little nervous, to be honest.

"Are you okay?" I ask, hoping I haven't somehow said something to upset her. "Are you feeling sick again?"

"No…" She shakes her head once…twice…and then sighs heavily as it falls back to the wall of the elevator with a thud. "My, uh…my sister…Isabella… she passed away too."

"What?" I question because there's no way that could be the truth. Isabella was always a vibrant, sweet, and kind girl. I adored her. And to wrap my mind around the fact that she's no longer here…it feels impossible. "H-how?"

"A little over six months ago," she explains, and her bottom lip quivers with emotion. "She and her husband both, actually. A tragic helicopter crash when they were on their way to the Hamptons for a vacation."

Both her mom and her sister? Fuck.

"Oh my God, Maria… I'm so sorr—"

"No." She clucks her tongue. "Please. I appreciate the sentiment, but one sorry is enough." She swipes one lone tear from her cheek. It makes my chest feel like it's cracked in half. "I swear, I'm not going to get all emotional on you. It's just…the way you talked about your sister and Wes. It just made me miss them—miss the way they were together. But I promise, I'm okay."

Maria's relationship with Isabella always reminded me a lot of Winnie and me. I honestly don't know how I'd cope with something like that.

"I don't know what to say, Ri. I wish there was something to say."

She laughs then, and it's startling. It's so out of sync with the conversation we're having, and once again, it puts me on edge for some reason.

"I don't think even God himself would know what to say here, Rem. This… situation is far more complicated than just me losing my baby sister and my brother-in-law."

I quirk a brow. "What do you mean?"

"Well…" She pauses, rubs a hand over her rounded belly, and her lungs let out a deep, emotional sigh. "This baby right here isn't my biological child. It's theirs. Isabella's and Oliver's. My sister and her husband."

"No." It's the only thing I can say, and I know it's not right. But I'll be damned if I can come up with anything else.

She nods, a little self-deprecating laugh mixing with a couple more unchecked tears. "She needed a surrogate and my uterus wasn't doing anything."

I know she doesn't want to hear one particular five-letter word again, but it's the only thing I feel like I can say right now.

"God, Maria. I'm so sorry."

She shrugs and rubs at her belly unconsciously. "I just wish I knew what the hell I'm doing. My life has revolved around my career for the past two decades, and now, I'm supposed to figure out how to be a good mom?" She shakes her head. "I never had time to be in a relationship with someone, and now, I'm supposed to know how to take care of another human being?

I mean, I didn't think I'd ever have kids of my own. I didn't… Well, I guess I didn't think a lot of things."

My mind wants to fixate on the reality that she's doing all of this alone. Without a significant other. Without her mom. Without *her sister*.

But I know that's the opposite of what she needs to focus on right now. She knows. God, she knows. The last thing she needs is me droning on about it.

No. Instead, she needs encouragement.

"That's where you're going wrong," I tell her, and her face pinches in confusion.

"What's where I'm going wrong?"

"Trying to know what the hell you're doing ahead of time. It's impossible. I've never met a parent who's said things turned out like they expected. It's always overwhelming. It's always a shitshow."

"But—"

"No." I shake my head and lean forward to squeeze her knee. "It's the truth, Maria. Kids are good at one thing, and that's being all the things you don't expect."

She laughs, frightened. "Great."

"I'm just saying, you think you're behind, but you're not. You're right on target with where you're supposed to be. When the baby is born…that's when you'll start to figure it out."

"I hope so."

"I know so. It's statistically proven."

Maria rolls her eyes. "Man, you haven't changed at all. Spouting shit like you know what you're talking about."

I smile. "Sounding confident is the key."

"Well, thanks. I think. It's not like I have a way out, so I'm just…making the best of it."

"It's going to be great. My niece Lexi is one of the best things that's ever happened to me. In fact, she's about the only human I would miss a meal for."

Maria giggles, joking, "You're a big, strong boy. You need fuel in the form of food."

"Yes. That is verbatim what I tell myself when I go for the second brownie."

"Sorry, by the way," she says, and I tilt my head to the side in confusion.

"Sorry for what?"

"Tossing all my crazy baggage onto you. I'm sure that's the last thing you felt like hearing while being stuck in an elevator," she explains, and I have the urge to pull her into my arms and tell her everything will be okay.

But I don't. It's nearly a thousand million degrees in here, and I can only imagine how little she wants to be smothered. Instead, I go for verbal reassurance.

"I'm glad you told me," I say, and I mean every word to my core.

"Yeah, well, I'm sure you weren't expecting that kind of reality when you saw my pregnant belly."

"No," I answer honestly. "But that's life, Maria."

"Yeah. That's life." She repeats my words. "And life can be a real bitch sometimes, you know?"

"Oh, trust me, I know." A soft laugh escapes my lungs. And then I can't stop myself from trying to make her feel a little better at my expense. "You want to know something wild about my life?'

"Um…*yes*. Please." She nods with wide, urgent eyes.

"I still see Charlotte," I tell her with a conspiratorial whisper. "She's married to Nick Raines, Winnie's ex and the father of my niece, Lexi."

Even though I'm truly okay with the whole situation now, it isn't necessarily one I enjoy talking about. But for some reason, with Maria, it's easy. If anything, I want to tell her.

"Seriously?"

"My niece's father is married to my ex-fiancée who left me at the altar." I nod. "It's almost some Maury Povich type of shit."

"Man, we really are two peas in a crazy pod of life, huh?" she comments through a quiet laugh.

"Yeah, babe." I chuckle. "We really are."

Smiles and silence settle over us, and it's all I can do to stop myself from ogling Maria in the time gap. Her brown hair and brown eyes both glow, and her lips—always plush and perfect—seem even more so in the dim light of the broken elevator.

Fuck. She's still painfully beautiful.

I don't know what's coming over me, but if I'm not careful, I'm going to be the kind of creepy guy who gets a hard-on at an unbelievably inconvenient time.

She's carrying her dead sister's baby, for fuck's sake, Remy. Show a little respect.

My phone chimes with a message, and I pull it out of my pocket to check the screen. For once in my life, I'm thankful for a distraction from my brother.

Ty: Bad news, bro. Lloyd's a fuckwit and can't do anything. We're waiting on the fire department.

Talk about being a little late to the fucking party. This is exactly why I called the fire department myself.

Me: Were they able to give you an ETA? When I spoke to them, they didn't have any idea.

Ty: My guess is that it'll either be before the power comes back on or after.

Me: How is it possible that you're tenured? How?

Ty: Tenured in English, bro. Not fucking elevator engineering.

Me: Thanks. Really. This has been helpful.

I tuck my phone back into my pocket and watch as Maria lifts her head from her own. Her thumbs are moving at warp speed, even while she's not looking at the screen, and I can't help but smile.

"Okay, is it just me, or are you not looking at what you're typing right now?"

She shrugs. "When you text and call as many people as I do in the real estate business, you can pretty much do it in your sleep."

"And you have little thumbs."

Her face pinches and curls with humor at the same time. "Huh?"

I hold up my hands and flash them around a bit. "I've got these giant meat clubs. It's hard to make them work in such a tiny area."

She raises a teasing eyebrow, and I immediately groan. "On *phones*, Maria. They work just fine in other tiny areas."

Her cheeks pink slightly, and a vise grip clutches my stomach as she murmurs three little words. "Oh, I remember."

Holy shit.

While the impulse to take a walk down Memory Lane is strong, I know now isn't the time for me to relive all of my favorite fantasies that revolve around Maria.

Definitely not a good time for that, bro.

I clear my throat once, and when that doesn't work, I clear it again. "Well. What should we do with our time?"

She flashes a knowing grin and digs in her purse for only a moment before coming out with a deck of cards.

My responding smile is nearly overbearing.

Back in the day, Maria and I never went anywhere without a deck of cards. We made many a bet and played many a game with each other with just a deck of cards when we dated in high school.

"How about an old-fashioned game of War?" she questions with a wink. "If you'll recall, it's excellent for passing time, and I always find a way to beat your ass."

"I cannot believe you still have a deck with you."

"Believe it or not, Remington Winslow, time, though powerful, doesn't always change everything."

She's right about that. Because time—as I'm finding out—well, it's maintained all the best parts of Maria Baros.

An hour and a half later, I pull Maria to my body and listen as firefighters pry at the doors from the other side. It takes them a minute or so to get the pressure to release, but when the doors finally open, I exhale the huge breath I didn't even know I was holding.

Thank fuck.

Because of where the elevator rocked to a stop, there's a small step up to climb out. Immediately, I usher Maria forward first, gently spotting her from behind, my hands gripping her hips, as she climbs out with the help of the two firefighters in front of us.

And I only look at her perfectly rounded ass once the whole time, which I'm counting as a victory for now.

Once she's cleared the doors, I follow her lead and make a jump up the couple of feet to the floor outside and smile. Finally. We're free.

I'm not exactly claustrophobic, but I'm not exactly *not* that either. Let's just say I do better in open spaces. Thankfully, the pregnant woman—an obvious choice to worry about more than myself—served as an excellent distraction.

Once we're both standing outside the elevator cart, still surrounded by firefighters, Ty spots us immediately.

"Holy shit, Maria?" he questions, looking at the blast from the past with wide eyes.

Grabbing Rachel's hand, he drags her over the distance between us, practically shoving the firefighters out of the way. They're pretty big and burly, though, and they don't budge as easily as my cocky brother expected. Everyone but Ty smiles as he settles for politely working around them.

"You guys okay?" one of the firefighters asks, grinning from his unmoved spot. I clap him on the back gratefully. I know it's his job to rescue people, but with the size of this blackout, I'm sure he's been slaving away all day.

"Yeah, man. Thanks for saving our asses."

"Hi, Ty," Maria greets, every ounce of what she's been through the last couple hours disappearing and giving way to her familiar friendly demeanor.

Ty looks at me and smiles. "Talk about a small world, bro."

I grin. "Tell me about it."

"Rachel, this is Maria. Maria, this is my Rachel," Ty introduces the ladies. Maria and Rachel shake hands immediately.

"Nice to meet you."

"I'm an old friend of this guy right here," Maria explains and nudges my side playfully. "From way back in our high school days. Though, it's been quite a few years since we've seen each other."

"Wow," Rachel remarks, surprised. "And you just so happened to get stuck in an elevator together?"

Maria doesn't even try to suppress her burst of laughter. "Yeah. What are the odds, huh?"

"It's good to see you." Ty steps forward to give Maria a hug and then turns to face me directly. "So?" he asks, so obviously eager for me to hand over the ring it's hilarious. He's g-o-n-e gone for this girl.

I discreetly slip it out of the front pocket of my backpack and hand it to him.

"Thanks, man," Ty says quietly, shoving the ring into his pocket as quickly as he can manage.

He's not as sly as he thinks, though, and Rachel's radar pings immediately.

"What is that?" she asks, suspicious.

"I'll show you in a bit," Ty responds, keeping his cool as he pulls Rachel to his chest and affectionately squeezes her shoulders.

"Okay. Well, then. It was good to see you two. Glad you're both okay. And now, if you don't mind, Rachel and I have something we need to attend to."

"Ty!" Rachel slaps at him over his perceived rudeness, but both Maria and I smile. We know what's coming, and we're not offended in the slightest.

"What?"

"Your brother and Maria were just stuck in an elevator for two freaking hours," Rachel scolds. "Don't you think we should invite them up for a bit?" Rachel looks at us imploringly. "Come upstairs so we can get you some water and food and whatever else you need."

"No, it's okay," I refute with a gentle smile. "We're going to head out, actually."

I've done my job, and Maria could use some fresh air. I know from experience that the last thing she needs to deal with right away is Mrs. Patricia Clemmons.

"That's great!" Ty exclaims, excitedly tossing Rachel over his shoulder and making her shriek.

"Ty!"

"Bye, guys!" He just laughs, ignoring a mortified Rachel completely and turning on his heel toward the stairwell doors.

"I'm so sorry he's a rude idiot!" she calls toward us. "And it was really nice meeting you, Maria!"

Maria smiles and laughs, looking up at me conspiratorially as they leave earshot. "Man, to be a fly on the wall to see what's about to come for her. Seems like she's going to be shocked."

I laugh. "I'm not sure how. Ty is the world's worst secret-keeper."

"He's in love. It's cute. Different from what I remember."

I chuckle again. "He was a little prick back in the day, wasn't he?"

"Oh yeah."

"Don't worry. He still is in a lot of ways."

THE REDO | 37

She laughs.

"Come on, I'll walk you out." Slow and easy, Maria and I make our way down the four flights of stairs to the street level. I place a gentle hand at her back as we walk through the lobby, and I hold open the front door for her to exit first. She smiles gratefully, stopping just outside to wait for me.

I look into her pretty caramel-brown eyes for a long moment before saying anything, and when I do, she opens her mouth to speak at the same time.

"Well, I should be going to meet—"

"Have dinner with me," I request because it feels like two hours together in the elevator wasn't enough. I want to chat more. To laugh more. To remember what it's like to be around a woman whose company I truly enjoy.

Her smile is soft but hesitant as she shakes her head. "I really shouldn't. I told Mrs. Clemmons I'd get in touch with her to reschedule as soon as I was out, and I have two contracts to write up tonight. Some other time, maybe?"

I want to push the issue—to fast-talk her into going with me anyway—but knowing what she's been through and how tired she potentially is, I realize it's a much better idea to lay the groundwork to have another opportunity at a less chaotic time.

"Some other time, definitely," I respond with a wink. "And I'm going to hold you to it."

Gently grabbing her phone from her hand, I type in my current phone number and save it to her contacts quickly. She watches me avidly, not bothering to hide the thick swallow she takes that makes her throat bob.

"I've really enjoyed seeing you, Maria," I tell her, and her responding smile is so genuine it makes my chest grow warm.

"It's been good to see you too, Rem."

"So...let's do it again, but under less stressful circumstances, yeah?"

She snorts. "Less stressful sounds perfect."

"You have my number now." I hand her phone back to her. "Use it, okay?"

She nods. "Sure."

I lean forward and kiss the soft skin of her right cheek to say goodbye, and then I watch as she walks away.

For the rest of the night? I wait, hoping she'll call or text or anything to return the exchange of numbers, but the communication never comes. Memories, however, do. Her *some other time, maybe?* reminds me so much of the first time I met Maria Baros, it's practically palpable.

THE PAST

THE START OF IT ALL

Twenty-Eight Years Ago...

Summer break, two weeks before school starts...

Remy

In less than two weeks, summer will be done, and school will be back in session. No more week-long trips to Uncle Brad and Aunt Paula's lake house. No more sleeping in. No more watching my brothers get kicked out of the community pool for being dicks.

Soon, I'll have to deal with homework and football practice.

It blows.

"Remy, my feet hurt," my little sister Winnie whines, her petite hand tugging at the material of my T-shirt. "I want to go home."

I almost want to laugh at her sudden change in mood. Prior to leaving the house, she was a six-year-old diva on a mission to tag along with me up to my high school to grab all the books and shit I need for the start of my junior year.

But after a subway ride and a ten-minute walk, she sure is singing a different tune.

"Winnie, we're almost there," I tell her, but she stops in the middle of the sidewalk. I turn to face her just as she stomps one pink-gym-shoe-covered foot to the ground.

"But, Remy! I'm so tired!"

"If I recall, you're the one who said you wanted to come along," I say, and both hands go to my hips. "I'm pretty sure I remember you *begging* me."

She pouts, and her face morphs into that infamous look of hers. The look that has everyone in our family wrapped around her little finger. "Can you at least give me a piggyback ride? Pretty please?"

I smile; I can't help it. My baby sister is too damn cute for words. "If I give you a piggyback ride, do you promise to stop with the whining?"

"I wasn't whining. I'm not a baby."

"You were definitely whining," I correct her. "So, if that's what babies do, then hello kettle, meet pot."

"What?"

"Never mind," I respond on a laugh and kneel down in front of her. "Climb aboard, Winnie."

She smiles like a girl who just won a battle of wills and doesn't hesitate to climb atop my shoulders. Once I'm certain she's secure, I stand up and proceed to finish walking the last two blocks to my high school.

I'm not surprised to find that the massive building looks exactly like it did when I walked out the doors the day before summer break.

The same red bell tower.

The same light bricks.

And the same smell of impending doom.

Ha. I'm kidding. *Sort of.*

"Are we getting Flynn's stuff, too?" Winnie asks, and I laugh.

"Hell no. Flynn can get his own shit."

"Remy!" Winnie exclaims and slaps one hand on the top of my head. "Those are bad words! I'm going to tell Mom!"

"If you tell Mom I say bad words, she'll never let you hang out with me."

That shuts her up.

"Fine. I won't tell," she mutters. "But I still think we should get Flynn's stuff."

"Even if I wanted to do that, I can't. Since Flynn is a freshman and I'm junior, our pickup days are different."

"When does Flynn have to go?"

"Tomorrow."

"Oh."

"You trying to plan another getaway from the house?"

"No."

"Liar." I smirk and walk inside the entrance doors of the building, heading straight for the main lobby area where I know the pickup table is located.

"Your school is so big, Remy! I hope I get to go here when I'm all growed up!"

I want to tell her high school isn't all it's cracked up to be, but I bite my tongue in the name of keeping the younger generation optimistic.

"Name?" a lady with glasses the size of Coke bottles and a brown perm asks from her seat once I come to a stop in front of the pickup table.

"His name is Remington Winslow," Winnie answers for me, still perched on my shoulders. "He's all growed up. Sixteen years old. He plays football and can drive, but he doesn't drive that much because we live in the city. Though, I really think he should've driven today. My feet hurt."

The woman smiles up at my baby sister. "And what is your name, sweetheart?"

"Winnie Winslow. But I'm not in high school. I'm only six years old and will start first grade this year. I'm the youngest in my family, and I have four brothers. Jude is in fifth grade. Ty is in seventh grade. Flynn is gonna be a freshman, and this is my oldest brother, Remy." She continues to tell this poor woman her whole life story as she pats the top of my head. "He's gonna be a junior this year."

Already knowing it's a useless endeavor to get Winnie to stop talking, I just stand there, smiling knowingly at the lady.

"Oh my goodness," the woman responds, and she flashes an amused smile at me before looking back up at my sister. "You know, I swear, I thought you were at least fourteen."

"Nope." Winnie giggles. "Only six."

"Well, you sure are a gorgeous, smart girl. And it's very nice of you to help your brother today," she tells my sister and then meets my eyes again, amusement still in place on her face. "Give me one minute, Remington, and I'll get your things."

Out of her chair and toward several shelves the staff have set up, she searches for my packet and books. And the entire time, the chatterbox on my shoulders doesn't stop moving her mouth.

"Do you know that man standing by the lady getting your books?"

"Yes."

"Is he a teacher? He looks like a teacher."

"Yes, he's a teacher, Win."

"What about him? The guy with the bright-red hair talking to that lady over there?"

"That's Freddy Harrison."

"Why aren't you saying hi to him?"

"Because I don't know him that well." And because he's an asshole.

"What about her, Remy? Do you know her?"

"Who?"

"That pretty girl over there."

Pretty girl? Say what?

Instantly, I look up to meet Winnie's eyes and then follow her little finger that's stretched out toward the other end of the room.

Dressed in jean shorts and a tank top, my sister wasn't wrong, the girl in question stands at another pickup table and is *definitely* pretty. Truthfully, she's way more than just pretty. Long brown hair, tanned skin, and the kind of big, warm eyes that make guys like me stupid, she's downright gorgeous.

And I've never met her before. Which is crazy because I pretty much know everyone who goes to Hidden Hills High.

Damn. Who is that? Is she new?

"Do you know her, Remy?"

"Nope." But I certainly want to.

"I think she has a little sister like you do. See that girl with her? I bet that's her sister."

My observant baby sister doesn't miss a beat. Standing right beside the mystery girl of my dreams is a shorter, younger version of her. She can't be older than nine or ten.

Instantly, I get an idea.

"She looks like she's close to your age, Win," I comment. "You should go say hi."

"Okay," Miss Chatterbox responds like it's completely normal to just walk up to random strangers and introduce yourself.

That's Winnie, though. Never met a stranger in her life.

Frankly, it's almost too easy.

I help Winnie off my shoulders and to her feet. And in a matter of two minutes, she's already across the room, chatting up the two girls.

"Remy! Remy! Come over here!" Winnie shouts toward me as the nice lady with the Coke-bottle glasses is handing me my stack of books.

The beautiful mystery girl and her sister look in my direction, and I silently thank the Big Guy Upstairs for blessing me with the most talkative six-year-old in history as my sister.

I close the distance between us, and it's no surprise that Winnie is the first one to speak when I come to a stop near their little group.

"This is him," she says proudly. "My big brother Remington. But you can call him Remy. Everyone else does. Isn't he handsome?"

I can't deny that my baby sister is about the best wingman I've ever had. No way Flynn or Ty or Jude or any of my buddies could create an opening for me like Winnie just did.

A giggle leaves Mystery Girl's lips, and I swear, it's music to my ears.

"Hi," I say with a knowing smile and hold out my hand. "I'm Remy Winslow. The handsome brother."

She giggles again, and it makes a cute dimple appear at her right cheek.

Fuck. She's beautiful.

"Hi. I'm Maria," she responds and places her petite hand in mine. "Maria Baros."

Maria.

Her hand is soft and warm against mine, and my nose catches just the hint of her sweet perfume. She smells like coconuts and summer and a girl I want to know.

"Nice to meet you, Maria," I answer, and the way her name rolls off my tongue could easily become my next addiction. "And who is this?"

"Her name is Isabella," Winnie answers for her, and I playfully nudge my baby sister in the side.

"If you haven't noticed, Winnie here is incredibly chatty."

Maria grins. "And adorable."

"Remy, can I show Isabella the fountains we saw near the front door?" Winnie asks, completely oblivious to the conversation around her. "And I need two pennies to toss in it."

"Sure, Win." I take two pennies out of my pocket but pause before giving them to an impatient Winnie, who currently has two hands held out toward me. "But only if it's okay with Maria."

"Can I?" Isabella looks at her sister, and Maria shrugs.

"Sure. But stay together."

I hand Winnie the two pennies, and she fist-pumps one tiny hand in the air. "C'mon, Isabella! Let's go make a wish!"

And then Maria and I are left alone, both of our sisters running toward the entrance doors of the building where the not-all-that-exciting fountain sits.

"Are you new—"

"Do you—"

We both start to talk at the same time, and a blush forms on Maria's cheeks.

"Sorry. What were you going to say?"

"It's fine," I respond with a smile that's probably too big for the occasion. "Are you new here?"

She nods. "Freshman."

"That's cool."

"What about you?"

"Junior," I answer. "My brother Flynn will be a freshman this year too."

Her smile is self-deprecating. "I take it Flynn realized he didn't need to be here until tomorrow?"

"Maybe." I grin. "But it's okay. Your secret is safe with me."

"So…you're not going to tell the whole school I'm a dumbass?"

"You're not a dumbass," I respond on a laugh. *But the most perfect girl I've ever seen? Yes. That you definitely are, Maria.*

Though, that's also a secret I'm going to keep to myself.

"Are you busy?"

She tilts her head to the side. "What do you mean?"

"I was planning on taking Winnie to grab some ice cream. Would you and Isabella like to come along?"

"We're going to get ice cream?!" Winnie exclaims, her presence a surprise to both of us. And Isabella is right beside her. "Oh my gosh, this is the best day ever!"

Maria quirks one eyebrow and whispers, "I take it she didn't know about the ice cream until now, huh?"

"That would be a negative." I shake my head on a laugh. "So…would you like to come with us?"

A frown forms at the corner of her lips. "I'd love to, but I really shouldn't. I promised my mom I'd have Isabella home by lunch." She glances down at her sandal-covered feet and then back up to me.

"Ah, rats," Isabella groans. "Come on, Maria. Ice cream sounds so good."

"Sorry, sis," Maria says and ruffles Isabella's hair before meeting my eyes. "Some other time, maybe?"

I smile. "Definitely."

"Wait…we're still getting ice cream, though, right, Rem?" Winnie chimes in, and I nod on a sigh.

"Yes, Win. We're still getting ice cream."

"Best day ever!" Winnie squeals.

And frankly, as I watch Maria wave and walk away, I can't disagree with her.

The only thing that could've made this day better was if that *some other time, maybe?* would've been a *yes*.

But lucky for you, in two weeks, you'll have a whole school year to make that happen.

All of a sudden, I'm excited for the start of my junior year.

FOUR

Friday, August 23rd

Maria

Tap-tap-tap-tap, my index finger bounces off the ledge of the passenger door of my taxi. A vision of what feels like miles of cars assaults my eyes through the windshield.

Early afternoon traffic on a Friday is never optimal, but today, well, it's downright dismal.

I should've never agreed to three showings so close together.

Talk about a real rookie mistake. Or, you know, a *Claudia* mistake.

"It's a damn parking lot out here," my cab driver grumbles, and it does nothing for my anxiety.

Scanning the nearest street signs, I note that I'm only two blocks away from my next appointment, a swanky building located in an area known as Central Park East. But when I glance at the clock on the dashboard, I see my time to get there has dwindled down to ten minutes.

Shit. Shit. Shit.

I stay rooted to my seat for about thirty more seconds, but when the traffic doesn't budge and my taxi driver starts to play a game of Yahtzee on his phone, I know I'm left without a choice.

Full-term pregnant or not, I'm going to have to finish this trip on foot.

I let myself savor the cool air conditioning of the taxi for another few seconds, and then I haul ass. Door open, I toss forty dollars toward my driver and quickly grab my purse and bag.

"What the hell, lady?"

"Sorry, but I have to go! Thanks!" I shut the door and carefully maneuver through the traffic, both hands on my belly, until I reach the safety of the sidewalk.

I know my cab driver is pissed at me, because my problem has now become his problem, but that's life, man. Not to mention, I paid him double the fare the meter on the dashboard showed.

He'll get over it.

Me, on the other hand? Well, I just hope my swollen feet can tolerate the long, hot trek inside these heels I decided to wear today. It's almost pathetic how my need to maintain a professional appearance still trumps my body's cries for comfort.

A bead of sweat runs down my back as I maneuver through the pedestrian traffic on the sidewalk. *Hell's bells, it's hot. Why is it always so hot?*

New York summers can be brutal, and like every other day for the past month and a half, today is no exception.

Suck it up, buttercup, and keep that preggo ass of yours moving.

Half a block into my blistering stroll, my phone buzzes with a new text message, and I quickly pull it out of my purse to see the very last name I want to see right now—*Patricia Clemmons*.

It's been four weeks since I got stuck in the elevator that was located inside the building of a Greenwich Village property she decided she wanted to purchase.

Four weeks since you told Remington Winslow you'd call him…which you still haven't done.

I roll my eyes at myself and focus on the task at hand—Mrs. Clemmons.

Ever since the Greenwich Village seller accepted the Clemmonses's offer, I've had an influx of calls and texts from Patricia, all of which revolve around her closing date. But not for the normal reasons you'd expect. Any rescheduling that's occurred is because her bougie ass likes to take last-minute, purely recreational trips to Fiji.

In the last several weeks, she's caused me more headaches than my assistant and this pregnancy combined. Which is saying a lot because Claudia sucks at her job and my due date is only two days away.

I swear, if Mrs. Clemmons tries to reschedule her closing again, I'm calling the seller myself and telling them to back out of the deal. I don't care how much commission I'll have to walk away from.

Patricia Clemmons: Mr. Clemmons and I can make the closing next week.

"Hallelujah!" I shout so loud I startle a fellow pedestrian in passing as I finish the last block of my hot-as-balls walk across Central Park. *Whoops.*

Determined to get this date in stone, I type out a quick response to Mrs. Clemmons and the seller's agent, solidifying the closing that I've already assigned to a new agent at my firm. I will most likely be busy with a newborn next week. At least, that's what my OB-GYN, Dr. Maddox, has told me.

I hope Daniel, one of two new agents that I hired out of desperation about a month ago, will be able to close the Clemmonses without any issues. I really, really *hope.* I've been trying to get both him and Brenda, the other agent I hired, up to speed, but I can't deny, four weeks before I leave on maternity leave isn't much time.

The building stands like a beacon in the distance, and it doesn't take my tired, currently swelling feet too much longer to get there.

My client, however, is already standing outside.

Shoot.

Sweat drips from my brow, and I reach up to discreetly wipe it away before Mrs. Allistair sees my approach. She's one of those women who's kempt at all times, no matter the weather, and while I appreciate working with people who smell good, it's not always easy to maintain my laundry-fresh scent when it's one hundred degrees outside and I'm carrying the next world-record-sized baby.

I don't actually know, of course, how big this baby is going to be, but I'm kind of doing the thing you do to figure out the tip at a restaurant—you know, taking the number of weeks and doubling it? That puts the baby's poundage somewhere in the seventies.

That's how I feel, at least.

There's a part of me that wishes I knew whether I have a little boy or little girl inside this belly of mine, but the need to honor Isabella's wishes has been too strong to deny. She wanted to be surprised, so looks like I'm going to be surprised whenever this baby makes his or her big debut.

And to think, that surprise is going to happen really damn soon…

Mentally, I'm well aware my due date is forty-eight hours away, but at the moment, I'm mostly just trying not to think about what I'm going to do when this baby is born until, you know, the baby is born.

Some might call it unhealthy avoidance, but I prefer to think of it as a woman trying to cope with the insane cards she's been dealt. I mean, if you show me a psychology textbook that provides the "correct" way to handle a situation like mine, I'm certain it'll be the day pigs can fly.

After crossing the street as fast as my waddling hips will let me, I wipe the dampness from my hands on the straight line of my maternity pencil skirt and face the real estate music. "Mrs. Allistair!" I call her attention, jumping up on the curb with a spryness I definitely don't feel and sticking out my hand for her to take. "So good to see you again."

"Does this building have on-site parking?" she asks instead of greeting me back and completely ignoring my outstretched hand.

I smile and cock my hand back to my hip. It's always the rudest clients with the deepest pockets. Every insult or dismissal might as well be a dollar sign.

"Yes. There's an underground garage with twenty-four-hour valet and security. You won't have to worry at all."

"Good," she says with a nod and an almost-smile.

Ah, she's warming slightly. I, however, am well past warm. If I wrung out my bra, I could probably fill a freaking bathtub.

"What about a concierge?"

"There's no official concierge, but the front desk manager Lukas has assured me that he handles many tasks for the residents of the building as an inclusion in your monthly fees."

"I suppose that would do." She doesn't look back as she heads for the front door of the building, and the doorman jumps to pull it out of her way. I smile gratefully and mouth a silent *thank you*, and he just nods and offers a secret, knowing grin in response.

Obviously, he's used to entitled people.

Lukas is standing behind the front desk in the lobby, but he moves swiftly to push the elevator button for Mrs. Allistair while I hold out a hand and shake his. I've spoken with him several times prior to showing this apartment, and he's always been the epitome of helpful and considerate. He's the reason we're able to get into this apartment while the owners are away on vacation.

"Lukas. Thanks so much for meeting us. This is Mrs. Allistair. Mrs. Allistair," I call, garnering her attention just enough that she turns to barely glance over her shoulder. "This is Lukas. The front desk manager of the building."

She doesn't recognize him with anything other than a blink of her eyes, and still, Lukas smiles. I take it as a good sign that the staff of this building has as many years of customer service under their belts as I do. At this point, rudeness just washes off me.

The elevator door opens with a prestigious ding, and Lukas gallantly jumps to stick his arm across the door to hold it while we enter. The mere idea of getting inside another elevator makes me hesitate for a brief moment—it has every single time I've done it for the last month—but I force myself to put one foot in front of the other and step inside.

Call me crazy, but getting stuck inside an elevator for a few hours in the middle of a New York blackout while you're pregnant doesn't exactly make you excited to step inside a cramped cart.

Sure, I've been in dozens of elevators since, and clearly, the time I got stuck turned out okay, but that was because the kind of man who might as well be a modern version of Prince Charming just so happened to be inside. Surely that can't happen every time, just as frogs don't really transform with a kiss.

Well, it could happen again. But only if you'd call him.

Despite my inner voice's urgency, it's pretty damn obvious why now isn't an optimal time to get in touch with Remington Winslow again. I mean, what's he going to do? Help me figure out how to use a breast pump while I have a newborn crying over our attempts at chitchat?

Yeah. No thank you. No one deserves that kind of chaos in their life. Especially not Remy.

As the elevator starts to make its journey up the building, I take several deep breaths and concentrate on getting myself together. I'm sweating profusely despite the crisp breeze of air conditioning, and my lower back is so tight it feels like I've rammed a rod inside it. Mrs. Allistair's inspection of this place will no doubt be swifter than some of my other buyers, but I'm still going to need to slap on a smile and walk her through.

Unfortunately, my belly decides it's the perfect time to tighten in a way you can see through my silk blouse, and I inhale a sharp, deep breath through my nose and release it out of my mouth as quietly as I can.

You're fine, Maria. You're fine. It's just a summer pregnancy. Millions of women deal with this every day.

I find a place of calm inside myself and smile over at Lukas, whose eyebrows have now pulled together in concern as he stares at my protruding, hard belly. I wave him off silently from my position behind my client and shake my head.

I'm good. Really, I'm good. Any woman who is full-term pregnant in August looks like this, I swear.

As the elevator opens on the top floor of the building, Lukas presents his arm again but this time doesn't move with us.

"I've unlocked the door for your ease of entry and will be downstairs if you need anything. *Anything* at all. Please, don't hesitate to call for me," he tells me gently as I follow Mrs. Allistair off and to the door across the hall. She opens it without pause, and I have no choice but to follow, smiling and waving at Lukas as I go.

Once inside, I kick off my shoes and start flipping on light switches as fast as I can. "This is the formal living room and parlor, and another living area is down the hall, adjacent to the kitchen."

"Window cleaning?" Mrs. Allistair asks brusquely.

"Once a week."

She nods then, clomping down the hallway in her heels without even considering removing them.

"Mrs. Allistair," I call, hoping she's not scuffing the floors. "Would you mind removing your heels as a courtesy to the sellers?"

"I mind," she says simply, disappearing deeper and deeper into the apartment.

A pain shoots from my lower back and stretches across my belly, and it's all I can do not to scream. Evidently, even the fetus inside me can feel the effects of snobby people.

Once the discomfort passes, I sigh and do the only thing I can do—follow Mrs. Allistair around this large apartment as she scrutinizes every nook and cranny.

Please, let this showing go quick.

Thirty minutes later and Mrs. Allistair has walked through every room, outwardly commented on anything that annoys her, and has remained unreadable on whether she even likes this apartment.

Normally, I'd do my best to coax her into a conversation that would help me figure out where her head is at with this place, but I'm too damn exhausted and uncomfortable to care. Completely unlike me, but I blame it on the heat and tiny human that appears to be throwing a party inside my uterus.

"I'll be in touch, Maria," Mrs. Allistair eventually says, but her attention is completely invested in the screen of her phone. Without another word, she walks out the front door of the apartment and departs with a short wave over her shoulder and a murmured "Ta!"

My stomach tightens, and a pain shoots from the back of my hip and finds a home inside my pelvic bone. *Goodness gracious.* I breathe through my mouth until the door shuts behind my client and then find the only relief I can by bending over to lean into the wall.

I don't know if it's the heat or the weight of my stomach or what, but God, these pains are becoming a real nuisance. Of course, since my due date isn't for another two days, I know they're probably what Dr. Maddox calls Braxton-Hicks—aka *fake* contractions. Nothing more than my body practicing going into labor.

At this rate, my uterus must be training for Olympic gold.

Since I have another showing in half an hour and it's located two blocks away, I try not to dillydally closing up the apartment. Or, you know, standing here dealing with these stupid fake contractions.

Once the pain eases a little, I stand back up straight and make my way through the three-thousand-square-foot apartment, shutting off lights and ensuring nothing is out of place. These owners might be summering in the Mediterranean for another four weeks, but that doesn't mean they wouldn't know if I left their place anything but spotless.

I make quick work of everything, only stopping once more to grind my teeth against this naggingly inconvenient pain, and close and lock the front door behind me. Slinging my briefcase bag onto my shoulder, I head toward the elevator bank, smashing the gold button impatiently to call the next available cart.

There are two elevators in this building, side by side, and I can hear the one on the left zooming toward the ground floor in a hurry. I cradle my stomach and hope with all my might that the one on the right will be swift to arrive.

Just as another pain shoots through my stomach, the doors open gallantly, and I stumble inside and hold on to the golden rail on the back wall.

God, why is the heat getting to me so badly today?

I take several deep breaths and lean into the wall, looking to the ceiling to find some kind of blind solace. You know, where you kind of black out a little, and everything that's plaguing you fades away for a bit?

If I could just black out for like two, three minutes, and then be on my way to my next—

"Ah!" I scream unexpectedly as the elevator jolts so hard it forces my feet to stumble forward. In a matter of seconds, the main lights flash off and the cart settles to a dead stop. "Oh my God!" I stomp my one heel to the ground and stare at the emergency lights, the only source of illumination inside this small, confined space. "Are you kidding me?"

I look around manically. Up, down, at the wall, at the floor, and when the elevator cart still doesn't budge and the lights don't come back on, I smash my fingers against every damn button I can find.

I will take any floor at this point. I don't care if I have to trek seven hundred flights of stairs. I refuse to be stuck in an elevator again.

But nothing changes.

I'm still inside the elevator, and the damn thing isn't showing any signs of life.

Oh my God! This isn't funny, universe! This isn't the blackout I meant!

FIVE

Remy

This kid, I swear. I laugh down at my phone as I read a message from Lexi.

I just dropped her off with Wes and Winnie after she spent the afternoon with me at Coney Island, but apparently my niece is none too thrilled with what her parents are up to.

Lexi: They're currently potting a vegetable garden and talking about the meals they're going to make with it, Uncle Remy. As if all of these plants won't be dead within the month.

My sister and brother-in-law have a track record with plants. A can't-keep-them-alive kind of sad reality. I know this because my annoyed niece always gives me the inside scoop.

Me: You have to give them credit for trying over and over again. That's determination.

Lexi: Or botanicide.

Me: Botanicide? Is that a real word?

Lexi: It would be if more people killed plants at the rate of my parents.

I snort and shake my head just as I'm nearing the door to my building. My doorman, Nathan, rushes to beat me there from his spot at the curb, assisting a fancy-looking woman as she climbs inside a black Escalade, but I'm five steps ahead of him.

"Sorry, Mr. Winslow," he remarks, making me purse my lips and shake my head.

"Don't be, Nate," I call over my shoulder. "I can open doors myself. Been training my whole life for it."

Once I step inside the fresh air conditioning of my building, I sigh in relief. It's another hot one today, and according to the meteorologist, it's only set to get hotter in the next couple of hours.

Lukas, my building's front desk manager, looks up and waves from his phone call as I pass him by, and I offer him a smile as I close the distance to the elevator. While glancing down at my phone and typing out a text to Lexi, I push the gold call button for the next available cart.

Me: Just let them revel in their blind, plant-growing ignorance, Lex. I mean, it's too late for these plants, but in the future, I'll try to help you stop your mom and Wes from committing any more botanicide.

Lexi: Fine. But maybe I'll pull up some plant facts from the web and read them off in their vicinity. Consider it a last-ditch effort.

Me: HAHA. Sounds like a plan.

Lexi: Why are you laughing? I'm not joking.

I bite my lip and chuckle to myself. Lexi is on the autism spectrum and sometimes doesn't interpret humor in the same way I do. She's also a million times smarter than me, however, so in all honesty, I usually just default to her opinion.

Me: Oh sorry, Lex. Of course. You can tell me some of the facts the next time I see you.

The left-hand elevator dings, and I step inside, the doors sliding closed in front of me.

Lexi: Are you considering a garden?

Me: No. Not exactly.

Wes and Winnie's brownstone has a backyard. My apartment is located inside a high-rise with only Central Park as the closest source of nature. Pretty sure I'd get arrested if I started digging up the grounds.

Lexi: Then why do you want to know facts about plants?

I chuckle again, shaking my head and poise my phone at my fingertips to type another response, but the elevator cart rocking to a hard stop forces my attention. Mere seconds later, the power goes out completely, and the emergency lights inside the cart illuminate.

You have got to be fucking kidding me.

I furrow my brow and hope this is only a momentary pause in power, but when nothing changes, it's pretty fucking obvious that I'm trapped in an elevator...again.

But this time, there's no gorgeous woman by the name of Maria to keep you company.

My mind could dive deep with thoughts of her *or* the reality that a month has passed without her following through on using my number, but clearly, I have something that's a little higher priority to deal with at the moment. Like getting the hell out of another elevator.

Get your shit together, New York power grid.

Even with the reliable staff of my building who are probably already on the case, there's no way I'm going to wait around to be rescued. After watching the firefighters work a couple weeks ago, I'm pretty sure I can get out of this fucker myself if I try hard enough.

I move to the doors swiftly, tucking my phone inside my pocket and studying the seam between them. They look spring-loaded, but there's enough of a gap that I think I can get just enough traction inside the seam to budge the entrance open.

I scrape my fingers into the notch between the doors and push as hard as I can until they start to give way and sluggishly slide open. It hurts like a motherfucker—my fingers, no doubt, will be bruised and bleeding—but once I manage five inches of space between the doors, they start to move easier.

Thank fuck.

I peer out of the cart and realize two things—I'm halfway between floors, and thankfully, the doors to the floor above me have glitched open enough that I can get my body through without having to strong-man them open. The fall to ground level is nothing to snub my nose at, but since I've never really been afraid of heights and have a long history of doing reckless shit with my brothers, I don't hesitate over the risks.

Right into action, I pull myself up and out of the cart and onto the sixth floor of my building.

I dust off my now-sore hands and push to standing, but when my ears catch the faint sounds of the word *help* coming from the other elevator shaft, I rush over and put my ear against the closed doors.

"Help!" I hear a desperate woman's voice call. "Can anyone hear me? I need help!"

"Hello! Can you hear me?" I yell back, hoping to reassure her that someone's here and that help is on the way.

"Hello?" she yells back, her faint, feminine voice sounding both strong and terrified at the same time. "Is someone there?"

"I'm here!" I scream again, this time a little louder. "Have you tried the emergency phone?"

"It doesn't work!" she yells back.

Of course it doesn't. *Fucking hell.*

"Do you know what floor you're on?"

"I think I'm on the sixth!" The panic in her muffled voice is unmistakable. "And I really need to get out of here! Please help!"

There is no way on God's green earth I can just leave this woman stuck inside an elevator when she sounds like she's in distress.

Okay, she's on the sixth floor. You can work with that. That's a good thing.

"I'm going to try to get the doors open and see if I can get you out of there, if that's okay with you?"

"Oh, well, actually, I was hoping to stay in here for a while. But if you must…"

If I weren't so over fucking blackouts in the city this summer, I might have laughed. I guess that was a pretty dumb question. Instead, I give her a simple but hopefully comforting instruction. "Hang tight."

My fingers are already torn up from my last battle with elevator doors, but my eyes quickly locate a bright-red fire case with an ax inside. Shirt off and wrapped around my elbow, I break the glass and get the fire ax out without slicing open my skin.

"Are you still there? Hello?" The woman's muted voice hits my ears again as I step back toward her elevator. "I really need help!"

"I'm still here!" I shout toward her as I position the blade of the ax inside the seam of the sixth-floor doors. "Just stand back while I try to pry the doors open!"

I lift the ax's handle to get some leverage before pushing hard to one side. The doors open just enough for me to get my hand inside, and I juggle the transition from the ax to my hands as carefully as possible. I'm not looking to lose any fucking fingers today.

Finally getting my footing, I push the doors with a strong heave, straightening my arms out until the doors have completely opened to the sides. Unfortunately, the only thing I can see is the top of the elevator cart below me. This one, it seems, didn't stop in as good of a position as mine did.

Thankfully, it's only a couple of feet down, and I can easily pull her out through the top emergency hatch if I need to.

"Can you hear me down there?" I ask toward the top of the elevator. "Are you doing okay?"

"Um…" She pauses, her voice sounding out of breath. "No. Not really." There's a small, almost indistinct whimper and then words that seemed dragged from somewhere pained inside her. "I don't think I'm okay."

My eyebrows draw together, and before taking even a moment to think, I'm on top of the cart, looking for the release to open the emergency hatch.

"Hang on," I tell the woman inside. "I'm coming to get you, okay?"

I find the latch and release it, opening the hatch and peering down below into the soft light of the car. The woman, it turns out, is a woman I know.

And from the looks of her strained position on the floor, she's in full-blown labor.

Fuck!

SIX

Maria

Everything inside me burns, and my heart is in my throat.

I grit my teeth as another contraction takes hold and sends any ounce of comfort I had left to the moon. It takes everything inside me not to cuss up a storm so violent it would put a hole through the bottom of this stupid elevator.

Oh, hellllllllll!

The pain is so intense, I have to squat and brace myself on the walls of the elevator. And when that's not enough, I find that my body is running on pure instinct and sets up shop on the damn floor.

Sweat pours off way more than just my brow, and my cream silk blouse's stainless past is history. I'm a walking swamp rat, except, of course, for the fact that I can no longer walk.

It's safe to say you've been having real *contractions all day.*

I thought first-time pregnancies were supposed to take a while. Like hours. Sometimes *days.* But why does it feel like this baby is trying to shoot out of my body like he or she has a six thirty dinner with the president?

Another contraction begins to grip my body, and anyone with a brain would recognize this is not good.

As the specific someone with both a brain and the uterus that's currently nuking itself to oblivion, I understand this isn't just not good; it's bad.

This is really fucking bad.

"Oh my *Gawwwd!*" I yell, just as the hatch above me pops open, and it startles me so badly, I feel like my bones jump through my muscles. The top of the metal structure creaks above me frighteningly, and all I can do is crane my neck to look up as I continue to puff tight breaths through tense lips.

I close my eyes briefly, wondering if I've somehow teleported to the beginning of a Superhero meets Villain movie, but when I open them again, I'm blessed with the stark and undeniable feeling of relief. The hatch is fully open now and the creaking has stopped, and one of the most beautiful faces I've ever laid eyes on is looking down at me.

He forms words quicker than I do, but seeing as I'm a little busy feeling like my body is trying to turn itself inside out, I give myself a pass.

"Maria?" he questions, the concern immediately evident in his rich voice.

"Remy? Oh God, oh God."

With quick movements, he shifts to put his feet in through the hole of the opened hatch and climbs down. He's shirtless and beautiful, and for the love of everything holy, I wish I could concentrate enough on anything other than the contractions that keep gripping my body like a vise to appreciate it.

He settles onto the floor and immediately kneels beside me. I wish I could say I was presenting myself as something other than a wadded-up ball of desperation, but I'm afraid not.

His smile is gentle and tender and makes me want to cry a thousand tears as he reaches up and wipes some of the sweat-slicked hair away from my face and whispers, "Honestly, Maria, getting stuck inside my building's elevator is a really strange way to see me again. You could've just called."

This is his building. Go figure.

"Very funny," I answer through a hard jaw as another contraction rolls through my body like a freight train.

"Seriously, babe. We have to stop meeting like this."

I nod fervently at that. "I never realized I'm even *in* elevators this much, for goodness' sake."

"Maria, I think it's safe to say, you're going to have a baby today."

I close my eyes and shake my head, full denial the only thing I'm still trying to hold on to. "No. No, I'm not. Maybe tomorrow? Yeah, probably tomorrow."

"Pretty sure it's happening now, hun," he corrects me with a soft but knowing smile. "But it's going to be okay. You're doing an amazing job. And just think, the hard part is over."

"The hard part is over?" I scoff. "Remy, last time I checked, the baby's still inside. I think there's a lot of hard shit to go."

He nods with a smile but reaches down to grab my hand and squeeze. "Yeah. But you don't have to do it alone anymore. I'm here."

"Just like having a doctor." It's a little rude and unnecessarily snippy, given that he's literally knight in shining armor-ing for me right now, but I'm in so much pain, I think I've earned some testiness. Still, I feel badly enough to wince and apologize. "Sorry, but it hurts."

"Maria," he says with a chuckle. "Don't worry about me. You can curse me up and down if it helps. You worry about you, and you worry about this baby. Let me deal with the rest."

"Am I really having my sister's baby today? I just…I need you to pinch me." Emotion clogs my throat as the gravity of everything in my life that's changed in the last several months hits me square in the chest. "I can't believe any of this is real."

Isabella should be here for this.

Remy strokes the hair at the side of my face again and squeezes my hand. "You can do it, Ri. I promise. I've never met a woman I thought could do it more."

I'm momentarily taken aback by the genuine nature of his compliment. "Really?"

"God yes. You've been through more than ninety percent of people I know and, somehow, managed to come out on the other side even stronger. Beautiful. Successful. Kind. You're going to be the best thing this baby can have with the hand it—she, he? Is it a boy or a girl?"

"I don't know yet. My sister wanted it to be a surprise."

"Looks like we're about to be surprised today, then."

I nod resolutely then, fully accepting the fact that this is happening, and I can do it. I *have* to. End of story.

"Okay, Rem. You can stop Tony Robbins-ing my ass. I'm ready and willing. God help us both."

He laughs. "I was going for a more Bear Grylls type of thing, but Tony Robbins works too."

"Sorry, Charlie. This talk was nowhere near tough enough for Bear Grylls."

"I can be tougher."

"No," I say through a half laugh, half groan. "Please. Don't."

"Okay, okay," Remy consoles with a grin. "I'll be good, I promise."

"Goo—ahhhhhhhhh—ood!" I try to respond while simultaneously howling in pain over a peaking contraction. "Holy chickens in a coop, this hurtsss!"

Remy rubs at my arm and my hand and my leg, seeming desperate to comfort the impossible. The truth is, babies fucking hurt. I don't care what people want to try to tell you when they're not in the throes of a currently epidural-less labor, but shooting a baby cannonball through a very small hole is one of the worst ideas someone has ever had on this planet. I'll sign a notarized statement and present it to a judge.

"Do you think you can stand up?" he asks, clearly trying to get me out of this elevator so I can have this baby in a hospital like a normal woman.

I want to nod yes. I want to agree and get to my feet and magically find myself in a hospital bed with a staff of doctors and nurses around me. You know, so they can give me all the drugs that will make this not hurt so fucking much.

But what I want and what my body wants are two very different things.

"I want to stand, I do, but the pressure, Rem. The fucking pressu—" I can't even continue to speak when another contraction takes root.

His eyes pinch together in worry. "Maria, how long have you been having contractions?"

"I don't know. Awhil—" I start to say, but the pain is back again, tightening my body in a way that makes anything other than breathing impossible.

"Just take deep breaths," he coaches and pulls his phone out of his pocket. "I might be able to get us out of here. I was in the other elevator and pried my way out. And I can already get an ambulance on the way."

"Ahhh! Sweet land of the living, I don't think we have time for that, superstar," I shout, and when the pressure becomes so intense it feels like someone just lit a match to my vagina, I turn into a crazy woman and slap his phone out of his hand.

And then, *pop!* The audible sound fills the elevator, and the feel of water dripping down my legs makes me very aware of my reality.

"Oh no."

"W-what?"

"I think…my water just broke, Remy. Oh my God," I grunt when the urge to push is undeniable. "I think the baby might be coming now. Like, right, right now. I feel like I need to push."

"Oh…oh shit," Remy says, glancing down to the space between my legs with a swallow.

"Oh my God, I want to push!"

"Shit." His eyes go wide. "Are you…Ri, I'm going to have to look and see what's going on. Are you okay if I…" He stammers a little, nerves and uneasiness about making me uncomfortable no doubt hurtling their way from his stomach to his throat, but pretty quickly, the man I've known nearly all my life gets it together. Steady, in control, calming—Remington Winslow has seen the options before him and decided for himself. There's only one thing to do here, and it's not going to do either of us any good to tiptoe around it.

"Ri, I need to check you and see if the baby's coming, okay?"

I nod fervently. "I'm well past modesty at this point," I admit easily through my pants. "Please help me. Help the baby."

He nods immediately, squeezing my hand before he lets it go, swiveling to reposition on his knees. Down between my legs, he eases up the hem of my skirt and props my feet up on his shoulders. As he gently maneuvers my underwear out of the way, the demands of my body cry out again, making me howl into the echoey space so hard I throw my head back until it nearly hits the wall.

Sweat feels sticky on my face, and the cloying heat of this summer blackout isn't helping a bit, but eventually, I find the strength to lift my head again and meet Remy's eyes.

And that's all it takes for me to know the truth—the baby is there. The baby is so there, he or she is practically a third passenger already.

"It's happening, isn't it?" I kind of want to cry. "I'm really about to have this baby in a fucking elevator, aren't I?"

Remy nods, his eyes sympathetic and his smile comforting. "I can see a head full of beautiful brown hair."

"Shit!" I scream, letting my head fall back again and throwing my arm over my face. I knew it was happening—I can very much feel it happening—and still, some small part of me was hoping it wasn't real.

And then the fear rushes back, making my mind race with all the things I was supposed to do and all the things I'm not sure I'm ready for.

"Oh my God, I don't think I can do this, Remy!" I grunt, trying to breathe through the urge to push. "I don't know if I can be a mom to Isabella's baby, and I still have so much to get done at work. Daniel and Brenda aren't ready to handle the ship while I'm busy with a newborn and Claudia is completely worthless and I think I need to hold the baby in until I get all my ducks in a row. You know, just, like…a wine bottle with a cork, but only the cork needs to be human-sized and—"

"*Maria*," he cuts me off, removing my hand from my face and making me look at him with a gentle press of his fingers to my chin. "Nothing else matters right now. You can do this."

The pain is still there, so excruciating it makes me wonder how some women willingly sign up to do this more than once. And I know my eyes must be wild, like an insane woman who is about to come apart at the seams.

Because, I *am*, for all intents and purposes, an insane woman who is coming apart at the seams. One very specific seam is ripping wide open right at this moment, actually.

"Maria, you can do this," he repeats. "I'm right here, and I'm going to do everything in my power to take care of you both. But I need you to concentrate and push when you have a contraction so we can get the baby out safely, okay?"

As much as I don't want to, as much as I'd love to be voted off the island right about now, I curl up my abs and lean in to the pressure as my insides light on fire once again. Remy strokes at my ankle, calmly reassuring me the whole time.

"That's it, Ri. You're doing it. I can *see* you doing it. The baby's head is moving down."

I use every ounce of my strength to finish off my push and collapse back toward the elevator floor as the tension in my abdomen recedes slightly.

"You've got this. You're doing so fucking good, it's ridiculous," Remy coaches, moving his hand between my legs again. He tries to be discreet, I can tell, but the feeling of him ripping my underwear completely out of the way under these circumstances is the kind of thing my brain will be trying to sort out for decades. "One more big push, okay? The baby is so close, Ri."

The next contraction comes, and I do the only thing I can do, I woman the fuck up. Lifting my head, I curl into the pressure and push as hard as I can. The intensity and the burning pain make me scream and grip my legs behind the thighs.

And Remy continues to reassure me with encouraging words while he leans his weight into my feet to help give me leverage without moving from the catcher's position.

"Keep going, Ri! Keep pushing just like that!"

I scream and I yell and I'm pretty sure I say some things about the pope that I'm going to need to confess the next time I go to church, but within a minute, the most beautiful cry in the world rents the air.

"It's a girl, Maria," Remy says, looking down at the wiggly, screaming ball of life in his hands. "A beautiful baby girl."

"Oh God. Oh my God, it's a girl," I cry, tears pouring unchecked down my face. "I did it. I did it, and she's really here."

Remy doesn't hesitate from his position between my legs, cradling the messy baby against his chest to check her nose and mouth the best he can, and then gently passing her up to me and laying her on my chest.

"You're the most beautiful baby I've ever seen," I tell her, and her cries begin to soften. "Welcome to the world, sweetheart."

There's a moment then, of complete and utter spirituality. A moment when everything in the world slows and my sister feels so incredibly present. Her sweet baby girl clings to my chest and wraps her fingers around my own, and all I can do is sob. I see casually through my tears that Remy has pushed himself back to the other side of the elevator and settled his back into the wall, wetness on his face too.

I wouldn't dare categorize it for him, but the raw emotion among the three of us is so powerful, I feel like I've been transported to another planet.

"I hope I don't sound like a dick when I say this, Ri, but my God, I'm so proud of you. And you should be proud of you, too. What you just did…" He shakes his head, and I swear a tear falls down one of his cheeks. "Incredible."

Just then, there's a bang on the outside of the shiny golden doors, and the muffled voice of one of New York's finest calls, "Hello in there! This is the FDNY. Is everyone all right?"

Remy clears his throat and climbs to his feet just inside the doors. "We're okay, but we've just delivered a baby. We need immediate medical attention."

There's mumbling outside and then another yell from the firefighter. "Yes, sir, understood. EMS is on the way! Stand back, please, while we work on getting this elevator switched over to the generator so we can get you guys out!"

Remy steps back and to the side, very pointedly blocking the baby and me from anything that could come from the direction of the doors, and I listen as they get started on getting us out of here.

The baby works her mouth at the fabric at my chest, and my abdomen contracts painfully about every minute or so. I know that my body is attempting to birth the placenta now—thanks to Dr. Maddox and Google-style prenatal education—and that now is the time when some medical professionals would be a really good idea.

I need to be monitored for hemorrhage, and the doctors need to check us both to make sure everything is okay. But I feel tired and weak, and staying awake and alert to the baby on my chest is about all I can do.

I hear hustle and bustle outside the doors, and then finally, the elevator jolts and eases up to the floor. I can hear Remy explaining the entire situation to the firefighters, and I can even almost see a couple of paramedics as they approach. But the details are hazy, my mind a fog, really.

Paramedics are around me now. I can feel their hands as they move up and down my arm to insert an IV, lift me onto the gurney, and wheel me out of the building through the same door I entered what feels like a lifetime ago. Remy trails behind steadily, and I wish with all my might I could find the strength to ask him to come to the hospital. I need to say more—to thank him.

"Remy?" I call for him, my voice a pathetic whisper. "Remy?"

It feels like it takes an hour for his response, but when I feel his hand grip mine and I look up and into the blue of his eyes, relief fills my chest. "I'm here."

"I'm so tired," I tell him.

"Then close your eyes and rest," he says and reaches out to brush loose strands of hair out of my face. "You and the baby are in good hands now."

"Will you…will you stay?"

"Of course, babe." His smile is so warm and cozy I want to wrap myself in it like a blanket. "Wouldn't want to be anywhere else."

I want to say more, but I can't hold my eyes open enough to speak, and the last thing I hear is the doors of the ambulance closing behind my gurney, Remy's hand on mine the entire time.

Wouldn't want to be anywhere else, my mind whispers his words. Words that I've heard before, on one particular day, many, many years ago.

THE PAST

SOME OTHER TIME

Twenty-Eight Years Ago...

Friday afternoon, the first week of school...

Maria

"Okay, ladies! I know it's the weekend, but I need full focus for another hour, okay?" Emily, the captain of Hidden Hills' varsity squad, shouts loud enough for all of us to hear over the football team practicing on the other end of the field. "It's time to practice the first two stunts of our routine. Chrissy and Kate, I want you to be bases! Eden, you're backspot. Maria, you're going to fly!"

Oh boy. My hands shake, and I run clammy fingers over the material of my shorts.

"Let's go, ladies! You can do it!" Emily exclaims as she stands off to the side, ready to watch me and three senior girls attempt a basket toss that kind of makes me want to puke.

Yes, I've done this type of stunt before, but I think the pressure of being the only freshman on the varsity cheerleading squad is starting to get the best of me.

"You ready, fresh meat?" Chrissy asks, and I push a smile to my face to cover my nerves.

No, not really. "Uh... Of course."

"Well, let's do it, then, girlfriend!" Kate chimes in.

I position myself between them, and with my head down, I inhale a deep breath.

You can do this.

I try to picture my little sister Isabella in the hope that I can draw some strength from her enthusiasm for all things cheerleading. The girl lives and breathes cheer. It's always been her dream for us to cheer on the varsity squad together. And although, it'll be another three years before that dream can even come to fruition, I figured I'd get used to it—establish myself on the squad before that.

And it doesn't hurt that cheering affords you a front-row seat to Remy Winslow playing football either.

"Ready!" Eden shouts from behind me and claps her hands together. "Okay!"

My cue comes faster than I'd like, but I dig deep and find the strength to follow through. Hands together three times, I jump to the tips of my toes and straighten out the muscles of my body while I brace myself on Chrissy's and Kate's shoulders. They lock their arms together by holding each other's wrists in a basket-weave pattern, and Eden grips my hips, counting it off, "One, two!"

With a bounce of my toes, I jump up to the surface of their hands, and Eden counts it again, "One, two!"

Chrissy's and Kate's hands move down under my feet and then up with amazing force. I'm catapulted up, my body flying toward the sky, and I focus on keeping my arm and leg muscles tight as I let my back stretch into the first flip of my stunt.

All is going well *until* my body starts its rotation into the second flip.

My equilibrium turns wonky when I forget to latch my eyes on to my spotting point, and my body overrotates all the way through the second flip and halfway into a third as gravity starts to pull me down. My momentum is too much for Chrissy, Kate, and Eden, especially in this awkward position, and as a result, the catch fails spectacularly. We have a rule in cheerleading—that a flyer *never* hits the floor. But even I have to admit, in this case, I've made it pretty much impossible for them to catch me. All that's left is the ground.

Ohhhh noooooo!

After that much height and rotation, the impact is so sudden it forces my left hand to hit the ground at an awkward angle, and an audible *crack!* assaults my ears.

The pain that follows is so dang intense, it makes my vision burst into a kaleidoscope of indiscernible shades of reds and yellows and whites.

"Maria!"

"Oh my gosh!"

Concerned voices fill my ears, but all I can do is lie there, on the grass, cradling my left arm to my body. The discomfort is so acute, so undeniable, that I know I probably broke something.

Oh God. I'm gonna puke.

To my right side, I tilt my body, and vomit shoots out of my mouth and onto the football field.

"Ew. *Gross.*"

"Shut up, Chrissy! She's hurt!" Eden scolds.

"Maria?" Emily's worried voice is right beside me. "Are you okay?"

All I can do is shake my head when I meet her eyes. I am definitely not okay.

"I think we need—" she starts to call over her shoulder, but something stops her midsentence.

Bright-blue eyes replace Emily's green ones so quickly it's almost as if she vanishes in a puff of air.

"Maria? You okay?" Remington Winslow, sweaty and still wearing a football helmet, is hovering over me, his eyes etched with the kind of unease that makes tears want to flow from mine.

I swallow hard against them and try to answer, but my words come out all stutter-y. "It…it h-hurts really b-bad."

I don't know why I want to cry. Because it hurts? Because I feel embarrassed?

Because I feel oddly thankful for the concern he's showing me? *Probably all three.*

"Is it your arm?" he asks, his fingers gently assessing me for injuries.

"The left one," I tell him through a shaky breath. "I think it's broken."

"We should probably call an ambulan—" the Great Disappearing Emily tries, only to get metaphorically shoved out of the way again.

"I got her," Remy says as he tugs off his helmet and tosses it to the ground. "Maria, just keep that left arm braced to your body, okay?"

But there's no time for me to answer before I'm being moved, up and into his arms and cradled close to his chest.

"Where are you going, Winslow?!" a husky male voice calls from somewhere in the distance.

"She's hurt, Coach! I'm taking her to the ER!" Remy yells over his shoulder, his body already jumping into action and somehow managing to carry me like I weigh two pounds.

There are definitely irritated words that follow from his coach, but I'm too busy staring up at the enigma jogging me across the field and into the Brooklyn parking lot where his car is located to hear what's said. Most high schools in Manhattan don't even have football teams, but ours does. Still, because of spatial constraints, that means we have to either drive or bus it over to Aviator Field in Brooklyn every day to practice. It's normally a pain in the ass, but then again, I don't usually get the opportunity to ride in Remy's car.

"It's going to be okay. Hang tight, and I'll get you to the ER as fast as I can," he says gently as he carefully adjusts the passenger seat belt over my body and shuts the door.

As a matter of fact, I've never been in a *boy's* car before. I'd expect to feel all awkward and nervous, especially since said boy is two years older than me and one of the most popular guys in school, but the pain in my arm makes it impossible for me to think about anything else.

Not even a minute later, Remy is in the driver's seat of his totally cool forest-green hatchback Mustang and taking a right turn out of Aviator Field's parking lot.

The pain in my arm throbs in nauseating waves, and all I can do is settle in for the ride, resting my head back against the seat and keeping my eyes firmly shut.

I can feel him shift forward and mess with the knobs near the stereo, and the soft sounds of a Van Morrison song fill my ears. "Into the Mystic." It's an oldie but goodie and makes me smile internally over his music choices despite the throbbing pain resonating from my arm.

When I open my eyes again enough to look at the display, I realize it's a CD. I kind of love that he didn't choose something that's in the Top 40 and often played on the radio.

Man, Remington Winslow sure is a different kind of guy.

The song is a balm to my racing heart and anxious mind, and if it weren't for the nagging discomfort in my left arm, I might even be able to relax and enjoy this momentous occasion of being in a car with a boy…alone.

"Thank you," I eventually find the strength to tell him, and he glances at me out of his periphery.

"For what?"

"For helping me." I state the obvious. But when a sharp pain shoots from my left elbow and into my wrist, I grimace and shut my eyes. "Pretty sure Coach Rydell is pissed off at you for it."

"Wouldn't want to be anywhere else, babe."

Babe. He called me *babe*.

And more than that, Remington Winslow wouldn't want to be anywhere else than with me, on our way to the ER?

Sheesh. If I weren't in so much pain, those words just might show my teenage heart what it feels like to be in love. Which is crazy. I mean, this is *Remington Winslow*. A junior who could get any girl at our school. Surely he wouldn't waste his time with a freshman.

Says the girl who just got rescued by him.

The thought makes me open my eyes again and turn my head slightly to take in the way his blue eyes are fixated on the road. His dark hair is damp with sweat, and the T-shirt that covers his body shows off every rigid muscle.

Goodness, he's hot.

"You hanging in there?" he asks, looking at me briefly before putting his gaze back to the road. "We're only about ten minutes away."

Probably the hottest guy…ever. Brad Pitt has nothing on him.

I kind of want to kick myself for not agreeing to go with him and his little sister for ice cream when I first met him. I wanted to, of course, but I was too nervous and made up some lame excuse about having to get Isabella home.

My sister definitely gave me an earful for that as we walked back to our apartment that day.

"That was so dumb, Maria. You should've said yes. He was so cute!" she'd said.

Which, she was right. It *was* dumb.

Ever since then, I haven't had a single conversation with him. Frankly, I only ever see him when I'm at cheerleading practice and he's busy playing football at the other end of the field.

The music switches to another Van Morrison song, most likely because the CD is a greatest hits, and the opening beats of "Someone Like You" start to fill the inside of Remy's car.

Someone like you? More like, someone like Remy. That's the kind of guy I'd like to call my boyfriend.

"Maria? You okay? You still with me?" he questions, and I realize I never answered him the first time he asked.

But I don't really care about that question. I'm too busy wondering about a different one.

"Is the some-other-time offer still on the table?" I blurt out, and he furrows his brow, his eyes shifting back and forth between me and the road.

"What?"

Blush heats my cheeks, but it doesn't stop me like it normally would. Call it pain, hysteria, or adrenaline, but I am, in fact, trying to ask Remington Winslow out. "A few weeks ago, when you asked me to get ice cream with you and I couldn't." I remind him of the first and last time we had a conversation. "I'm just wondering if that some-other-time offer is still on the table."

"Are you asking me out, Maria?" His smile is almost too big for the inside of his car. "Right now? While I'm driving you to the ER?"

Instantly, mortification starts to set in, and I feel like the world's biggest moron. I mean, how could I confuse him helping me get medical attention with him being interested in me?

Idiot. You're such an idiot.

"Uh—" I start to find a way backtrack, but he cuts me off.

"Because if that's the case, the answer is yes. A *hell* yes." He winks and reaches out to gently pat the skin of my knee. "Though, I only have one stipulation."

"And what's that?"

"Let's get that arm of yours seen by a doctor first."

"Good idea." I laugh. I can't help it. But the movement jostles my left arm in a way that makes me whimper.

"We're almost there." Remy squeezes my knee once more and then focuses his full attention back on the road.

Me, though? I float off into a place of euphoric disbelief, far too giddy for a girl who is on the way to the hospital with a broken arm.

Remington Winslow *just said yes to going out with* me.

SEVEN

Late night, Friday, August 23rd

Remy

Night has consumed the sky, and the blistering heat that caused another damn blackout today has dissipated to a tolerable seventy-five degrees.

I can't believe that, just five hours ago, I arrived at this very hospital, in the back of an ambulance, with Maria and her baby. Hell, her baby whom *I* delivered. Inside a fucking elevator.

I have Maria's car seat and hospital bag clutched in my hands, and the hospital doors open automatically as I enter. The night shift security guard flashes a wide smile in my direction.

"Congratulations, Dad," he greets, the items I'm carrying putting off what he assumes is an obvious signal.

In fact, in his tenure here, I'm sure he's encountered lots of new dads arriving at the hospital in a bluster of panic and excitement and stupidity. No matter how prepared, how ready they are to be fathers, the transition is both sudden and rude. There's no going back from being responsible for another human being. No redos, no second chances, no pushing the pause button.

I don't bother discrediting his assumption, as an explanation would be a lot more labor than I'm prepared to take on, instead grinning in his direction and bowing my head in a nod of acknowledgment as I head toward the bank of elevators in the lobby.

Truthfully, I imagine many a spectator would think I *am* the father. I mean, I am the guy who arrived alongside Maria in the ambulance with an obviously flustered appearance—*and with a shirt that has seen some shit*—and waited nervously for news of the doctors verifying that both mom and baby were okay. And then, I even talked my way into her hospital room as her support person.

Maybe I shouldn't have done that, but I couldn't find it in me to do anything else but stay by her side. Didn't *want* to do anything else but that.

An empty elevator is ready and waiting, and I scoot inside with all of Maria's baby loot in tow. The maternity ward is only a short ride to the fourth floor, but it's long enough to have a brief moment of realization—I'm not really connected to this woman and her child, other than being a part of the birth.

Sure, Maria and I have a past. *History.* But it's been years since we were together. Two decades worth, in fact. Other than someone she used to love a million years ago, I'm simply a man who knows as much about her life now as she knows about mine—very little.

God, I hope I'm not making her uncomfortable by hanging around and semi-forcing her to let me run the errand to her apartment for all the planned items she didn't have with her. But without any family showing up to replace me, it doesn't feel right leaving her alone. She really is a one-woman show, and wholly welcome or not, I won't leave her to that. *Can't* leave her to it.

She's doing a lot of things alone right now, and the thought of adding to that pile makes my stomach churn.

When the doors open on the fourth floor, I step off and make my way down the hall, the nurses offering friendly waves as I pass their station. They recognize me by now, our story of birth in an elevator becoming hospital lore in a flash of a second upon our arrival.

I smile glancingly, knowing that staying in the good graces of the nursing staff in the hospital is about the smartest thing you can do, but mostly focus on making my way to Maria and the baby.

The door is cracked as I step up to it, the tiniest sliver of light from the hallway cutting into the darkness of the entry hallway. I push it open gently, careful to be quiet, and pause at the corner by the bathroom when I see that both Maria and the baby have fallen fast asleep.

It's a sweet vision, to be honest, and I refuse to be the bastard who wakes them up.

Backing out slowly, I set the car seat and bag on the chair by the door and head back toward the nurses station. Several of them are milling around as they scarf down their midnight snacks, so I belly up to the counter and raise a finger to get their attention.

"Yes, sweetie?" the one with hot-pink scrubs and barely graying hair asks me with a wink.

"I was just wondering if one of you could point me in the direction of the gift shop. I thought I might pick up a few things while mom and baby are resting."

"Sure, sugar," offers another nurse, this one older and hungrier, if you know what I mean. Maybe she can smell the singledom on me, but something about a woman trying to pick me up in the maternity ward of a hospital when they know I arrived here with another woman seems wrong. "Want me to show you? I have a little break."

I smile broadly, keeping the tone light and easy. "Thanks for the offer, but I think directions will do just fine." She frowns a little, and I cock my head to the side slightly. "I'll be sure to have them call up here for you if I need help carrying stuff, though."

She laughs at that, as do the others, and the easiness of casual acquaintances washes back in.

"You just have to take the elevator back to the bottom floor and then follow the signs toward the cafeteria. The gift shop is right across from it and open twenty-four hours, so you're in luck."

"Great," I reply with a slap of my hand on the counter. "I appreciate it."

Turning back for the elevators, I push the call button, climb aboard, and make my way back down to the ground floor.

The security guard's eyebrows rise when he sees me exiting so soon, and I shrug with a grin in an effort not to let him down. "They're sleeping. Figured I'd get some food and reinforcements."

"Good thinking."

My chest pings a little with memories of how I'd intended my life to go. How I'd imagined I'd be married young with kids and a house and, frankly, a different life entirely. Instead, I'm in my forties, single, and pretending to be the father of a kid who belongs to a woman I've barely seen in the last two decades.

Yeah, but she's not just any woman. It's Maria.

"Don't worry, sir." The man tries to reassure me about the things he thinks he knows. "You're gonna be good at this."

"Thanks," I murmur, my enthusiasm slightly muted by the realization that I'm just playing house rather than making it.

"You bet. Enjoy the quiet time while you can."

I chuckle a little and give him a jerk of my chin before making my way down the hall. A blue stripe runs along the middle of the wall the entire way, and I'm sure it means something to someone. To me, though, it just reminds me of high school—of high school with Maria.

Our school colors were blue and gold, and our mascot was a strong and wild mustang. Maria cheered at all my football games, and even now, after all these years, I can remember the way her legs looked in that bright-blue uniform, stretched out inside the passenger seat of my car.

She was special, even then, and all the guys in our school knew it, including me. Normally, as a junior guy with the prospects I had, I never would have dreamed of dating a girl two years younger than me. The freshmen were practically considered an entirely different class of humans at the time. But not Maria Baros.

She was in a class of her own. Vibrant, beautiful, kind—she drew people to her like a magnet. I can hardly remember a time that I didn't find her deeply enveloped in the grasp of someone else, someone desperate to talk to her, desperate to share even just a minute of her time between classes.

She loved to laugh, and she did it often, whether she was the one telling the joke or not. She made people feel good about themselves and about life, and I found myself ninety percent happier any time I was around her.

Clearly, only a dumb shit eighteen-year-old would let a girl like that go.

The gift shop is obvious once I reach the end of the hall and turn the corner, though at this hour, it looks mostly deserted. Lights shine on big blue and pink teddy bears, and balloons billow in the gentle breeze of the air conditioning.

A young brunette girl sits behind the counter playing on her phone, and for the briefest of moments, I almost think she's the fifteen-year-old Maria of my memories, it all feels so fresh.

She stands up and smiles, setting her phone down on the counter when she notices my presence.

I glance around the store and then back to her, and her eyes widen in question. "Something in particular you're looking for?"

"Something that won't be super annoying for a new mom with a newborn."

She laughs. "I don't know that such a thing exists. From what I hear, the sleep deprivation is hell."

"Okay," I say through a soft chuckle. "Something she'll at least appreciate, then?"

She purses her lips in thought and then nods. "Oh, I know. We do these custom signs. With the baby's name and height and weight and stuff. My mom did one for me, even a long time ago, and she's still got it. In a closet, but still. She says it's one of her favorite things."

I almost say yes to the sign, but then I realize Maria hasn't decided on a name yet.

"How about some flowers and balloons? Those wouldn't be too obnoxious, right?"

She smiles. "Not at all."

"What about one of the life-sized stuffed bears?"

She grimaces. "I'd steer clear unless you want to throw caution to the wind."

I laugh. "That's what I was thinking. Especially in the city. Unless the bear can pay rent, it's not a good idea."

"Totally. Also, if you find a bear to pay rent, let me know. I could use the help."

I laugh at her good humor and pull my wallet out of my back pocket to pay for the goodies I've requested. While she wraps up my flowers, my phone buzzes in my pocket, and I pull it out to find a string of texts from my brothers, pissed off that I'm a no-show for guys' night.

The first messages occurred earlier in the evening, most likely when I was busy helping Maria get comfortable in her hospital room.

Ty: I've been elected as investigator in the matter of Remy Winslow's disappearance. If anyone has any information regarding his whereabouts—ie, not at fucking Thatch's house like he's supposed to be—please contact me at this number promptly.

Flynn: For the record, I did not vote in this election.

Jude: Me either

Ty: Fuck you guys. All I've heard from you for the last thirty minutes is bitching about where Remy is and why he's not here on time, and I'm the only one with the nuts to send a message.

Jude: Did you just accuse Flynn of having no nuts? While he's in the same room as you? Do you have a death wish?

Ty: His wife likes me too much for him to kill me.

Flynn: You're her least favorite, actually.

Ty: THE FUCK?

Tonight was poker night at Thatcher Kelly's house. A man who is one of my brother-in-law Wes's best friends, and who has, over the years, become not only one of my investment clients, but a good buddy, too.

Honestly, Thatch is one of those people that once he's in your life, you can't get rid of him. He's like a lovable parasite.

I scroll down about twenty text messages and finally land on some words of actual concern for my whereabouts. It's not like I was wishing for them to worry so much they sent out a search party, but given the length of time it took them to reach a true manifestation of an emotional connection to their eldest brother, I won't be listing any of them as my emergency contact in the future. My sister and my mom will have to bear that burden.

Jude: Remy? Earth to Remy? Where the fuck are you?

Ty: Is it just me, or does it feel like he's standing us up? You think he's okay?

Jude: Remy? ARE YOU OKAY? Text YES if you've been abducted by aliens.

Ty: That'd suck if he got abducted, but it'd also be cool, you know? To have a relative who lives on another planet?

Flynn: I don't have time for space travel visits. We just got the twins on a sleep schedule.

I scroll down to the most recent messages, and they make it apparent Flynn is the only sober brother left.

Jude: Whats a ducking bastich you Rem. You standed us up.

Ty: Duckwit.

Flynn: Hey, idiots, our cab is here. Stop texting, close your tabs, and get the fuck outside.

Jude: Damn, Flynns mads.!.

Ty: So pisses

Jude: HAA. Now I gotta piss.

Ty: You think Rems dies?

Jude: He okay bub

Flynn: I will kill you both if you don't move your asses.

I'm left wondering how in the hell poker night at Thatch's place turned into my two youngest brothers getting hammered drunk at a bar but choose to find the answer to the question some other time.

Crazy assholes.

On a silent laugh and a roll of my eyes, I lock the screen of my phone and shove it back into my pocket. It might seem cruel not to at least let them know I'm okay, but trust me, with the number of times they've left me wondering whether I'd find their bodies in a ditch somewhere, this is the least they deserve.

I did, however, answer Lexi earlier in the night, who was still very concerned by the care her parents were showing in their garden. I talked her off a ledge while Maria and the baby were getting their checkups, and I even said hello to my sister briefly. So, I'm not a total monster. One member of my siblingdom knows I'm alive.

"Here you go," the girl behind the register says and hands the flowers and balloons to me.

"Thanks again," I tell her over my shoulder as I start the trek back to the maternity ward.

It's a short, uneventful trip in the elevator, and I hold the balloons in front of my face to avoid eye contact with Ol' Hungry Eyes as I pass the nurses station. When I get back to Maria's door, a dim light is on, and I can hear her murmuring to the baby on the other side of the room.

Slow and easy, I push through the door and announce my arrival with a soft, "It's Remy. Can I come in?"

"Of course," Maria says, turning to face me as I walk inside her room. On the bed, the baby is sprawled out in front of her, fussing a little as she gets her diaper changed.

A smile lights up Maria's face when her eyes meet mine, and I can't pretend it doesn't spread a warmth throughout my chest.

"Well, this is a nice surprise," she adds. "I saw the bag and the car seat and thought you went home for the night."

"And miss the look on your face when changing your first dirty diaper? No way."

She laughs. "My God, it's like tar!"

I pad into the room and stop just short of her so I can lean around to see the baby. "Don't worry, little lady. My mom said the same about me."

Maria rolls her eyes, and I put the flowers on the table by her bed and tie the balloons to the window lock so they're out of the way before returning to her side as she's securing the tabs of the baby's diaper.

"So…what are we thinking about her name?" I ask. "Have you decided yet?"

She shakes her head solemnly, and I rub her shoulder in comfort. "It's fine. She doesn't need a name yet anyway. Honestly, she won't even know the sound of it for a couple of months, so you could try out a bunch of stuff if you want to," I tease, trying to lighten the mood, and Maria turns to shove my shoulder playfully before picking up the baby and cradling her.

"You're ridiculous."

"No, no." I scoff. "Me being ridiculous would be suggesting you name her Otis. Or Kone. Or Schindler. Or ThyssenKrupp."

"Are those…" Her eyebrows pinch together as she concentrates. "Are those elevator companies?"

"They might be," I admit with a wink, and she bursts into melodic laughter. I smile so big my face hurts.

"How in the eff do you know all those elevator companies?"

"I think the real question here is, how do *you* know?" I challenge, crinkling my brow.

"You first."

"I'm an observant person. I notice details." I shrug one shoulder. "I also might have a strong understanding of how each of those companies is doing in the market right now."

"Stocks. Of course." She laughs. "Well, I'm in real estate. And you wouldn't believe the things clients ask sometimes."

"Are there really elevator-brand snobs? Here? In this city? Sharing my air?"

"Yes. Lots of them. And, well, honestly, after the run I've had with elevators lately, I'm starting not to blame them."

I walk to the chair on the other side of the room and settle into it while she eases herself and the baby down onto the bed. I want to offer to help, but her body language seems closed off from that, and I completely understand. We've gotten supremely intimate today, and she's finally getting back a little bit of her personal space and control.

"If we're going to point the finger, we should probably do it at the power grid," I comment. "He's the bad guy here."

"Nah. I choose not to believe that. The city's power grid is a mint antique with a lot of charm. At least, that's how I'd describe it if I were writing it into a listing."

I chuckle. "I love a good spin. In my business, we do the same thing. *Oh yes, Mr. Jones. The market is simply coasting through some expected volatility. We're looking for the law of averages, not the law of extremes.*" I roll my eyes at myself. "Meanwhile, Mr. Jones just lost $100K in a two-day bottom."

Her smile shows she gets it. "It's the job, right?"

"Yeah," I agree. "And sometimes the job is shit."

She tilts her head in question. "You don't like it?"

"Eh," I admit. "Most days are okay. I like the security it's built me in my life. I like the security I've been able to give my family. And I like the numbers. I like the game of it. But the all-consuming hours I put in? That's starting to get old."

"Oh, so it's not just me whose job consumes their life?" she retorts on a snort. "I mean, it's probably completely normal for a pregnant woman to schedule three showings in a row two days before her due date, right?"

"Wait…is that why you were in my building?"

"Yes." She grimaces.

"Damn, Ri. I think you work too much."

"Says the guy who just admitted *he* works too much."

I laugh at her cheeky grin, and somewhere deep inside me, I remember how good the two of us used to be together. How we always laughed and had the kind of back-and-forth banter that made me pull all-nighters with her on the phone, despite my mom's irritation.

"So, the hours, then?" she questions, and I meet her eyes again. "That's what you don't like about the job?"

The hours can be brutal. Sure, the stock market's opening bell rings at 9:30 a.m. sharp, but the true trading, if you manage to claw your way into the investment in-crowd, starts around four. If you want to make the *real* moves, you're up and trading before the sun even thinks about rising.

"That's part of it," I answer honestly. "But if I had to choose what bothers me the most, it's the pressure and stress that come with messing with someone else's hard-earned money."

"That's exactly why I try not to be too judgmental, even when people are pricks. I mean, it is *their* money they're spending. They just want to protect it. I can understand that."

"Nah. Anyone who's rude to you must really be an asshole."

A giggle jumps from her throat as she pats the baby's back with a gentle hand. "And why's that?"

"Because you're special and kind and considerate. A whole trio of things that are a rarity in this city. In this world, really. Anyone who can't see that has their head up their ass."

In an instant, her eyes turn warm and vulnerable in a way that makes me want to walk over and pull both her and the baby into my arms.

"Remy?"

"Yeah?"

"Thanks for showing up today. I don't know what I would have done without you."

Knowing what I know now, I don't know what I would have done if I'd missed it.

EIGHT

Maria

The war inside my chest could be in history books one day, I think to myself as I stare down into the newly opened eyes of the most beautiful baby girl I've ever seen.

She's so delicate and tiny and innocent and the perfect combination of her parents, and my heart squeezes at the hurt of them never getting the chance to see her—of Isabella never getting the chance to hold her.

My sister loved babies and wanted them with a fierceness that I never understood. I was content to be alone—content to pour all my time and energy into myself and our business and my sister and her family.

Now, I'm all the family this sweet angel has got.

When it comes to her living relatives, it's just me and Oliver's parents that are still in the picture. But they live across the pond, all the way in Italy, and aren't in good enough health to travel. Aside from FaceTime calls, I'm not expecting to see them anytime soon.

I'm literally all she has.

And she's all the family you have, too.

I was supposed to be her fun aunt.

But now, I'm her mother...*right?*

"You okay over there?" Remy asks quietly from his spot across the room, and my gaze jerks up to meet his. "Your thoughts look heavy."

How he could possibly read me that well after all these years is beyond me.

Right now, I look at him, and I see nothing—understand nothing. I would give almost anything for a tiny window to see inside. For the chance to know what he's thinking at this moment.

I mean, it's one in the morning, we've been at the hospital for several hours with nothing more than a lot of diaper changes, feedings, and bumbling on my part, and still, he hasn't left other than to go to my apartment on an errand for me and to the gift shop to get me flowers and balloons.

Frankly, he hasn't even gone home to change his torn-up T-shirt that became a casualty in the war against the elevator.

Is he planning on staying the rest of the night? The whole time I'm here? I can't figure it out, and with the state of my emotions this soon after giving birth to my sister's baby, I don't exactly have the capacity to ask.

"I'm…okay, I guess. It's just a lot."

Remy nods sympathetically, his eyes so soft I'd almost swear he'd lost a sister and subsequently given birth to her baby himself.

Perhaps, though, the adult version of the boy I loved is just an empath of sorts.

"I know. You have all the right in the world to feel anything you need to feel. There's no certain way this is supposed to happen."

"No certain way this is supposed to happen?" I scoff a little, a bitter twinge firing in my chest and making me say the words I've been thinking out loud. "I was *supposed* to hand her over to my sister while I watched joy overwhelm her. I was *supposed* to be the fun aunt. But now, I guess, I'm her mother."

"Yeah, Maria." His smile is sad, but also hopeful. "You are her mother. And she's so incredibly lucky to have you."

Those words disarm me. They make me drop my verbal weapons and meet his eyes. "Y-you think so?" I ask and glance down at the beautiful baby in my arms.

"I know so, babe."

"I'm sorry," I say with a groan. The last person I want to lash out at is Remy. He's the only one here for me—the only one here for…

Just like that, it hits me. My sister can't be here, but I can do my damnedest to make it seem like she is. She wouldn't mope or cry or even let the exhaustion get to her. She'd joke and laugh and love and tease, and she'd do it all in earnest.

The best thing I can do for her daughter is embody her spirit.

"Isabella Olive," I say aloud, making Remy raise his eyebrows slightly. "That's what I'm going to name her. After her mom and her dad. Isabella and Oliver. And I want to call her Izzy."

"Izzy." He tests out the name on his tongue. "I love it."

I smile then. "Yeah? You don't think it's too cheesy?"

He shakes his head and climbs to his feet, strolling over to look down at Izzy's now-sleeping face. "Maybe for some other baby. Some lesser infant. But not this one," he says proudly. "This one can carry it."

I laugh, wiping a lingering tear from my face and smiling down at my girl. "She does look strong."

Remy hums from right next to me, and a wave of warmth from his body settles the chill in my spine. "Oh yeah. She looks like she can do anything…" He laughs. "Aside from feed and care for herself for the next several months, that is. But other than that, she's got this world handled."

That makes me feel good. Confident. Like the world isn't turned completely upside down, if only for a moment.

Still, it feels a little too intimate—too vulnerable. And I do what I've always done as a protective mechanism. I make a joke.

"Good thing you weren't this into female empowerment in high school, Rem. We would have been famous for female spontaneous combustion."

He smirks and shakes his head as he steps away and drags the chair from the side of the room closer to the bed to sit down next to me. He crosses one jean-covered ankle over the other knee and leans back into the seat. He looks so damn sexy, I swear, if my vagina didn't hurt so bad right now, she'd probably be revving right to life.

"Oh, come on," he denies through a laugh. "I wasn't anything special in high school."

"Wow," I say with feigned insult. "Are you trying to say I was with a dud?"

"Obviously. That's probably why you're still single now. I scarred you for life."

I blow out a humored puff of air and rock the baby in my arms on instinct as she starts to whimper. "Oh yeah. That's *exactly* why I'm single."

Remy just shrugs like his crazy words hold any merit. "As far as I can tell, that's the only logical reason. If you wanted to be with someone, you would."

"What? What do you mean?"

"You're a catch, Ri. A real one-in-a-million bachelorette. I bet the men nip at your ankles every chance they get."

I snort. "They don't."

"Pull at the hem of your skirt, then?"

"Pretty sure that would be sexual harassment," I tease. "And no, they don't do anything."

He considers me closely. "You must just be too intimidating, then. Too awesome and strong and successful for them." He lowers his voice to a conspiratorial whisper. "Don't let anyone know you heard this from me, but the truth is, most men are big old babies. Afraid of rejection. Wounded ego. Insecure. We're mostly worthless."

"Don't worry. We, the women, already know," I say through a soft laugh and flash a wink in his direction.

He groans and falls back into the chair with a bang, pretending to stab himself in the chest with a knife and twist it, as though I've wounded him greatly. I know better. Remington Winslow may be a representative of the male community, but he's absolutely none of the things he just listed. He's confident and kind and completely secure in his manhood without having to be a pompous twat.

"Honestly, I'm probably single because that's the way I've wanted it," I admit, and he looks at me for a long moment.

"You've *never* wanted to settle down with someone?"

No one besides him *when you were a love-sick teenage girl*, my mind reminds me, but I keep that information to myself.

"Not really. I've always been too career-focused, I guess. What about you?"

"What about me?"

"Oh, c'mon, Rem." I squint when a knowing smile crests my lips. "You know what I mean. Why is a great guy like you still single?"

"I already attempted the marriage thing once," he responds and runs a hand through his hair. "As you know, that didn't exactly work out."

His words make it seem like his past has jaded him. Like it's closed off the possibility of love and companionship. My heart twinges with discomfort for him.

"So…you never see yourself settling down with someone?"

"Honestly?" He shakes his head. "No."

Well, damn. Like, no marriage…no relationship…*ever?*

I'm tempted to push the question, but Remy beats me to the punch and redirects the conversation altogether.

"Well, unless the relationship involves free Chipotle burritos. Then I'd consider it."

I snort. "Rem, that's a reward card. Not a relationship."

"Oh, then, I guess I want to settle down with a reward card," he says with a big ol' grin that reminds me of the past and how something as simple as talking to Remy was always so much fun.

Laughter, teasing quips, and lots of smiles, that's how it always was with him.

And that's exactly how it is with him now. We fill more hours of the night, teasing and joking and laughing while Izzy is cradled in my arms for ninety percent of the time. I know people say to put babies down from the beginning, but I know my sister wouldn't let go for a beat unless it was to give Oliver a short turn.

And Remy makes it easy on me anyway. Taking her without my asking to change her diaper, and moving to the other side of the room when it's time for me to breastfeed her. He even gets the nurse for me when I'm having issues with getting her to latch.

He respects my privacy while remaining at my side, and after more time passes, I'm not even sure I care to know what his plan is anymore. I'm just thankful for his company. Thankful for the time he's spent making me feel like I'm not alone.

Now, though, it's a little after five in the morning, and finally giving in to exhaustion, Remy's fallen asleep in the hard wooden chair on the other side of the room, and his neck is craned awkwardly to the side. After all he's done for me, I can't stand the thought of being the reason he can't look to the left for a couple of weeks.

I start working on shifting my weight in the bed to get up and wake him, when a new nurse comes in to introduce herself and let me know she's taking over for a couple hours because my previous nurse got to go home early.

She's blond and bubbly and efficient, writing her name—Deb—on the whiteboard at the side of my bed and then glancing over to Remy sleeping in his chair.

She smiles conspiratorially. "The dads are always more exhausted than the moms at this point. I think it's because they spend the entire pregnancy worrying."

A small ping of something I can't distinguish makes my belly flip at Remy being referred to as the "dad." I don't know what it's about, but I can only imagine it's another blip of grief for my sister and her husband.

And I can't find it in myself to correct her.

"I can get loud if you want… Wake him up?" she offers, pulling me out of my thoughts and making me laugh.

"That's okay. Thanks for the ride-or-die attitude, though. I appreciate it."

She winks. "I'll be back in a little bit. Let me know if you've changed your mind."

As she leaves the room, I find myself staring at the fan of Remy's dark lashes on both of his closed eyes. They're as long as I remember—as though they're extensions.

Why do men always have to have such great eyelashes? It's completely unfair.

His face is relaxed, almost like he didn't deliver my baby in an elevator several hours ago, and that's when it strikes me. *I think I'm getting a little* too *comfortable having him here.*

It's relaxed and companionable and, quite frankly, easy reassurance of why I loved him so fiercely back in the day.

But God. My life is the absolute epitome of complicated, and Remy is the least deserving person I can think of trapping in my chaotic web.

Gingerly, I climb from the hospital bed and cross the distance to his chair on the other side of the room. His chest moves up and down with ease, and his lips are parted just enough to let out the tiniest puffs of air.

He's gorgeous, and I'm probably becoming a little too smitten all over again. Which is why I need to do this now—before I lose my nerve.

With two shaking fingers, I reach out to his shoulder and shove gently. It takes half a dozen pushes before he wakes up, but when he does, it's with a jolt.

"What...what's happening? Are you okay? Is Izzy okay?"

All thanks to raging postpartum hormones, I nearly burst into tears at the sweet concern in his voice.

"We're fine. Everything's okay."

He sits up straight and wipes the sleep from his eyes to look me over. "Do you need me to do something?"

I soften my face with a smile I don't really feel. "Go home. Get some sleep. In an actual bed."

"But I thought… Maria, I can help."

"I know, Rem. And I appreciate it. But watching you sleep sitting up in that chair is giving *me* a crick in my neck. Go home and rest. I'll be okay, I promise."

"Are you sure? I can stay. It's no prob—"

"I'm sure, Rem."

He considers me for a long moment and then nods. "Okay. If that's what you want."

"It is," I say and try to mean it. "But trust me, the jury's decided. You officially saved the day. Thank you for being there for me."

"I wouldn't have wanted to be anywhere else."

With words like that, I almost have the urge to tell him to stay forever, but I know that would be ridiculous.

"However, you should know, my departure comes with stipulations," he says and stands to his feet.

"Stipulations?"

"Yep. *Stipulations.*" He smirks as he pulls his cell phone out of his pocket and holds it out toward me. "I'll head home…once you give me your phone number."

In an instant, I feel like I've been transported back in time.

THE PAST

ONE OF MANY FIRSTS

Twenty-Eight Years Ago…

Friday night, the first week of school, after leaving the ER…

Maria

Remy comes to a stop in front of my building, and I stare down at the brand-new, bright-pink cast on my arm. The ER doctor confirmed that my suspicions were correct; I *did* break my arm, but apparently I was lucky it was a clean break to only one bone. And after six weeks of walking around with this colorful monstrosity attached to my body, I'll be as good as new.

Another oldie but goodie plays from Remy's stereo, a song I've heard my mom play a thousand times while she's making dinner. It's one of those songs that just…I don't know…gives you goose bumps. Pretty sure some guy named Otis sings it, and the title is "These Arms of Mine."

I look toward the driver's seat, where Remy sits, and I don't know if it's the music or the dose of pain medication the ER gave me to take the edge off, but I feel…something. Something that I don't really understand but makes me want to lean over the console and find out what Remington Winslow's lips feel like against mine.

But that's crazy, right? That would be a crazy thing to do. Especially for a girl who has only kissed one boy in her entire life, and it was just a small, little peck of nothing exciting.

"You think your mom is going to be mad?" Remy asks, and I'm thankful for the distraction. Goodness knows, my mind wasn't heading anywhere good.

"Well…" I look at him with wide eyes and a smile that's equal parts terrified and amused. "I don't think she's going to be happy that I didn't call her."

Instead, the nice nurse in the ER was the one to let her know her eldest daughter broke her arm while verifying insurance information and parental permission to be casted by the good doctor. Pretty sure I'm about to get an earful of anger and worry and disappointment when I walk through the door.

I *did* end up talking to her, more so to calm her down and so she didn't burst through the hospital doors like a madwoman than anything else, but still. I *at least* did that.

Thankfully, her inability to leave work at a moment's notice gave me more time with Remy. And after she talked to *his* mother on the phone, she gave a disgruntled go-ahead for him to drive me home.

Well, *you better bring your ass right home*, were her exact words.

Considering Carmen Baros never curses, it's safe to say, I have a heap of trouble waiting for me.

"I should've told you to call her first." He grimaces. "You were just in so much pain, all I could think about was getting you to the ER."

He just might be the sweetest guy I've ever met.

"Don't be silly. You helped out a lot by getting my mom in touch with your mom."

"Just so you know, Wendy Winslow wasn't too thrilled with me either," he says through a half laugh, half grimace. "I'm not really supposed to be driving everywhere on my own yet. I only have my permit."

"Eek. Looks like we both have long nights ahead of us."

He nods dramatically. "Yeah."

"Thanks again for…everything," I tell him for what has to be the one-hundredth time of the evening. "I don't know what I would've done without you today. You saved my butt."

"You can stop thanking me. I wanted to help."

"No, I should *definitely* thank you. Like a million times, in fact. I owe you big-time, Remy," I say, wishing I could repay him for his kindness. "If you ever get hurt or something and need someone to drive you to the ER, I'm your gal," I say. But then quickly add, "But obviously, I hope I can help you in a different way that doesn't involve you getting an injury. I definitely don't want that. But if an injury would occur, *which I definitely don't want that to happen,* I'm not the gal who can physically drive you because that would be illegal unless it happens two years from now, but I'll definitely be the gal who will call you a cab *and* keep you company."

Oh my God, what is wrong with you? You sound insane.

I almost cringe at my nearly incoherent ramble, but when an amused laugh jumps from Remy's lungs, I find myself smiling instead.

"Sounds perfect, Maria," he says, smiling right back at me. "I'll mark you down as my emergency contact if cab transportation is an option."

I giggle. "Great."

Silence stretches between us, and when I look down at my cast again, I get an idea.

"So…" I pause and hold out my arm. "Do you want to sign my cast?"

He grins. "You want me to be your first?"

You want me to be your first? That question plays in my mind on a loop, and I can't help but wish Remy would be my first for *a lot* of things. Not all of which my mother would approve of.

"Yes, please," I answer and hold out the black Sharpie one of the nurses in the ER was nice enough to give me before I was discharged.

"I'm honored, Maria," he says, but then a secret grin kisses his perfect mouth. "But my signature comes with stipulations."

"Huh? What do you mean?"

"I'll sign your cast," he explains. "But only if you give me your number."

My heart dances inside my chest. "You want my phone number?"

"Yeah," he says with the kind of smile that makes my stomach feel all gooey inside. "I have to make sure you're going to follow through with our *some-other-time* plans."

"Are you asking me out after I've already asked you out, just to make sure we go out, Remington Winslow?" I tease, using his earlier words, and it's no surprise to me that he takes it in confident stride.

"Maria, I am most definitely asking you out after you've asked me out to make sure we go out. Soon."

Holy moly. He's asking me out! Remington Winslow wants to go out with me! My inner cheerleader does three flips in the air. Although, I'm certain she actually manages to stick the landing.

"You have a deal." I hand him the marker.

He grins at me from beneath his lashes as he takes the Sharpie from my hand and writes his name on my cast. His handwriting looks exactly how a boy's handwriting should look. A combination of messy and sharp, and I don't know why I like it so much.

Once he dots his "i's" and crosses his "t," he gives the marker back to me and holds out the palm of his right hand.

"Your number please, milady."

I giggle, thinking he's joking, but when he doesn't move his palm from its outstretched position, my jaw nearly hits the tops of my thighs. "But…but this is a permanent marker?"

"Exactly," he says. "No way I'm going to risk losing *Maria Baros's* number."

He says my name like I'm someone special, and it makes my belly feel all fluttery inside.

I want to let out the giddiest squeal, but I hold it back, acting as laid-back and chill as I possibly can, and simply write my number on the palm of his hand.

"Thank you." He stares down at the numbers like they mean something to him, and I stare at him like he's the type of guy who could quickly mean something to me.

When he looks up at me from beneath his lashes, I can't find the power to look away.

The stereo clicks off from the engine being idle for too long, and a hush fills the car. The air around us is so quiet that my ears feel like there's a radio inside them, trying to find the right frequency.

Remy searches my eyes, and I can't look away from him. Don't want to look away from him.

He shifts his body closer to mine, the only thing between us the center console of his Mustang. He lifts his hand and uses his fingers to brush loose strands of hair that have fallen from my ponytail and slide them behind my ear.

His touch. It feels magical. Otherworldly.

For the briefest of moments, I flicker my eyes down to his lips and wonder again what they feel like.

"So, when I use this number…" His voice is the first thing to break the silence. "You're going to answer my call, right?"

I nod, look at his lips again, then find myself licking my own lips.

His gaze catches sight of my tongue's movement, and he's back to searching my eyes again.

I wish I could see inside his head. I wish I could know what he's thinking right now. I wish I could find out if he's thinking about kissing me like I'm thinking about kissing him.

I've never felt the urge to kiss a boy before. Not like this. It feels strange and good and crazy all at the same time.

I bet he's a good kisser. You can't have lips like that and not be a good kisser.

His face moves closer to mine, and my heart kicks into overdrive inside my chest.

Oh my gosh, is it happening? Is he going to kiss me?

And then…his lips are on my face, pressed softly against…*my cheek.*

I'm almost disappointed, but he doesn't give the emotion time to form a pit in my belly.

"I wish I could stay here with you all night like this, Maria," he whispers into my ear. "But I know I need to let you go inside." And he presses one more soft kiss to my cheek before moving his body back into the driver's seat.

"I'll call you tomorrow."

"And I'll answer."

"Good night, Maria."

"Good night, Remy."

Holy shit. Remington Winslow is going to call me! Tomorrow! It's all my mind can think about as I climb out of his car. Once I make my way inside my building, I lose every ounce of cool and dance in the lobby like a fool.

Sure, I'm about to get yelled at by my mom.

And I have six weeks of healing ahead of me. Which means I'll have to sit out cheering at some football games and competitions.

But Remington Winslow holds *my* number inside the palm of his hand.

If he keeps this up, soon, he'll have your heart there too.

NINE

Remy

The sky is a dusky denim color from the light of the sun, the ball of fire just barely starting to make its way above the horizon, and the normally bustling city streets are filled by a few lingering delivery trucks and the scent of fresh bakery flour. Only the weary are up at this hour, preparing for the rush of the rest. They are the backbone of the community—the holders of the coffee and the start of so many's days.

A yawn catches me off guard as I step off the curb in front of the hospital and cross the street to the other side. I pull my phone from my jeans pocket to glance at the time, only to find I've not only missed a message from the illustrious Cleo, but an entire text thread that further explains what my brothers were up to last night.

C: Sometimes, if we're lucky, life gives us the kind of second chance that reminds us how right it was the first time.

If that isn't the most vaguebook shit I've ever read, I don't know what is. I know she's trying to bait me into something here, most likely revolving around her trying to give me one of her kooky predictions, but I'm not biting.

Truthfully, I don't even know what I would respond with if I had the energy, and I decide to leave it for now and thumb into the chat that contains more details on my brothers' shenanigans.

Thatch: Yo, Remy, we're all wondering where in the fuck you are? What gives, man? Truthfully, your ass better have a damn good reason that revolves around something awesome like a set of magically growing tits or else I'm gonna be pisssssssed, son.

Obviously, Thatcher Kelly initiated this thread, and about ten minutes after I didn't respond, the conversation rolled on like I wasn't even in it.

Thatch: Seriously. Where's your brother?

Jude: Hell if I know.

Ty: Apparently he's decided being a little bitch is way more important tonight.

Wes: Guess we should cancel poker night and head home.

I kind of want to laugh. Surely the stress of spending all day with my sister, planting a garden that's most likely going to die, has worn my brother-in-law out.

Thatch: We're not canceling.

Kline: I'm kind of a fan of canceling. Georgia and I are two seasons deep into Game of Thrones, *and I have a strong suspicion she secretly started season three tonight after the girls went to bed.*

Kline Brooks is also one of Wes's best friends and has become a good buddy to the Winslow family. However, his continued presence is more by choice since he's one of the nicest, chillest guys out there. Unlike Thatch, who just takes it upon himself to set up shop in your life.

Wes: Yep. It's settled. You should definitely go home. And so should I.

Thatch: You guys are dicks.

Wes: Says the guy who is texting instead of dealing the fucking cards.

Jude: I can't believe you've talked us into texting the whole night, Thatch. This is the most ridiculous shit I've ever been a part of, and trust me, that's saying something.

Thatch: Listen, if you want to be the one to tell Cassie that she can fluff off about her No Noise Rule, go ahead. I like my nuts where they are.

Ty: You're scared of your wife, dude. You realize that, right?

Wes: Honestly, I don't blame him on this one. I'm a little scared of her too.

Kline: Me three.

Thatch: I knew I loved you supportive bastards for a reason. Now, type a little quieter, would you? Less aggression in your thumbs. Once Remy gets here, we can just play instead of texting so much.

Flynn: He's not coming.

Thatch: What? Did you talk to him?

Flynn: No.

Ty: Not gonna lie, you guys are boring the shit out of me.

Jude: Same, bro. Same.

Wes: Yeah, I'm out. Bye.

Thatch: Goddammit, Wes! Don't you dare leave!

Kline: If Wes can leave, then so can I.

Thatch: FUCK YOU GUYS. I TAKE THE ASS-KISS BACK. YOU AREN'T SUPPORTIVE AT ALL.

Jude: Holy shit, they really left.

Ty: I think we should leave too. To a fucking bar where I can get a drink. It's either that or I'm going home to my beautiful woman.

Jude: I second this. It's either a bar or I'm going home to Sophie. No in-between.

Thatch: Harry's?

Flynn: No.

Ty: THAT'S WHAT I'M TALKING ABOUT!

Jude: YESSSSSSSS

Thatch: Majority rules, Flynn. Looks like you're going to Harry's.

Flynn: Fuck.

The thread goes eerily quiet for about two hours after that, and then, their downfall is apparent.

Thatch: Cass iz gonna so pisses at me. Ty you dumb. I hate you soon much.

Ty: you luv me bros. tequila!

Jude: You drunk

Thatch: NO YOU DRINK.

Jude: Yes sirrrrrr

Ty: HAHAHAzs.

Thatch: I haves to leaf. Cass is comin to get me. She so mud.

Jude: baby donts go

Thatch: byez bro luver you

Flynn: I hate all of you.

God, my brothers—and Thatch—really are a hilarious bunch of assholes.

I roll my eyes, but I smile too, as I type out a message so simple it's almost criminal within the confines of the thread. But I'm certain I should be excused on this one. After today's events, my mind isn't exactly working at optimal level.

Once I get to my apartment and my head hits the pillow, I imagine it won't be but a couple of seconds before I'm out for the next twelve hours.

The subway car shrieks to a stop at my station, and I have to use Herculean effort to pull myself up out of the seat and drag my tired ass out the doors and up the steps. There are only a few people who get off with me, having partied a little too hard the night before.

It's just a two-block walk to my building—or what will now be referred to as *the scene of the crime turned miracle of life*. Part of me knows I'm crazy for chancing a ride in another elevator at this point, but twelve floors of stairs is just a little too much to attempt while I'm this bone-weary. Besides, the elevator at the hospital managed not to fail me. Maybe I've met my quota.

But, hey, if it stops, it stops. I'll curl up on the floor and sleep.

The cart dings its arrival, and I step inside the same elevator I first found myself in yesterday afternoon. It's not the one in which Maria gave birth, but the memory of the whole thing comes rushing back all the same. It feels like just moments ago, and at the same time, feels like a lifetime has passed.

A wave of warmth washes through my chest as I remember how strong she was. Courageous. Determined. It's not every day that a woman is faced with the magnitude of obstacles she's been, but it's even rarer that they do it with as much dignity and grace as her.

I swear, she's the strongest woman I know. And I'm a fucking Winslow. I know a lot of strong-as-hell women.

I wish I'd had this same foresight at the hospital—I wish I'd had the awareness to tell her how awed I am by what she managed to do in this very building. By what she's managing every day, despite the grief I know she's carrying.

It's almost surreal as the elevator arrives at my floor and opens, and I step off with a lingering look back. I don't know that the short trip to my apartment will ever feel the same.

I mean, holy shit. I delivered a baby. Like MacGyver or Chuck Norris or motherfucking Superman.

You'd think I would've been scared shitless, but I don't know, between seeing how strong Maria was in that moment and feeling the poignancy of what we were experiencing together, I just…couldn't be anything but the man she deserved to have by her side.

A quick trip down the hallway and a turn of my key and I'm inside the solace of my apartment. It's spacious—both for New York and bachelorhood—but it's the only place that ever felt like a good fit. It's richly traditional in style, very old New York, and just snobby enough to make me feel proud of everything I've accomplished.

It's dumb, really, but sometimes this apartment is what reminds me my life hasn't been a waste. It's so different from what could have been; and yet, it has the memories of Lexi taking some of her first steps by the floor-to-ceiling windows and Ty and Jude fistfighting when they found out they'd gone on two dates with the same woman several years ago.

It's the home of several family Christmas dinners and has been a haven for my drunken, sloppy brothers on more than one occasion. It's the door my sister knocked on in the middle of the night when she didn't know what to do to comfort Lexi at the age of four—now known as the year she wouldn't stop crying.

This apartment is full of all the echoes of the decision I made a decade and a half ago. For me, my family is everything. They're all I've ever needed. And for the longest time, with the decades-long absence of our good-for-nothing father, they've needed me, too.

But it feels so quiet now. There's no baby crying, no mess to tend to, no one to take care of.

It feels odd—almost eerie, really—and I can't put my finger on why. Yesterday morning when I left, the walls felt close, the space felt cozy. But right now, it feels like they're retreating, opening into a chasm or a void without anything to fill it up.

My sister is married now, her husband one of the good ones, and my niece Lexi is well past needing her uncle Remy for much of anything besides entertainment. Even my three brothers have grown up and settled down.

It's different; my role in their lives is different. And I imagine, the role of this apartment and the memories it carries going forward are going to be different too.

Stripping off my torn and dirtied white T-shirt, I pull out the sliding cabinet in the kitchen and pitch it into the garbage. I don't think there's any salvaging it at this point.

But before I can close the cabinet, something grips me in the gut and makes me pause. I reach into the can and take it back out, shaking it out and tossing it in the laundry room instead.

I don't know why, but it almost feels wrong to get rid of it.

Fishing my phone out of my pocket, I scroll down through my contacts to the number Maria gave me.

I want so badly to check in and see how she's doing, but I'd hate to wake her up if she's finally getting some rest.

I hover on the fence for thirty seconds more before realizing I've known the answer all along. After everything we've been through together in the last twenty-four hours, there's no way in hell I'm leaving any shade of doubt with Maria. I need her to know that she can reach out to me anytime.

Fingers to the screen of my phone, I do just that and hit send.

TEN

Maria

I stare down at a message from Remy, reading his words for what feels like the hundredth time.

Remy: Thanks for letting me be a part of this experience, Ri, whether you really had the choice or not. I'll remember this for the rest of my life. PS: Don't forget to use this number if and when you need me—or if you just want to chat. I'm always here.

Goodness, he's so damn kind, so considerate, so…Remy.

Even after all these years, he's still the same sweet guy who made my teenage heart fall hard.

Sure, he's rougher around the edges now, jaded about things like marriage and relationships, but deep down, at his core, he hasn't really changed.

I honestly don't know what it would've been like to have Izzy if Remy hadn't been there. Sure, it would've been nice to deliver her in a hospital, where a freaking epidural could've been utilized and I wouldn't have had to feel like my vagina was lit on fire and used as a damn cannon, but I would've been experiencing her birth…alone.

And that would've made it a million times harder.

Sure, I have friends and acquaintances in this city, but grabbing a drink or dinner is not the same as wanting someone witnessing you push a baby out of your hoo-hah.

For me, there's no one who could replace my mom and sister. They would've been the only two people I would've wanted by my side when I delivered Izzy.

Luckily, you had Remy.

I war with myself over whether I should respond to him.

I even type out at least ten different texts but end up deleting every single one of them before hitting send.

I just…I don't know… It feels wrong to bring him into my web of crazy complications. It feels like I'd be taking advantage of his kindness or something.

"Knock, knock." The soft sounds of a woman's voice pull my focus toward the door, and that's when I see a new face in a pair of pale-blue scrubs.

"Good morning. I'm Christina. I'll be your nurse today," the day shift nurse greets as she steps into the room. She erases Deb's name from the whiteboard and fills the empty space with her own. "How are you feeling?"

"I guess I'm doing pretty good for a lady who delivered a baby in an elevator yesterday afternoon," I tell her with a knowing smile, and she laughs.

"Talk about a wild birth story, huh?"

"Pretty sure I might have to deal with some minor PTSD every time I get in an elevator now."

"Girl, you had a baby in an elevator, in the middle of a blackout, on one of the hottest days of the summer. *Without* an epidural. You're officially my hero." Christina flashes a wink and a smile at me before walking over to where Izzy is currently lying in the hospital bassinet. "And just think, one day when this little lady is older, you'll be able to tell her how much pain she put her mother through."

"Yeah," I say and swallow past the emotion that all of a sudden threatens to close off my throat.

Her mother. For better or worse and lack of any other option, I *am* her mother.

And for a reason only a newborn can understand, Izzy takes that as her cue to start crying.

"Uh-oh, looks like she has some things to say about her birth story, too," Christina muses as she checks to see if Izzy has a dirty diaper. "Girlfriend, let me tell you, your momma is one strong woman."

I wish I felt as strong as Christina seems to think I am. Truthfully, I mostly just feel like I'm trying to survive. Trying not to fail.

"I think she might be hungry," I tell the nurse after she updates that Izzy's diaper is surprisingly clean and dry. "But I've been having a lot of issues with getting her to latch."

If there was one thing my sister was incredibly adamant about, it was breast-feeding. She was even planning on taking medication to hopefully induce her milk supply so she could be the one to do it.

Hell, when I was only eight weeks pregnant, she was already trying to get me to agree to pump my breast milk if her own milk supply couldn't be induced.

Isabella wanted Izzy to have the best of everything. The best source of food and nutrients. The best pediatrician. The best schools. She and Oliver were even preparing to shift their work schedules so they would never have to use a nanny.

Goodness, I hope I can live up to my sister's wishes.

"Would you like some help?" Christina offers, and I nod dramatically.

"Help would be greatly appreciated."

The nurse lifts Izzy out of the bassinet, and I glance down once more at the phone that's still in my hands. Remy's text still sits prominently on the screen.

But the crying baby heading my way quickly becomes my priority.

Which, I guess, is the way it should be. And while there's a part of me that would relish support from someone like Remy, I know my truth.

From here on out, it's just Izzy and me.

ELEVEN

Maria

When I was about seven months pregnant with Izzy, I watched a documentary where a forty-year-old woman ran a marathon, one week after her six-week postpartum checkup, *with* her baby in a stroller.

She made it look so easy. Like, she was all healed up and just crushing the whole motherhood thing so much that she had time to fit running 26.2 miles into her schedule.

Naïvely, after seeing that, I thought I'd be rocking and rolling just like her when I reached this point. Like my six-week postpartum appointment was going to be some kind of momentous occasion where I'd feel victorious.

Hence, why I thought I could fit it in during Dr. Maddox's Saturday hours, on the same day as a listing appointment with a new client, and somehow juggle it all with a big-ass smile and happy baby to boot.

Ha. The joke is very much on me. And I now know that documentary woman was either a psychopath or a robot.

"It's okay, sweet girl," I tell Izzy, but her cries only get louder, bouncing off the walls of the small exam room in piercing waves.

To her? It is most definitely *not* okay. Apparently nothing is okay right now in Izzy's little life.

Her cries only get louder, and I pull the flimsy paper gown around myself, trying to hold it in place with my right hand as I rock her stroller back and forth with my left.

Izzy's been cranky around this time every day for the last several days in a row, and no matter what, I never know how to fix it. It's as if she's opposed to the angle of the sun—except she's inside in a room without a window.

Gah, I just wish there was a way to know what's upsetting her.

I rock the stroller faster and faster until the hiccup in her cry is less shaky, and I glance at the clock yet again. The doctor is evidently running behind this morning, and for someone on as tight of a schedule as I am, it's the last thing I need.

Izzy's pacifier falls to the side, and I grab it as quick as I can and push it back into her mouth. Her eyes are fluttering just enough that I know sleep has to be somewhere on the horizon. It'd be helpful if the horizon seemed a little closer, seeing as I'd like to spread my legs for my physician without holding a baby at the same time and then make it across town to my listing appointment without trying to tell my client *"The hardwood floors are original!"* over the sounds of Izzy's wailing.

Her eyes blink heavily, and I have to caution myself not to rock the stroller faster with my eagerness. Finding something that works with a baby is a lot like finding something that works with sex. Don't go faster, don't go harder, don't change the rhythm—don't move a fucking muscle that you're not currently moving.

And what exactly do you know about sex these days? It's only been eleventy billion years since you've had it.

I hear the doctor chatting with a nurse outside the door and grit my teeth while appealing to the universe. *Please, I beg of you. Let them come into this room as quietly as they possibly can. Like church mice, in the middle of a priest's sermon, with the Virgin Mary herself standing at the altar.*

As Dr. Maddox and her nurse continue to chat about a new upscale Japanese restaurant in SoHo, I will Izzy to take the plunge into dreamland. Back and forth, back and forth, I watch as the tension in her tiny body finally leaves on a whimpering sigh. She's still in the twilight stage of sleep, but I can attest to the fact that she's due to pass out—we partied all night together last night—and her body's needs should take over soon. At least, I hope.

I really, *really* hope.

Finally, there's a knock on the door, just two quick raps of knuckles and then the door is swinging open, and it all occurs without startling Izzy. *Thank everything!* I shift back onto the table and rearrange my gown—a practice in modesty I don't really understand, given the fact that the whole purpose of this appointment is for the good doctor to spend some time between my legs.

"Hi, Maria." Her smile is warm as she greets me. "How are you feeling?"

I keep my voice low and soothing—a hint I'm hoping her medical degree will help her pick up on—and answer to the best of my ability. "Great, Dr. Maddox. I mean, tired, sure, but great. Things are really great. I'm great. Izzy's great. We're great."

Wow, Ri, don't oversell it.

Dr. Maddox's brow automatically pinches together, and I don't blame her. I sound about as confident in how things are going as I would if I were preparing to perform an operation with only a ten-minute YouTube video serving as my training.

"Are you still breastfeeding?"

Ugh. Two questions into this appointment and I already feel like a failure.

"I…uh…tried, but…yeah, I had to switch to bottle-feeding."

To say I tried is putting it lightly. After having issues with Izzy's latch from day one in the hospital, I continued to try even after I was discharged. I even hired three different lactation consultants and private nurses to make home visits to help, but all breastfeeding ever brought me was lots of stress, tears, and sore nipples.

I still hate that I couldn't do it, knowing how important it was to my sister.

"Let me guess, issues with latching?"

"And my milk supply wasn't exactly stellar." I frown. "Though, I did keep pumping until my nipples were bleeding and I was only getting air back."

"Well, that's okay." Dr. Maddox tries to reassure me. "The most important part, Maria, is that your baby is getting fed." She glances at a gloriously sleeping Izzy and grins at me. "And by the looks of those adorable, chubby cheeks, I'd say you're doing a good job."

A good job? *Ha.* If I had to rate myself, I'd say I'm struggling to reach *World's Most Mediocre Mom.*

"And what about rest? Are you getting sleep when you can?"

"Um…" I laugh nervously. *Is that a real question?*

Her smile turns upside down. "Rest is truly crucial for recovery from childbirth, Maria. I know it can be tough—"

Can be *tough?* Has she actually met a baby before?

"But the first six weeks postpartum aren't just about bonding with the baby. They're about actual physical recovery for the mother, too. And although you were incredibly healthy prior to your pregnancy and maintained that state of health during your pregnancy, you are considered advanced maternal age. You need rest, Maria."

That's her nice way of saying I'm old.

I almost counter her words by telling her about the fortysomething documentary lady who was running ten miles a day by week three postpartum. Surely her "old" ass wasn't getting that much rest either.

"I…well, I'm doing what I can."

"Would you be able to arrange for an extended leave from work?" she asks, turning to type on her iPad. "From what I'm hearing, I think that might be wise."

I wince. How in the hell do I tell her that I already went back to work… two weeks ago?

Even if I wanted to stay on maternity leave, I didn't have a choice. Without my sister's and Oliver's help running The Baros Group show, it's all on me, and we have an enormous load of clients who aren't willing to wait around while I "heal." Not to mention, the agents I hired are still learning the ropes. They aren't ready to be thrown into the shark-infested waters of high-end real estate without it turning into a Jaws-like situation.

She notices the look on my face, and evidently, I don't have to tell her at all.

"Oh, Maria," she chides softly, and I look down at the paper gown across my legs so I can fiddle with it. She sighs again, and it's the weirdest feeling. For as much as she's scolding me, I should be annoyed. I should feel attacked and righteous.

But I know, deep down, that she's right. What I've been doing isn't sustainable long-term. I just haven't figured out a way around it yet.

"I'm definitely not going to ask when you went back to work because I have a feeling I'm not going to like your answer, but tell me this, you've hired a nanny, right? Maybe even a private nurse to take over some nights for you, too?"

I already failed breastfeeding. No way I can fail Isabella's wishes related to nannies.

"Do you want an answer that's going to make you happy or…?" I cringe, and Dr. Maddox lets out the kind of laugh that doesn't come from humor.

"What am I going to do with you?"

That, Dr. Maddox, is a fantastic question. One I currently ask myself and Izzy about one hundred times a day.

"I tell you what," she says finally, rolling over on her little stool to look up at me where I can't avoid her eyes. "After the exam, I'm going to get you some numbers for support groups. Being a new mother is difficult, but it's even more so when you're doing it alone and *without help*." She states the last two words with pointed emphasis. "I personally attended one of these after having my first, too, so you can rest easy that I'm not sending you to a cult or something."

I smile thankfully. "Okay."

"But you need to consider getting a nanny and accepting help from other people too, okay? Friends, family, anyone who's holding out a hand. And I promise, someone is there and waiting for you to ask."

I almost scoff in A minor. I'm pretty sure that's the note of loneliness.

Although, there is one person who would help in a heartbeat…

By God, he's already done enough. Unless I'm on the brink of insanity, I refuse to put this on him.

"I'll ask for help. I'll get help," I lie, knowing it's the only thing that's going to get her moving and Izzy and me out of this office. The urge to glance at my watch and check on my timing for my appointment is strong, but I don't dare. I don't need the postpartum police checking me in to a ward somewhere and screwing up a potential five-million-dollar deal.

She eyes me closely, likely knowing that I'm a big fat liar. Still, she smiles at me then, but this time, it holds an edge of sadness.

"Okay, Maria. Let's scoot down to the end of the table and get the fun part over with, shall we?"

Oh yeah, this is going to be great.

⌒⌒

"Oh, Izzy, please," I beg. "This is an apartment on Fifth Avenue, sweetheart. You can't cry about Fifth Avenue. It's, like, a rule."

My cherub-faced angel only seems to cry harder at that, and a bout of desperate nonsense kicks in. I don't even know what I'm saying. I just need something to sink in. "I'll buy you a pair of Jimmy Choos and Chanel and, oh, oh, Louboutins too. Everyone loves the red sole!"

Izzy's cries intensify, and I direct the stroller over to the side of a building where I can safely get her away from the bustle of the Manhattan sidewalk. She calms slightly, but at my first breath of relief, her cries are renewed.

I feel like I'm going crazy, the stabbing pain of her wails nearly enough to send me into a tailspin. I'm drowning. I'm failing. A tear catches inside the corner of my eye, and a sob hitches in the back of my throat.

I want to do this for my sister and the way that she wanted. Without help, and with the loving nurture of a mother's patience.

But I'm not Isabella, and I don't know what I'm doing. She was a natural—a goddess. All I know is that you'll never find a worthy two-bedroom in Uptown for under a million.

Izzy's nap that started at the doctor's office has fallen short-lived, and if I don't start walking again soon, I'm never going to make it the two blocks I need to in time for my listing appointment with the Downfellers.

It's a great listing, in a great location, worth a hell of a lot of money. But something tells me, even if I make it there in time, I'm never going to win them over with a crying baby in my arms. They're extremely picky and discerning, and it's taken over a year to convince them to join our team.

I feel like the earth is crumbling beneath my feet, but with one look at Izzy's sweet, desperate face, I make a decision.

I'm not making the appointment today. Instead, I'm going to go home and take care of my girl—even if it sullies my business just a little bit.

I fire off a quick, but what I hope is professional, text to the Downfellers— *I'm so sorry to do this last minute, but I've had a family emergency and need to reschedule. I assure you this is a one-time event and not how I handle business on a regular basis. I know you're eager to get listed, so let's set up another appointment for another day this week.*

I ignore the numerous texts and emails from my staff, put my phone back in my purse, and pull Izzy out of her stroller, putting her up on my shoulder to offer what I hope is a comforting hug while I focus on getting us home.

Izzy cries harder and harder and harder as I weave my way through the New York tourist crowd. It's thick and suffocating for everyone else, but lucky for me, because of Izzy's shrieking cries, everyone gives me a pretty wide berth.

Oh, Izzy girl…what in the world are we going to do, me and you?

TWELVE

Remy

I take a sip of my first beer of the day and stare down at a new text from Miss Cleo.

C: It's okay to have uncertainty if it means you feel like the possibilities are endless.

Me: Your investment portfolio is rock solid, Cleo. Still low-to-moderate risk with steady growth. You have no need to be uncertain. I got you, boo.

Obviously, I know she's not talking about her portfolio, but I can't resist screwing with her.

C: You know I'm not the one who is uncertain, Remington. Just remember, uncertainty can be a good thing, if it means you're open to anything that can come next.

Me: I can't be sure, but it kind of feels like you're trying to engage in the kind of conversation we've established (about a billion times) is off the table.

You'd think after fourteen years of this, she'd give up on trying to go all fortune-teller on me, but evidently, old habits die hard.

C: I have no idea what you're talking about, my dear.

Me: But shouldn't you know? I mean, you ARE the psychic.

C: Oh, right. I guess I forgot. The reminder is greatly appreciated.

Me: Very funny.

C: 😊 Enjoy your day, Remington.

On a half laugh, half sigh, I slide my phone back into my pocket and stare out into the backyard of Wes and Winnie's brownstone. Immediately, my eyes spot the vacant pile of dirt in the far-right corner that sits beside a small shed within the privacy fence.

Looks like another vegetable garden has officially bitten the dust.

I smile to myself and move my attention back to my family, the entire Winslow clan together again for a Saturday afternoon barbecue. Since the Mavericks have a home game this week, Wes and Winnie offered to play host.

Lexi puts on a song from her phone, a party beat that everyone in the world knows by name, and Howard doesn't hesitate to stand up from his seat with a jovial clap of his hands.

"Oh yeah! I know this one!"

"Get it, Howard!" Jude cheers him on, a beer in his right hand and his left arm wrapped around his wife Sophie's shoulders.

My mother's boyfriend has now not only garnered her and my youngest brother's attention, but the entire family's attention too. Uncle Brad and Wes grin from their spots by the grill. Aunt Paula and Mom and Winnie giggle from their seats on the deck. An amused Ty stands behind Rachel with his arms around her waist. Flynn and Daisy stand side by side, each one holding one of their eight-month-old twins on their hips—Ryder on Flynn's and Roman on Daisy's.

And I move to stand by Lexi as she continues to blast the familiar music from her phone.

My nephews giggle and clap their chubby little hands as Howard swings his hips in a circle and jump-turns by ninety degrees. And it doesn't take many more of his dance moves before everyone falls into laughter so hard that Winnie can't hide her infamous piglike snorts.

I never knew a man in his early seventies could know the Macarena this well, but as I've learned over the last several months of his courtship with my mom, Howard Sulken is full of surprises.

In calf-height crew socks, white New Balance shoes, and a tucked-in polo and jean shorts, Howard is the epitome of a "dad." It's ironic, really, for a man who's spent this many years of his life without kids to fit so well into a family with five of them. But he's good to our mom, he's ridiculously funny, and I've never met someone who owns their style as much as he does.

I can't do anything but like the guy. For once in my life, I feel like there's someone there to take care of my mom. Lord knows Wendy Winslow certainly deserved this a whole hell of a lot earlier in life, but I'm grateful she finally has it now.

Once the song comes to an end, good ol' Howard bows dramatically to the applause that surrounds him. "Thank you! Thank you! I'll be here all night!"

"Yo, Howard! Do that thing! The thing you do with the word association!" Ty shouts excitedly, not even bothering to make himself seem aloof or disinterested.

For a guy who, in the beginning, was as skeptical as a police officer during an interrogation with a pathological liar about our mother dating someone she met on the internet, he's the exact opposite now. If he weren't engaged to Rachel, I'd think he was going to propose to Howard himself.

"You got it." Howard, ever the people pleaser, nods, dusting his hands off in preparation like any good dad would do. "Who do you want me to start with?"

"Remy," Ty says and shines a sarcastic, I'm-a-real-asshole kind of smile in my direction. "Definitely Remy."

I almost groan aloud, but I know damn well that would result in way too much sibling satisfaction. Instead, I shrug, cross my arms over my chest, and raise my eyebrows as I wait.

"I like a man who is ready." Howard snaps his fingers. "Okay, Remy. The point of the game is to answer as quickly as possible. No time for thinking. No second chances. I'm going to throw a one-word question at you, and you have to answer back with the first word that comes to mind."

I nod. "Sounds simple enough."

"Ha! That's where you're wrong, bro!" Ty exclaims through cupped hands around his mouth.

Seriously? How bad can a one-word game be?

"Shoes?" Howard asks.

And of course, all I can think to say is, "New Balance."

Immediately, all eyes go to Howard's feet, but he's a good sport and responds by grinning and wiggling one New Balance-covered foot around like he's a model.

"Only $39.99 at the Shoe Carnival!" he announces, and I can't not laugh.

"Nice. But the real question, Howard, is did you get the BOGO?"

"Does Ty have the biggest mouth in the Winslow family?" he retorts, grinning at me like a man who most definitely knows his way around a good sale. "Of course I got the BOGO, Remy. There's an identical pair of these babies in the closet, just waiting to be used in the future."

"I can confirm this!" my mom calls out with a grin.

"Give me a break. I do not have the biggest mouth of the family," Ty tries to counter, but even his fiancée Rachel gives him a look that calls him on his bullshit. "Okay, fine. Whatever. But what are you doing here, Howard? The point of the game is lightning-quick. Not minute-long intermissions to sell us sneakers."

My mom's boyfriend just grins but meets my eyes and continues. "Fun?"

"Family," I respond instantly, and Jude bursts into laughter immediately.

"How fucking wholesome."

"*Jude*," my mom starts to chastise his language and glances at Lexi, but when she sees that her granddaughter is not affected the way her mother used to be when she was that age, she just shakes her head on a sigh. There was a time when Lexi informed everyone, in the middle of a Winslow family dinner, the use of curse words is a sign of intelligence, and Jude has been using that to his advantage ever since.

Basically, even powerful women like Wendy Winslow tire of being one-upped by an adolescent girl who has the IQ of Einstein.

I bite my lip to smother a laugh and turn back to face Howard as he continues the game.

"Excitement?" he asks, settling himself into a good old-fashioned dad pose, his feet shoulder-width apart and his arms across his chest.

Maria. She is the one word, the one name, that immediately comes to mind—one that won't make a bit of sense to anyone on this deck and isn't exactly business I'd like to share. But the excitement of six weeks ago is still so fresh that, if I tried hard enough, I could convince myself it happened just yesterday.

But then again, the month and a half of hoping she'll call, hoping that she'll let me lend a helping hand, haven't passed by quickly either.

Other than one text from her, right after she got home from the hospital, letting me know they'd been discharged and were apparently doing well—and no matter how many times I've attempted to reach out to her since then—it's been radio silence when it comes to communication with Maria.

"Uh…Rem?" Ty's far-too-amused voice grabs my attention. "Again, the name of the game is quick, bro."

I ignore him and glance around the backyard at my family. "Wait…how many turns do I get? Doesn't it eventually rotate or something?"

"Ohhh shit." Jude laughs annoyingly. "Sounds like someone is feeling the heat."

Of course, Ty is all about it. "The kitchen is cooking, bro."

I flip both of them off, and my mother can only sigh. She's been trying to reform her foul-mouthed, crude children for over forty years at this point. I guess, given our inability to change, she's just about given up.

"I'm cool as a damn cucumber," I retort. "I'm just wondering when someone else gets to join in."

Howard is more understanding of my questions and holds up a reassuring five fingers. "Each person goes five times. Then it moves on to the next person."

"And the excitement builds every second like you're on the boat in the Gene Wilder version of Willy Wonka," Ty chimes in.

"What are you, the cruise director?" I ask him. "Trying to build interest and participation?"

"I've just seen it in action, bro. That's all. Howard's a wizard."

I shake my head but turn back to Howard. The faster we get this over with, the better. Most of these other yahoos like being the center of attention—I, however, do not.

"Excitement?" Howard repeats again.

This time, I answer, with a much vaguer version of the same story that instantly came to mind. "Blackout."

"Interesting choice of words, Rem!" Ty shouts himself back into the game. "I recall a time when you—"

"Keep 'em coming, Howard." I cut Ty off at the knees. I already know what that word sparks in his mind, but that doesn't mean I have to subject myself to his response.

"Next?" my mother's boyfriend tosses out quickly.

And I respond with a swift, "Future."

Howard's eyes light up mischievously as he repeats my answer—this time, in the form of a question. "Future?"

My answer is immediate. "Undecided."

Winnie and my mom both make a sad, disappointed sound that lets me know that one word has the power to bring a shitstorm of questions my way. Questions they've been pestering me about for years, their focus on my constant state of bachelorhood a little too intense for my liking. Hell, it'd be too much for any single man on the planet's liking—and if there were men inhabiting Mars, they'd want to avoid their damn questions too.

Flynn and Jude groan, and I know it's because they're just as aware of what I've set off in the females of the family as I am. I wouldn't be surprised if Daisy and Sophie and Rachel all join in now, trying to help poor, single Remy find the purpose for his life.

Although I did reach the five-word mark, it's clear I've put a damper on the future prospects for the game when the women start to shift toward one another.

And when my phone starts to ring in my pocket? I immediately excuse my-self and make my way off the deck and away from the Winslow women's plotting. I don't care if it's a telemarketer at this point—I'm taking the call.

Someone who wants to sell me life insurance? Let's do this.

One of those annoying fuckers who want to extend my car's warranty? I'll even give them the damn VIN number if it means they'll keep me busy un-til Uncle Brad and Wes finish grilling the burgers. At least then, food might have the ability to keep my mom and sister too busy to play life coach.

I'm so amped for this distraction, I put the phone to my ear without looking at the screen to see who it is first.

"Hello?"

"The baby won't stop crying! And my phone won't stop ringing because I had a million work things to do and couldn't! And I'm losing it!" The voice is feminine, frantic, and one I know like the back of my hand—Maria. "And I don't think I know how to do both things at once, but if I don't figure it out, Izzy and I are going to be homeless." She pauses only very briefly to take a breath, but I don't hesitate to cut in.

"Text me your address. I'm on my way."

"Okay, maybe not homeless, but definitely need to move to something smaller," she keeps rambling, apparently too worked up to even hear me. "And I can tell you right now, this place is big, but it already feels tiny with all the crying and vomit and toys and blankets and bottles. And Dr. Maddox said I should hire a nanny, but I can't do that because I know that's not what my sister wanted and I don't even know my name anymore and I know it's crazy of me to ask anything of you, given the fact that I already owe you my life, but I just didn't know who to call or what to do or if I'm going to make it and I—"

"Maria," I call with a little laugh, both to remind her of her name and to get her attention. "It's okay. Take a deep breath. I'm on my way."

"Wait… Really?"

"Just text me your address, and I'll be there in thirty minutes, tops. Promise."

"But what if I keel over from exhaustion between now and then?"

She's teasing, I can tell, but I'm pretty sure she half believes it's possible, too. The desperation in her voice is unmistakable.

"You won't. Just hold on until I get there, okay?"

"Okay…and Remy?"

"Yeah?"

"Thanks."

"No thanks needed. I'll see you soon."

I hang up the phone with a small grin curling the corners of my mouth. Once I get her text with her apartment's address, followed by the words "thank you" in all caps with twenty praising-hands emojis, I tuck my phone into my pocket with an amused shake of my head.

But when I turn around, everyone is looking at me.

And I do mean *everyone*.

I am a fish in a bowl.

"Uh…can I help you?" I ask, trying not to get too defensive right off the bat. With this much of the Winslow family interest piqued, that'll only make it worse.

"You going somewhere?" Ty asks, a sly smirk on his face as he takes a pull of his beer. I bet the bastard heard me say her name, and now he thinks he knows a secret.

"Yeah, actually," I admit simply. "A friend needs help."

"A *lady* friend? By the name of Maria, maybe?" Jude asks smartly, a teasing titter in his voice, and making it apparent Ty wasn't the only one who overheard my conversation. Sophie smacks him in the chest with the back of her hand, but his smile only grows. "What? It's a simple, very easily answered question."

If only these two idiots knew the truth.

"I probably won't be back," I say instead, approaching Lexi to give her a hug and a kiss on the top of her head.

She leans into the affection—something I feel privileged by since she doesn't do that with everyone—and then calls me on my shit, just like she does with everyone else.

"Is Maria the Maria you dated in high school?"

"Um…" Surprise furrows my eyebrows. "How do you know about me dating Maria in high school?"

My brilliant niece doesn't bat an eye, and I don't miss the way the rest of the family is using their absolute highest concentration to listen.

"I looked through your yearbooks when I stayed at your apartment two weeks ago."

"I thought you went to sleep."

"I did. After I looked through your office completely."

"Great. Find anything else good?"

"Just that Shawn Williams's portfolio is outperforming Mark Cohen's portfolio twofold this quarter. Their portfolios are nearly identical, but I think Mr. Cohen's tech shares, while small, are the missing link and should be switched into the S&P dividend ETF that Shawn Williams's portfolio is utilizing until the NASDAQ finds its bottom."

I blink. *What the fuck?* "Right. I'll, uh, look into that."

"How is *Maria*, by the way?" Ty asks, waggling his eyebrows like an idiot and thinking he has the inside scoop because he was a witness to my first stuck-in-an-elevator-because-of-a-blackout experience with her.

"Is she okay?" Winnie asks, while at the same time, my mom says, "Do she or the baby need anything?"

Both of their eyes soften with the kind of look that shows they are the only two people in the family who know the full details of Maria's situation and my part in Izzy's birth.

But back in the day, when Maria and I were together, my mom loved Maria and her family dearly, and Winnie and Isabella were friends. I felt compelled to tell them. Felt like it was something they deserved to know.

"Baby?" Jude asks, utterly puzzled and so far out of the loop he should be in another country. "Maria Baros has a baby?"

When Ty looks like he's seconds away from opening his big mouth, Winnie walks over to him and slaps her hand across his face. "You better go, Rem."

"Wha thu ellth?" Ty mutters around her palm, most likely confused as to why our sister is letting me off the hook so easily.

I take that as my cue to leave.

One day, in the near future, I'll explain the whole situation to my brothers, but now isn't the time. Now, I have somewhere important I need to be.

"Thanks for hosting, Win!" I call over my shoulder and quickly make my way to the back gate, where I exit and head for the subway stop a couple of blocks from my sister's brownstone.

It's a day I thought would never come and I'd about given up on.

The day Maria Baros finally used my number.

I make it to Maria's place in record time. Frankly, it's almost crazy how close her building is to mine. All these years and we've been one short walk across Central Park from each other.

I step over the threshold of her front door, and all I can think is…*holy shit*.

What I think used to be a pristine, mostly all-white, warm but stylishly minimalist apartment has become a place that could be taped off as a crime scene. Well, if said crime scene involved a robbery where the burglar was a crying baby and her sidekick was a frazzled mom who looked like she hadn't slept in days.

Maria's hair sticks out to the side at an unnatural angle as though it's a compass and the disaster that her apartment has become its north. Debris dots every surface in sight, and half-empty coffee mugs litter the kitchen counter in a continuous stream.

Baby Izzy cries in her arms, clearly unhappy with the current state of the world and probably, if I had to guess, feeding off the emotional exhaustion of her momma.

"Here," I offer immediately, not bothering with the time-suck of a hello that I guarantee Maria cares nothing about, reaching for the baby, and making Maria's eyes widen comically. "Why don't you let Izzy hang with me while you take a shower?"

Her voice is ragged as she tells me, "I can't get her to stop crying. I've been trying for hours, and nothing is working. I don't know what to do or what to—"

"Maria," I cut in, interrupting her gently. "Go take a shower, babe. Take a few moments for yourself. I've got Izzy. We'll be good. I promise."

Her face nearly crumples with relief as she finally nods and turns without another word to retreat down the hall. I know she doesn't have the energy for anything else right now, and I know she feels like she'll never feel normal again. My sister went through it with Lexi, and Daisy went through it with the twins. Going from independent to responsible for kids is a hard transition.

But I know the other side of the tunnel. I've witnessed the light that lives there. I just have to convince Maria it's real.

Izzy's sweet little face pinches with her cries, and her normally beautiful crystalline eyes are hidden from view. The sound is manic, confused even, and I have the very strong feeling that little Izzy is feeling just as exhausted as Maria.

But damn, I can't believe how much she's already grown.

It's been a month and a half since I first held her in my arms, the moment she took her first breath, and I can't believe the changes that have already occurred. Her cheeks are fuller, and her cute little body is heavier in my arms. Her eyes are still blue, but I have a feeling when they eventually change, they'll end up a caramel shade of brown like Maria's because Isabella was basically her mini-me.

"It's so good to see you again, sweetheart," I whisper down toward her.

Slowly and calmly, I tuck her tight to my chest, cradle her head, and swing side to side with a bounce. I pick up singing just a whisper of an old Van Morrison song, mostly for the effect I know the vibrations in my chest will have on her. I hum and dance and swing and bounce, and it's only a matter of five minutes before Izzy is passed out in my arms, her little body lax and her tearful cries nothing but a memory.

I smile down at her delicate features, trying to match them to those of Maria and, from what I remember from decades ago, those of her sister Isabella.

There is no doubt, this little lady will be a stunner when she gets older. Back in the day, Isabella was a pretty little girl. And Maria, well, she's always possessed the kind of beauty that gets more than a second look. She's also kind and warm and really fucking funny when she's not on the brink of a breakdown.

Frankly, she's always been the full package, the kind of woman that men fight for, so I know she wasn't kidding when she admitted to me that being single was something *she* wanted.

Obviously, I get it. I do. I mean, much to my mother's and sister's dismay, I *am* the perpetual bachelor-by-choice.

And I can't see that as anything but a good thing right now. I'm the perfect candidate for Maria to lean on. She needs a friend with time and energy to give. And since I'm only responsible to myself and work, I'm more than capable of giving it.

Nonetheless, I have a feeling convincing her of this fact is going to be a hard sell. Women as strong as Maria have taught themselves not to need anyone. They can fend for themselves. Even now, she could go it alone, and I know she'd succeed. But she shouldn't have to. Not when I'm ready and willing to help.

She deserves to have some kind of support system by her side through this. She *shouldn't have to go it alone,* and from the looks of it, that's exactly what she's been doing. Handling all of this—taking care of Izzy, running a business—by herself. Without even the help of a nanny.

In an instant, I decide. From now on, I'm not going to wait for her to ask.

THIRTEEN

Maria

I pause in front of the sink, turning to the mirror only after I've stripped off my spit-up-soaked clothes and tossed them on the floor.

"Oh hell!" I shriek on a whisper, a hand going to my chest as I take a step back. The dark circles under my eyes could pass for UFO crop activity, and my hair looks like I stuck my finger in an electrical socket. I am a dark-haired Christopher Lloyd in *Back to the Future*, and the clock tower is chiming.

On a groan, I slap my hands over my eyes. "How did I get this bad in a day?"

I mean, sure, I've been struggling for the entire six weeks since Izzy was born, but I pulled it together this morning. I put on Valentino, for God's sake. Now I look like a gutter rat who lives under the subway.

Shaking my head at myself and pointedly avoiding looking in the mirror again, I lean into the shower to turn on the water and let my naked body sink to the floor while I wait for the spray to warm.

I look to the ceiling and take a deep breath.

"I'm trying, Isabella," I whisper as my eyes fixate on a barely there crack in the white paint above me.

Truthfully, I don't know if some spiritual part of her can hear me or not, but I find myself saying it anyway.

"I don't know what I'm doing, and I didn't prepare well enough," I continue quietly, hoping my sister isn't disappointed in me. "I always feel like I can't quite be who Izzy needs, you know? I miss you. I'm sure Izzy misses you. And I just wish I could figure out how to be second best."

I can't explain it, but a shiver moves over me as I hear a clank from Remy in the other room. I listen harder then, and that's when I realize that the crying has stopped.

Calling him was a good start, the words move through my mind. *You don't have to go it alone.*

My head falls back into the solid wood of my bathroom vanity, and the steam from the hot water of the shower starts to roll out over the glass door.

Get up, I tell myself. *Get up and get in the shower and just keep putting one foot in front of the other.*

I stand and open the door to feel the water. It's almost scalding, just like I need it to be to wash away the stress. To sterilize me to the point of a fresh start. To remind my nerves they can feel something other than the overstimulation of motherhood and Izzy's cries.

I've had a lot of long days since having her six weeks ago, but none that has felt quite as hopeless as today. I don't know what I would have done if I hadn't had Remy's number, and if he hadn't dropped everything to come over here.

I dip my head under the spray and let my whole face drown in the rush of water. It's intense, but frankly, it's the kind of thing I need.

When I pull my head out, I instinctually start to listen for the sounds of Izzy's discontent. I don't know if it's the volume of the shower or if my ears have simply numbed, but I don't hear the high-pitched wail anymore.

Goodness. I swore I'd hear that in my dreams.

The tension in my shoulders finally starting to ebb, I take a deep breath and lean a tired hand into the stone wall. My feet are the only thing I can see, and after about thirty seconds, even the vision of them starts to blur.

My mind wanders, first to the memory of what my body used to feel like—something very different from this tired, aged thing—and then to the day I had Izzy in that elevator with Remy at my side.

I can see the flex of his rigid, shirtless abdomen as if it were yesterday, only this time, thankfully, I don't have to feel like I'm being split in half from between my legs at the same time.

His hard muscles, his strong, fearless demeanor—he looked like an Adonis that day as he came to my rescue.

And his smile…it's a little older and a little wiser, but it's still the best thing I've ever seen in my life, encompassed by a strong, defined jaw, straight white teeth, and the sweetest of laugh lines in his cheeks. His eyes are the show-stopper most of the time, but when he smiles, that's all I can see.

Without planning, my hand finds its way to the space between my legs and starts to explore. Dr. Maddox gave me the spiel that I was physically cleared now for everything, *including* sexual activity. I didn't think much of it then, given my life of solitude and singledom, but now that I'm touching myself, I'm remembering how good it can feel.

Damn, it really feels good.

As my head falls back, the spray of the water centers on my chest, sluicing down my abdomen and right around my active hand.

I shut my eyes and Remy's smile appears in my mind, and before I know it, my brain builds a scene around it.

Him, on top of me, naked and smiling with his hands clutching at the sides of my head. His hips are moving between mine, and he's almost laughing he's enjoying it so much.

Me, though, I can barely think, barely even see. If it weren't for the feast-worthy sight of his arms and shoulders and perfect fucking chest, I imagine I'd just give up the fight of keeping my eyes open altogether.

There's no dialogue, really—my brain is too tired for that—but the action says more than enough. Remy and I, we're a matched set physically. It's easy and exciting all at the same time and, in all likelihood, the reason I, a young, smart, cautious girl, chose to give herself over to him in the first place.

I thought maybe I was just hormone-struck at the time, but I can tell you now, teenage Maria knew what she was doing when she chose him.

I stroke at the flesh gently, circling my clit and putting pressure in the center at the end of every cycle. I can feel my pleasure building, the need to come taking on a form of its own.

Remy runs his hands down my sides, settling them on my ass and lifting me to meet his strokes. I deepen the action of my fingers to mimic the fantasy and am caught off guard when my orgasm grabs me in a vise, sending me over the edge in a rush. *Oh God, Remy!* my mind silently calls out.

Coming down from the high, I bury my face in the spray once again and let my weight collapse into the wall. It feels so good to be free, so good to give myself a moment of attention outside of the baby.

But more importantly, did I really just masturbate to thoughts of Remy while he is in my apartment taking care of Izzy?

Guilt and embarrassment consume me like wildfire. And without wasting any more time, I finish washing and cut off the water with shaky hands.

It only takes me a few minutes to throw on some leggings and a T-shirt and brush out the knots in my damp hair. But when I make my way back down the hallway toward the main living area, I swear I've been transported to a different era altogether.

Izzy is quiet, peaceful even, and Remy is laying her down in the swing on the far side of the living room. She doesn't startle or wake, and he buckles her in with the utmost ease and care. I watch silently, my disbelief so potent I'm surprised it doesn't blow Remy over.

When he turns around and sees me, he smiles. "Feel better?" he asks in his soft voice, just a notch above a whisper.

My cheeks heat at the thought of just how much *better* I feel—and *why* I feel that way—so I settle for a nod instead of testing the control properties of my tongue. I cannot believe he managed to put her to sleep in the time it took me to shower. *And touch yourself to the thought of him.*

"Sometimes, they just need someone who's not so invested in their going to sleep," Remy comforts with a laugh. "You know?"

I shake my head and flop down onto the messy couch like a rag doll. "I don't know anything, Rem. Nothing at all. My brain is a vast empty space at this point."

He laughs, walking across the room and taking a seat on the other end of the sectional. "You should go take a nap. I can handle keeping an eye on Izzy for now, and when you wake up, we can go out and get some fresh air."

I look around at the absolute volcanic rubble of a mess around me and shake my head. "I should pick up. I should—"

"You should sleep, Ri. Don't worry about the mess. We'll handle that later. Get rest, and get refreshed. You can't tackle a mountain without any energy."

The concept of sleep *is* really tempting.

"Go. Rest. I promise I'll make sure Izzy is fine if she wakes up, but I have a feeling she needs the time too."

"And, what? You're just going to hang out?"

I don't know if I can fall asleep knowing he's just out here…on my couch.

"College football is on," Remy says with a shrug. "It's not like I'd be doing anything different at home."

Considering him closely, I can see that he's not going to take no for an answer at this point. Whether I like it or not, Remy is here to stay, and I…well, I have the freedom to take a nap.

"Her formula and bottles are in the kitchen," I tell him in a rush. "But she shouldn't be hungry for at least another two hours or so. But if she is, she's been taking five ounces. And she did have a little bit of a diaper rash, so use some of the Aquaphor that's near the diapers and wipes on her changing table if you have to change her."

"Five ounces of formula. Aquaphor for diaper rash. Got it," he responds, but when I don't move, he adds, "It's all good in the baby hood, Ri. Promise. I've got it covered."

I nod then, succumbing to the inevitable and handing him the remote from the side table.

"If you need anything—"

"I'll manage," he interrupts gently. "Go rest."

I nod again and retreat back down the hallway, climbing into the center of my bed and pulling the big white comforter over myself. I spend about two minutes feeling weird and wondering if I'll be able to shut my brain off, and then suddenly and without warning, I'm out.

Checked out from the world and any and all chaos in it.

And it's all thanks to the handsome knight in perfectly washed-out denim in my living room.

FOURTEEN

Remy

When Maria comes out from her two-hour nap, she looks like a different person. The light and life I've come to know in her eyes are back, and her shoulders aren't slumped toward the ground anymore.

Izzy, on the other hand, is sleeping calmly in her swing that's remained at a gentle, back-and-forth lull since I put her in it again twenty minutes ago.

"She's *still* sleeping?" are the first words Maria says.

"Well, technically, she's *back* to sleeping after I gave her a bottle and changed her," I admit with a wink. "Feeling better?"

"So much." She rounds the sofa and coffee table and takes a seat in one of the plush white chairs on the other side. "Honestly, I don't even know what to say to you. Thank you doesn't feel like enough."

I smile. "No need to say anything, babe. Happy to help." I'd like to tell her that I wish she'd called me sooner, but on the outside chance that it adds to her stress, I don't. I don't want her to feel like she's failed somehow by waiting it out.

She fought the good fight, and she called when she needed me. That's all that matters.

Seemingly awakened from a deep slumber, she peers around the apartment, her eyes widening and catching on the mess. "Dear God. It looks like a bomb went off in here."

"No, it looks like a child lives here. Trust me. Even my sister had a messy house during Lexi's infancy. And she's like a machine."

"I just… I don't normally live like this," she says then, a mild bout of embarrassment coloring her cheeks.

"Maria, stop. Seriously. I'm a forty-four-year-old bachelor. You think I keep my place pristine all the time?" I shake my head. "Not a chance."

When her eyes flit over the mess again, I know I'm going to have to remove her from the space if there's any hope of preserving the rest and relaxation I've managed to get her to take.

"Listen, I think we should get out. Get some fresh air. Exercise our lungs. That sort of thing."

"What did you have in mind? I didn't do my hair after the shower or anything," she says, and a self-deprecating smile follows. "So I'm not exactly ready for a night on the town."

"I think you look perfect for any occasion, but I was thinking a walk in the park. Not a walk on the red carpet. You can rest assured that all of those expensive heels you love to wear can stay in the closet."

"Are you knocking my red soles?"

I grin. "I'd never think to do something like that."

Truthfully, those heels I've seen her wear, they're sexy as hell, even on a woman who was full-term pregnant at the time.

"So…how about that walk?"

"Okay. Yeah." She lets out a soft breath, and some of the tension eases from her shoulders. "A walk in the park sounds nice."

"Good." I stand up to get Izzy out of her swing. Her eyes are open now, but she's mostly just peering at the world. No fussing or cries for help. "Why don't you get some stuff together that you think we might need for the bambino here, and I'll occupy her time."

She nods gratefully. "Sounds like a plan."

Little does she know, I'm planning a little something else.

When she retreats down the hallway to Izzy's nursery, I snag my phone out of my pocket and scramble to text the one person I know can help me. I wish I had enough time to do it all myself, but just like I've been telling Maria, sometimes you need to outsource.

Me: Hey, I need your help. I need your housekeeper who does the rental properties to add another one to her list. I'll give you the money, but just get her on the books.

Winnie: Okay, I can do that. Did you just buy another rental place or something?

Me: No, just helping a friend.

Winnie: You have friends?

I very nearly roll my eyes. My sister is the nicest smartass I know.

Me: Very funny.

Winnie: I know, right? I'm hilarious. And I take it this friend is Maria?

Me: That would be correct.

Winnie: She doing okay?

Me: She's doing as well as a mom with a baby can do.

Winnie: So, she's trying to survive, then.

Me: Exactly.

Winnie. Send me the address, and I'll call them. When do you need them to come?

Me: In the next two hours. I'll leave the door unlocked when we leave.

Winnie: If this weren't for Maria, I'd definitely bitch at you for the last-minute request. Luckily, the whole fam has FINALLY left my house, and I have some time on my hands.

Me: You say that like you don't secretly love playing hostess for Winslow get-togethers.

Winnie: I say that like a woman who loves playing hostess but has to clean up after Uncle Brad.

Our uncle has always been a bit of a sloppy dude. I'm certain that's why Wes never lets him grill alone.

Winnie: Oh, and you can thank me later. Wes has my list of jewelry needs.

I have to mute my guffaw as it rolls up and out of my throat.

Me: Jewelry? You take an awful high hourly rate for this stuff, huh?

Winnie: It's all supply and demand, dearest brother. You need me, and I need jewelry. It goes hand in hand, really.

I roll my eyes at her again but laugh at the same time.

Me: Send me a link and sizing.

I think on it for half a second and send another quick text.

Me: Lexi's too.

Winnie: There's a reason you're my favorite brother most days.

My smile is still engaged and I'm shaking my head slightly when Maria comes back into the living room with a big diaper bag and a baby carrier, a little bout of curiosity pinching the skin between her eyebrows together. She's pulled her hair back into a low ponytail and changed into a pair of jeans and a loose-fitting sweater.

"You seem awfully amused."

Knowing I can tell the truth without spoiling the surprise, I rock my phone back and forth in the air and remark, "My sister."

Maria plops down onto the couch beside Izzy and me. "How is Winnie doing? I bet she's busy these days since football season is in full swing."

"She's actually here this weekend because the Mavs have a home game. And she's good. Still a smartass who can always connive exactly what she wants out of her big brother, but good."

Maria reaches out to run a soft finger over Izzy's cheek. "Sounds like not too much has changed since the last time I saw her."

"Yeah." I laugh. "She might be an adult now, but she's still the same old Winnie. I'll have to get the two of you together sometime. I know Win would love to see you."

Truth be told, I'm sure it was taking everything inside my sister not to pry with more questions regarding Maria and the baby. Of course, those will certainly come the next time I see her.

Maria's smile is soft but genuine. "The feeling is very much mutual. I'd love to see her again."

I reach out and grab the baby carrier from her hand, and once I'm certain Izzy is lying safely on her back between two couch pillows, I stand up to start strapping it on.

"Uh…?" Maria's eyes are wide and white. "What are you doing?"

I chuckle, nodding down at my torso as I clip the buckle at the side. "Putting on the carrier."

"*You're* going to carry her?"

"Yeah. Why not? Give your back a rest."

I finish doing up the straps and then open the front wide to ready it. I bend down to scoop Izzy up, and once again, Maria's eyes take on a saucerlike quality as I load the baby into the carrier and fold it up to secure it.

After checking to make sure Izzy's head is supported properly, I assure myself that she's getting enough air in the space in front of my chest and give all the straps one last tighten.

"You ready to get our walk on, Ri?"

"Let's do it." Maria stands then too, swinging the diaper bag backpack over her shoulder before I can stop her.

"Hey, no," I say, reaching for it immediately. "Give me that too."

"But you're already carrying Izzy."

"So?" I retort with a shrug. "You carry them together all the time, don't you?"

"Well, yes, but—"

"But nothing. One in the front, one in the back. It'll balance me out."

"Remy…"

I raise my eyebrows as I wait for her to lick her lips a couple of times.

"I…thank you…" She pauses again, but eventually continues. "Thank you so much for rushing over here today and for everything you've done for me so far. Like, seriously, I feel human again, and that's because of you. But you don't have to do all this for us. It's Saturday. I'm sure you have things to do and places to be—"

"You're right, Ri. I don't *have* to do it. I *want* to do it. And right now, the things I have to do and the places I have to be are taking a walk in the park and carrying all of your shit like the pack mule God intended when He made these big, huge muscles of mine."

She laughs at that, and finally, a carefree smile breaks loose. *There's the girl I remember.*

"All right, Mr. Muscles. Fine. Carry my stuff. See if I care." She holds out the backpack for me to take, and I swing it up and onto my back gently, so as not to jostle Izzy too much. Her little eyes are looking sleepy again, and if I play my cards right, I have a feeling she'll be back to baby dreamland by the time we step outside.

"Come on, ladies," I say, ushering Maria forward and putting a soft hand to her back. "The park awaits."

Maria's smile is noticeable as she glances back over her shoulder at me, and I give myself a mental pat on the back for helping to put it there. It's empowering—being able to be the thing that someone needs when they need it most.

In the past, I've mostly taken that role for my siblings, but this…I don't know…it feels even better.

Since it's only a short walk across the street from her apartment, it doesn't take us long to reach Central Park. It's pretty busy, but no more than I'd expect on a Saturday in early fall. The crowd isn't cloying or suffocating, just present.

The sun feels warm, and I roll up my sleeves to let some of it soak into my skin.

After Maria snags one of Izzy's hats from the backpack on my back and se-cures it on her little head, she follows my lead and does the same, rolling up the sleeves of her sweater and letting the sun hit her skin. She even closes her eyes occasionally and turns her face up into the warmth.

I watch, involuntarily enthralled by the sight of her face so at ease. She's truly one of the most beautiful women I've ever seen, and I don't even mean that in the affectionate, subjective way that can happen when you care about someone.

Her beauty is an eleven on a scale of ten in the most intrinsic of ways. Anyone who meets her can see that.

We've been mostly silent for the first ten minutes of the walk, but now that we're nearing a mile into it, her vocal cords start to limber up. "Okay. I have to admit, this is pretty freaking fantastic. I honestly didn't realize how good doing some exercise that doesn't involve rushing to a showing or listing ap-pointment could feel."

"Everything feels different when you've had a nap and a shower." I nod down toward a sleeping Izzy at my chest. "Even she knows that."

"Well, thanks. I owe you."

"You don't owe me anything. This is what you do for people you care about."

"Are you sure you don't want anything?" she asks, and her tone is light and airy. "A new set of golf clubs, maybe?"

I laugh. "It'd have to be a first set. I don't golf."

"Shoot. For some reason, I was getting that vibe about adult Remy."

"A golfer? Really? I'm giving that vibe?"

She shrugs, her smile climbing her cheeks and right into her eyes. "Well, yeah. But I don't think I've ever met an actual golfer, so I guess you can take it with a grain of salt."

"What else? What other crazy things is my aura telling you about me?"

"Your *aura?*" she questions on a cute guffaw. "Who have you been hanging out with, Remy? New age crystal healers? Psychic mediums?"

"Fortune-tellers," I answer, but she has no idea how true that statement is. "My aura. My vibe. Whatever you want to call it, babe. What other crazy things is it telling you about adult Remy?"

"Hmm." She smacks her lips together and tsks her tongue dramatically. "Okay, let me see. I'm getting a weekly gym rat vibe and twice-a-day shower thing from you. I think you're a pretty routine guy. Love to frequent the same restaurants and can't start your day without a black coffee. Although, I have a feeling, every once in a while, you go wild and order one of those sugary coffees with whipped cream. It's a guilty pleasure of yours and probably has an unhealthy amount of caramel." She scrunches up her nose in disgust. "And I also get the overwhelming feeling that you secretly love the early episodes of *Sex in the City.*"

She hit the nail on the head on all but one thing.

"Can't say I've ever watched that show." I waggle my eyebrows. "But I've always liked the title."

She grins. "You'd like the show too, trust me. Not in a, like, oh man, I love this storyline kind of way. But you'd, at the very least, get a kick out of Samantha."

"Samantha?"

"She's brutally honest, hilarious, and very sexually open."

"Sounds promising for this adult me you've envisioned. Maybe I'll fit in a few episodes after my next golf outing."

Maria laughs. "What do you see about me, then? Now that we're old?"

I roll my eyes. "*I'm* old. You're beautiful."

She turns her head to the side a little, just enough to absorb the compliment in some privacy, and my phone buzzes in my pocket. Normally, I would ignore it and enjoy the view of Maria blushing a little at my words, but since I'm hoping it'll be an update from my sister, I quickly check the message.

Winnie: Cleaners are going there next. Should be done by 6 or so.

Perfect. Everything is going to plan.

Me: Thanks, sis.

I tuck the phone into my pocket and return my focus to Maria and her question. *What do I think of her as an adult? I think she's fucking flawless.*

"Okay, let's see. Maria Baros as an adult." I ponder for a moment, letting my eyes search hers as though all the answers are just inside. A bevy of secrets and clues, just floating around in her pretty brown gaze.

"I think you stay up late sometimes, even when you know you have to be up early, just to rebel against your neat and tidy schedule a little. You watch late-night infomercials and order products that you end up donating or hiding in the closet when you see them in the light of day. And you still make time to watch that ridiculous soap opera *General Hospital* every day, even with how busy you are with work."

She laughs. "Hey, don't knock my show. *General Hospital* has some of the longest-running relationships I've ever known."

I laugh, remembering just a tiny sliver of detail from our days of watching it together after school. "Are Sonny and Carly still together?"

"Not right now. But they have seven kids and, as you know, are always on-again, off-again."

"Aha!" I declare. "So, I was right. You do *still* watch it."

"Not every episode!" she defends through a giggle. "I don't have the time. But I catch about one every two weeks or so, and it's easy enough to keep up."

"I love that. Makes me almost feel like we're kids again."

Maria's eyes hold mine as we walk, and I have to glance away to make sure we don't bump into anyone in our path. We've gotten pretty deep into the park at this point, and when I see something up ahead, I can't resist having a little fun.

"Stay right here," I tell her as I start to climb the giant rock in Central Park, her eyes widening to the point of strain.

"Remy—" she calls, clearly concerned by my climbing while wearing Izzy, but I know with one-hundred-percent confidence that this moment will be worth her temporary freak-out. I'm also a pro at this rock from back in my wild childhood days. My brothers and I utilized it often for sneak attacks on one another.

"It's fine," I call back, being careful with my foot and hand work as I pick my way to the top. Izzy coos a little in the carrier at my chest, having just woken up and enjoying the ride. "I promise. She's liking it!"

"Remy, she's six weeks old. She'd probably like razor blades and needles if I let her!"

I laugh at that; I can't help it. Maria has always been funny, but I'm pretty sure she's gotten even funnier with age.

"You're right, Ri. We'd better be careful," I call down as I climb. "Forget pre-schools. Let's start looking for a good toddler rehab."

"I don't appreciate your jokes right now, Remington Winslow."

"Oh wow," I whisper down at Izzy. "She must be serious. She's using her mom voice."

"I can't hear what you're saying, but I just want you to know I can tell you're talking about me."

I laugh and turn around carefully to wink down at Maria. "I was just telling her how beautiful you are."

"You're so full of shit."

I pretend to cover Izzy's ears as I make it to the top and turn around dramatically. "Language, Maria. There are little ears here."

"I hope your dry cleaner is good with blood."

I chuckle as I grab my phone out of my jeans pocket and search until I find what I'm looking for.

"Remington Winslow, get your ass down here!" Maria calls toward us, but I'm already working to unbuckle Izzy from the carrier.

I turn her in my arms to swing her slightly as she fusses a little. I give her nose a quick brush of mine that makes her relax, and then I turn and present her to all of Central Park Prideland. As planned, the music from *The Lion King* crashes into full volume from the speaker of my phone, and I fall into my stance with pride.

"An heir!" I yell into the distance so loud that strangers start to turn and look.

Maria's face turns beet red in an instant, but there's a subtle smile there too as she buries her face into her hands.

Of course, that reaction only makes me yell louder. "An heir has been born!"

And Izzy is my ride-or-die, stretching her little neck like she's watched this movie before.

A couple of passersby amused by our display stop and even bow down to the new Queen of Pride Rock. "Congratulations!" one exclaims. "She's gorgeous!"

"Lord help me, you're crazy!" Maria shouts up toward us, her embarrassment receding and giving way to the kind of genuine smile I was going for. She plays it cool, though, just to keep me on my toes. "And where are Scar and the hyenas when you need them?"

"You wish harm on poor Simba?" I call, tucking Izzy to my chest and covering her ears dramatically.

"No, no. Just Mufasa. The big, cocky prick."

A couple of straggling strangers laugh at that, and a smile spreads from one corner of my mouth to the other.

"Can you come down here now?" Maria requests with a stubborn hand to her hip. "Or do I have to call your mother?"

I laugh. "Wendy would be thrilled to hear from you."

"You know, I think a couple of decades hanging out with your brothers has really had an effect on you."

"Yeah?"

"Yeah," she confirms with a nod. "Baboons tend to breed more baboons. Just ask Rafiki."

"Was Rafiki a baboon?" I find myself asking, and Maria rolls her eyes.

"How about you come back down here, and I'll tell you."

I smirk, satisfied with the awakening of Maria's humor that my little stunt has caused. That was the goal. To cut through the exhaustion with fresh air and antics and remind Maria that she's human. That even when she's feeling like she's trapped at the bottom of a deep well of darkness and unknowns and unexpected motherhood, the breath of fresh air she's looking for is just a short walk away.

God, it's good to see her again.

When I don't move, Maria tosses out both of her hands in front of her and eyes me with a squint. "Remy? What are you doing?"

"Just trying to decide if I should come back down. Does trouble await me at the bottom?"

"You know, I almost forgot how freaking ridiculous you are." Her smile is so big it clones itself, jumps onto the rock beneath my feet, rolls up through my toes, and reveals itself on my own face.

"What's the verdict? Am I in trouble?"

"Only the good kind, you lunatic."

Only the good kind.

Man oh man, do those words give me déjà vu.

THE PAST

THE KISS GAME

Twenty-Eight Years Ago…

Junior year, early October

Remy

"It's going to be okay, babe," I tell Maria as we walk out of her doctor's office.

She's about four steps ahead of me, and my words make her stop in the middle of the sidewalk and turn around to meet my eyes.

"*Okay?*" she retorts with irritation that makes her lips part and eyebrows draw together. "I have to keep this stupid cast on for another two weeks! I won't be able to cheer, and I'm pretty sure this means I'm on the bench for the rest of the season! It is most certainly *not* going to be okay."

Today's appointment was supposed to be a splendid occasion where the doctor took off Maria's cast and gave her arm the all clear for physical activity.

The pink cast *was* removed, but when they did an X-ray, the doctor felt it was wise for her to keep a cast on for another two weeks to ensure that it's healed properly.

Needless to say, my girl, sporting a *black*—"*because it matches my soul right now, Remy*"—cast, is none-too-pleased.

And since Mrs. Baros got stuck at work and she's had six weeks to warm up to me, *and six weeks to become friendly with my mom*, I'm the one who drove Maria here. Which means, I'm the one who has the privilege of trying to help her feel better about the whole situation.

"Babe, I know you're upset, but—"

"There is no *but* here, Remy," she cuts me off before I can continue. "There is nothing you can say or do that will make me feel better about this."

She turns on her heel, flips her long brown hair over her shoulder, and stomps toward my Mustang that's parked across the street from the medical center. Located just outside the city, her physician's office is only about a twenty-minute drive from home and has street parking. Which, if you know New York, you know that's like finding a unicorn.

My only choice is to follow behind her.

If it were any other girl, I might be annoyed, but Maria has this special way of being cute when she's angry. Honestly, after spending the last month and half dating, I've yet to find a moment when she's irritated me. It's strange but kind of awesome at the same time.

Jude and Ty love telling me I'm "whipped" like the little assholes they are, and Flynn looks at me with serious eyes a lot. Of course, Winnie is Team Maria because she *loves* the fact that Maria has a little sister too. It means she has more opportunity to try to tag along with me.

I dutifully beep the locks when Maria reaches the passenger side, and I hop into the driver's seat just as she's closing her door.

"Are you okay?" I ask her carefully, trying to get a feel for where her head is at.

"I'm fine, Remy."

One look at her and I almost want to laugh. Her arms are crossed, her brow is furrowed, and a little pout has found a home at the corners of her pretty mouth.

But I don't dare laugh. I may just be a sixteen-year-old dude, but I'm way smarter than that. It's *never* smart for a guy to laugh when a girl is angry. I'm also aware that the word fine doesn't mean fine at all when it's coming from a girl's lips.

Her earlier words replay in my mind, *There is nothing you can say or do that will make me feel better about this.*

I take those words as a challenge. I know I can find a way to make Maria smile. She just needs a little pick-me-up, that's all.

I slide a CD into my stereo, and a few seconds later, the band KISS is playing. The song is "I Was Made for Lovin' You," and normally, Maria bobs her head along to the beat and sings along with all the *do-do-do*'s.

"Seriously? Gene Simmons is not ideal for a time like this, Remy," she grumbles and lets out an aggravated sigh. Her eyes stay fixated on the windshield, even though, with the car still parked, the scenery isn't changing.

I grin. Okay, fine. No KISS.

Truthfully, songs from this band have a bit of a history. One that Maria utilizes every time she's trying to get me to kiss her. I know it sounds crazy, but I'm the one who isn't ready for our first official kiss.

Well, *I* am ready. Trust me, *I'm ready*. But I just want to make sure *she's* ready. She's a little younger than me, and I don't know…she's not like any of the other girls I've dated.

She's different. Special. I don't want to fuck any of it up.

And Gene Simmons and his band have spurred a game of "kiss" between the two of us. Maria puts on one of their songs, trying to get me to kiss her, and I kiss every part of her face *but* her lips.

It drives her nuts. But man, it's kind of amazing at the same time. Although it's probably also dangerous because it drives me nuts too. So nuts, in fact, that by the end of the night, I have to throw my ass in a cold shower when I get home. Let me tell you, blue balls aren't a myth. They are the real deal.

I slide in another CD, but this time, the new song doesn't cause a volatile reaction from Maria. It doesn't exactly make her turn all happy either, but still, it's progress.

It's a Supremes greatest hits CD, and the song currently playing is called "Baby Love."

I start to sing the lyrics out loud, giving my best Diana Ross impression. I even do a few doo-wop-style dance moves from the driver's seat. But all I get is the side-eye from the pretty girl beside me.

Okay. Yeah. It's time to bring out the big guns. The song Maria calls her "happy song."

CD switched *again*, new song on, and Maria crosses her arms over her chest when the opening beats I know she knows like the back of her hand begin to play.

"Man, I love this song," I say, and she refuses to look in my direction. "It always makes me happy. It's almost like it's my *happy song*, you know what I mean, Ria?"

When she doesn't say anything, I add, "It's too bad my favorite singing partner is mad at me. Marvin Gaye is feeling a little lost over here without his Tammi."

"I'm not mad at you, Remy," she says quietly but still loud enough for me to hear over the music. "I'm just mad in general."

I don't respond. Instead, I hold up an air microphone in front of my face and start to sing the opening lyrics.

Maria rolls her eyes, but it only takes another ten seconds before she's watching me. And the more I sing, the more I notice her shoulders start to relax away from her ears.

"Was I being mean to you earlier?" she eventually asks me over the music, and I shrug.

"A little, maybe?"

"I'm sorry," she apologizes with a small frown, and I hold out an air microphone toward her.

"Don't worry, Tammi. I know just the way you can make it up to me."

The hint of a smile starts to show on her lips.

"C'mon, Ria. You know you want to."

Her smile is visible now, and she pretends to take the air microphone from my hands.

And then, we sing our hearts out. Eventually, both of us fall into it so much, we have to share the same air microphone.

Maria giggles when I really go nuts and start trying to mimic Marvin Gaye's voice, and by the time it comes to an end, she can't swipe that pretty smile from her lips.

Hell yeah. I knew I could cheer her up. Just call me the World's Best Boyfriend.

"You just couldn't let me be mad, could you?" she asks, turning her whole body to face me.

"Nope." I smile. "Am I in trouble now?"

She searches my eyes for the longest moment, and when her gaze flits down to my mouth briefly, she looks back up at me with a mischievous-as-hell grin. "Only the good kind."

"The good kind of trouble? What does that mean?"

"It means I'm going to kiss you, Remington Winslow."

Maria has never actually said those words to me. She's hinted at them but never voiced them in a way that made me feel like she was ready to take the bull by the horns.

"Yeah?" I gulp. "And when are you planning on doing that?"

"Right now."

Right now? Holy shit.

She reaches out to place her hand on my cheek, and I don't miss the way her fingers shake a little, vibrating against my skin. I half expect her to hesitate, to let her nerves get the best of her.

But she surprises the hell out of me.

Leaning forward, she places her lips to mine, and the first, ever so gentle brush of her mouth occurs. Light as a feather, the kiss lingers like that long enough that I can feel my heart getting off-balance in its spin cycle in my chest.

The urge to take it further overwhelms me. I slide my fingers into the hair at her neck and kiss her, *really* kiss her, right there in front of the medical center. Our mouths part and our tongues dance, and I don't know if I've tasted anything as sweet as this.

It's not my first kiss, but damn, it feels like it. Every other kiss before this one feels like an impostor. A fake.

They weren't hesitant but hungry like this one. More experienced, but not nearly as mind-blowing. If I'm not careful, I just might end up falling in love with this girl.

Actually, you just might already be.

FIFTEEN

Still Saturday, October 5th

Maria

Who would've thought that a simple walk around Central Park would make me feel better?

Certainly not me. Somehow, though, the tightness in my chest has eased, and I no longer feel like my shoulders are trying to relocate to my ears.

If anything, I feel relief. Rejuvenated. *Human.*

"You have to admit, Izzy and I put on one hell of a show," Remy says with a big-ass smile as we stand off to the side of the huge rock he just climbed down from. "We should probably take this on the road. Hit all the major cities."

The man just presented her to all of Central Park from the top of that big rock like she was freaking Simba, while the soundtrack from *The Lion King* played from his phone.

The two of them were such an amusing spectacle that even random strangers stopped to clap and laugh.

"The next time you rock climb with my baby, I'm calling the cops," I retort, and the teasing tone in my voice can't be missed.

"Hold the phone, babe. I thought you said I would only be in the good kind of trouble when I came back down?"

"This *is* the good kind," I tell him with a playful point of my index finger. "The bad kind would be me kicking your ass."

He laughs at that. "Well, I'm more than happy to take the heat because my little stunt achieved what I needed it to."

I raise an eyebrow at him, and he nods toward my face.

"You're smiling."

You're smiling. He did all that to make me smile?

After everything he's already done for me, I don't know what to do with that information. I almost feel undeserving of his kindness. I mean, I'm losing count of how many times he's saved my ass… And what have I given him in return? Stress? A crying baby?

Izzy begins to fuss in her carrier, but when Remy bounces his knees a little, she calms down and her eyes start to fall shut.

"Is it just me, or does this baby like to be in a constant state of motion?"

I laugh. "Oh, it's not just you. Girlfriend definitely likes to be on the move." I should know; I've been dealing with that issue since the day I brought her home from the hospital—I often wonder if my fast-paced work habits during my pregnancy created this dilemma.

He grins. "Looks like we better get this walk moving again, then."

At an easy pace, and in the name of keeping Izzy happy, we continue our walk. And after we've managed a quarter of a mile or so, I look beside me, where Izzy sits in the baby carrier across Remy's chest and see that she's snug as a bug and sleeping again.

The day is uncharacteristically warm for early fall, midseventies and sunny with a few clouds. They're the perfect conditions to get some fresh air without having to stress whether Izzy is too cold or too warm or the wind is blowing against her skin too much or the sun is too hot on her little face… or you know, a million other things that you'd never think would be a stress until you're responsible for a tiny human being.

It's almost crazy how, when a baby comes into the picture, your life changes in a matter of seconds. Everything that used to be a priority is forced into an afterthought, and worries you never thought you'd have are suddenly all you can overthink about.

"How about you give your back a break and let me carry her," I suggest, but Remy looks over at me and shakes his head.

"No thank you."

"C'mon, Remy. Let me carry her."

"Listen, missy, I'm not giving this sweet baby up," he comments and nods his chin toward the top of her head. "Plus, look at her. She's too cozy to be moved."

"So, what you're saying is that you're a baby hog?" I tease, and the small smile that crests his lips makes my heart get all wonky inside my chest. My reaction is strange, but I blame it on that smile of his. It's all too familiar and has the power to take me back years into the past.

"When it comes to this little cutie? Yes. I am most definitely a baby hog," he answers. "Plus, I think me and Iz are quite the adorable sight. No doubt, the ladies of Central Park are appreciative."

"Ohhhh…so what you're really trying to do is pick up hot chicks with my baby?"

"Yeah, right." He winks. "Why would I want to pick up hot chicks when I'm with the two most beautiful girls in the world?"

"Are you trying to charm me, Remington? Because it's starting to feel like you're tossing an awful lot of smooth-talking my way today." I quirk a defiant eyebrow at him, and he just shrugs one shoulder.

"That depends."

"On what?"

"Is it working?"

I roll my eyes. "When I was sixteen? Most definitely. But now? Not after I got a look at myself in the mirror before we left my apartment."

"Don't be ridiculous," he retorts. "You're freshly showered and gorgeous."

"I might be showered, but I'm still a sleep-deprived, overworked, postpartum mess of anxiety," I correct him. "I'm *surviving*. That's about as far as it goes."

Seriously. This isn't even me being insecure. It's my current reality. There is no way on God's green earth that my current frazzled state lands me in the top one billion of beautiful women. Being a new mom is not easy. Especially when the term "new mom" holds so much more weight than I ever thought it would when I first found out I was pregnant.

"Well, *I* think you're gorgeous. And I'm certain, if Izzy were awake, she would agree."

I snort. "Izzy can't talk."

"She'd think it."

"Pretty sure that's not how it works, but okay."

Remy just grins and places a gentle hand to my lower back to guide us toward a park bench. "She's out. I think we can take a load off for a minute."

We sit down just as a young, thirtysomething mother runs past us, trying to wrangle a small toddler back into his stroller.

"Henry!" she shouts, and he just giggles and giggles, his fat little legs churning faster whenever his mom gets close.

Henry the toddler screeches like a pterodactyl, and his poor mother exhales an exasperated breath, sweat already starting a path on her brow. "Henry, honey, it's time to go home."

"No!" Henry shouts and stomps one gym-shoe-covered foot to the ground. He crosses his fat little arms over his chest and tries to stand his ground, but his mom isn't having any of it. In an instant, she whisks him up and into her arms and toward the stroller he keeps refusing to sit in.

The toddler screams and cries the whole way, his little arms and legs kicking and smacking his mom as they go.

Holy moly. What's it going to be like when Izzy is no longer an infant, but a toddler like little Henry over there? Will she be just like him? Screeching and demanding and not listening to anything I tell her? God help me.

I can't manage Izzy and my work schedule as it is, and she's only six weeks old. Even when she's crying or upset, I can at least keep her secure in my arms or in her stroller or baby carrier or her vibrating swing when I'm really desperate.

But when she's a toddler? What in the hell am I going to do?

"Maria?"

Evidently a liar wrote the last book I read, talking about how it gets easier after the newborn stage.

"*Maria?*" Remy's voice stresses, his extra effort at getting my attention obvious now.

"Hmmm?" I respond, but I still can't pull my eyes away from little Henry and his mom as she fights to get him strapped into his stroller.

"You okay?"

I have no idea how long I've been sitting here, falling down the rabbit hole of future fears and watching Henry turn into the Incredible Hulk, but the concerned look in Remy's eyes says it's been a few minutes too long.

Am I okay? No. Not really. I mean, the current circumstances of my life would probably equate to most people not being okay, but I refuse to drag Remy into my pit of anxious misery. He's already done enough for me as it is today.

"Yeah, of course." I offer a little white lie and force a small smile to my lips. "I'm good."

"I think it's time for a little change in scenery." He reaches out to pat a gentle hand to my thigh. "What do you say we go grab an early dinner? I mean, truthfully, you've still left me hanging since the first time I asked you."

I raise a questioning brow. "The first time?"

"After we got trapped in the elevator in Ty's building," he expands. "Consider it a redo, kind of like how we got to experience the blackout-elevator situation *twice*."

"But only, with this redo, you won't have to deliver a baby," I state on a snort. "Because I sure as hell am not going through that again."

"The only baby in attendance will be this one," he responds on a soft chuckle and reaches out to brush a rogue piece of hair out of my eyes. "A much more laid-back redo, if you will."

"Laid-back sounds perfect."

Remy carefully stands up from the park bench, one hand providing stability on Izzy's back as he gets to his feet. And then, he holds out his hand toward me. "C'mon, Maria, let's go enjoy a meal together."

I look down at his hand and then up and into his blue eyes. They are bright and warm and all the things that turned me into a bumbling teenage girl back in the day.

To distract myself, I try to sneak a peek at Izzy's face.

"Don't worry, she's still asleep," he adds, still holding his hand out toward me. "And I have a sneaking suspicion that you haven't eaten much today."

He's not wrong. Between juggling a cranky baby and my six-week postpartum appointment and work calls and a showing that I eventually had to cancel, I managed to scarf down half a banana and a granola bar…but that's it.

"Okay. Yeah." I nod and place my hand into his. "Let's do it."

Remy smiles, and once I'm on my feet, I expect him to let go of my hand, but he never does. He just keeps holding it as he guides us toward the closest exit out of Central Park and onto 84th Street.

"Where are we going?"

"It's a surprise," he says and waggles his brows as he places his hand on my lower back and guides the three of us across the street.

"A surp—" I start to ask, but he cuts me off with a smile and a chuckle.

"A surprise that you'll find out about in exactly two blocks."

"Is that your way of telling me I don't get to ask questions?"

"Yep." He grins down at me. "I know how horrible you are at letting people surprise you."

"I'm not that bad!" I respond on a giggle and playfully slap his arm.

"The week of your sixteenth birthday, you damn near ruined your own surprise party, Ms. Super Sleuth."

"You're being dramatic."

"You interrogated all of my friends. My brothers. Even my baby sister."

I bite my lip through a smile. "And Ty almost spilled the beans."

"Because Ty is shit at keeping secrets, and you basically turn into a fucking CIA agent attempting to sniff out an international spy ring when you're trying to ruin a surprise."

"It's not that I'm trying to ruin a surprise. I'm just nosy."

"And impatient," he teases and reaches out to grab my hand again.

"Whatever, Rem." I roll my eyes, but I also shut my trap because I can't deny the truth. I'm incorrigible when it comes to surprises. If I have any inkling there's about to be a surprise of some sort, I can't stop myself from trying to figure out what it is.

Birthday presents. Christmas. You name it, and I've probably ruined many a surprise throughout my life.

We walk another block or so before Remy guides us onto another street, and it's not long before he's coming to a stop in front of a rustic-looking brick building.

"Surprise," he says, and I look at him curiously before allowing my eyes to read the sign above our heads.

"Jacob's Pickles?"

"You ever been here?"

"No." I shake my head. "Can't say I have."

"Do you still love pickles on your sandwiches as much as you did back in high school?"

I laugh. "I can't believe you remember that, but yes."

"Maria, I used to go with you to that little diner near the public library after school because you were obsessed with their chicken sandwiches. *Extra pickles on the sandwich and extra pickles on the side,*" he repeats my old order.

"I even recall a few times you convinced me to play hooky at lunch just so I could help you satisfy your crazy pickle cravings."

"Excuse me? Crazy cravings?" I put a hand to my hip. "Pickles on chicken sandwiches are everything. Anyone who thinks otherwise needs their head checked."

Remy just grins. "Well, let me be the first to introduce you to the best fucking pickles that you'll ever taste in your life."

My eyes go wide. "I hope you realize those are some big promises."

"Promises I stand by, Ria."

Not Maria or Ri. But *Ria.* That's what Remy always used to call me back in the day. He was the only one to use that nickname, and when I was a high school girl with first love in her eyes, it felt like *everything.*

It still kind of does.

I let Remy guide me inside the restaurant, and in a matter of minutes, we're seated at a cozy booth in the back corner. A request made specifically by the man still wearing Izzy on his chest.

"Here," I say and hold out both of my hands. "I can hold her while we eat."

"Ah-ah." He shakes his index finger at me. "She's still sleeping. So, we're good just like this."

"But how are you going to eat with her strapped to your chest like that?"

"I'll manage," he answers without hesitation and hands me a menu. "And you work on figuring out what you want to eat."

"Are you sure? Because I can—"

"Ria, can you do me a favor?" he asks, and I tilt my head to the side.

"What?"

"Will you try to relax and just…enjoy this meal?" His eyes turn soft, and he reaches out to place his hand over mine. "Don't worry about me or Izzy. Just…order all the fucking pickles your heart desires," he says while grinning.

"And relax. You deserve it. You're a great mom, and great moms deserve a break sometimes, okay?"

For some insane reason, I want to cry at his words. But not because they make me feel bad. Actually, they make me feel so good the relief they provide is overwhelming.

All I can do is swallow hard against the emotion and nod.

"Okay. Deal."

"Lovely doing business with you." He gently squeezes my hand before letting it go to grab his menu. He peruses the dinner options, and I just sit there, looking at my own menu.

But mostly, my mind races and wonders, *How, after all these years, is Remy Winslow here, with me?*

In the blink of an eye, he'd gone from someone I hadn't seen in so long to the first person I called when I felt like everything was falling apart.

The only person I wanted to call, actually.

Rem tilts his head away from a still-sleeping Izzy on his chest and carefully lifts the rest of his chicken sandwich to his lips, all the while avoiding inadvertently dropping food onto an incoherent baby's cute head.

Izzy stirs ever so slightly as he takes one final bite, but her tiny cherubic face stays lax and her sweet little body just keeps on snoozing.

I don't know if it's exhaustion from giving me hell today or if Remy has cast some kind of secret baby voodoo on her, but somehow, someway, she stayed asleep through the *entire* meal.

"Okay, let me hear it." Remy wipes his hands off with a napkin and tosses it down onto his now-empty plate. "What did you think?"

"You want my review on Jacob's Pickles?"

He nods and rests his hands at Izzy's back. "You bet your cute ass I do."

My cute ass? I kind of want to tell him my ass isn't looking all that cute after having a baby six weeks ago, but I bite my tongue and focus on his real question.

"Well…" I feign a small frown. "It was…okay."

"Okay?" He narrows his eyes and nods pointedly toward my plate. My very empty plate that used to hold seven different flavors of pickles, French fries, and the best flipping chicken sandwich I've ever had in my life. "My surprise was just…*okay?*"

"Yeah." I shrug and bite my lip to fight the urge to smile. "I mean, I appreciate the thought behind the surprise. So…I definitely give that five stars. But the food?" I shrug again. "It was…okay."

"You're so full of shit." He laughs. Outright. And then he reaches out across the table to gently run his finger along the side of my cheek. "And I know this because this dimple right here is your tell."

"I do not have a tell." I quickly lift my hand to cover the traitorous dimple in question, and immediately, his mouth turns up in a megawatt, proud-as-a-peacock smile.

"Oh, but you do, Ria. It's that dimple right there, and it only reveals itself when you're lying."

"How would you know that?"

"Because I know *a lot* of things about Maria Baros." He waggles his brows. "All sorts of awesome things, in fact."

"Watch yourself, buddy." I playfully point a finger at him. "Because I just so happen to know *a lot* of things about Remington Winslow too."

He chuckles at that. "We had a lot of good times back in the day, didn't we?"

"Yeah, we definitely did,"

Oh man, did we ever…

Instantly, my mind joins the stupid dimple in its traitorous behavior and goes straight toward memories of what it was like to be the girl on Remy's arm.

To spend nearly every waking hour with him. To be the person who made him laugh and smile. To be the girl he kissed. And *touched*.

To experience what it felt like to have Remy slide inside me.

Stop it.

Still, even though I know it's not good for me, I can't stop myself from taking in how painfully cute he looks, sitting there, with Izzy.

He was right. The ladies of Central Park were definitely appreciative of this view.

Honestly, it's almost criminal how perfect he looks with Izzy or how good he is with her. Like a baby whisperer, but only, so insanely attractive that every pair of ovaries within a hundred-mile radius is at risk of exploding.

Hell, he should probably be restricted from walking around like this in public; he's a danger to biological clocks everywhere.

When his phone vibrates on the table, he lifts it up to check the screen for a brief second before setting it back down. But other than that, he doesn't say anything. Doesn't even respond to the sender.

"What do you say we start heading back to your apartment?"

I nod, assuming he probably has somewhere he needs to be. Lord knows his Saturday plans probably didn't include spending it with a frazzled mom and her baby. "I think that's a solid plan. Izzy is going to need to eat soon."

Rem makes quick work of getting—and paying for—the check, and before I know it, we're back on the street and heading toward my building.

And it's not long before we're at my apartment and I'm unlocking the front door.

But when we step inside, I stop dead in my tracks.

Clean. *Everything* is *clean.*

"Uh…" I look around my living room and kitchen and even head into the guest bathroom to find it so clean I could probably eat off the tile floor. "I think I've been robbed…but only, they didn't take anything. They…cleaned."

Remy's soft chuckle fills my ears, and when I walk out of the bathroom, I find him easing Izzy out of her carrier and putting her still-sleeping body in her vibrating chair by the couch.

"So…I have a bit of a confession," he says, and his mouth morphs into a slight grimace. "Don't be mad, but I hired someone, *very* trustworthy and highly recommended by my sister, mind you, to come clean your apartment while we were out today."

"Mad?" I question. "Why would I be mad? I feel like a million pounds of stress have been lifted from my shoulders."

"Really? So…you're okay with this?"

"Remy, are you kidding me?" I retort and walk toward him to wrap my arms around his waist and hug him tightly. "I'm…I'm…just…thank you."

"You're welcome," he whispers back and hugs me tighter. "So, you also won't be mad that I've made arrangements for the same very trustworthy cleaning team to come to your apartment once a week and clean."

I lean back and search his eyes.

"You have too much on your plate," he adds and taps his forehead against mine. "And I know it's not a lot, but I just…want to help you however I can."

This man. What am I going to do with him?

I'm in awe of him.

This day was a dumpster fire. I was stressed to the max and overwhelmed, and I felt like I was failing at being a mom to Izzy…failing at work… failing at pretty much everything, and all it took was one phone call to Remy for him to swoop in and turn everything around.

He was everything I needed him to be.

"You're pretty awesome, you know that?" I whisper toward him, and he searches my eyes, our bodies still wrapped up in a tight embrace.

"So are you," he whispers back, and his blue eyes flit down to my lips.

Our bodies are the closest they've been in I don't know how many years, and it just…does something to me. Out of nowhere, a surge of arousal makes itself known in my belly and I find myself stepping even closer to him, sliding my hands up his back and wrapping them around his neck.

Our eyes meet again, and his hands are wrapped around my waist and my breasts are now pressed up against his chest, and I don't know what we're doing but I know that I really like how it feels to be right here, in Remy's arms.

And I like how it feels to have the warmth of his body next to mine.

And I *really* like how it feels to be this close to him.

"Maria," he says my name, but it's not in question. It's for something else. Something I can't quite discern.

I move my face closer to his, my gaze flitting between his blue-as-the-sky eyes and his full, lush mouth.

And he's doing the exact same thing.

Is Remy going to kiss me?

Am I going to kiss Remy?

I move my mouth closer to his, mere millimeters, but it feels like a mile.

But the other person in the room? The tiny, adorable baby in her vibrating chair?

Well, she has plans of her own.

Big plans that include belting out the kind of cry that makes Rem and me jolt away from each other as if we were about to commit a crime. Or you know…*kiss*.

Holy hell, was I really going to kiss Remy?

But I don't have time to contemplate that question or what kissing him would have meant, because when you're a mom and your baby is crying her little lungs out, her needs are all you can focus on.

And I'm not the only one whose focus has shifted.

Remy walks over to Izzy and picks her up, pulling her into his arms. "Aw, Izzy girl. Are you hungry? Or do you need to be changed? Or maybe we're dealing with a combination of both?" he questions and cuddles her closer to his chest.

"I have a feeling it's probably both." I hold out my hands to take her from his arms, but he shakes his head.

"I'll change her. You get the bottle."

Izzy belts out another cry and Remy heads into her nursery, and I don't think twice before going into the kitchen to get her bottle ready.

It's almost surreal how easily we fall into a routine.

And by the time Izzy has a fresh diaper and her bottle is in her mouth, I plop down on the couch beside Remy while he feeds her because he refused to have it any other way.

She sucks at the nipple like she's starving, like she hasn't been fed in days, and it urges a soft laugh to leave my lips. "My oh my, you were a hungry girl."

Remy flashes a wink at me. "Kind of like you when it comes to pickles and chicken sandwiches."

"Whatever, smartass." I roll my eyes on another laugh, but I also yawn.

"Tired?"

"I am, but that's probably par for the course when you have a baby, right? Tired all the time."

"My sister would agree. And definitely Flynn and Daisy. Twin boys are no joke."

"Yeah, I don't even want to think about having two Izzys right now. I can barely handle one as it is." I grimace through a giggle, but when my eyes grow heavy, I find myself resting my head on Remy's shoulder while he finishes feeding Izzy the bottle.

I'm just going to rest my eyes for a little bit, I mentally remind myself. *Once Izzy is all fed, I'll let Rem off the baby-caring hook.*

Just a little catnap. That's all...

SIXTEEN

Remy

My eyes pop open when the muscles in my leg jerk, and I jam my foot into something really fucking hard.

Ah, shit. That hurt.

I blink the remnants of sleep from my vision, looking around at surroundings that aren't my apartment. When I note the fancy marble coffee table and practically all-white décor, I realize I'm still at Maria's. One look to my left and I see Izzy sitting in her favorite vibrating chair. One look to my right and I find Maria sleeping beside me, still sitting up and her head resting on my shoulder.

Somewhere along the way, after I fed Izzy her bottle and put her in her swing, I decided it was a good idea to just…rest for a hot minute on Maria's couch. She was already asleep, so I sat down beside her, but what I didn't plan on doing was passing the fuck out.

What time is it?

As careful as I possibly can, I grab my phone off the coffee table, but when a soft groan leaves Maria's lips, I freeze into a statue and silently pray I didn't just wake up a sleep-deprived new mother for the mere purpose of checking the clock.

Once I'm certain she's managed to stay asleep, I peek at the time and see it's a little after eleven and I have a shit-ton of missed texts from my brothers.

I open our group chat and scan the messages that started a few hours ago.

Jude: What do you guys think about meeting up for a drink tonight? Say, in about an hour?

Ty: I think that's a grand idea.

Flynn: We just saw one another at Winnie's.

Jude: Yeah, but we didn't get to bro-out, you know?

Ty: Exactly. We should definitely bro-out tonight. And I vote that Remy has to join us.

Jude: For sure. Rem, you HAVE to come.

These fuckers. I know exactly what they're trying to achieve.

Flynn: Remy is going to see right through your bullshit.

Obviously, Flynn knows too.

Jude: What bullshit? How is wanting to spend time with my brothers bullshit?

Ty: Yeah, Flynn. What's the deal? You sound like an asshole right now.

Flynn: If I'm an asshole, then you two are pussies who won't just come out and ask Remy what is going on with him.

Bingo bango.

Jude: You know, I wasn't even thinking about that, but now that you bring it up, Flynn, I am curious. What's going on, Rem? You left the barbecue today in a rush.

Ty: You did leave in a rush, man. Right after you were on the phone with your old high school flame Maria. It's all pretty strange if you ask me…

Jude: Very strange. Not to mention, it usually only takes Flynn this long to respond.

Flynn: You guys are fucking idiots.

My thoughts exactly, Flynn.

Jude: Remy, are you really just going to leave us hanging, man?

Ty: Talk about a real dick move.

There're still another twenty or so messages in the chat, all of them revolving around Jude and Ty trying to con me into telling them what's going on, but in the periphery of my left eye, I see Izzy's little body is just barely starting to stir from the kind of deep sleep only a baby can achieve.

She pouts her lips and squirms her tiny legs, and I know I'm going to have to move my ass if I want to get to her before she starts crying and wakes up Maria.

Gently, as I stand up from the sofa, I ease Maria off my shoulder and place a pillow under her head. But when that doesn't feel like enough, I snag a white blanket out of a basket-thingie that every woman I've ever known seems to have and place it over her still-sleeping body.

"Okay, Miss Izzy," I whisper toward the baby as I lift her out of her chair and into my arms. "What do you say we take this little powwow into your nursery so your mommy can sleep?"

Izzy's big blue eyes stare back at me, and since she's not crying or fussing, I take that as my cue that she's on board with the plan.

Into her nursery, I shut the door behind us and lay her on the changing table across from the crib that Maria says she hates sleeping in.

"How many hours has it been since I last fed you?" I grab a fresh diaper and start unbuttoning her sleeper. "Three? Four, maybe?"

She lets out a wail once her bare legs are exposed, and I almost want to laugh at how quick she is to give me an earful when she's not happy about something.

"You're the kind of girl who doesn't take any shit, huh?" I tell her while I make quick work of cleaning her up. "I can respect that. It's a good quality to have in this world."

Izzy cries some more, but I know the score. All she needs is a clean ass and the promise of a bottle, and she'll be good to go.

"You know, it feels like forever ago I was doing this exact same thing with my niece Lexi," I say and finish buttoning her sleeper back up. "She's much older now. Almost eleven, to be exact. But man oh man, she's something special.

Crazy smart. Hilarious. Lexi is one of my favorite people in the world. You'd love her." I lift Izzy into my arms and cuddle her close to my chest.

A few more cries leave her little lungs, but eventually, she settles down and appears content with just staring at me, her blue eyes looking almost too big for her face as she tries to understand the world around her.

"Don't worry, Busy Izzy, you're something special too. I know we've only known each other for a very short time, but trust me, you are."

I stare down at her and take in all the little details that make up this tiny human being. The way her nose has a little rounded curve at the end. The way her lips are so full and so adorably pink. And the way her little brow furrows in the center and the hint of a dimple appears in her cheek.

Just like Maria's.

My mind drifts to the almost-kiss in the kitchen.

Fuck me. How did that happen?

It was like one minute she was hugging me, and the next she was staring up at me with those pretty brown eyes of hers, and a rush of feelings I haven't had since I was a rowdy teenage boy consumed me. Between one breath and the next, I'd thought of a hundred different ways to kiss her, touch her, lick her, *fuck* her.

And if it weren't for Izzy belting out her need for a bottle, I don't know what would've happened.

"You have some seriously interesting timing, little lady," I tell her and sit down in the rocker beside her crib.

I honestly don't know what would've happened if we hadn't been interrupted.

It goes without saying that I still care about Maria, but I don't think you ever stop caring about the first person you fell in love with. And young Remy Winslow was obsessed with Maria Baros. Consumed by her. *In love with her.* At one point in my life, she was everything to me.

All of that mixed in with the now makes it hard to distinguish my current feelings.

"Izzy girl, sometimes in life, things don't turn out how you expect."

She just blinks her big eyes at me.

"It's not necessarily a good thing or a bad thing, though, just...the reality of life."

I reach out to caress my thumb over the soft skin of her cheek, and she reaches up with her tiny hand to wrap her fingers around mine.

"Damn, you're cute, you know that?" I grin at her, and she starts to suck on her bottom lip. "And probably hungry too, huh?"

I stand up from the rocker and hold Izzy secure in my arms as I toss her dirty diaper in the diaper pail. "Now, before we go out into the kitchen to grab your bottle, you have to make me a promise, okay? We need to stay as quiet as possible so your mom can keep sleeping. No offense, but you've been a bit of a handful lately."

Izzy wiggles her little legs.

"Do we have a deal?"

When she just stares up at me, I take that as her silent agreement and head out of the nursery and toward the kitchen to make Izzy a bottle.

And as I pass by the couch, I'm elated to see Maria is still sound asleep.

"Looks like we're about to have a sleepover tonight, Izzy," I whisper to her as I step into the kitchen. "Surely as long as I keep the bottles coming, you won't mind, right?"

When her tiny butt lets out a loud fart against my hand, I take that as her approval.

My phone buzzes in my pocket as I prep Izzy's bottle, and I take a quick glance at the screen to see more messages from my brothers. A *lot* more messages, in fact.

I decide it'll be best for them—and *especially* for me—to put them out of their nosy-as-hell misery. With my free hand, I type out a quick text.

Me: Listen, you crazy fuckers, I'm a little busy tonight, but I'll give you the scoop soon.

Just like with my sister and my mom, at one point, Maria was a big part of their lives too. They deserve to know the truth. Deserve to know the circumstances surrounding Maria's life. Deserve to know that two people who were a part of their youth are no longer with us.

Jude: Fucking finally!

Ty: How soon?

Me: I can free up some time tomorrow after I take Lex to the Mavs game.

More texts vibrate through, but when Izzy squirms in my arms, I ignore them, put my phone back in my pocket, and look down at her. "Keeping you happy and giving your momma rest is the priority tonight, sweetheart."

Everything and everyone else can wait.

SEVENTEEN

Sunday, October 6th

Maria

For the first time in I don't know how long, I wake up simply because my body decides it's time. Not because there's a tiny human screaming or a cramp in my still-recovering uterus or because I had a dream that babies suddenly can't breathe if their moms are asleep. My body's clock finally got to ring its own bell, and the feeling is somewhat disorienting.

I rub a hand down my face and sit up, only then realizing that I'm not in my bed. Instead, I'm on my couch, and the waistband of my jeans has officially fused itself to the center of my stomach.

"Ow," I mutter, rubbing softly at the harsh indentations in my skin.

Looking from side to side, sleep confusion still clinging to the edges of my consciousness, I search the room for something. There's something important, something I need to—*oh my God, Izzy! I have a baby named Izzy!*

I shoot up to standing like I'm a bullet being shot from a gun, her empty bouncy chair making my heart kick into overdrive.

Where is she? What in the hell time is it? How did I forget about her for even a second?

I run from one end of the living room to the other, thought and strategy both things of the past. The sun is so bright it blinds my sensitive eyes, tripping me out even more. *Holy shit, it's morning already?* On my next panicked jog from one end of the room to the other, I catch sight of the clock beneath the TV—9:03 a.m.

Oh my God. OH MY GOD.

It's then, in a desperate effort to prevent self-destruction, that my brain calculates the events of last night, and I remember that Remy was here.

Oh yeah. Is he still here? Does he have Izzy? Please, God, let him have Izzy.

"Remy?" I call out and sprint into the kitchen, for what, I don't know, only to backtrack and make a beeline toward her nursery.

"Remy!" I shout, my voice rising with panic.

Did something happen to them? How in the hell did I sleep through at least two of Izzy's feedings? Is she okay? Is she alive? Holy shit, I'm the worst mom in the whole wide world!

Instantly, tears prick my eyes, and my bottom lip quivers.

"*Remy!*" Emotion hovers along the edges of my voice as I move like a madwoman down the hallway, turning to crash through her door like the Kool-Aid man, when a hard body stops me and pushes me back and away from the door slightly.

"I'm right here," Remy consoles, his two strong hands working gently on my shoulders.

"Where's the baby?" I nearly shout. "Is she okay? Did something—"

"Hey, it's okay. She's okay," he reassures in a hushed voice. "I just fed her a bottle about two hours ago, and she's sound asleep in her crib."

Her *crib?* Somehow, he got her to sleep in her crib? Izzy *never* wants to sleep in her crib.

What kind of Twilight Zone have I woken up in?

"Just take a deep breath, Ria," he adds with the kind of gentleness in his voice that could melt concrete into a puddle. "Izzy is fine. I promise."

"Okay." I nod and inhale, but all I can manage is an unsteady breath. "Okay." I put a hand to my chest and try like hell to slow my racing heart. "I just panicked when I woke up and didn't know—"

His face is gentle with remorse. "I'm sorry your morning had to start with an adrenaline rush. Definitely not how I was hoping it would begin."

I nod. I know he didn't mean to cause this—hell, if anything, I should be thanking him. I just have to get my body to open the memo somehow.

Thankfully, under the coaxing of his firm hands, the tension in my shoulders eases, and the cloud of fear hovering around us starts to dissipate.

Okay, yeah. God. His hands feel good.

I let my head fall back and take a final deep breath, expelling all the rest of my worry at once.

"There's my girl," Remy remarks on a whisper, bringing a smile to my face and my neck back to upright.

And that's all it takes to kick my heart back into an uncharacteristic rhythm.

Remy is practically *naked*.

I'm talking bare chest, wet hair, water dripping down the firm muscles of his stomach and biceps naked. Only a single white towel around his waist stands between his penis and me and a permanent stutter.

"Y-you took a shower?"

A wry grin forms at the corner of his lips. "We might have had a little accident this morning."

I tilt my head in confusion, trying to force my body into taking the right cues—you know, the ones that come from him talking to me, rather than the ones coming from my imagination's rabid attempt to mock up a picture of what I'd be seeing if the towel weren't blocking my view.

"It was a blowout kind of situation," he explains, but despite my best efforts to stop perving, I'm still hardly listening.

Good God, the muscles. There are so many of them, and they make the perfect little obstacle course for several persistent drops of water. I don't know if my screams left him with no time to dry off or if the water is just as desperate to lick around the perfect V muscles at his waist as I am, but I'll be damned if I haven't been willing every single droplet that travels that path to be the tipping point to the loosely tied knot on Remy's towel.

Is he still as big as he was back then? If I could, I'd roll my eyes at myself. It's not like dicks get smaller—well, unless they're in cold water or something. *But what if it's bigger?*

No, no, it can't be.

I mean, Remy was eighteen years old the last time I was with him in *that* way, but surely, a penis is full-grown by then, right?

"I hope you don't mind, but my clothes are in your dryer," he continues, speaking words I can barely register around the dirty fucking places my mind is going.

It might be *highly* inappropriate considering the circumstances, but hell's bells, I can't stop thinking about what it was like to *be* with him. He was my first real lover, and he did *not* disappoint. If anything, he set the bar really high for all the men who came after him.

Maybe that's why you almost kissed him last night…

"Maria? Everything all right?" he asks, obviously tiring of his one-sided conversation. I blink out of my walk down Sexy Memory Lane.

"Yeah," I say, clearing the cobwebs from my throat. "O-of course. I'm fine. Everything is fine."

He smiles down at me, and I almost hate how there are so many gorgeous parts of him, I can't even figure out where to look.

In an instant, I mentally put my foot down on the crazy vortex my mind wants to suck me into. I am *not* going to go there. I *can't* go there. My life is a train wreck of epic proportions and thinking about kissing Remy or seeing him naked is the very last thing I need to be doing. I've had my fun, but now, well, it's over. Time to concentrate on the head that doesn't ejaculate.

"So…you stayed last night?"

He nods, and I swear, his grin almost looks as though he can hear what I'm thinking. For my sanity, I ignore it completely. "You looked so peaceful sleeping."

I snort a laugh. "Wild Saturday night, huh? I hope you didn't have plans."

"I didn't. But even if I had, this was more important."

My chest squeezes with memories of just how amazing of a guy Remy is and how it feels to be on the receiving end of it, but I try my damnedest not to pay attention to any of it.

"You should've woken me up."

"No." He shakes his head. "I did exactly what I needed to—let you get some well-deserved sleep."

"I feel bad," I say and step back to put some much-needed distance between us.

He furrows his brow. "Why would you feel bad?"

"Because it's not your job to take care of Izzy. You shouldn't be put in the position of rearranging your night just so you can help me."

"Ria," Remy says, stepping toward me and closing off the distance I gained less than a minute ago. "I stayed because I wanted to. Not for any reason other than that. Your guilt is unnecessary, okay? Don't think twice about any of it. I wanted to be here. I wanted to help you."

All I can do is nod.

But then I also add, "Thank you." Because hell, it's been weeks since I've gotten a full night of sleep. One hour here, two hours there, that's about all I've managed since Izzy was born.

And let me tell you, that starts to make you feel like a crazy person.

"Why don't you go grab yourself a cup of coffee, and I'll finish up in here?"

"Yeah, okay." *Anything to get me away from your deliciously naked body.*

Once he's safely behind the closed door of my bathroom, I can't stop myself from walking into Izzy's nursery to verify she's okay with my own eyes. Not that I don't trust Remy, but the maternal instinct is too strong to deny. I swear, I spent the first week of her life checking her every ten minutes to make sure I could see her chest rising and falling with breaths of air.

But I find her exactly where Remy said she was—sleeping inside her crib.

"Girlfriend, I'd really love to know why you refuse to do this for me, but for Remy, you're all in," I whisper down toward her, smiling at the way her eyelids flutter in her sleep. "I guess I can't really blame you. He just has a way about him, huh?"

She doesn't answer, but then again, she doesn't have to. I wouldn't be Mr. Miyagi-ing myself out of sexual thoughts every second and a half if Remington Winslow didn't have a *way* about him.

Her eyelids flutter some more, but her eyes remain closed and her breathing steady. I'd say she's going to be out for a while. Releasing the guilt, I pledge to savor the hour or so of calm before she wakes up so that I can be better and more present when she wakes up.

Back down the hallway, past the bathroom where my brain tries to remind me that a naked Remy resides, I head into the kitchen and make myself a fresh cup of coffee.

Man, what a strange turn of events the past twenty-four hours have been.

The past twenty-four hours? More like, the past year. I can hardly believe everything that's happened in such a short amount of time. Everything I've gained, everything I've changed—everything I've lost.

I shake off the impending thoughts of grief and confusion. The last thing I want to do is turn into a blubbering mess thinking about my sister. And truthfully, I know that's the very last thing she'd want for me, too.

"Hey, Maria." Remy's voice startles me out of my thoughts. I turn around to find him fully dressed and with his phone, wallet, and keys in his hand.

"Are you heading out?" I try to keep the question light, but I'm afraid the effort to do so makes me sound more like Screech from *Saved By the Bell* than easy-breezy. *Why on earth am I feeling disappointed? Remy has a life of his own to live, and he's been here all of yesterday and last night.*

"I promised Lexi I'd take her to the Mavericks game today."

"Oh, okay." I force a smile to my lips. "That sounds like fun. I hope you have a good time."

He steps into the kitchen and takes it upon himself to pull me into a hug. "Promise me, if you need me, you'll call me."

I lean back and look into his eyes. "I'm sure we'll be fine."

"Maria, I'm serious," he says, still hugging me with his arms wrapped around my waist. "I don't mind helping you and Izzy. It's not a job, okay? I want to be there for you."

When I don't say anything, he reaches up to tap one gentle index finger against my nose. "I'm not leaving until you promise."

"O-kay." I roll my eyes. "I promise."

"And what do you promise exactly?"

"Seriously, Rem?" I scoff, but he's persistent, refusing to let me go until I acquiesce. "Fine," I say through a sigh. "I promise I'll call you if I need you."

"Fantastic." He places one soft kiss to my cheek and releases me.

I'm generally not the type of girl who goes back on her word, but I don't know if that's a promise I can keep. Remy shouldn't have his life uprooted with emergency calls from me because my life is chaos.

No one deserves that. Especially not him.

And selfishly? I'm not so sure I'll be able to stop myself from getting used to having him around.

EIGHTEEN

Remy

Lexi and I show our VIP passes to the security guard at the secret back door entrance to the Mavericks' stadium, and he nods and gestures us through with a nonchalant wave of his hand.

My niece's petite hand latches on to mine as she all but drags me down the long hallway.

"In a rush, Lex?" I question on a chuckle, and she blazes me with a roll of her eyes over her shoulder.

"I want to see the team before they take the field."

"Huh?" I furrow my brow. "How are you going to do that? Aren't they getting ready for the game?"

"They're in the locker room, Uncle Remy, not the president's bunker. We can get in."

"Whoa, whoa, whoa. The locker room? We can't go into the locker room."

She rolls her eyes again. "Yes, we can."

Taking an almost eleven-year-old girl into an NFL locker room pregame? I don't think that's a great idea. I imagine they're both rowdy and lightly dressed. I don't need to take my impressionable niece on a swim through a swinging-dick river. *Christ, I'd never hear the end of that.*

"Lex, honey, they're probably getting ready. I'm not sure your parents would want—"

"I'm allowed. I do it all the time," she interrupts, dragging me through staccato steps to the doors in question.

I glance at the solid black doors, a white sign emblazoned with *Authorized Personnel Only* in the center and the sound of absolute mayhem on the other side. "Wes lets you come into the locker room—*this* locker room—before—"

"Yes," she cuts me off again, pushing through the doors like she owns the fucking joint.

Hurriedly, I reach out to stop her momentum with my hands on both of her shoulders, and then I slide one hand over her eyes so I can scan the room for the kinds of things a young girl shouldn't see.

There are a few bare chests, but pants appear to be on. *Thank fuck.*

"I can't see anything," Lexi states the obvious and shoves my hand away.

Teeny Martinez, one of the Mavericks' best offensive linemen, is the first to notice her presence.

"Lexi Lou!" he shouts as his big body barrels across the room to pick up my niece and put her on his shoulders. "Boys, we can all relax now! Our good luck charm is here!"

I guess Lex wasn't bullshitting me? She really comes in here before the games?

An authentic laugh spills from her lips, something Lex reserves for only the worthiest of times, and I watch on in amusement as she's carried around the room to give high fives to some of the Mavericks' star players. Quinn Bailey, Sean Phillips, Cam Mitchell, Leo Landry, and nearly a dozen others, they're all joining in on the fun, smiling and slapping Lexi's hand, despite the fact that they're scheduled to take the field in less than thirty minutes.

"How many TDs, Lex?" Sean, the Mavericks' leading wide receiver—who also flexes into the running back position—asks.

"Statistically, you've been averaging two touchdowns per game, but Philadelphia's defense is number two in the league, and they'll be double-covering you. Which makes the probability of you meeting your average below thirty percent."

If it wasn't already obvious, she's a bit of a statistical genius. Feelings don't matter so much when hard facts are on the line. I can't help but smile at the disappointed look on Sean's face.

Cam Mitchell, otherwise known as the best tight end in the league, bursts into laughter. "Uh-oh, Sean. Looks like I might have to pick up your slack today."

Sean flips Mitchell the middle finger behind his back and feigns a pout at Lexi. "C'mon, Lex. How you gonna do me like that? Double-covered or not, you know I got the skills, girl."

"I think what our girl is saying here, Phillips, is that you're going to have to get your cocky as—I mean, butt in gear today, bro," Teeny comments, still holding Lexi on his shoulders.

Of course, my niece just shrugs, stone-faced and not affected in the least. The girl lives and breathes numbers and the kind of mathematical concepts most grown-ass adults can't comprehend. If these fuckers weren't ready to hear the hard truth, they shouldn't have asked.

Quinn Bailey, the Mavs' QB, reaches up to take Lexi off Teeny's shoulders and squats down to converse with her face-to-face. "What do you think, Lex? Are my guys going to pull out a W today?"

"Philadelphia's defense is going to be tough." She taps her fingers to her chin. "They're averaging four sacks per game, and when they played Seattle, they shut down touchdowns and only allowed two field goals. They started out the season in second to last place, and they're coming off a three-game rally. Rallies have a statistical tendency to give an advantage."

Quinn just grins. "So…what you're telling me is that we need to come to play."

She nods, and Quinn reaches out to place both hands on her shoulders.

"Don't worry, Lex. We've come to play."

The smallest hint of a smile crests her lips as Bailey stands up to face the rest of the team.

"Ain't that right, boys?" he shouts at the top of his lungs. "We came to play!"

"Hell yeah! Fuck Philly!"

Just as my brother-in-law Wes walks in through a door on the opposite side from the one we entered, the team starts chanting "Fuck Philly" in perfect synchrony. He shakes his head on a laugh and walks over to Lex and me.

"You brought my daughter down here to listen to my idiot football players drop f-bombs?"

"This is an important part of the pregame." Lex rolls her eyes for what feels like the one-hundredth time today, and I just shrug on a laugh as I reach out to shake Wes's hand.

"She insisted, man. Pretty much refused to go to our seats without stopping in the locker room first. Not to mention, she said you let her do this."

"Oh, she said that, did she?" Wes grins at Lexi. "I guess I should just be thankful you chose to come down after they're mostly dressed."

"You and me both."

I glance down at Lexi, figuring she has some kind of response to that ready to fly from her lips, but I notice she's no longer paying attention to us. Instead, her eyes are busy looking around the locker room, taking in each player as they finish getting ready for the game. I know whatever she's doing, she's doing it with a point, so I don't bother interrupting.

"Where's Winnie?" I ask Wes instead, and his smile is both exasperated and amused.

"Probably in the PT room, making sure everyone's getting taped up exactly how she prefers."

I smirk. "Isn't that a physical therapist's job?"

"You'd think since we hired one of the best physical therapists in the damn country, she'd be able to relax a little, but you know Win. She likes to keep the reins tight."

"I trust you know this from experience?" I tease. "My sister keeping you on a short leash?"

Wes just chuckles, too far gone in love with my sister to even think twice about my jab. "She can keep me on as short of a leash as she wants."

Back in the day, when Winnie first started dating Wes Lancaster, I was suspicious. Hell, I wasn't easy on him at all. But she's my baby sister, and I'd seen the bullshit she'd been put through in the past. Her relationship with Lexi's biological dad was real fucking rocky up until a few years ago.

"You know, back in the day, Jude and Ty would've given you some serious shit about that comment, but now that they're in the same sappy fucking state of love as you, I think I'm the only one left to comment."

Wes waggles his brows. "And don't you think it's time to fix that, Rem?"

"He will," Lexi chimes in, and I look down at her in surprise.

"Excuse me?"

"Your personality shows traits of being a thoughtful caretaker, especially to the females in your life. Psychologically speaking, in order for you to feel fully content, you need to find a partner who not only makes you happy but whom you feel like you can take care of. It's a prosocial behavior that is considered a positive personality aspect by psychologists most of the time. However, it can also be considered negative if it leads to burnout, stress, and self-sabotaging coping mechanisms."

"I'm sorry...what?" I question, just as Wes snorts.

"Lex, have you been reading your mom's old med school textbooks?"

"Yes," she answers matter-of-factly. "Lately, I've been finding human behavior and psychology incredibly stimulating." She looks up at me and pats my arm. "Uncle Rem, most psychologists would say your biggest obstacle in finding a potential partner is that you need to find someone whom you want to take care of out of love but not obligation, and someone whom you will let take care of you, too. There needs to be a balance in relationships."

Wes looks at me with raised eyebrows and the kind of smile that's a little too fucking amused.

"Well, now that you've psychoanalyzed me, how about we start heading back into the stadium so we're in our seats before kickoff?"

Wes chuckles at that. "Things getting a little too real for you, Mr. Caretaker?"

I purse my lips and discreetly flip him the middle finger.

And Lex, well, she's already walking around the locker room high-fiving the players and giving her final game-day advice.

"We'll meet you down here after the game?" I ask Wes.

He laughs more. "Nice avoidance."

"I'm not avoiding," I retort. "But I'm also not going to take relationship advice from a kid."

"A really smart kid, mind you," he adds with a smug grin. "Hell, Thatch takes advice from Lex all the time."

"Because Thatch is a fucking lunatic."

"I won't deny that." Wes chuckles, and I can tell by the way he's looking around the room for someone in particular, his mind is already forming a plan.

"Hey, Gossip Girl, your giddiness to replay this conversation to Winnie is almost showing."

He smirks. "You and I both know Win would have my ass if I didn't tell her all about this. Especially the look on your face while Lex was psychoanalyzing you."

"I didn't have a look."

"Trust me, you had a look. And it should be noted Winnie had *a lot* to say last night about you helping out Maria and—"

"You think maybe you should get back to focusing on, I don't know, the game today, or do you want to bring the child psychologist over here and have her evaluate me some more?"

"She got you good, Rem." Wes laughs. "She got you really good."

He offers one final pat to my shoulder before heading back toward his office.

Smug bastard.

I love my niece to pieces, but the last thing I'm going to do is start reevaluating my life based on what she's read in a fucking psychology textbook from Winnie's medical school days.

She might be Albert Einstein-level smart, but she's still just a kid.

A kid who doesn't understand half of the shit I've gone through in the past.

Sure, I've made amends with Charlotte since then. Hell, I even understand why that marriage, that relationship, didn't turn out. But that doesn't remedy the fact that taking another leap like that, experiencing that kind of heartbreak, well, it's not something I want to volunteer as tribute for. My life is fine the way it is without that kind of complication.

Yet, you seem real keen on staying in contact with Maria…and her life is far from uncomplicated.

Obviously, my niece's commentary has fucked with my head a little bit.

Maria is someone I've known for a very long time. I care about her. Will always care about her. It only makes sense that I would want to be there for her. The shit she's had to go through is insane. Honestly, it makes my whole being-left-at-the-altar past trauma pale in comparison.

She deserves to have a support system. Someone by her side to help in whatever way they can. And I'm more than happy to be that person for her.

But does that include almost kissing her? Or fantasizing about what it would be like to slide inside her?

I mentally shake those thoughts out of my head and focus on finding Lexi.

It doesn't take long for me to spot her over by Quinn Bailey, her hands-down favorite player on the Mavericks.

"Ready to go, Lex?" I call toward her, and she meets my eyes briefly before turning back to give Quinn one last high five.

"See ya later, Lex!" Teeny tells her as she walks by him, giving her a high five as well.

"Glad our good luck charm is here today," Leo Landry adds, offering a little wink.

Once Lex reaches me, her lips are etched into a permanent smile, and her cheeks are so pink and rosy it's like she's blushing.

But my niece doesn't blush.

"Are you feeling okay, Lex?"

"Yes. I'm not experiencing any current symptoms that would raise suspicion for illness." She nods and I take her hand, but as we walk out of the locker room and down the main hallway that leads toward the inside of the stadium, I about trip over my own feet when she says, "Almost all of the Mavericks have firm butts. Like, really firm butts. Is that what women like on men?"

"Uh…" I blink one thousand times. "I'm sorry, *what?*"

She looks up at me. "I said almost all of the Mavericks—"

"Lex, I heard what you said," I cut her off before I have to hear the rest again. "I'm just trying to figure out why you're saying it."

"It's an observation, Uncle Rem. I've never noticed it before, but I kind of like seeing it. Is that normal?"

What the fuck is happening right now?

"Probably? I don't know…uh…" I pause, and instead of facing this head on like a man, I quickly pull our tickets out of my pocket and decide it's a conversation she should have with her mother. "What seats are we in again, Lex?"

She lets out an exasperated breath. "Uncle Rem, we're in the same seats we always sit in. First row on the fifty-yard line."

"You know, kid, you're lucky you've got friends in high places," I comment, trying like hell to keep this conversation heading as far away from football-player butts as I can. "When I was your age, never in my life did I get to sit on the fifty-yard line at an NFL game. Hell, even as an adult, I wasn't scoring these seats until your mom married Wes."

She just shrugs off my comment and points toward a concession stand. "Hungry, Uncle Rem?"

"Is this your way of telling me I need to buy my date a hot dog?"

"I am hungry." She smiles. "I would like a hot dog plus a soda plus a bag of M&M's."

"Man, you're an expensive date," I tease.

"$21.15."

"What?"

"That's how much it'll be with tax," she says, having already calculated the cost in her head. "And you should go on real dates, Uncle Rem. Not just pretend dates with me. That's the only way you'll find a potential partner."

Oh, here we go again…

"How about we cool it on the Uncle Remy needs to find a potential partner thing for the rest of the game, and I'll buy you two bags of M&M's?"

"Then, it'll be $26.72."

"Fine by me."

Candy for the win. *And your mental sanity.*

In the second quarter, Quinn Bailey throws a beautiful thirty-yard pass to Sean Phillips, who runs it another ten yards into the end zone, and the Mavericks officially take the lead over Philly.

Both Lex and I jump from our seats, cheering and high-fiving each other as we watch Phillips showboat in the end zone with one of his signature dances.

"Looks like Phillips might hit his game average today, Lex," I comment, and she grins like a little devil.

"He will."

"Wait…what?" I question and tilt my head to the side. "Were you playing him back in the locker room?"

"What do you mean by 'playing him'?"

"Were you messing with him when you were telling him statistically the odds were against him? Were you lying to him a little?"

"Oh," she responds, and her mouth forms a little O. "Yeah, I think I was." She shrugs as we sit back down in our seats. "Sean Phillips statistically plays his best game when he thinks he has something to prove."

"I see," I answer through a soft laugh. No wonder Wes loves when she talks to his players. She's fucking brutal.

"Uncle Rem, I need to run to the bathroom."

"Oh, okay," I say and start to stand up, but she lifts one hand toward me.

"I can go by myself."

Well, shit. That's a new one.

"Are you sure? Because I can go—"

"I'll be back in about…" She pauses and glances at her watch. "Five minutes, if the bathroom line is the usual forty-five-second wait. And I have my phone if you get worried. Though, the probability that something could happen to me on the way to the bathroom in the middle of a stadium with security at every entrance and exit is around 0.0001 percent."

I quirk an amused eyebrow. "I take that as you telling me not to worry?"

"Yes."

"Well, okay then," I tell her and stand up from my seat to let her pass by me. "I'll give you six minutes, but after that, I'm most definitely calling you."

She snorts and rolls her eyes heavenward. "Fine."

As I watch her walk up the stadium steps, I can't stop myself from thinking about how it wasn't that long ago that Lexi wouldn't have gone to the bathroom by herself. Hell, she wouldn't have done a lot of things by herself.

But now, she's a girl who wants independence and notices football players' butts.

Sheesh. Where did the time go?

I turn my attention back to the game, and when the Mavericks force Philly to a fourth-down punt, I find myself pulling my phone out of my pocket and checking for any missed messages or calls.

But the odd sensation of disappointment fills my gut when all I find is one text from the illustrious Cleo and a boatload of messages within the group chat with my brothers.

I prioritize by level of sanity, checking the least crazy first.

C: Memories are there for a reason.

Looks like she's back at it again…

I almost want to laugh. I know *exactly* what she's trying to do, but I'm not taking the bait today. Quickly, I shift into my brothers' chat.

Ty: Fifty bucks says Bailey hits Mitchell for a TD.

Ty: PS: Remy, when and where are we meeting tonight?

Jude: Yeah, Rem. What's the plan? And you're wrong, Ty. He's going to Phillips.

Ty: So…you're taking that bet?

Jude: Of course I fucking am.

Three minutes later, Jude *was* gloating like a prick when Phillips scored that touchdown.

Jude: HAHAHAHAHAHA TOUCHDOWN! PHILLIPS IN THE END ZONE! You owe me fifty bucks, sucka!

Jude: Oh, and hey, Remy, if I don't hear from you by the time this game is over, I'm coming to your place.

Ty: I second this plan.

Flynn: I am not a part of this plan.

Finally caught up on all the message, and while I appreciate Flynn's solidarity, I'm actually good with their plan. It'll be better for me in the long run if I just get it over with rather than suffer through thousands of text messages like these.

Me: Actually, my place works. Meet me there around 6.

Jude: Perfect.

Ty: Count me in.

Flynn: I am now a part of this plan.

It goes without saying, my brothers are ridiculous.

And they're the opposite of who you were hoping to hear from…

I can't deny that ever since I left Maria's apartment this morning, I've been silently hoping things are going better than they were yesterday. Several times, I've nearly texted her, which is probably why I can't stop myself from doing exactly that right now.

Me: How are you? How's Izzy?

I'm surprised—and thankful—when my phone vibrates with a response a minute later.

Maria: She's good after having a whole night sleeping in her crib because, evidently, the baby whisperer stayed at my place last night.

"Who is the baby whisperer?" Lex asks, and I realize she's standing patiently beside me, waiting for me to let her get to her seat. And, evidently, reading my messages.

I quickly move my legs and she sits down, but when I don't answer, she asks again. "Uncle Rem, who is the baby whisperer?"

"Apparently, it's me," I tell her, but I also add, "You know it's rude to read other people's text messages, right?"

"I do, but you made it hard not to look. I could see your whole screen while I was waiting for you to let me through to my seat." She just shrugs. "You stayed at Maria's last night?"

"Uh, yeah, I did." I go with the simplest response I can manage, but when she tilts her head to the side, I know there're more questions coming my way.

"And she has a baby that you took care of last night?"

"Yes." I nod. "Her name is Izzy, and she's a tiny baby. Just a little over six weeks old."

My phone chimes with another text, and I look at the screen to find a picture of Izzy resting on Maria's chest, her face lax with sleep. And the words *See? All good here.* follow.

"Is that Izzy?" Lex asks, still keen on being nosy.

"Yep."

"She's really cute."

"She is," I respond with a soft smile. "You know, I used to take care of you a lot when you were that small. You were really cute too."

Lex grins, but then her attention is back on my phone. She points toward the picture. "Is that her mom? Maria?"

"Yes."

"She's really pretty," she says and looks up to search my eyes. "Her face is almost completely symmetrical. Don't you think so, Uncle Rem?"

This kid. I swear.

"Yes," I answer honestly. "Maria is a very beautiful woman, some might even say symmetrically so."

"You should date her."

I snort. "It's not that simple, Lex."

"Why not?"

"Because it's just not. Relationships are more complicated than that."

"Doesn't seem that complicated to me. You think she's beautiful. You like her baby. You should date her."

"I'll keep that in mind," I say because it's the only fucking way I'll get out of this crazy loop of conversation.

Thankfully, my tactic works, and Lexi goes back to watching the game. Her eyes are fixated on the field as the Mavericks complete a first down.

While the nosy little eavesdropper's eyes are busy, I snap a quick picture of her and send it to Maria.

Me: This is where the baby whisperer got all of his baby experience. Though, now, she's a ten-year-old girl who is apparently noticing that football players have tight butts. Not even kidding. Those words were said to me today, and I think I died a little inside.

Maria: Oh nooooooooo.

Me: Yeah. Talk about a kick in the gut for her Uncle Rem. My sweet, innocent little niece is starting to act like a teenager more and more every day.

Maria: She's gorgeous. It's almost crazy how much she looks like Winnie.

Me: Definitely Win's mini-me.

Maria: Now you should go back to enjoying the game. I promise all is well over here.

Me: You trying to get rid of me?

Maria: LOL. Just go enjoy the game with Lexi.

Me: Before I go, I want to remind you that you promised to call me if you need help. I'm expecting you to keep that promise…

Maria: I'm rolling my eyes at you right now.

Everyone is rolling their eyes at me today. I probably shouldn't feel so damn amused by it.

Me: Because you're stubborn.

Maria: And you're relentless.

Me: Bye, Maria. ;)

Maria: GOODBYE, REMY.

A soft laugh leaves my lips as I shove my phone back into my pocket.

If I know Maria at all, I know that she'll do just about anything to avoid asking for help.

Which is why I'm going to keep checking in on her until she gives in, instead of waiting for her to ask.

NINETEEN

Tuesday, October 8th

Maria

Sweat dots my brow and my arm aches as I finish blow-drying the last few pieces of my dark hair.

I love my hair, I really do—I've been blessed with the kind of thick locks most women would kill for. But let me tell you, it's no easy feat getting this hair of mine to dry in a practical amount of time, and it's even harder now that I'm not the only person I have to get ready.

I steal a glance at Izzy in the mirror, still calm and quiet in her bouncy chair—thank God—and then check the clock on the far side of my vanity. With only an hour left until my showing across town, I'm going to have to move double time.

More sweat dots my brow, and I stop mid-brush to fan my face.

Holy hot tamales. I shouldn't be sweating like this fresh out of the shower, but that's what forty-five minutes of blow-drying will do to a girl.

Confident my hair is as good as it's going to get, I add a little extra deodorant and spin on my bare feet to look directly down at my girl. Her cheeks pull up in what I'm convinced is a barely there smile, and my heart clutches. *I don't know that I'll ever get over being the center of someone's universe.*

I don't have time to get sentimental and teary-eyed right now, though, so instead, I get sassy.

"Girlfriend, we have to get our asses moving if we're going to make it to the showing in time," I tell her with a hand to my bare hip. "I have to get dressed. I have to get you dressed. And then, I'm sure, you're going to want to eat."

She sucks on her bottom lip.

"Oh, I know, honey. Food is always your top priority," I say and reach down to pick her up. "It's mine too. But today, we have to do clothes first."

Into the walk-in closet of my bedroom with Izzy on my shoulder, I grab a bra, underwear, my favorite black Chanel pencil skirt and matching jacket, and a black silk top to match.

Normally, I'd go with a white or soft pink blouse, but spit-up is a real and constant hazard in my life these days, and black hides mess better. I walk back out to my room, and the clock on my nightstand glares at me with hard facts.

I only have forty more minutes to get us dressed and get Izzy fed if I'm going to have a full fifteen minutes to get across town—which, honestly, is pushing it. Sure, to most people, even me a year ago, that sounds like plenty of time. But once you add a baby into the mix, time seems as if it evaporates.

Come on, Maria, pick up the pace.

I gently lay Izzy in the center of my bed while I get dressed and slip on some heels, and then I pull her back into my arms and head into her nursery.

"What are you going to wear today?" I muse as I scan her closet for options.

A pink onesie with kittens? No.

A yellow dress with bumble bees? Nope.

Balloon onesie with "I'm a floating baby" in big letters on the front? *Hell no.*

"All you have is frilly lace dresses and sleepers with cute animals on them," I say out loud as I run my fingers along the clothes hanging in her closet. "This isn't the vibe we need right now, Iz. All these things scream 'I'm a baby,' and Eleanor hates babies."

I need a power suit. A pencil skirt. A sporty blazer, at the least.

It sounds crazy, I know, to want to dress Izzy up like a business professional, but since leaving her alone in the apartment isn't exactly an option at this ripe age, I'm kind of in a bind.

The last time I showed Eleanor Waverly an apartment, when she spotted the fourth bedroom that was being used as a playroom, she said, "Ew. I hate kids."

Nerves clutch my belly. *Man, I hope she doesn't get pissed that I'm bringing Izzy with me to this showing and, like, curse her out or something. People don't cuss at babies, right?*

I'd push this off onto one of my new agents, Daniel or Brenda, but they are *not* ready for someone like Eleanor. She's tough-as-nails, rude-as-hell, and the revenue she'll generate for the company is too much to risk.

When I glance down at Izzy's denim-blue eyes, she doesn't look nearly as concerned as she should be.

"Yes, I'm fully aware you *are* a baby, but I need you to not look like a baby," I tell her. "You're a very small adult, okay? *Very* small. Start getting into character now."

Izzy sucks on her bottom lip, her mind more consumed with food than anything else.

"All right, all right. You're a foodie. We can work with that," I state crazily, carrying Izzy back to my bedroom and into my walk-in closet.

Scanning my clothes again, I spot my smallest business jacket and wonder if I could make it work. I tilt my head to the side. There'll be a lot of origami folding and safety pinning involved, but if I tuck it at the seam and roll the three-quarter sleeves, I might be able to use it as a business-y swaddle.

I look at Izzy and then back at the jacket and then at Izzy again.

"Am I cracked? This is freaking nuts."

I look at the black suit jacket again and imagine Eleanor smiling down at Izzy in her current giraffe onesie. The image pops immediately, blown up by impossibility. *Eleanor's going to have my soul for lunch.* I look back at the jacket one more time, groaning.

"I mean, we'd match, which wouldn't be a bad thing, right? We'll look cohesive. Like a kick-ass team. Co-agents." I scoff. "Not that you really earned the title, but whatever."

I shake my head. *Jesus, I'm losing it!*

But the commission alone on this deal could be almost a million dollars.

Izzy sucks on her bottom lip again, and I press a soft kiss to her forehead and inhale her sweet baby scent. "I'm sorry, baby. I'm sorry, but I have to do this to you. It's for college, okay? I'm thinking about you here." I snag the jacket off the hanger and head back into her nursery.

Determined, I grab a black sleeper with fancy gold buttons on the front and frilly lace on the butt. I lay her on the changing table and start the process of changing her diaper and getting her dressed.

She fusses when cold air hits her bare skin, but a quick pacifier to the mouth proves to be just the trick in keeping her calm. Once she has a clean diaper and her sleeper is in place, I doctor the jacket as best I can and begin to put it on her.

"So, yes, I know this is big on you, but trust me, that's a good thing. When you get to be my age, everything starts to get tight and uncomfortable."

Izzy fusses, and I nod as I adjust her pacifier in her mouth.

"Don't let it bother you, honey. Eleanor not liking kids says everything about her and nothing about you. I, personally, think you're the most fantastic thing in the whole wide world."

I slide both of Izzy's arms into the sleeves and roll them up as much as I possibly can.

"But for today, I need you to think Hollywood. You're just a very tiny, very privileged adult…who prefers to be pushed around in a stroller."

Izzy stretches out her little legs, her feet pushing the material of the jacket away from her body.

"Just think of yourself as a rich Manhattan socialite who has been fed from a golden spoon your whole life." I pick her up from the changing table. The jacket hangs way past her little body, but the rolled-up sleeves at least give her some room to hold her little hands together like she always loves to do.

She sucks on her paci, and I stare down at her. "Today, you're a diva. But not, like, a fussy, crying diva. A diva who shows her annoyance through silence. Understand?"

Izzy pushes the paci out of her mouth with her tongue and immediately starts crying.

"I'll take that as a no, and hey, I understand your frustration, but this is not the vibe we need, girlfriend."

Her cries get harder, and all of a sudden, I kind of want to cry too.

This is *insane*. Like, I'm truly approaching the criteria for being committed.

I mean, how in the hell am I going to get through an entire showing with Eleanor Waverly, a true Manhattan socialite who could very well be crowned the biggest bitch on Fifth Avenue, while pretending my very real, live-action baby isn't a baby?

God help me.

Izzy's cries continue, and I head into the kitchen and make quick work of a bottle. Once I pop it into her mouth, she lets out a few quivering breaths and starts sucking.

"You have about ten minutes to finish this thing off and then we should probably change you again and then we need to go. *Capisce?*"

Izzy sucks harder on the nipple, and I take that as her silent agreement.

I hear my phone chime from somewhere in my bedroom, and while I juggle Izzy in my arms and her bottle in her mouth, I hurry down the hallway and start the process of trying to find the damn thing.

Thankfully, I spot it on the bathroom counter and snag it off with a quick hand while my chin keeps Izzy's bottle stable to her greedy lips.

I almost roll my eyes when I see the sender, but a big, obnoxious smile gets in the way.

He just can't help himself.

Remy: How are things going today?

How are things going today? Ha. That's the question of the hour.

I consider lying, but as my anxiety sucks at the organs inside me, I think better of it. *The truth will set you free.*

Me: It could be better.

Remy: Uh-oh…what's going on?

I sigh and snap a quick picture of Izzy and send it to him.

Me: Client hates babies. Fingers crossed she just thinks Izzy's a really tiny adult.

His reply back is instant.

Remy: Holy hell, Ria. LOL.

Me: I KNOW. It's so ridiculous it's comical, but I'm trying to juggle all the things today. And, well, juggling all the things when you have a baby to take care of ends with you having to go to a showing with said baby, even though the client loathes kids.

Remy: Still staying strong on your "No Nanny" rule, huh?

There is no way I could ever get a nanny. I just…can't do that to my sister. It was one of two things that were important to her when it came to raising her daughter.

The other one was breastfeeding her, and that only panned out in failure. I can't disappoint her again.

Me: Staying strong? The jury is still out on the official verdict, but I'm definitely trying. Does that count?

Remy: You're doing awesome, Maria. Don't forget that. And…don't be jealous, but I happen to be heading to an appointment with an investment client who LOVES babies…

I am most definitely jealous.

Me: Ugh. Can we switch clients?

Remy: How about we just switch Izzy? I can come over and pick her up and take her with me.

Dammit. I should've known he was gearing me up for something.

Me: Remy, don't be ridiculous. You don't have to do that.

Remy: I know I don't. But I WANT to do it.

I look at Izzy and back at the screen of my phone. *Can I really let him do this? Take Izzy with him to a meeting?*

No. I can't. That's asking for way too much.

Remy: Don't overthink it.

Me: I'm not. It's just too much, you know? You shouldn't have to bail me out all the time.

Remy: I'm not bailing you out. I'd say you're doing pretty damn well managing right now. Plus, this is really for me. I could use a distraction with this client, and Izzy is the cutest distraction I can think of. I'm coming over to get her.

Me: REMY. No. We'll be fine.

Remy: It's happening. I'll be there in about 10 minutes.

I sigh and even try to call him, but all I get back is his voice mail and another text.

Remy: 8 minutes.

I look at Izzy, who has just finished up her bottle, and blow out a breath.

"Well, honey, forget everything I told you about real estate and start thinking about things like the Dow and the S&P 500 and any stock-focused things your little mind can handle. Looks like you'll be specializing in investments today because Remy just can't help himself."

The thoughtful bastard.

TWENTY

Remy

As I step onto the elevator and hit the button for the twentieth floor, my phone pings in the back pocket of my jeans. I check the screen to find a rambling text message from the woman I just saw about thirty minutes ago.

Maria: Are you doing okay? Is Izzy behaving? God, I hope she sleeps through your meeting. I mean, even people who love babies don't necessarily want to deal with a screaming baby in the middle of talking about their investments.

I start to text her back, but when Izzy fusses a little from inside the baby carrier against my chest, I stop and glance down to find her little face scrunched up into a grimace as she attempts to suck on the material of the ridiculous suit jacket Maria dressed her in today.

A baby. In a suit. Add that to things I never thought I'd see.

With one hand gently stabilizing the back of the carrier, I use my free hand to reach into the front pocket of the backpack diaper bag that Maria packed up for me and locate Izzy's pacifier. Once I pop it into her mouth, she sucks on it like a real-life Maggie Simpson and begins to settle down.

I don't hesitate to snap a quick picture of the victorious moment and send it to Maria.

Me: After a hearty debate on whether you should invest on a monthly basis no matter what the market is doing or wait to buy the dip, Izzy has decided she needs to ponder her investment strategy before revealing her final answer.

Maria: I take it this is your way of telling me all is well in the land of baby watching?

Me: You are correct.

The elevator dings our arrival and I step off the cart, but I pause halfway down the hall toward Thatcher Kelly's office when another message from Maria chimes in.

Maria: Have I already told you that I'm forever thankful you're doing this? Because I am.

Me: About one hundred times before I left your apartment. And like I've said one hundred times myself, no thanks needed.

Maria: Don't be crazy. I owe you. Big-time. You saved my ass today.

Me: You can make it up to me in compliments about how amazing and studly I am and a promise of dinner tonight.

Maria: You got a deal on the dinner.

Me: And the compliments?

Maria: REMY WINSLOW IS AMAZING AND STUDLY. OH MY GOSH, HE'S, LIKE, GOD'S GIFT TO ALL WOMEN.

I grin and type out a quick response.

Me: Hmmm… Why do I sense sarcasm?

Maria: What? No way. I totally meant every word.

Me: Go sell an apartment. I'll take a rain check on the compliments.

Maria: *rolls eyes*

Me: *smiles like the studly, awesome man that I am*

Phone back into my pocket, I smile down at a now-sleeping Izzy and finish the walk toward the office that will hold today's meeting with Thatcher Kelly. About a year into knowing each other, he conned me into collaborating on some of his investments because that's how shit goes with Thatch. He is something of a financial genius in his own right, so he doesn't need me, but he's the type of guy who can convince you to do just about anything without you even realizing it's happening.

And his wife Cassie, one of my sister Winnie's best friends, is the same damn way.

I offer a friendly smile to Thatch's assistant, and her eyes go wide for a beat when she spots Izzy, but she silently gestures for me to go inside while she finishes up a phone call.

I find Thatch sitting behind his massive desk, his legs kicked up on the wooden surface and his arms stretched out behind his head.

"What the fluff, Kline?" he retorts with a furrow of his brow. "I thought you said—" He pauses midsentence when he spots my arrival, and then his gaze moves downward to my chest, where Izzy sleeps in her carrier. "Uh…I gotta jet, Special K."

"You're such a di—" Kline Brooks's voice starts to chime from the speaker, but it's cut off with a click before he can finish.

"Uh…I'm not sure if you know this, but…" Thatch drops his voice to a whisper. "You have a baby strapped to your chest."

"I'm aware."

"Okay…" He squints and stands up from his desk. "And how exactly did you get this baby?" he asks, but then he holds up his hand toward my face. "Wait. Don't answer that. First, let me add that if you stole this baby, keep that shit to yourself."

I laugh. Outright. "I didn't steal this baby."

"If you bought that baby off some kind of black market, *again*, keep it to yourself. I'm fluffing good at keeping secrets, but not when the FBI is involved."

I start to open my mouth to set his crazy ass straight, but he's already diving headfirst into one of his insane rambles as he steps closer to me and Izzy, his eyes taking in her suit jacket.

"So…she's a little lady. But, like, a very professional little lady," he comments. "Shit, this is the most professional baby I've ever seen in my life. Is she famous? Did you steal a famous person's baby? Wait… Don't even tell me this baby is a mobster."

"Yeah, Thatch," I retort with a roll of my eyes. "She's a mobster baby who's here to collect."

He looks at me. Then back at Izzy. "I ain't sleeping with no fishes tonight, honey. I can tell you that."

Izzy just keeps sleeping.

"And whatever dark world Remy has found himself in," he continues, "I can tell you, I can't join in. My wife is far scarier than a mobster. She'd literally castrate me if I became someone's drug mule or some shit."

I stare at him. "Are you done?"

"I think so." He smirks. "Wait…unless that baby is connected to my wife and she's sent you here to try to slyly convince me that another kid is a good idea. Then I'm going to have to ask you and your professional baby to leave."

"Her name is Izzy, and I'm doing her mom a favor."

He eyes me suspiciously. "So, she's not in the mob?"

"No."

"And you didn't steal her?"

"Also no."

He scoffs. "Well, fluff, this story is far more boring than I was hoping."

"You're insane."

Thatch just grins. "Would you and your baby like to take a seat?"

"Only if that means we're actually going to converse about investments."

"You wound me, Rem." He feigns a pout. "You act like I'm not the most entertaining friend you have. Which, you and I both know, I am."

Despite my better judgment, I sit down in one of the chairs across from his desk, but I'm surprised when, instead of walking back around to his big leather throne, he sits down beside me.

And then he proceeds to carefully pull Izzy out of the carrier and cuddle her tiny body in his big arms. One sniff to the top of her head and he grins.

"Ah yes, honey. You have that addictive baby smell." He sniffs her head again like some kind of fucking addict.

"You do realize you're being really weird right now, right?"

"Hell if I care." He shrugs. "You can't bring the cutest boss baby in the whole wide world into my office and not expect me to hold her. Do I know her mom?"

"No." I shake my head. "She's an old friend from high school, actually."

"Is she married?"

"The baby? No."

He snorts. "Her mom."

"No, Maria is not married."

"Oh, so…it's *Maria?*"

"Yes." I roll my eyes. "Her mother's name is Maria."

He grins at me like a fucking lunatic. "And this Maria isn't married… Is she engaged?"

"No."

"Is the father involved?" he questions, and I shake my head.

"No, but it's a really long story that I'm not going to get into with you because it's none of your business."

"So…you're taking care of Maria's baby. A woman who is an old friend but is also single…*and* you're protective over her business? I take it back—this is starting to get *very* interesting." He waggles his brows. "Give me the scoop, Rem. I'm all ears."

"There's no scoop."

"Oh, there's scoop. I can tell. We're already well on our way to my two favorite tropes of all time—friends-to-lovers and second chances, baby."

"You have to stop reading romance novels, bro."

You might think I'm kidding, but I'm not. Thatch is a lover of romance novels. Hell, I've heard rumors about a book club that my brother-in-law Wes was even roped into, but I've still yet to get the real truth out of him.

Thatch laughs like I've just said the most ridiculous thing in the world. "Get real, son. Besides my wife's t-i-t-s and p-u-s-s-y, there's nothing better in this world than a good romance novel."

In order to achieve the entire reason Thatch had me come to his office today, I know I'm going to have to get this crazy train back on the rails. "So…are you planning on holding the baby the entire time we're sharing information, or should I put her back in the carrier?"

"Fluff that," he huffs out on a snort. "I'm not giving up this little cutie until I have to."

"You say Cassie is the one who wants another baby and you don't," I retort. "I call bullshit, bro."

"Yeah, well, I'm calling bullshit on you too, bro."

I quirk a brow. "Excuse me?"

"You don't think I noticed the careful avoidance. The pointed distraction you just provided. C'mon, Rem. I know what's up."

I roll my eyes. But also, I ignore the metaphorical carrot he's dangling in front of my face. One comment about what he just said, and I might as well settle in for a three-hour tour.

So, I do the only thing that's going to prevent me from having to tell Maria I can't bring Izzy home tonight because we have to sleep in this lunatic's office because he won't shut up. I pull my phone out of my pocket and hold it up toward Thatch and Izzy.

"Mind if I take a quick picture?" I ask. "Winnie would get a kick out of this."

What I *really* mean is...*Cassie* would get a kick out of this because there is no way my sister wouldn't share this with Thatch's wife.

His eyes flare. "You motherfluffer."

"What?" I feign confusion. "My sister would love to see you holding this baby, looking like a man who wants another baby."

Checkmate, bro.

"Put the phone away," he says and walks around to his desk, still holding Izzy in his arms. "And give me the rundown on what you're thinking next quarter. If I like what you have to say, I'll share some of my secrets too."

I grin. *Yeah. That's exactly what I thought.*

TWENTY-ONE

Maria

I stand inside the massive living room of a six-thousand-square-foot penthouse located smack-dab in the middle of Manhattan while my client bitches at someone on the phone.

Just another day at the office.

"Anna, I already told you I want an exclusive with Page Six. Why are you coming to me with this *Cosmo* stuff? It's like you think I'm pathetic or something. Fix it. *Now.*" Eleanor Waverly scoffs and hangs up her phone, flipping her long blond hair over her shoulder.

This is the fourth phone call she's taken since I started this showing. The first three were about some kind of emergency menu change for a charity function next month. Apparently, salmon is an *atrocity* she wouldn't wish upon her worst enemies.

Back to her penthouse scrutiny, she narrows her eyes as she takes in the expensive floors that sit below her red-bottomed heels. A sigh escapes her lungs as she adjusts the white Hermes Birkin bag hanging prominently on her arm. "Hardwood is so overdone these days."

With a point of her nose toward the air above her, she moves into the kitchen.

Her heels click-clack across the floor with precision, and I try to maintain a neutral but happy expression on my face despite the reality that I'm dying a slow death in this woman's company.

For the third time since we stepped into this penthouse, the kitchen receives the same scrutinizing attention from Eleanor. Silence stretches across the room for a good five minutes until she breaks it with more critiquing commentary. "I like it, but I wish the kitchen were all marble."

I look around, confused, my eyes scanning across the marble counters, kitchen island, *and* floors. "Just out of curiosity, what else would you like to see in marble?"

"Everything, Maria," she retorts with pursed lips. "*Everything.*" She points toward the ceiling, cabinets, even the fridge.

A marble freaking fridge. That's a new one.

"Anyway, it's nice, I guess," she says with a small shrug of one pointy shoulder. "But I don't think it can really showcase me as a person." She twirls her fingers around. "I need an apartment that matches my level of sophistication, Maria."

She lifts one eyebrow in my direction.

This is her not-so-silent warning toward me. Despite the fact that this penthouse literally checks off all the boxes from her list, she doesn't feel it's a viable option. Especially not one I should've wasted her time with.

Normally, I'd be determined to make her happy. To find exactly what she wants, no matter how impossible it might feel. But right now, as I stand here, watching Eleanor snub her nose at a highly coveted penthouse that will no doubt be sold by the end of the day, I can't find the desire to care.

Maybe it's lack of sleep.

Maybe it's the fact that I'm finding it hard to focus on anything but wondering how Remy and Izzy are doing.

Or maybe it's simply that I am tired of dealing with clients like Eleanor.

Frankly, I don't know what it is, but I'm certain I want to be done with this showing. Done with this client. Done with this workday.

I want to go get Izzy and go back to my apartment, take off these godforsaken heels, order some takeout, and just...relax on the couch.

"Maria, I'm done here," Eleanor says and pulls out her phone to text her driver, who's probably double-parked somewhere nearby. "Call me if anything worthy of my time comes up on the market."

Goodness, I really should be trying to make her happy. But again, I can't find it in me to care today. I don't think there's a person alive who could make Eleanor Waverly happy. A billionaire on a private jet asking for her hand in marriage with a ten-million-dollar diamond ring and no prenup wouldn't even urge a smile to her lips.

"Okay, Eleanor." I offer a sugary-sweet smile and walk with her down the long hallway leading to the foyer that holds the entrance to the private elevator.

Yes, this penthouse has its own private elevator. Not to mention five bedrooms, six bathrooms, an actual sauna and hot tub room, and a rooftop terrace that photographers would drool over.

I'm about to let her leave, to throw in the towel and go back to the drawing board, when something hits me—something that feels a hell of a lot like a freight train of confidence.

"You know, Eleanor, I truly think this is the apartment for you. It's got everything on your list of desires and then some, and it has incredible potential to grow exponentially in value. I wouldn't dare assert a decision on you, but I do want to express how big of a mistake I think you're making if you walk away."

My breathing is labored and my eyes suddenly feel incredibly watery, but I stand my ground as she works her glacial gaze across my face.

With one final nod, she spins on her toe and steps directly into the elevator without another word.

The doors close on the Wicked Witch of New York, and I all but jump for joy.

Thank everything. I might have blown my relationship with Eleanor completely, but at least I spoke up for myself, and right now, that's something I'm going to choose to be proud of.

Maybe I won't be when I'm trying to find a way to pay for private preschool and everything that follows, but for now, I'm at peace.

Before starting the process of shutting off the lights and locking up, I pull my phone out of my pocket and start to fire off a text, but I'm downright shocked when a notification pops up on my screen before I can manage to type a single word.

Eleanor Waverly: Tell them I'll give them list, but I want the Picasso that's hanging in the library.

Is she kidding me? She wants the fucking apartment?

Holy, holy shit. I can't believe standing up to her worked!

There's a part of me that wants to tell her to go fuck herself just to feel the buzz, but the big commission check that gleams off in the distance wins out.

Me: I'll reach out to the listing agent now.

I quickly shoot Carl Morrow, the penthouse's listing agent, an offer via text, but once I hit send, I don't wait impatiently for his response like I normally would. Instead, I open my chat with Remy.

Me: How is Izzy? Are you still surviving?

Simultaneously, my phone chimes with two messages, one from Carl and one from Remy. I open Remy's first. Inside our chat, I only find a photo. It's a picture of Izzy, sleeping peacefully, with a note taped to her chest. **I'm a very happy hostage. (Not fussy at all because I've been a little angel all day.) PS: You will only get me back if you agree to eat dinner tonight with a handsome, studly, amazing man named Remy.**

A laugh bubbles up from my lungs and comes out as a cackle.

Me: You are nuts. And I already agreed to dinner.

Remy: Yes, but I need to make sure you're going to follow through.

Me: When have I ever not followed through?

Remy: Ha. Lots of times, babe. Take today, for example. I told you on Saturday to call me when you needed help, but you didn't. Luckily, I texted you this morning to see how things were going.

He's not wrong, but that doesn't make my reasons for not reaching out to him invalid.

Another text from Remy fills the screen.

Remy: How did your day go, by the way? Did you sell the apartment?

Oh shit, Carl!

Quickly, I open Carl's last message.

Carl: Great news, Maria. Looks like we have a deal. Owner agrees. Draft up the contract and send it my way.

Me: Fantastic. Thanks, Carl. My buyer will be pleased.

Before I let Eleanor know the news, I update Remy first.

Me: Actually, yes. I did sell the apartment. So, tonight, dinner is on me. I hate to ask this, but can you manage Izzy for another hour or so while I get contracts finalized at my office? Meet me at my place around 6:30?

Remy: See? That wasn't so hard, was it? Asking me for help when you need it? And I can definitely keep Izzy with me. It's not a problem. So don't even bother asking, "Are you sure, Remy?" ;)

Remy: PS: Congrats on the sell. Dinner is on ME.

Me: You're so stubborn.

Remy: Hello, pot. I'm kettle. Nice to meet you.

Me: I'm rolling my eyes at you again.

Remy: Yeah, but you're also smiling too.

I both love and hate that he's right.

Remy: See you at 6:30, Ria. I'll be the guy at your door with the cutest baby in the world plus dinner from your favorite Italian restaurant.

Me: And which restaurant would that be?

Remy: Pfft. Like I'd ever forget your love for Buca.

How does he remember *everything?*

The real question here is, how does he keep being everything you need?

TWENTY-TWO

Maria

The sight of Izzy perched on the kitchen island in her favorite bouncer chair is the first thing I see when I walk through the door. And the second is Remy pulling containers of takeout from a large brown paper bag that reads *Buca*.

The smell of garlic and cheese and pasta fills my nose and my stomach growls, but also, my mouth quirks up into a smile.

"Italian takeout was a glorious idea," I comment as I lift Izzy out of her chair and into my arms. "I sure missed you today," I whisper to my girl and place my lips to the soft skin of her cheek. "And I *really* hope you behaved yourself."

Izzy shuts her eyes in contentment when I nuzzle my face against hers.

"She was an angel," Remy answers, and I look up to find him smiling at me over his shoulder.

My eyes can't stop themselves from taking inventory of him. Dressed in black slacks and a white collared dress shirt that has the first two buttons undone and the sleeves rolled up his forearms, the man looks almost as delicious as the food.

Nice try. He looks more *delicious than the food.*

I want to smack my inner self for being so ridiculous. Obviously, I know he's an incredibly attractive man. Hell, I've known that since I was a teenage girl who had hearts in her eyes every time she saw him.

But now is not the time to obsess over his physical attributes.

What about his other attributes? Like the fact that he saved your ass again? Or the fact that he just might be the most thoughtful, considerate man on the planet? Is now a good time to obsess over those?

"Hungry?" Remy asks, and I have to blink myself out of my thoughts.

Quickly, I realize I've just been standing here, holding Izzy, while also staring at the way the muscles of Remy's forearms flex and stretch with his movements.

"Um...yeah. Starving, actually. I didn't have time for lunch," I finally answer and busy myself with inhaling Izzy's sweet baby smell again. Surely a baby is the perfect distraction from the ride o' randy thoughts my brain keeps trying to take me on.

"You didn't eat today?" He tsks at me. "Am I going to have to start sending food to you during the day? Packing your lunch?"

"You've already hired a cleaning service for me. I'll manage my own food, thank you very much."

"You have to promise me you're going to make sure you're eating."

"Okay, Dad. I promise I'll make sure I eat."

He smiles, but he also states, "I'm serious. Promise me."

"You're real big on the promises these days, huh?" I tease, but his eyes are unrelenting, damn near boring holes into my skull until I acquiesce.

"Fine," I say on a sigh and hold up my free hand in the air. "I promise. Sheesh."

Of course, his responding smile is victorious. "Good."

Truthfully, prior to Izzy's arrival in my life, I can't remember a time when I'd simply forget to eat. Hell, I'd schedule client appointments around my lunch schedule. But everything about my life has felt off ever since I got the call about Isabella and Oliver, the one that changed my life forever.

It's like the anxiety and stress and grief and every other hard emotion rolling around inside my heart have made some of the simplest things feel like impossible tasks.

The first week after their funerals, I was pretty much a nonverbal, insomniac zombie, just kind of meandering around my apartment. I couldn't sleep, could hardly eat, and I cried what felt like every hour of every day.

Isabella wasn't just my sister; she was my best friend. She was my family. My only family in this life. And now, all I have left of her is this sweet little baby in my arms.

I stare down at Izzy and silently wonder if we're going to be okay.

It's just you and me, kid, I mentally whisper. *Just you and me.*

When the threat of emotion starts to migrate into my throat, I clear it and distract my heavy thoughts with something else.

"So…uh…how did your meeting go, by the way?" I ask Remy as he pulls two plates out of my kitchen cabinet.

"My client spent the entire meeting holding Izzy."

My jaw drops. "What?"

"I told you he loved kids," he answers with a soft laugh.

"And seriously, Izzy didn't give you any problems?"

"Like I said, she was an angel. Slept the entire time."

Thank goodness.

I lean down to kiss the top of Izzy's head. *Good job, sweetheart. Good job.*

Remy starts to dish our food onto the plates, but when his cell phone rings, he pauses to answer it. "Hey, Phil. How's it going?" he greets the caller, but before his conversation progresses further, my phone starts ringing loudly from my purse.

With Izzy held securely in my arms, I snag the phone out of the front pocket, and even though I don't recognize the number, I answer. "Maria Baros."

"Hey, Maria. It's Michael Longview."

My smile is genuine. "Oh wow. It's been a while. How are you and Shelly? How's Paris?"

About two years ago, I helped Michael and his wife Shelly sell their Nolita apartment so that they could move to France. Their architectural firm had landed a big project just outside Paris and required their full-time attention.

"We're great," he answers. "Paris is great. But we're missing having some New York roots. We'd like you to fix that for us."

Izzy starts fussing, and before I can even blink, Remy is already pulling her out of my arms and setting her in her vibrating chair. His phone still pressed against his ear.

"I'd love to help," I tell Michael as I get to work making a bottle while Remy busies Izzy with a pacifier in her mouth. "You want to find something in Nolita again or branch out to a different neighborhood?"

"Definitely Nolita."

"And square footage?"

"Nothing smaller than four thousand."

Once Izzy's bottle is ready, I turn and relieve Remy of pacifier duties and lift her out of her chair. Both of us still on the phone. He goes back to plating our food, and I take Izzy into the living room to feed her on the couch while Michael gives me an idea of what he and Shelly are hoping to find in terms of bedrooms, bathrooms, and views.

Per usual, Izzy girl goes at her bottle like a woman starved.

"We shouldn't make any changes until the markets open…" I hear Remy say into his phone as he sets our plates on the coffee table.

"We can come into town in about two weeks," Michael comments into my ear. "Would that work for you?"

"I'll make anything work for you and Shelly."

Michael is pleased. "I'll have my assistant send you over our flight and hotel details."

"Great. We'll talk soon," I say and hit end on the call, but just as I set my phone on the coffee table, it starts to ring again.

This time, though, I know the caller—Eleanor Waverly.

Despite the dread in my belly, I blow out a breath and answer by the second ring.

"Maria, I think I made a mistake," she says, avoiding a greeting entirely. "I'm not sure if that penthouse is the right one."

I blow out another breath. *Oh, for fuck's sake.*

"Well, you did sign the contract," I explain to her. "So, it wouldn't be easy to just pull out of the deal without a valid reason that won't go against the legal terms you've agreed to. Mind explaining why you're having second thoughts?"

"I don't know… I mean, is it truly the right place for a woman like me? I have a reputation, a responsibility to this city to only showcase the best."

I shut my eyes for a brief moment, and when I open them, Remy is offering a soft smile in my direction as he takes Izzy from my arms. And while he finishes feeding her, I stand up from the couch and begin to pace the living room.

"I know you can't possibly understand the kind of pressure a woman in my position is under, but this is a big decision, Maria," Eleanor states. "I need to make sure it's the right one."

It's safe to say, she is beyond the point of living in reality. Her money, her entitlement, her entire lifestyle, make her so self-involved, she can't tell her foot from her ass.

This woman has no idea the kind of pressure I'm under. Not a freaking clue.

And normally, yes, this would be a big decision for pretty much anyone. But Eleanor Waverly changes apartments more than Izzy goes through onesies. Over the past two years alone, she's purchased and sold five different New York properties and one beach house in Malibu.

"I understand," I say, even though I really want to tell her she is driving me batshit crazy. "Why don't you tell me what it is exactly that's giving you second thoughts?"

"I don't know…" She pauses, and when I feel something touch my hand, I look down to see that Remy is handing me a breadstick.

I almost want to laugh, but I also don't hesitate to take it gratefully.

Three bites in, Eleanor finally breaks the silence. "At first, I thought it was the lack of marble, but then I think the kitchen is fine the way it is. And then, I thought it was the fact that the master bathroom had a soaking tub with a walk-in shower, but I guess it would be nice to have both. And then, I thought, maybe I want my walk-in closet to be bigger, you know? But I guess it's about the same size as the one I have now… So… I don't know… Maybe it is the right decision…?"

It's probably for the best that technology hasn't reached the point where we can physically reach through the phone. Because it's highly likely I'd be strangling her right now.

I inhale a quiet but deep breath and force myself to go to the place where I'm a real estate agent who can handle clients like this without batting a fucking eye.

"Well, all aspects you just mentioned will be great selling points if you ever decide to put it on the market again," I state. "So, even if you would eventually decide to sell it, you'd have no problems finding a buyer. Truthfully, there are six buyers with backup offers right now, hoping you'll decide not to follow through."

If there's anything that gets to Eleanor Waverly, it's knowing she has something other people want. She lives for that shit.

"They're still leaving the Picasso, right?" she questions.

"Yes. They have to. It's in the signed contract."

"Okay. Fine. Yeah. I'll buy it," she says, quickly adding, "Gotta go. Toodles!"

Then *click*. She hangs up the phone.

Goodness. I swear, that woman is a roller-coaster ride from hell.

"Everything good?" Remy asks as I sit back down beside him.

"Besides my client being a certifiable psycho? Yes, everything is good to go."

He grins at that, but when his phone starts ringing, he sighs and mutters, "Fucking hell."

"It's fine," I tell him and take Izzy from his arms. "Answer it, Rem. Trust me, I get it."

He sighs again but answers the call, and I attempt to juggle Izzy and eating while Remy talks to someone about market reactions and how he thinks the Fed's announcement about interest rates is going to affect the stock exchange's open tomorrow.

And once he ends his phone call, it only takes a minute for my phone to ring.

"What the hell is going on tonight?" I question around a mouthful of pasta, and Remy just laughs and takes Izzy from me again.

"A sign from above that we need to quit our jobs and move to a deserted island."

I smirk and point a finger in his direction. "Don't tease me like that."

"Oh, I never tease. You should know that by now." Rem grins, and I shake my head on a laugh.

"Your clients would lose their shit if you left them high and dry," I whisper toward him as I answer my incoming call by the third ring.

"So would yours," he mouths.

"Our clients suck," I mouth back just as Daniel's voice is filling my ear and asking me a question regarding a contract he's trying to draw up.

Rem nods at me with wide, knowing eyes and takes a bite of his pasta as he keeps Izzy close to his chest.

And the night pretty much moves on like that, Rem fielding market calls and me fielding real estate calls, while both of us attempt to eat and take care of Izzy at the same time.

By the time the clock strikes eleven, I feel so exhausted that I just throw myself onto my bed once we get Izzy to sleep in her crib.

To my surprise, when I look up from my facedown spot, Remy is climbing into bed beside me.

"I might need to rest for a minute before I head home."

Both of us are still fully dressed in our work clothes, but the idea of switching into something more comfortable sounds more uncomfortable than sleeping in my skirt and blouse.

"Just sleep here," I tell him without a second thought. "Is it just me, or was tonight a long one?" I whisper toward him, and he nods, yawns, and adjusts the comforter so it's covering both of our bodies.

"Nope, not just you. I still think my deserted island idea is the way to go."

I snort. "You're nuts."

"And you're nuts for not agreeing with me."

"If I weren't so tired," I say through a yawn, and my eyelids start to feel impossible to keep open. "I'd have a better comeback. But I have nothing."

"Same, Ria," Remy whispers back, and his voice is already thick with sleep. "Same."

TWENTY-THREE

Wednesday, October 9th

Remy

All I feel are softness and curves. Over me. Around me. Pressed against me.

This is a good fucking dream.

The smell of the most delicious flowery perfume engulfs my head, and the sound of soft panting fills my ears.

Damn, that's sexy.

Hands grip at the material of my shirt, and the feel of warmth rhythmically pressing against my thigh makes my cock take notice. Like, *really* take notice. So much so that I no longer feel like I'm sleeping.

I feel awake. *Really* awake.

I blink my eyes open, and the light of the moon coming in through the windows is the first thing my brain can understand.

The second? *Maria.*

Her long hair fans over my shoulder, and it's *her* hands that grip my shirt, tugging at the material with her fingers. Her full breasts are pressed against my ribs, her thigh is stretched across mine, and the rhythmic sensation against my body is her. *Grinding* against me.

Holy fuck. Definitely not dreaming.

Her breaths come out in more soft pants and brush across my neck, and in an instant, my cock is at full attention.

Fuck me.

I think she's still sleeping. I don't know. I can't tell, but when a sexy little moan leaves her lungs, I have to find out.

"Maria," I whisper her name, my voice already strained with my undeniable arousal.

But she doesn't answer. Just keeps *grinding* herself against me.

"Maria," I whisper again, and it's then that her eyes pop open and meet mine.

Her gaze is sleepy but still shining with heat and desire, and I can't stop myself from thinking about how beautiful she is. Maria has always been beautiful to me, but there is something about seeing her raw and without inhibitions that makes me feel crazy with need.

The need to touch her.

Feel her.

Kiss her.

Slide my cock inside her.

Slowly, I reach down and brush my knuckles over her breasts, and her nipples are hard beneath the material of her silk shirt.

She whimpers, and her hips jolt forward against me.

I move my hand farther down her body, but when I grip her thigh, something changes behind her eyes. It's like she's finally fully awake. Completely aware of what's happening.

"Oh my God, I'm so sorry," she whispers and starts to avert her eyes from mine, guilt and shame lowering her chin. "I don't know what I was doing… I think I was… I—"

"Maria," I cut her off, not giving her space to apologize for something that's done the opposite of make me uncomfortable. And then I tell her the only thing that makes sense right now. "I want you too."

I lift her chin with my index finger and search her eyes.

When she doesn't pull away this time, I slowly, carefully, lean forward until our mouths are just a breath away from each other.

"Remy," she whispers as she grips my shirt tighter and she presses her body into mine.

Fuck. I have to kiss her.

I can't not kiss her.

TWENTY-FOUR

Maria

Kiss me, Remy, my mind whispers as my eyes search his.

His eyes are hooded and his lips are parted, and I don't know what we're doing right now or how we got here, but I can't find any reason to stop.

Please kiss me.

I almost say the words out loud. I almost open my mouth to tell him, but somehow, he already knows. Lips to mine, Remy *kisses* me.

It's slow and gentle at first, a careful exploration of each other. But eventually, it doesn't feel like enough, and I find myself kissing him back with a fervor, a deepness and desperation, that makes me feel greedier than I've been in I don't know how many years.

God, he tastes good. Like sunset and sex and all of the things my body forgot I love to feel.

A moan slips from my throat when he flips me onto my back and settles himself between my thighs. His hands are in my hair and his tongue is in my mouth and his cock is pressed against me, grinding against the one spot that aches and throbs for him.

I pant and writhe beneath him, desperate for more of whatever he has to give. My hips follow his movements, and I silently wish we had a lot fewer clothes on than we do.

He leans back and slides his big hands over my breasts and begins to unbutton my silk blouse, and I do the same with his sleep-wrinkled dress shirt, my hands shaking with intensity as I bumble to remove it.

In a flash, our shirts are gone, and he's licking and kissing at my exposed skin.

I moan, writhe, *pant*, my body begging him to keep going.

His mouth creates a path down my breasts and all over my belly. His fingers undo the side zipper of my skirt and move the material down my legs as his mouth goes lower and lower and *lower*.

I ache and throb, and my hips move of their own accord at the feel of his lips against my skin. I feel overheated, oversensitive, like a woman who will only be satisfied if she can crawl inside Remy's body while he manages to do the same thing with hers.

He grips the waistband of my panties, and he deftly moves them down my legs. I'm completely bare now, and his gaze is on me, staring at my exposed flesh. "Fuck. You're beautiful."

His words make me moan and my legs fall open and my back arches as his strong, skillful hands slide up my thighs.

His face hovers between my legs, just inches from where I need him to be. Just a breath away from his mouth *touching* me *there*. And I feel crazy with the need for him to close that distance. Put his mouth on me. Slide his tongue across where I ache and throb for him.

But something happens.

Like a needle to a balloon, the moment is popped by a singular sound—Izzy's little cry.

TWENTY-FIVE

Remy

One minute, my hands grip Maria's thighs, my mouth greedy and eager to taste her, and the next, I'm a fucking statue. Hell, so is she.

Both of us are frozen, intently listening, and wondering if the cries of a baby we've heard are real or figments of our imagination.

Two sharp wails crack the air, followed by a full-on hiccuping sob, and our debut as stone sculptures is nothing more than a memory.

Maria jumps out of bed and furiously pulls on her discarded robe from the ottoman at the confirmation of Izzy's cries, and I take off down the hall in nothing but the black dress slacks I fell asleep in.

Gentle but swift, I push through Izzy's bedroom door to find her writhing in her crib, arms and legs kicking and squirming outside of her no-longer-intact swaddle. In full distress, she has her little pink mouth screwed up into a frown that pinches the delicate skin between her eyes, and her cheeks are mottled with red splotches.

I feel absolutely terrible for her.

Once I undo the Velcro on the disheveled swaddle, I scoop her out of her crib and boost her up to my shoulder, patting and rubbing at her back in an effort to help her calm down. This is the most upset I've seen her, and the earnest sharpness of her cries stabs me like a knife to the pit of my stomach.

"It's okay, Iz. I'm here," I comfort, swinging her from side to side and falling into a bouncing motion without thought or planning.

Maria trails through the door behind me, having stopped briefly to grab Izzy's favorite pacifier from where it got left behind in the living room last night, her eyes wide and alert as she gets a load of just how upset Izzy seems to be. This is a true cry of some sort of pain or discomfort, not the softer lull of her normal complaints.

But even her favorite pacifier appears to be a useless endeavor.

"Oh my goodness, you poor thing. You're even too worked up for your binky," Maria whispers and reaches out to gently caress the skin at Izzy's cheek and forehead. She looks like a mom who is equal parts worried and eager to calm her sweet baby down. "She doesn't feel like she's running a fever or anything, but she seems really upset. You think I should get her a bottle? Even if she's not hungry, maybe the sucking sensation will soothe her?"

"Worth a shot." I nod, and she turns to quickly head out of the room, but I call out to stop her. "Wait, Ri!"

She spins quickly to meet my eyes.

"Warm it a little extra."

She nods fervently and then disappears down the hall to take action. It's one of the most prominent parts of Maria's personality—the action. She's not a wait-and-see kind of gal. She's a doer. She needs to feel like she's trying, even if she's spinning her wheels.

I look down at Izzy's tiny features all scrunched up and rub at her back and sides, hoping to ease the pain. Her current state reminds me of Lexi and how a trapped gas bubble used to make her miserable when she was a baby.

Surely that's what this is, a gas bubble stuck in her teeny torso, and without the ability to understand the mechanics and whys of it, she's traumatized.

Ironically, I don't think she's the only one. Maria's face as she jumped out of bed, putting a pause button on our unexpected but well-appreciated activities, didn't tell a story of a woman who was confident in her understanding of what was happening between us.

And I can't say I blame her. Because I don't really understand it myself. One minute, we were falling into bed with exhaustion, and the next, we were... *not exhausted.*

My dick, in fact, was *all in* prior to the distraction that came from the cries of this little girl. Thankfully, he's old enough to understand that sometimes personal responsibility comes before pleasure. Although, the rest of the feelings and sensations in this situation are a little too complicated for him. Meaning? Fallout? Far past his pay grade.

And my brain, well, for the past decade and a half, it's just as inexperienced with anything other than short-lived flings.

Izzy takes a big gulp of air before letting out another sob, and I pat at her back continuously. I hate watching her little face in pain when she can't understand why.

I can hear Maria scrambling around in the kitchen with every bang and smash of the cabinets, and it makes me smile. She's frantic—just like any mother would be.

She's a mom.

She might feel strange calling herself that, but I've never seen someone with more unconditional love in their heart. Maria is a mother to Izzy, no matter the details of how that came to be.

As Izzy squirms, I lay her down on the ottoman of the rocking chair in her room and churn her legs toward her chest in an effort to find some sort of relief for her hurt. A trick my mom showed me when Lexi was about this age.

She fights the motion, but with every bicycle turn of her legs, her shouts ease a bit. In a sudden snap, Izzy releases a burp and two little baby toots in a row, and straightaway, all the pain in her features flees.

She's crying still, disturbed by the whole experience, but she's not in actual discomfort anymore.

Maria rushes back into the room with her bottle, and I scoop Izzy up and into my arms so that I can take a seat in the rocker.

I take the bottle from Maria, but not before catching her hand in mine and rubbing the back of it with my thumb. "She's good now. Just a whole lot of gas trapped inside."

"How did you know that's what it was?"

"Happens to Jude every time he eats broccoli," I tease, and Maria laughs softly.

"I actually knew from my niece," I explain the real truth of my knowledge, while giving Izzy her bottle. She drinks eagerly as I offer the nipple at her lips, and the room settles into blessed silence. "When Lexi was around Izzy's age, Winnie called me in the middle of the night at a complete loss over what to do with a baby who wouldn't stop crying. Being a single guy with no kids, hell if I knew what to do either. But Wendy Winslow saved the day after getting dragged out of bed to come help. I swear, it only took her two minutes before she had it handled."

"I've always thought your mom was a superhero for being able to raise all five of you by herself. Marvel should consider adding her to the lineup."

"She did manage to keep Jude and Ty alive." I raise my eyebrows in amusement. "A near-impossible feat, if you ask me."

"Yeah." Maria snorts, but her eyes are back to being fixated on Izzy. "I remember the crazy things they'd attempt back in the day. Absolute daredevils. It was terrifying."

She's not joking. Both Jude and Ty took many a trip to the ER for the consequences of their wild actions. Between the two of them, they've probably broken every damn bone in the human body.

Silence stretches between us, and the only sounds filling the room are Izzy's little breaths between pulls of formula. Maria is still standing beside us, only now, her hands appear to be working an invisible weave in front of her.

She's uncertain. Nervous. And I have a feeling it has everything to do with the moments leading up to Izzy's late-night cries for help.

She fidgets with the material of her robe with her fingers, and I don't know what it is about seeing her like this, but I can't help myself. I have to break the tension.

"So…that was one way to end a…uh…*make-out session*, huh?"

Maria guffaws on a startle, her hand jumping to her mouth at the completely unladylike but cute-as-hell noise. "Uh…yeah… It was an interesting end to the…uh…*make-out session*."

Obviously, we had far passed the point where that could've been classified as just kissing, but I knew it was the exact right terminology to use if I wanted to distract her from her busy thoughts.

"Certainly, something I've never experienced before, you know?" My mouth curves up. "And for a single bachelor in his forties, that's really saying something."

Maria laughs then. "The kinkiest finish you've ever had?"

I wink. "Definitely."

In the dark room, the two of us stare at each other for a long minute. Only the moonlight streaming through the curtains and a princess night-light in the corner illuminate the space enough to see each other.

I study the lines of her throat and the way her breasts push against her robe and how her bare legs peek out from the small slit down the center. And I remember the image of all of it just moments before she covered herself. *Fucking stunning, every inch of her.*

"God, Remy. I'm sorry. You must be exhausted," Maria starts, clearly taking my study of her features out of context in one way or another. Because trust me, if Maria Baros knew what I was thinking about right now, she wouldn't be apologizing for anything. "I should have—"

"Ria. Come on. I'm good."

And I am. With Izzy curled against my bare chest and Maria looking at me like she knows the feel of my bare skin against her own, I don't think I've ever been better.

Down deep, I know Maria's angst isn't about sleep deprivation or caring for Izzy right now. Lord knows she can handle all that. She's been handling it like Wendy Winslow on steroids, even when it's put her at the breaking point. Even when she's questioning herself if she can really do it. I don't know anyone who could've handled the first six weeks of their baby's life by themselves.

This is about what we were in the middle of when we got interrupted. It's about not knowing if she would have gone all the way if we hadn't been. And it's about wondering if I'm thinking all the same things.

"I was thinking," I add, "you should know that I normally last longer than that."

"Last longer?"

"Yeah," I say through a secret smile. "During s-e-x."

Her embarrassment is still under the surface, but she suppresses it enough to smile slyly. "But I thought it was a make-out session?"

"Same difference."

"*Same difference?*" she questions, now completely entertained by the path of this conversation despite the slight hue of pink that's still showcased on her cheeks. "Your definition of make-out sessions has certainly changed over the years."

"Well, I suppose I've learned a thing or two about *make-out sessions* over the years." I waggle my brows, and I can't help but reach out to pull her closer by the belt of her robe.

On a giggle, she falls to sitting on the ottoman by my feet.

"So, you've learned a thing or two about make-out sessions, but not about s-e-x?" she volleys back, and it makes my chest vibrate with hilarity. "I should probably make a mental note of that."

"I almost forgot how damn good you are at comebacks," I tell her with a smirk. "You could put all three of my brothers to shame."

Izzy shifts in my arms, squirming a little as she tries to find sleep again. I adjust her body an inch, and sadly, Maria's focus changes.

"Here, let me take her."

I start to shake my head—I'm perfectly content where I am—but the clock on Izzy's wall with a little pink balloon design in the center catches my attention.

It's nearly three in the morning, and the foreign markets will be opening soon. A couple of my clients' portfolios have me particularly attuned to Tokyo and the way all the shuffling on trade deals is going to affect things on a global scale.

I really need to be home, in my office, if I have any hope of keeping up with everything when the markets open.

Fuck. I wish things didn't feel so unfinished with me leaving.

I have to go, though. I *have* to. Billionaires don't exactly look the other way when you play fast and loose with their money.

I glance down at the tired baby in my arms once more and then up to an unsure Maria. She's shifting from one hip to the other, self-conscious in the gap my silence has left.

"Yeah, actually. But only because I have to head home." I snuggle into Izzy's sweet scent and smile down at her. "No way I'd leave if I didn't have to, little girl."

Maria leans forward, taking Izzy out of my arms, standing up, and turning to sway her way to the other side of the room. I can't shake the feeling that she's avoiding something…avoiding *me.*

I hope she's not taking my leaving personally—relating it to what happened before Izzy's cries. If she is, I'm going to have to do something about it before I leave if I want any hope of concentrating on the market at all.

Not yet, though. Right now, I need to get myself ready and give her some space to gather herself, and then, *then,* I'll give her a lesson in assuming.

Because I don't regret anything about our almost-encounter other than the fact that I have to use the qualifier of "almost."

I run a hand through my hair briefly, pausing to watch them for a moment before heading back to Maria's room to gather my stuff. It's a short, silent trip down the hallway, and the absence of Izzy's cries now is a stark hole for my own.

On the inside, of course. I mean, I'm not bawling out loud, but I've never wanted to stay somewhere more in my life.

The bed is rumpled and the covers askew, both from getting up in a hurry and from what we were doing before that.

And I can almost feel the warm flesh of Maria's thighs in my hands and taste the promised land of what's in between.

I lick my lips and force myself to move to the side of the bed, grabbing my shirt that's on the floor and throwing it on with rough, irritated movements.

We *will* try this again. One way or another, Maria and I will finish what we started.

Unfortunately for me, it just won't be right now.

Taking a quick trip into the bathroom, I wash off my face and run a hand through my hair to tame it a little and give my teeth a scrub with my finger and toothpaste.

I feel at least a little refreshed, and now I'm ready to take on not only my day at work, but also saying goodbye to Maria.

As I head out of her bedroom, I flick off all the lights other than the soft lamp at the side of her bed, grab my phone and keys off the nightstand, and walk back down the hallway toward Izzy's room. I can still hear the faint sounds of Maria shuffling around in there, despite absolute silence from Izzy herself.

Just before reaching the threshold of the nursery, my phone buzzes in my pocket, making my eyebrows draw together. *Who the hell is texting me this early in the morning?*

I unlock the screen and scroll into my messages, where a brand-new one from "C" sits right at the top.

Part of me knows I shouldn't open it, but another part of me is too curious not to.

C: Sometimes when opportunity knocks, it's from the same side of the door you're already on.

Okay, why did I open this thing again?

Annoyed by Cleo's vagueness, I click out of her text without answering and shake my head at my phone. Just below her message, though, is an old thread with Maria, and an idea hits me.

Quickly, I type out a message and hit send, confident that her phone is still in the bedroom on her nightstand, and tuck my cell back into my pocket.

Not wanting to disturb them if Izzy's almost asleep, I only peek into the nursery, holding on to the jamb of the door and leaning inside. But I'm surprised to find that Izzy is already back at rest, fast asleep in her crib, while Maria paces the room doing mundane chores.

"Ria," I call softly, getting her attention just as she's tucking some outfits into the top drawer of Izzy's dresser. Her head jerks up at the sound of my voice, and she glances back at Izzy, who hasn't even shifted an inch.

I wave Maria out of the room, and she comes—hesitantly.

I wait just outside the door for her and then nod toward the living room when she stops right in front of me.

She takes the lead, and I watch her hips sway powerfully from side to side. I practically have to bite into the flesh of my lip to stop my groan.

I cannot fucking believe I'm leaving right now. What a fucking douche adult Remy has turned out to be. Seventeen-year-old Remy never would have made this same decision. Not in a million years.

No, when it came to Maria Baros, seventeen-year-old me had balls *and* brains.

THE PAST

THE PRIORITY

Twenty-Seven Years Ago…

Senior year, Friday night in early October

Remy

Two steps out of the locker room and my arms are full of cheerleader. Excited, exuberant, and enthusiastic, Maria never waits for me to get any farther before throwing herself into my arms, win or lose.

But this time, with a win against our biggest rivals in the county, she has so much energy she nearly knocks me over.

"You played awesome!" she squeals into my ear and plants a smacking kiss to my lips.

I spot Winnie and Isabella giggling over Maria's shoulder, always amused by how "lovey-dovey" the two of us are. But Wendy Winslow always taught me to show affection for the people I care about. *It's like writing a story*, she always says. *You have to show them, not just tell them.*

"Thanks, babe," I tell her and return her affection with several playful, sweaty kisses all over her face. I don't stop until she's giggling me away.

A couple of the guys coming out of the locker room catch sight of our display and start mocking me with smacking kissing noises and wrapping their arms around themselves.

Idiots.

"Coming to pizza, Winslow?" a linebacker named Chris pipes up.

"Or are you too busy playing house with the wife and kids?" another guy named Nate adds with a nod toward Maria and our little sisters.

Maria shifts away self-consciously, and Winnie and Isabella stop laughing. My hackles have risen, and I'm just about to tell Nate to go fuck himself when Coach Rydell approaches and claps a hand on my shoulder.

"Probably a good idea for the team to go out together, boys. Just because you got a win tonight doesn't mean you can quit putting in the work. Go eat pizza and talk about the shit you need to fix for next game."

My jaw hardens as Maria backs away completely, a hollow version of her earlier excitement as she wraps her arms around Winnie's and Isabella's shoulders and smiles down at them. "No worries, guys," she tells our sisters. "The three of us will go eat and meet Remy after."

Her eyes are understanding and compassionate and completely fucking sad.

And I'll be fucked if I'm going to leave her like that to go to dinner with douchebags like Chris and Nate. Truthfully, it doesn't even matter that a lot of the guys on my team are good buddies. I have somewhere else more important to be.

"Sorry, Coach, but I already have plans tonight that I can't break. Next time," I state definitively, not leaving any room for argument before walking away.

Chris and Nate guffaw and cut up under their breath, and I'm sure Coach is wearing none other than his steeliest of jaws. But I don't give a shit.

And when I catch up with Maria and Winnie and Isabella and see the resulting smiles on their faces, I don't regret my decision.

Football is just a game. Nothing less or more than that.

But Maria and our sisters? They're my priority here. Period.

TWENTY-SIX

Still Wednesday, October 9th

Remy

"Maria, if it weren't for work, I wouldn't be leaving right now."

Younger me knew better. Younger me left no fucking doubt. *Well, at least the younger you that understood what he had when Maria was on his arm. The moron who let her go right before leaving for college—and then dropped out after a year to day trade anyway—clearly had a serious lapse in judgment.*

She stops just outside the living room and turns to face me with the kind of neutrality on her face I know has to be forced because the dimple in her cheek shows her truth. "Remy, you don't have to feel bad about leaving. Of course you have a job. A life. More important things to do."

More important things to do? It doesn't fucking feel like it.

Even with her feeling so unsure about how I'm feeling, I'm sure enough for the both of us, and I don't hesitate to show her.

I charge, right into her space.

Sinking my hands into her hair, I lift her chin up to mine, and without wavering, sweep my tongue over the line of her lips to get access before diving inside.

I swallow her gasp of surprise and kiss her like I've never kissed anyone before. This is a declaration—this is a point being made. This is a promise.

Our tongues dance, hers giving way to mine as I take complete control of the kiss and her mouth.

Her taste is so familiar, so beautifully and hauntingly her, that my mind almost spirals into despair at the thought of not tasting everything—every single part of her.

"God," I groan, pulling away just enough to lick across the line of her lips again. She whimpers, and all the planning, all the moments that have led to this one come into focus. No questions. No small talk. Everything that needs to be said is said with this kiss.

Leave no fucking doubt, Remy.

This isn't the end. And if it's the last thing I do on this earth, I will make sure we pick up where we left off.

When I finally pull away, Maria is breathing heavily, and her eyes are soft. "Wow."

I laugh. "Yeah."

"I guess I'll see you again sometime, then, huh?"

"Just try to keep me away, and see what happens."

She quirks one amused eyebrow at me. "Is that a threat?"

I shake my head. "It's a promise. And you know how I am about keeping promises."

She laughs then. "Adult Remington Winslow is all about the promises."

"Damn straight, babe."

With one last peck to her lips, I grab the remainder of my stuff from the kitchen counter and head for the front door. She follows easily, holding it open for me while I walk through it.

But before I leave, I turn in the open door, my hand firmly clenched around the outer edge, and lean back into the apartment. Maria is surprised by the motion and, as a result, doesn't have time to put up her defenses. Instead, I'm in her space—enveloped in her smell and, hopefully, trapping her with my own. She might have thought I was heading out, but there's no way in hell I'm leaving without a detailed plan. I cannot leave without knowing precisely when I'm going to see her next.

"Come to dinner. Friday. At my sister's house."

"Family dinner?" She shakes her head, her mind a swirling mess of thoughts I only wish I could read. "Rem, I don't know—"

"It's not formal. You know everyone anyway. And they'd love to see you. Plus, there will be other babies and kids and Lexi and plenty of adults to step in so you can enjoy a dinner with two hands."

"Rem—"

"Please?" I find myself whispering, the want hanging plainly in my voice.

Her head bobs back and forth for a moment of torture, but in the end, *finally*, she gives in. "All right. Text me the time and address. I'll be there."

"I already did." I smile unabashedly. I'm proud-as-a-fucking-peacock for convincing her, and to be honest, I feel no need to hide it.

"What? When?"

"When I was getting my shit together. While you were with Iz."

Her cheeks carve into a smile, and I feel the expression all the way in my chest. "You're cocky, you know that?"

"I've been told before."

"Well, you need to be told again. Dear lord, the ego of Remington Winslow is going to be the size of a semitruck by the time I'm old and gray."

I chuckle. "Fine by me. As long as you're at dinner on Friday night."

"Like I said, I'll be there."

The best part is, I believe her. I can see it in her eyes that she's going to follow through.

And I'm the lucky son of a bitch waiting on the other side.

TWENTY-SEVEN

Friday, October 11th

Maria

"Here goes nothing, Izzy girl," I whisper down to where she sits cozy in the baby carrier strapped to my chest, but as I start to lift my hand to rap my knuckles against the fancy wooden door in front of me, something makes me pause. Hesitate.

Truthfully, my heart is in my throat as I stand on the threshold of Winnie Winslow's Uptown brownstone, memories swirling about a young girl doing something very similar years ago.

Of course, then, I didn't have a baby in tow and, ironically, felt like I knew myself well enough to take on a family of this size. Back then, Isabella and I waited with bated breath for sixteen-year-old Remington Winslow to open the door to his childhood home. For me, it was because I was in love—starry-eyed, notebook-doodle-causing, heart-thumping love—with one of the cutest boys I'd ever known.

Isabella seemed to have a little crush on Remy too, but even in her preteens, I imagine she saw the way I looked at Remy and understood it. It was powerful, all-encompassing. So, for her, the excitement came in the form of three seriously fine-looking younger brothers and her then-good-friend Winnie.

It's crazy that I had more confidence as a teenager than I do now, but I've entered a whole new phase of life that I'm still trying to sort out.

I don't know who I am or who to be or who I wish I was. All I know is that if I don't get up in the morning and love Izzy with all I have, no one else will. I imagine that's how Remy felt back then, all those years ago, having to be the head of his family since his father took off.

Sure, Isabella's and my dad took off, too, but it was shortly after Isabella was born, and I was barely four. Plus, I only had one sibling to watch out for, and the memories of our absent father were foggy at best.

The thought makes me look down at Izzy again, and my heart aches with the irony that she had a dad who wanted to be there for every waking moment of her life, but he got taken away from her too soon.

You have to cut this out, I silently coach myself. *Now is not the time to go there, of all places.*

I inhale a deep breath.

I can do this. I *can.*

Bouncing Izzy up and down to give her a little bit of faith in my feelings, I smile big and dare myself to be bold. Dare myself to lean into the moment and just take the night as it comes.

It's a big ask, and I don't know if I'll be able to. But I'm sure as hell going to try.

Although, before I can bite the proverbial bullet and knock on the door, my phone buzzes in my bag. I juggle Izzy enough to pull it out of the front pocket of her diaper bag that's slung over my shoulder and check the screen.

Claudia: *I feel like you might've told me to move tonight's showing to tomorrow, but I can't remember. Anyway, there's still a showing tonight.*

Oh no. This is bad. This is really bad. Furiously, I type with my one free thumb.

Me: *Claudia, what the hell??? I sent you three emails about this. You need to MOVE that showing. Tell them I have an emergency or something, but I CAN'T make it there tonight.*

For the first time in her life, Claudia texts back promptly, but it's not with anything that's going to lower my blood pressure. In fact, it's quite the opposite.

Claudia: *Just chatted with the old guy. Told him you were having an uncontrollable bout of diarrhea and were indisposed.*

The "old guy" she's talking about is Mr. Conrad Blakely, owner of one of the biggest grocery store chains in the damn city. *He's also a man who now thinks his Realtor is at home with the shits.*

The anger I feel is all-consuming, bubbling up from my toes and hitting every damn nerve in my body until it finds an escape from my mouth.

"You have to be fucking kidding me!" I shout, but unfortunately for me, the words fly from my lips at the same time the fancy wooden door swings open and Wendy Winslow's face comes into view.

Oh my God! Tell me those aren't the first words I just said to Remy's mother after nearly three decades!

Instantly, my insides fizzle as if I'm going to spontaneously combust.

"Maria?" she questions, as though she doesn't even recognize me as an earthly being. And I can't blame her. I might as well be a tomato for as red as I feel all the way to my core.

"Oh, Mrs. Winslow," I say, clearing my throat several times to talk around the humongous lump inside it. "I'm so, so sorry. Please excuse my language." I cringe. "Those words were not at all intended for you. I-I... Well, I hadn't even knocked. I didn't know anyone knew I was out here and—"

"Winnie has one of those Ring cameras," she explains, nudging her shoulder toward the glaring thing. *Damn. How on earth did I not notice that thing? What kind of Realtor am I?*

"Again, I'm so sorry. I didn't think—"

"Oh, Maria, please," Wendy clucks, stepping forward without delay and taking my face into her hands in a way only a mother can do without making you feel uncomfortable. "Stop apologizing. I have four boys who would make what you just said look like a children's program."

I laugh a little at that, despite the heaviness of my lasting embarrassment.

Wendy looks at me, smiling warmly, just like she did when I was young—just like my own mom used to—and a pang of longing for the unconditional love of her parenting hits me hard.

Man, I miss her sometimes. Her guidance and understanding and just flat-out love.

"Look at you, lovely girl," she whispers, making my nose sting and my lips curl up into my mouth. "My goodness," she states reverently, studying my face. "You grew up beautifully."

A blush creeps its way from my chest to my neck, and I find myself gently rubbing at Izzy's back to give myself something to do. "Thank you. It's really great to see you."

"Can I?" Her smile overwhelms her put-together face as she reaches for Izzy, asking for permission with her eyes, and I carefully lift my baby out of her carrier and hand her over while observing.

Izzy is comfortable with Wendy from the get-go, and I can't help but wonder if she can sense some piece of Remy in his mom. Because for as little as she knows of him, there's an almost unspeakable comfort there when she's in his arms.

Truth be told, I can't blame her. I know the feeling all too well. Remington Winslow's embrace *is* comforting.

"Wow," Wendy whispers as she looks at Izzy in awe. "She sure is precious."

Once Izzy is settled in her arms, Wendy backs out of the space of the door and ushers me in with the soft voice of a woman talking to a baby. "Come in, come in, both of you," she muses, focusing mostly on the baby in her arms. "Everyone is ready and waiting to see you!"

"I'm so sorry that I'm running a little late, by the way," I apologize as I quickly set my baby carrier and diaper bag down by where everyone's bags and purses appear to be.

"Nonsense, sweetie. Dinner isn't formal around here." She scoffs a little, laughing. "Nothing is formal with Jude and Ty around. They may be a lot older than the last time you saw them, but I can guarantee they haven't changed a bit."

Jude and Ty were always the most rambunctious of the four Winslow boys.

I follow her down the spacious front hall, studying the photos on the wall of Winnie, her nearly identical twin of a daughter, and a handsome man

I assume is her husband, and several with Remy in them too. He smiles the biggest in the ones with his mom and Winnie and Lexi, and a tickle of warmth fills my chest.

He's always been the most complex mix of grumpy and loving, but around me, he's pretty much been the latter. I can't think of a time he wasn't patient with me when we were teenagers or even a moment when he raised his voice.

He was like a different guy with his brothers, always teasing and grumbling and shooting insult arrows in their archery tournament of banter.

But to me...he was always sweet.

As Wendy clears the opening at the end of the hallway, a chorus of cheers erupts toward the baby in her arms—my baby—and several asses shove off from their spots leaned into the kitchen counter and come forward with their hands extended.

Winnie and Ty are at the front of the race, and Ty hip checks Winnie out of the way.

"Gah! Ty!" she shrieks, but her brother is completely unfazed.

"Too slow!" Ty snarks back. "Last time I saw this little bun, she was still in the oven. I have to hold her first as a kind of ceremonial thing. You understand."

Wendy grins at me knowingly, her eyes silently saying, *See what I mean?* as she passes Izzy over to Ty.

He cradles her softly to his chest, looking down at her with big, moony eyes. It's such a change from the little shit-stirrer I remember from my childhood that it almost doesn't compute.

Love, it seems, really does have the power to tame some of the wildest men.

"Maria, I know you remember Ty and Jude and, of course, Winnie," Wendy starts to introduce me to everyone in the room. "This is Rachel, Ty's fiancée. Sophie, Jude's wife, and Wes, Winnie's husband."

Everyone greets me with genuine smiles and kind words, and I try hard to keep all the names and faces sorted in my head.

"The only new people we're missing are my Howard, Flynn's wife Daisy, their twin boys Ryder and Roman, and Winnie's daughter Lexi," Wendy updates, but I'm starkly aware that we're also missing Remy.

I don't know where he is, but without him here reassuring me, I kind of feel like I'm going to puke.

"It's so good to see you, Maria," Winnie says from my side, rubbing a kind hand down my forearm and startling my attention away from the crowd with my baby. "I'm so glad you came. There's a lot of testosterone in this group, so we're always in need of a couple more hits of estrogen. You and Izzy are more than welcome to fill the role."

I smile at that, glancing at all the big, powerful men cooing over my baby once more. It's very *Three Men and a Baby*-esque, and the simple thought reminds me of my mother. She always had the biggest crush on Tom Selleck, and Isabella and I never let her live it down.

One Halloween when we were teenagers, we even dressed up as him just to freak our mom out. The laughter that ensued between the three of us has proven to create one of my most vivid, core memories.

"Thank you. I really appreciate you all having me. It's been…well…nearly two months since I've had a home-cooked meal."

Winnie laughs. "Oh man, I remember those days. One blending into the next. It's awful. And worth it." She pauses briefly. "And awful."

We both laugh at that.

"Don't ever hesitate to call me, okay?" she adds then, her voice so sincere I can't even bring myself to dismiss it.

"Okay. Thanks."

"No," she says with a shake of her head and a little grin. "I mean, *really* call me if you need anything, which is why I'm going to make you give me your phone right now so I can put my number in it."

Her hand held out toward me, I have no choice but to acquiesce. It reminds me so much of how persistent and determined little Winnie Winslow was back in the day.

"Anytime, day or night," she says and hands my phone back to me, her contact information now saved. "I remember what it's like. We moms have to stick together."

I swallow hard on the word mom. Even though I know it's what I am—what I have to be for Izzy—it still feels completely foreign coming out of someone else's mouth.

"Damn, she's a beauty," Ty muses as he approaches me with Izzy, and a shallow breath I didn't know I was holding finally releases. "Rachel, I want to have ten of these cuties after we get married."

I stretch out my arms to take her back, even get my hands on her tiny baby sides, when his fiancée smacks him on the shoulder softly and chastises, "What? No! If I'm supposed to birth a football team for you, I deserve to be able to hold the inspiration."

Ty passes Izzy to Rachel before I can even put my hands down from the space where they were prepared to clutch her. And Rachel nuzzles her face against Izzy's cheek.

My girl appears to enjoy it, her little eyes squinting in comfort, but my heart is still beating a million miles a minute.

Remy is across the room now, finally appearing from wherever he's been hiding in this beautiful brownstone. I recognize his brother Flynn standing beside him, and I assume the beautiful woman next to him is his wife Daisy. Which means the two adorable-looking boys on their hips must be their twins, Roman and Ryder.

My eyes are wide, and I can practically feel them stretching to the limits of my face as I try to telepathically yell to Remy when Winnie steps into my line of vision and fills it completely.

Her face is a friendly smile full of amusement. She reaches up and squeezes my shoulder comfortingly as she explains, "By the way, there's a rule here. You never have to take care of your own kids. It's group-parenting, sister-wife-ing, whatever you want to call it. But there are enough of us, and enough of us who *get* it. Take the break and enjoy it. I promise Izzy will be in good hands."

"Okay," I reply as calmly as I can manage, trying to squash the overwhelming need to hover obtrusively.

Winnie giggles. "Man, Maria, I'm impressed. Not many moms pretend not to be shitting themselves as well as you."

I slam my hands into my face and groan before smiling back at her. "Am I that obvious?"

"Only because I've been there," she says. "I can remember when Lexi was that age, and I felt like someone had removed my arm whenever I wasn't holding her. You're doing great. I promise."

"Thanks," I murmur, surprised by how nice it feels to have that kind of encouragement. "Truth be told, I kind of feel like I'm bumbling my way through this whole motherhood thing."

Winnie nods supportively. "That means you're doing it right."

"Really?"

"*Oh yeah*," she enunciates. "We're all big fakers without a flipping clue."

"Yo, Ty, when are you going to pay up, bro?" Jude shouts so loud from the other side of the kitchen that it startles Winnie's and my attention. He slaps Ty in the stomach with a hard hand. "You still owe me fifty bucks for Phillips's TD."

"Ow, you fucker," Ty grunts, and Wendy steps between them with a stern face.

"Knock it off, you two. I brought you into this world, which means I can take you right back out if I want."

"Mom, how many times do you think you've said that to us?" Jude asks, grinning like a real smartass.

"Apparently not enough."

Winnie gives me a look and points conspiratorially at her mom. "Even Wendy's still faking it. Though, I can't blame her. Who the hell would know what to do with these hooligans?"

"Certainly not me." I grin. "I always wondered if your mom was superhuman."

"Girl, I still wonder that," Winnie says through a laugh, but when Wendy calls her over to the oven, she gives my shoulder one last gentle squeeze. "Looks like I'm being beckoned back to food duty. Talk to you later."

I nod then, putting my hands to my hips and then my pockets and then crossing them over my chest when neither of those feels right. For two months, I've done nothing but hold stuff. Bottles, babies, toys. My hands don't know how to just hang anymore.

I spot Remy again as he moves to his mother to give her a quick hug. And when he turns around with a heart-stopping smile and scans his siblings and their significant others, it's all over.

He spots Izzy in Rachel's arms and doesn't hesitate to steal her.

"No way, Rach, this is my girl. I always have dibs," he says, and Rachel gives him the stink eye but also grins at his dramatics.

For the first time since I got here, I start to relax a little. But when he meets my eyes over the top of Izzy's head and winks at me, all relaxation flees again.

How can one man whom I've just started to really get to know again make my heart race so much?

TWENTY-EIGHT

Remy

My sister's house is bustling with the entire Winslow gang, but my attention is pulled across the room to where Maria stands in the kitchen. Her eyes are busy keeping track of Izzy as Ty's fiancée Rachel holds her, and although Maria looks a little out of sorts, she also looks fucking beautiful.

Damn, I've missed her.

Even though it kind of feels like a lifetime, it's only been two long days since I've loved on Maria and Izzy. The urge to scratch at least one of the itches is nearly uncontrollable. That said, I'd wager it'd be slightly inappropriate to scratch things with Maria in mixed company, so I swoop in and steal Izzy from Rachel instead.

Rachel voices her annoyance with me, albeit more amused than anything, but Maria *smiles*.

And the small shadow of her happiness makes the victory of my acquisition feel even more significant. I wink at her over Izzy's head, snuggling her sweet baby smell so deep it'll stay with me forever, and then cross the room to the woman I haven't stopped thinking about since I left her apartment.

"Package acquired," I say under my breath, spinning around to push my hips into the counter next to Maria like I'm some kind of international spy.

"You're an absolute weirdo," she replies, crossing her arms over her chest in an attempt to seem disinterested. She's out of luck, though, because the angle of her body and the twinkle in her perfect eyes say otherwise.

Which is probably why Jude picks that very moment to turn into a fucking child and stick a wet finger in my ear. My brothers are the best in the world—bar none—at ruining a moment.

"Dammit, Jude," I gripe, shifting out from under the power of his wet willy and passing the baby to Maria, so I don't have to multitask while I'm kicking his ass.

"Boys!" my mom shouts, putting a hand against my chest just as Jude skirts out the back door and sticks his tongue out at me like he's eight years old again. On a sigh, Wendy glances from the door her youngest son just escaped out of, back to me, her eldest son, and rolls her eyes. "You know he's not worth the effort. Toddlers never understand rationale or reasoning."

My sister and even Jude's wife Sophie laugh at that, and I instantly decide my mother is right and let Jude act like an idiot alone.

Maria is waiting where I left her, but now, she's wearing a smirk. "Even after all these years, I see nothing has changed."

"Jude has a wife instead of a bedroom that smells like dirty old gym socks, but that's about it."

Her smirk morphs into a big smile. "I like it. It feels…familiar or something."

"Uncle Remy, is this Maria?"

I look down to find Lexi standing there, looking up at us, but Maria is already quick to introduce herself.

"You must be Lexi," she says, and my niece holds out her hand.

"Yes. I'm Lexi. Nice to meet you."

"The feeling is mutual." Maria engages in the handshake with the hand that isn't holding Izzy and glances at me with an amused gleam in her eye. "I've heard so much about you. I'm glad we finally get to meet."

"You knew my uncle Remy when you were in high school," Lex says, but it's not a question. "I saw you guys in his yearbook. Is this your baby, Izzy?" she asks, a true question this time, as she stands on her tippy-toes to peek at the baby in Maria's arms.

"Lexi, this is Izzy. Izzy, this is my niece, Lexi."

Lexi's smile nearly consumes her face as she gazes at a now-sleeping Izzy, and I swear, it pulls at my heartstrings like a motherfucker.

"She's so tiny. And cute."

"That she is," I agree.

After a few quiet moments of staring at Izzy, Lexi's gaze homes in on Maria and me again. Her brow is furrowed as she glances between us, but whatever she's thinking, whatever she's about to say, is stopped in its tracks by my mother's voice.

"Come on, guys! Time to get your grub on!" my mom shouts over the din of several conversations. "Appetizers in the living room!"

"Gotta go!" Lex says, her mind now focused on the food.

Which, comically, is a lot like her uncle Ty. The call of appetizers is all he needs to hear to grab Rachel and head in the direction of the living room, stopping briefly at the back door to shout for Howard, Wes, and Jude on the back deck.

Winnie, my mom, Sophie, and Daisy grab the last few dishes filled with appetizers and follow. And Flynn brings up the rear with a giggling twin in each arm.

"Here," I prompt Maria, reaching for Izzy. "Let me take her. That way, you can eat."

"What about you?" she protests. "Aren't you hungry?"

I shake my head. "I can wait. I was grazing a little before you got here until I got slapped out of the way."

Maria laughs. "Ah, I see."

I grab Izzy underneath the armpits and pull her close to my chest, shooing Maria in the direction of the living room. "Go on. You know how the Winslows are. You need to get in there before the locusts destroy it all."

"Says the man who was eating it before it was even ready."

"Exactly, Ria. They're worse than me, and that's saying something."

She giggles again, finally skirting past me and heading into the living room after the crowd. I follow behind with Izzy in my arms. She's still calm, but her eyes are slightly open, and I give her a conspiratorial look, asking her to keep my secret as I stare at Maria's ass unabashedly.

It's round and thick and makes the perfect heart shape in her skinny-style jeans. *Fuck me, she's sexy.*

Izzy coos a little and wiggles, and I'm convinced she's trying to spill the beans. I hold her closer and whisper softly in her ear. "Come on, Iz. Don't rat me out. We don't want to scare her off." I change my accent to my best version of an Australian in the Irwin family. "She's a flighty bird, right? Gotta be extra careful with this one, mate."

Izzy just stares at me, in the way that she does when she's content and trying to understand the world around her. It might be because of the funny change in my voice, but I like to think it's because she understands exactly what I'm saying and agrees.

By the time we make it into the living room, three-quarters of the food is gone, and Howard is full swing into his infamous word association game. No doubt, Ty's put him up to it again.

I take a seat on the arm of the couch with Iz, keeping one eye to Maria as she grabs a plate at the end of the TV table and starts to fill it up with food.

"Yard," Howard says, to which Rachel immediately replies, "Work."

Flynn laughs the loudest, remarking ironically, "I guess we never have to worry about Ty and Rachel moving out of the city."

His face is relaxed and bright, and I'll be damned if he isn't a completely different man from the one I knew before Daisy. He's still quiet, sure, but he's also lighter and quicker to laugh. He's *happy.* It's written all over him.

Maria surprises me by holding a plate out in front of me, filled with all my favorite foods.

"What's this?" I ask in a stupid whisper.

She laughs softly before sitting down next to me. "I fixed you a plate so you don't miss out." She mimes what I imagine is supposed to be a locust, and I smile so big my face hurts.

"Hotel," Howard prompts Rachel, everyone eagerly paying attention other than me. I'm focused on the fall of Maria's hair as she looks down at her plate and picks up a mini quiche.

"Carlyle," Rachel responds in the background, and I have to admit, even without my focus, just the sound of that word makes the hairs at the back of my neck stand on end.

"Don't go spilling all of our sexy secrets, Rach," Ty chimes in, and Rachel winks at him.

"In my defense, *you* are the one who chose the Carlyle, not me."

The fucking *Carlyle*.

It's been a hell of a long time since Charlotte took off on the day of our wedding and left me to smash half the breakables in my groom's suite at the Carlyle Hotel, but it's something of a core memory. It's a day that shaped and polished me into the person I am now.

A day that, no matter what else happens in my life, or how right I know she was to call it off, haunts me. It reminds me of parts of myself I'm not proud of. Of emotions that have a long-standing history of making me feel out of control.

Winnie notices my face and steps forward to take Izzy from me and pass her to our mother. She walks up to me then—already engaged and ready to play peacemaker.

I don't want to do it; I want to let it go. But before I can stop myself, I'm butting into the game to ask the exact thing I know I shouldn't. Fucking with Ty over the whole *left-at-the-altar thing* has evidently consumed the dark humor part of my soul.

"Did you say the Carlyle?"

Rachel glances at Howard, and then Ty, and then back to me before tentatively nodding. "Um, yeah. Why?"

The room is almost painfully silent now, and Maria is looking at me with questions in her eyes, but now that I've opened this can of worms, I can only see one way to close it.

Rachel is uncertain, glancing again to Ty for help or advice or direction—I'm sure none of this is making sense to her—and he groans, piping up to explain.

"I took Rachel to the Carlyle for a week when we first got together, okay?"

"The Carlyle?" I ask, just as Jude lets out a half groan, half laugh, his mind torn between being amused and concerned over what's brewing.

"Yeah, dude."

"Seriously, Ty?" is all I can say.

"Seriously what, Rem?" he snaps back. "I mean, are we just supposed to ignore one of the nicest hotels in New York for the rest of our lives because you've got a bad memory there?"

"What's going on?" Rachel whispers, to which Winnie steps forward and grabs her arm with a shake of her head.

"A bad memory?" I challenge, my voice edging toward angry. I mean, it's all fun and jokes until he starts to act like he wasn't there to witness the whole huge thing.

"Yeah. So, your wedding crashed and burned there a fucking decade and a half ago. It's not like it was the hotel's fault! They even refunded some of the money!"

A warm hand settles on my back, the scent of Maria enveloping me from behind. I can feel the flow of her comfort as she infuses it into me with all of her strength. She thinks I'm upset about Charlotte, about the wedding, about stupid shit that doesn't matter to me anymore. Everyone does, honestly. But it's so much fucking deeper than that.

Still, the last thing I want is to upset her or make her nervous that I might overreact in some way. I force myself to relax.

She must feel the tension leaving my muscles, because the pressure on my back shifts then, turning into a comforting rub.

"You're right, Ty," I admit. "It's not the hotel's fault. Not a big deal."

Ty's eyes widen to the point of bursting, and the rest of the room takes a collective breath. It's a little alarming how much they all expected me to flip out, and even more disturbing that if it weren't for Maria looking on, they probably wouldn't have been wrong.

Fuck. That is not the man I want to be. Maybe it was the man I was okay with being for a long time, but I'm not okay with that now. I don't want to model that for the next generation, and I certainly don't want that to be what I'm known for by the people I love the most.

Howard, the smart bastard, goes back to the game, pulling everyone's attention away from my outburst, and I decide to head out onto my sister's back deck for a minute. I just need a second to breathe. A gulp of air to figure out why on earth I reacted at all.

Ty, for once in his life, is right. It was ages ago. I'm over it. *I've been over it.* Charlotte is married to Lexi's biological father. And yet, still, I can't seem to find the place inside myself that doesn't go back to that day when I hear something related to it. Even my long-running joke of busting Ty about it has to be rooted somewhere, right? The normal thing to do would be to let it fucking go.

I lean into the rail to think, and the door cracks open behind me. I'm expecting it to be my mom or my sister, so when Maria calls out to me, I'm surprised.

"If you want me to go back inside, I will. Just wanted to make sure you're okay."

I jump and turn, standing up straight to face her. Her expression is one I can't stand—cautious and unsure of her place out here.

I have to fix it straightaway.

"Please, no. Stay. I'm fine. I promise."

She steps forward then, coming to stand next to me and mimicking my position with her ass at the rail. It takes several moments of silence before either one of us says anything, but when she does, I'm reminded swiftly while I always enjoyed Maria's company so much.

"So…how about the hotel that rhymes with shmar-myle?" she asks with a secret smile. "You give them a bad Yelp review or something?"

I burst out laughing with a shake of my head, pulling her into my side and then swaying her back and forth like we're just a couple of teenagers again.

Finally, I finish my laugh with a groan. "I like Howard, really, but his stupid word game always seems to be trouble."

She raises her eyebrows, and I roll my eyes before I continue. "Honestly, it's really not about what everyone thinks it is at all. It's not the *Carlyle*. And it's not the wedding or Charlotte or any of that shit. I'm more than over it. The only reason I usually even react is to bust Ty's balls, but today just caught me off guard and felt a little different. Maybe it's going back in time, spending all this time with you, but the past feels a hell of a lot fresher than normal, you know?"

She nods then, her face awash in understanding. "I get it. Boy, do I get it. Seeing Winnie today all grown up… God, Rem, she's really something. And it just makes me think of her and Isabella as kids—going everywhere with us, doing everything we did. Winnie's life is so vibrant, and I just wish…"

She doesn't even have to finish for me to know exactly what she's going to say. "I know."

The fact of the matter is, Isabella got fucked and so did Maria. They don't get the futures that Winnie and I still have a shot at. They don't get a future together at all.

A single tear falls down Maria's cheek, and she hurries to wipe it away while I pull her into a hug. "God, Ria," I whisper into her hair, hugging her tighter into my embrace. "I'm so sorry."

"So am I," she murmurs back, and I find myself hugging her a little tighter. Everything just feels better with her in my arms.

A feminine throat clears at the door, and both of our heads come up as Maria pulls out of my arms. I'm fairly certain I'm shooting laser beams in Winnie's direction because her eyes are light, and the corner of her mouth is lifted into a mild but contrite smirk.

"So sorry to interrupt, but Izzy is a little fussy and I wanted to make sure it'd be okay if I gave her a bottle. I already found them in her diaper bag, so you don't have to move a muscle."

Maria jumps forward to go in, but I stop her with a gentle hand to the elbow. She looks back at me with drawn eyebrows, but I don't look at her—not yet. Instead, I focus on my sister.

"Actually, Win, I thought I might ask you a favor. Do you think you'd be interested in keeping Izzy tonight?"

Maria's head whips back toward me, but again, I keep my eyes on my sister, whose face has turned downright Cat Who Ate the Cream at this point.

"A whole night with that sweet baby?" She's over the damn moon. "Are you kidding? Both Lex and I would flipping love that! Plus, I'm sure I can convince my boss to give me the morning off to give you time to pick her up," she says with a wink.

Ah, the convenience of having your husband be your boss.

"I have all the baby stuff I need, too, so you don't need to worry. While Daisy was looking for a nanny, I kept the twins twice a week."

When Maria looks at me with uncertainty in her eyes, I lean down and whisper into her ear, "Just trust me, okay? There's a reason for this. And if anyone can take good care of our girl, it's Winnie."

Maria leans back to search my gaze. She's still a little uncertain, I can see it in every fucking line of her perfect body, but she doesn't peep a word of protest. Instead, she nods and then proceeds to rush past Winnie and into the house, no doubt to squeeze the life out of poor little Izzy for another thirty minutes or so.

I know it might seem like a big ask, having Maria go a whole night without Izzy, but it's important. Necessary. This much, I know for sure.

Winnie raises her eyebrows and waggles them after the door shuts behind Maria. "Well, well, well."

I shake my head, smiling slightly. "Shut up."

"Oh, don't worry. I will shut up. For now. For now, I'll go in there and wrestle that baby from Maria's arms so you can do…whatever it is…that you're planning."

"This isn't about putting the moves on her, Win. This is about Isabella."

Winnie's eyes shutter then, remembering her vibrant childhood friend and the tragic news I shared with her not too long ago. Her whisper is solemn. "Oh hell, I didn't even think. Did we… God, I hope we didn't make her feel—"

I shake my head again, cutting her off before she rakes herself over the metaphorical coals. "Win, it's not something you did or even have control over. It's all the things we get to do that she never will again. It's this conversation, right here, that she can't have with her annoying little sister anymore. And she needs a night to try to work through all those things she's been burying deep."

Winnie nods, wiping a tiny tear as it forms in the corner of her eye. "I have a bottle of really good tequila. Take it with you when you go."

"Thanks, sis." I give her shoulder a squeeze on my way to the back door.

"Remy?" she calls, stopping me before I can get there.

"Yeah?"

"A word of caution from personal experience?"

I wait, my brows lifting marginally.

"The song is right, big bro." She grins like a damn devil. "Tequila really does make the clothes fall off."

"You realize that is the absolute last thing I want to hear from my baby sister," I grumble as I head inside, but she's quick to get the last word before the door shuts behind me.

"Doesn't make it any less true!"

TWENTY-NINE

Remy

Maria snags the bottle of tequila by the neck again, tips it back and swallows a huge, shot-like gulp. I watch her sleek, tanned throat work around the liquid and shake my head subtly to clear it.

She's so fucking beautiful, sometimes I have to remind myself to breathe. To blink. To stand upright and basically exist. I honestly don't think I've ever known someone whose whole being shines as brightly as hers. There's beauty at the surface and underneath, and then under that—that's where she keeps the pain.

She wipes the excess tequila off her lips and closes her eyes, humming as the liquid burns its way down her throat.

After we got back to her empty apartment, it took about an hour or so for her to get comfortable taking shots. But now that she's committed, she's gone full bore. We're nearing the halfway point of the bottle with no slowing down in sight. *Shit, I might have to DoorDash another one if we keep this up much longer.*

I take the bottle back, needing a distraction of some sort, and take another pull.

It's the most godawful straight liquor ever made, I swear, but I'll do anything to make this woman feel at ease tonight. Ironically, it's the same damn liquor I utilized several nights in a row after breaking up with Maria in high school.

I've never liked the shit since.

On the plus side, if I'm passed out in the bathroom, my dick will be much more likely to get the memo. This isn't about him, much to his dismay. This is about Maria. About her sister. About the grief she so obviously made herself bury when she lost her.

The body is tricky with emotion. It holds it and stores it and wears it even when we don't realize. There's a reason and a need for a purge, so that we can function without the weight.

Maria was never a drinker in high school—and though we were only in high school, that was a rarity. As I found out tonight, however, it seems that part of her never really changed. Her first glance at the bottle when I explained that my sister was going to watch Izzy and we were going to imbibe was not one of a woman who felt completely comfortable with the plan.

But I didn't push, and within a minute of consideration, all of that swung in the other direction. She grabbed the bottle from my hand, reaching back to grab me with her other, and we left Winnie's house with determination.

The ride to her apartment was made mostly in silence, but I can't blame her for that. Tapping into a part of yourself you've kept hidden for this long is beyond scary. You just never know if you're going to be able to stuff it all back inside.

Upon arrival at her place, we quickly found home bases on the floor in front of the couch and started swigging. Up until now, that's felt like enough. We haven't chatted or delved deep or even mentioned her sister's name. She's been dealing with her emotions privately, and I can respect—

"You know the last thing my sister said to me before she got on that helicopter?"

I pop my eyes open, the unexpected beginning enough to scare a man sober. I'm glad she's talking—so fucking thankful, honestly—I just never imagined this would be the place we *started*.

I shake my head, murmuring only a soft "No" into the space between us. She nods then, smiling long enough to steal the bottle back and tip it for another swig.

"She said, 'I'm pretty sure Orlando Bloom is going to be at this party. If you send your tits with me, I'll have him sign.'"

I blink one, two, three…sixteen times. And then, I burst out laughing. Out of the myriad of things I expected her sister to have said in their last moments before her death, this would come in last place.

"You always expect it'll be something deep, you know? Something with meaning you can take with you in their absence, something to apply to your life." She giggles hard. "And all I have are Orlando Bloom and my tits."

"Well, I can't speak for Orlando Bloom personally since I've never met the guy. But I have seen your tits, and Ria, they're not a bad thing to be left with."

She laughs again, and I can't help but smile as she snorts. She's in a deep vortex of messy feelings, but I'm glad to be here with her.

"I honestly forgot how funny your sister was," I admit then. "But she was always making me laugh when we were kids. You both were."

"We loved to cut up, that's true. Oliver always said he was going to record us and submit it to a stand-up comedy competition." She rolls her eyes. "He never did, obviously, because he was a man, and, no offense, but as a whole, your follow-through isn't the greatest."

I put up both my hands in surrender. "None taken."

"We were supposed to start doing Lamaze together—all three of us," she says with a shake of her head. Her gaze is longing and distant as she reaches through memories she's long since locked away. "Man, I'm sure that would have been the talk of the town. A sight to see, really. I can just imagine all of New York society gossiping about Oliver and his harem." She cackles. "He was so conservative. He would have died."

Her face straightens suddenly at the unsavory play on words, and my eyes widen in return. She bursts into laughter then. Completely unbound, uncontrolled, *One Flew Over the Cuckoo's Nest*-style hilarity.

It's a great sound. One I know is laced with pain, but necessary. If she doesn't get it out, that's what will be festering inside her.

When her laughter slows, she takes another pull of tequila and dives right into another story. I make sure the bottle finds its way back to upright on the carpet and listen intently.

"The day she got married, she actually freaked out so badly, she almost made me put on the dress and go in her place." She bites her bottom lip and lies down on the floor, staring at the ceiling as she talks. "I had to remind her that we weren't twins, and that I was pretty sure Oliver would know the difference."

I don't cut in to tell her that's how Jude and Sophie met, after she switched places with her twin sister, Bella. I don't cut in to say anything at all. Because Maria is there and, at the same time, she's not.

She's where she needs to be, years ago, in a room with her living, breathing, crying, laughing, loving sister.

"It was just stupid cold feet. I couldn't have handpicked a better match for her—a better brother-in-law, really. He was always the soft support we needed."

"I bet he was a great guy."

She snorts. "He had to be a great guy to put up with the two of us. Every Monday when we got to the office, both of us spent at least half an hour complaining about being back in heels. The same complaints, *every* week, and he listened every single time. Never told us to do something about it or wear flats or asked us to stop. Just listened and laughed while the two of us bitched and bitched."

I smile. "I bet it was worth the hours of entertainment."

"We were miserable, complaining shrews. But he didn't care."

I get it immediately. I get it so much, that I find myself grieving for a guy I never met. Because looking at Maria right here, right now, I wouldn't care either. I'd listen to her and Isabella complain all damn day if they wanted to.

"Although we bitched a lot, my sister took good care of Oliver. Always made shit fun. I know for a fact that she surprised him with nothing but an overcoat on more than one occasion."

My eyebrows rise and my eyes widen.

"How do I know, you ask? Ah, well, one time, I just so happened to be in the office with him when she busted in and ripped off that overcoat, revealing her *whole* self, bare as the day she was born."

"Oh man," I remark with a laugh.

Maria giggles. "Oliver jumped up so fast, I swear he set a land speed record."

"To try to cover her?"

"Ha! No way. He was like the freaking Flash with how quickly he got me out the door of his office and dropped the blinds." She smiles and smacks her hands together in a speedy gesture, remembering. "It was the one, singular time in my adult life that I ever wished to be married. That I ever felt sadness for not going the traditional route. That I mourned the house and the white picket fence and the two and a half kids."

My smile cracks a little, her sadness becoming my own.

"But I never experienced anything remotely close to what they had. I never had the *rush to the office in nothing but an overcoat* kind of feeling for someone, you know?"

I nod. *Fuck, but do I know.*

She shrugs. "I was content anyway. I almost never even thought I was missing out. But now, I can see… Now, I see all the things about living every day like you have no more left, and they make a whole lot of sense."

I swallow hard against telling her something like *it's okay, you've done what you were meant to* or platitudes equally as dismissive to her feelings right now. It's in my nature to fix things, but as in this case, some things really aren't meant to be fixed.

"What about you?" she asks quietly. "You never thought about it again…you know…after Charlotte?"

I shake my head.

"Do you still think about her?"

The question almost catches me off guard, but it's not hard to understand why she might think I would. Just tonight, I acted in a way that suggests I'm still harboring those demons. But the truth is, none of my demons has a single thing to do with Charlotte. If anyone deserves to know what really goes on inside me, it's Maria.

"Charlotte and I were not meant to be. I know that now, and, to be quite frank, I knew it then."

Her eyes widen slightly, and she sits up, turning her back to the couch again so she can face me, and I sigh, running a hand through my hair.

"The only thing that haunts me about what happened with her is the way I acted." I pause. "I've never told anyone this, but Charlotte only did the leaving because I forced her to."

She sits up straighter, suddenly looking more sober than I'd like. "What do you mean?"

"She wanted me to move to California with her. She got a job offer, a major opportunity. I said no. Me or the job." I scoff. "A fucking ultimatum." I shake my head. "What I didn't understand then that I do now is that I wanted her to *need* me, and she didn't. It's a stupid thing, wanting someone to need you like that—I get that now. Someone can need you around without having to depend on you." I shrug. "Back then, I just didn't know the difference, and I guess she did."

Maria studies me closely, and I turn to glance out the dark window just so I don't have to watch as she does it.

"We weren't right for each other at all because it wasn't easy. And it's never been easy with anyone else." I laugh. "And that's the tale of my long-standing run of bachelordom."

"Worked out pretty good for me." Maria smiles at me. "I don't know if I'd be surviving without your help at this point."

"Crazy," I remark, making her eyebrows pull together.

"What?"

"It's crazy..." I repeat, studying her beautiful face just a little bit closer, "... how a favor for you can feel like it's doing so much for me."

She stares at me for the longest time, her eyes intently searching mine, trying to find something I don't quite understand. She does this for so long that I honestly start to wonder if my words came out wrong.

But then, she surprises the hell out of me in one fell swoop.

Mouth to mine, Maria *kisses* me.

THIRTY

Maria

I don't know what came over me, but between one breath and the next, I went from a woman thinking about kissing Remy to a woman who *is* kissing Remy.

He's shocked at first, his lips parting out of pure surprise, but when I coax my tongue inside his mouth, I feel him give in to the moment.

He tastes like tequila and Remy and all the things that make me feel good inside.

"Maria," he whispers and slides his hands into my hair. His mouth has become as determined as mine, and the first inklings of arousal start to make themselves known by the ache that's formed between my legs.

I just…want to be with him. Feel him. Taste him. Touch him. Do all the things I've been thinking about doing since the morning we were interrupted.

"I want you," I say to him, the alcohol flowing through my veins making it easy for me to just tell him how I feel. "I want you," I say again, and this time, I know he understands.

And the heat in his eyes tells me we're on the same page.

It doesn't take long before we're off the floor and stumbling down the hallway, our persistent mouths kissing the entire time.

The bedroom spins around me as Remy turns me toward the bed and falls forward, taking us both down onto the mattress with a bounce. His lips stay firm on mine, and the smell of his cologne is like a warm blanket around me.

We're both so different than we were back in the day, and yet, it feels so, so familiar.

I'm feeling needy and anxious and like Remy being inside me is the lone answer to all my questions and prayers. Like some part of him will fill some part of me the instant we come together.

Rationally, I know that's probably not true, and realistically, I know I've had way more than my share of tequila. But with God as my witness, if having sex with Remington Winslow isn't the true desire of my heart, I've obviously never experienced such a thing.

Because I want him badly, wholly, so fucking completely that my limbs feel tingly all over.

The moment we entered my apartment together with that bottle of liquor and no baby, I knew this was where we'd end up.

I knew that the draw to him was too strong, the itch to feel him against me too much to ignore. And the way he spoke about all the help he's been giving me—as though it's been a gift to him—sealed the deal.

Now, I'm ready…eager. I want to feel pure, unadulterated pleasure, and I want to feel it without regret, even if it's only for a moment.

Remy pushes up off me enough to unbutton the front of my shirt, and I suck in a breath at the lust in his eyes. It's potent and so, so obvious.

Regardless, as the cool air of the bedroom first hits my bare stomach, a wave of uncertainty rolls through me. Not about the decision to fall into bed with Remy—the thing about knowing him the way I do is that I know he'll handle me with care. He has the history of my virginity and the many times following as a track record.

But my body is very much different from the way it was in high school—hell, it's different from how it was a year ago.

It's grown and nurtured a human, and it's lived the aftermath of little sleep, no help, and a much less consistent gym schedule.

My skin is marked and striped and doesn't sit quite the same over the flesh underneath. I know Remy isn't so shallow as to point out my less than peak condition, but I can't help but wonder in the back of my mind if he'll notice. If the mushy fat of my abdomen will feel off-putting against his wall of muscle.

I move my hand to cover the half-outie nature of my new belly button, and Remy, being as observant as he is, notices immediately.

A small hiccup of nerves sticks in my throat as I imagine him plying me with heady words about how perfect my body is when, to me, it's anything but.

Instead, though, he stays silent, only moving my hand to replace it with his own. I watch avidly as he studies the flesh there, moving his hand from one side to the other and then putting his lips to the skin. His words are only a whisper, a backup singer to the sweet kiss he places there. "You know, I still can't fucking believe I got to be a part of it. That Izzy, the Izzy I snuggle and rock and dance with, made a home in here for nine whole months. That she was happy and cozy and safe, and that I got to be there at the exact moment she chose to take a chance on the outside world."

My breath catches in my chest at the reverent way he speaks of both Izzy and the experience of her birth. I know she's a miracle, and I don't take that for granted. But I definitely take the role my body played in the whole thing for granted. *Definitely.*

Remy's dark head shifts then, his magical blue eyes coming up to meet mine and his smile climbing all the way to his eyes. "I swear, Ri. I think that elevator with you, watching you bring her into this world despite all the challenges you had…I think it's the best moment of my entire life."

"*Remy.*"

"It is. I've never felt anything like it, and I doubt I'll ever feel anything like it again." He smiles, closing his eyes and laying his forehead on my chest. "I close my eyes, and I can still see it. The moment you went to war with yourself—the moment you didn't know if you could do it or not—and won."

"You see all that just from looking at my stomach?"

"I see all that every time I look at you."

"Wow."

He chuckles. "Yeah. It's hard work living up to a superhero every second of the day."

I scoff. "Oh, please."

"A real-life Wonder Woman, Ria. That's you."

"Remy, stop it."

"Why?" he asks with a sly laugh. "Worried you're going to start to feel good about yourself? Worried you might realize your own power? Worried that if you really let go of everything else and just enjoy yourself with me right here, right now, you'll be ruined forever?"

"Honestly?"

He nods.

"All of the above."

"Do you want to do this with me?" he asks then. Blunt and unfiltered, his delivery leaves no room for dancing around the answer. "Because I can tell you, I want to do this with you. I want you, Maria. I want to feel you. Be with you. Be inside you. More than I've ever wanted to do anything with anyone."

My heart is beating so hard I swear it's shaking my rib cage, but I give it to him straight. When it comes to Remy and me and all my fantasies, not a single fucking one has started with me saying anything but, "Yes."

Remy doesn't say anything else aloud, but let me tell you, he definitely fucking says something.

Diving forward, he closes his lips over the pink lace of my thin bra, and my back arches dramatically off the bed. I can't even blame myself. At the very least, most women who birth a baby got it on approximately nine months ago. I mean, it's kind of part of the process.

But me? I haven't had sex in three years. Three. Years. I honestly can't even let the thought sit in my head too long or it'll make me pass out.

I've come pretty often thanks to my own pursuits, but the true nature of this partner activity has been lost on me for a while.

But I'm not lost now.

Holy *shit*, I'm not lost now. Remy knows how to make a woman feel found.

He moves carefully down my body to the button of my pants, undoing it with one hand while the other explores and caresses. His lips work over the skin of my stomach, and amazingly, I'm not feeling so self-conscious about it anymore.

Within a moment, my pants and panties are gone.

Remy's hands skate down the sides of my body and down the length of my legs until they close around my ankles and squeeze. My heart jumps as he spreads my thighs gently, placing my calves on his shoulders and looking at me bared in all my glory. His eyes are hungry, powerful. I can hardly control the shake of my hands as he leans forward and swipes just one single lick up the center of my heat.

Sweet merciful everything, I don't know if I'm going to survive this.

Because for as sweet and unassuming and helpful as Remy has been over the last week, he hasn't lost any of his intensity. Even in the peek of his smile and the light in his eyes, there's a darkness that lurks deep inside him. A side untapped, unchanneled, unchallenged. It's the steely quiet of his past and the abundant possibility of his future. He controls his destiny—that much is for sure. I just wish I weren't starting to feel like I'd be okay if he controlled mine too.

"Remy," I whisper, my whole body giving over to the feeling in one location.

The warmth and steady pressure of his tongue.

The soft certainty of his moves.

I can't think about anything else.

My initial instinct is to close my thighs around his head—to squeeze him like a vise to assure myself that he can't and won't escape.

But as always, Remy knows better than me, moving my thighs apart with the soft push of his hands and challenging me with a look that could ruin women forever—strong, determined brow, twinkling blue eyes, and the most enchanting curve of his perfect, soft lips.

"Leave them open, Ria. Give me room to work."

I nod then, feeling more confident in my ability now that I've been ordered to comply. I don't have a whole lot of Dom/sub-style daydreams, but I'll be damned if it doesn't feel really good to submit when the rest of your life is made up of decisions and responsibility.

Remy's tongue strokes and prods, and my stomach tightens with all the tension that's left the rest of my body. Languid and light, my limbs have given over to the feeling of nonexistence. I'm nothing but my clit right now—and the torturous rub of Remy's perfect fingertips at the pinnacle of my G-spot.

My head lolls back and my eyes feel heavy, overcome with sensation. I reach out to gather a chunk of Remy's perfect hair in my hand, and he hums a moan against me.

It feels like heaven—vibrating, pulsating, debilitating heaven.

"You taste so fucking good, Ria. I thought I'd forgotten, but now that I've felt you on my tongue again, I know I didn't. Best fucking pussy on the planet."

Okay, holy shit, that's some Grade A dirty talk.

I have to admit, his level of skill in that arena has changed a little since our teenage days. He was good then, but he was just a boy. Now, he's all man.

I don't want to come like this, though, with Remy all the way down there. I want to come with him inside me, his face in my hands, his eyes staring into my own.

"Rem," I murmur, the softness of my voice the only volume I'm able to manage. "I want you inside me."

He sucks harder on my clit, pushing my back up off the bed and forcing my eyes to roll back. It's all I can do to hold off the rolling wave of pleasure pulsing at the base of my spine.

"Remy!" I cry, just as he climbs up my body and covers mine with his. I don't know how anything happens from that moment to the next, but before I can complain again, he's inside me, a condom in place on his cock.

I can't exactly see the protection from this angle, but I can feel it. And as much as I appreciate his care with safety, I fucking *hate* it. Loathe that I can't feel him skin-on-skin without the risk of conceiving a baby the traditional way.

All that thankfully flies out of my head when he starts to move, in and out of me with his elbows on the bed at the sides of my head.

The feel of his thighs on mine is one I'm not likely to forget anytime soon. It might be a weird thing to focus on, but aside from the actual penetration, there's nothing to me that feels more intimate.

Remy moves his thumbs over my face, then tilting my chin up gently to gain my attention. He makes short work of locking his gaze with my own, and I take even less time to get lost in it.

Vivid, swirling blue, his eyes are the kind that tell stories of their own. Of pain and loss and triumph and joy. Their beauty isn't just surface-level—they're vibrantly multidimensional.

He groans richly, his head falling forward to meet our foreheads as his pace slows and deepens.

My throat dries out and my back arches and my eyes fall closed without my permission. I don't…I don't think I've ever felt anything like this. The need, the build, the perfect, exquisitely torturous pace.

Being connected with Remington Winslow is an experience like no other.

Being reconnected with him over half my life later is an experience beyond description.

"Rem," I whisper, knowing with intense clarity that I'm oh so close to losing myself over the edge. "Remy," I repeat, forming the only word I can.

He nods against my forehead, putting his lips to mine to whisper back, "Me too."

His tongue flicks out to lick across mine, and the taste of tequila on him is markedly better than the stuff that comes straight from the bottle. I moan, and even though I didn't think it was possible, Remy's stroke deepens—intensifies.

It's all I can do to exist now, the more basic functions of my throat and eyes and the speed of my thumping heart giving themselves completely over to the moment.

I don't know if it's because I haven't had sex in so long or if the sex is just that powerful, but the clench of my orgasm is so strong, I swear on all that's holy I pass out for the briefest of moments.

I, Maria Baros, temporarily left my body and watched over it from above while it absorbed the most pleasure it has ever experienced in this lifetime.

Remy's groan moments later is an indication that he's finished the race as well, but I'm ashamed to admit, I don't have the mental capacity to bear witness to nearly enough detail. I can't tell you the position of his face or the shift in his eyes or even the parting of his lips. All I can tell you is that I want nothing more than to do it again.

Over and over and over again, if I'm honest.

But I'm merely a passenger on the journey of tonight, and my body's reached the point of exhaustion. I can't move or breathe or chat.

All I can do is fall asleep, the feel of Remy still inside me and his weight atop me only the faintest of details. Exhaustion trumps embarrassment; bone-weary trumps boning.

Tomorrow, though, after I've slept, I have the distinct feeling I'll feel differently. Very, *very* differently.

THIRTY-ONE

Remy

At first, I don't know what wakes me up, but when I look at the clock on the nightstand, I realize it's nearing three in the morning.

But then, I know *exactly* why I'm awake. Maria's naked body is stretched over mine, her eyes lax with sleep, and my cock, well, it feels like he's harder than he's ever been.

It's only been a few hours since I was inside her, since I felt the way she pulsed around me as she gave in to her pleasure, saw the look in her eyes when she came.

But fuck, I feel insane with the need to do it again.

Her hips shift in a way that makes her bare pussy press against my thigh, and it does nothing for my current state of arousal.

I know I shouldn't wake her up. I know I should let her sleep.

But what I know and what I need are apparently two different things.

"Maria," I whisper toward her and reach out to brush her hair out of her face.

She stirs a little, and I lean down to press my lips to hers. Gentle at first, I coax her mouth with soft, brushing kisses at the corners. But I'm more than thrilled when her eyes flutter and her lips start to move with mine.

I should probably feel like an asshole, I know, but I can't find it in me to care about anything else but being with her again.

She moans into my mouth and our kiss deepens, and any inkling of willpower I might have had is shattered like a hammer to glass.

Her eyes are open now, staring directly into mine, and I'm too far gone on this woman to beat around the bush. "I need you," I tell her. "Fuck, I need to be inside you again."

"Yes," she whimpers and grinds herself against my thigh.

I don't know if it's the remnants of tequila still running through our veins, but we're acting on instinct. On raw, pure, unadulterated need.

It's all I can do to keep some control, to not attack her body with mine and put my mouth and tongue and hands and cock in every fucking place I can find. It's insanity. It's consuming. And it's fucking intense.

I pull her body over mine, and she sits up so that her legs are straddling my hips and her hands are pressed against my chest.

Her dark hair falls forward and her eyes are hooded and her lips are parted, and this is, hands down, the sexiest fucking sight I've ever seen in my life. I wish I had it in me to slow it down, to savor each second of this vision, of this perfect fucking view of her on top of me, but I can't.

I'm shocked I even find it in me to don a condom.

But the name of this game is rush-to-get-inside-her-before-I-fucking-explode, so that's exactly what I do. No pausing, no uncertainty, I am a man driven by only need.

I fill her up then, driving my hips upward to fill her with my cock inch-by-motherfucking-inch, and fuck me, it feels so good, I have to shut my eyes on a groan for the briefest of moments.

She moans and her head falls back, and the movement pushes her breasts out in a way that I have to reach up to grip them in my hands.

Her hips move then, her body giving in to the pleasure that sits before us.

"Yes," I nearly growl as I watch her in action. Watch her make herself feel good. Watch her ride me in a way that's hotter, sexier, more mind-blowing than any fantasy my mind has ever been able to come up with.

I don't know what the consequences of the morning will bring, but I know I won't regret this.

I know this because, even as I can feel her around me, feel the way she pulses with each thrust of my cock, feel the impending climax this will bring, I know this won't be enough.

I don't know if it'll ever be enough.

THIRTY-TWO

Maria

I startle at the sound of two sharp buzzes from my nightstand, my eyes flicking open dramatically before closing again in an instant.

Ugh, gah. Why is it so freaking bright?

I rub at my eyes then, willing them to work and adjust as I open them to small slivers and take stock of the room.

The covers on my bed are on but disheveled, and the curtains I normally close are wide open. Hence, the overbearing sunlight, I suppose.

My head feels like it weighs approximately one million pounds, and my stomach turns over on itself more than once. Several city salt trucks must have dumped their loads on my tongue too.

Tequila. Yuck.

I shift slightly again before coming to the realization that I have no fucking clothes on whatsoever, and then I glance to my left before doing a double take.

My gasp is audible. "Oh, holy shit," I whisper, my gaze snagging on a sleeping—also nude—Remy.

He's not even under the blanket, for goodness' sake.

Without taking my eyes off him—okay, *without taking my eyes off his penis*—I hold the comforter to my chest with one hand and reach back for my phone on its dock charger with the other.

It pops off the magnet easily, but I have to bring it fully into my vision—directly between myself and Remy's *member*—in order to look at it. I mean, *damn.* That beautiful, giant thing was inside me last night.

Twice, my mind reminds me.

My breathing escalates at just the thought. Evidently, despite my very best intentions and my drunken, orgasm-blurred confidence of last night, I'm actually *not* emotionally prepared to handle the situation like a full-blown adult.

Oh my God! Remy and I slept together last night. But, like, without the sleeping. Holy, holy shit.

My mind continues to taunt me, reminding me of last night's events in flashes of visuals that are most definitely NSFW.

His head between my legs as he sucked and licked and tasted me.

The heady look in his eyes when he slid himself inside me.

The way he practically growled "I need to be inside you again" when he woke me up in the middle of the night.

It's all so much and too much at the same time, and I force my vision to tunnel on my phone once again as a distraction.

"Oh no," I mutter, a new text message notification only adding to my anxiety.

Any message from Claudia this early is the first sign of bad news, but when I tap the screen to read its contents, things only get worse.

Claudia: So, I think I forgot to tell you last night that I got the showing rescheduled to this morning. 8:00 a.m. sharp.

Eight a.m.? I glance frantically at the time. *It's almost forty after seven right now!*

The Blakely family isn't one you just *cancel* on twice. The Blakely family owns a third of the available freaking real estate in Nassau County! Getting in on the ground floor of their wanting to expand their portfolio in Manhattan is a once-in-a-lifetime opportunity.

And Conrad Blakely isn't the type of man that tolerates bullshit.

Claudia has hung me out to dry with them twice now. Actually, three times, really! Because anytime anyone overshares about the shits, it counts for double.

I jump from the bed, thoughts of both termination and murder swirling in a completely psychotic mix inside me. Oh yes. A brutal, torturous, messy murder. Guantanamo Bay will have nothing on me when I get my hands on Claudia after this.

I'm never going to make it on time, and if I do, I'm going to look like I just got out of an intense laundry spin cycle.

"Shit! Shit!" I yell, scrambling from one side of the room to the other without even focusing on anything. I don't know where to go first, what to do.

At the sounds of my frantic voice, Remy sits up ramrod straight in bed, and a whole other wave of panic washes over me. His…his penis…it's sitting up straight too.

Okay, universe, one crisis at a time, please!

THIRTY-THREE

Remy

Sleep sticks to my eyes as I force them to focus on the blur of Maria as she runs back and forth from one side of the room to the other, shouting expletives as if it's her main goal in life to use every single one of them.

It'd be cute, honestly, on any other day, but after the way last night ended, I'm not sure this is the best sign.

"What's wrong?" I ask, jumping from the bed and hurrying after her. She doesn't answer, instead turning on her heel again and changing directions with a very random sock in her hand.

"Ria. Hey, what's going on?" I plead again as she zooms by, the wind from her speed creating a breeze against my face.

"My assistant is a curdled cheese bag!" she shouts nonsensically, and my eyebrows pull together.

"Your assistant is…a what now?"

"She's an idiot!" she clarifies, whizzing past me yet again. "And so am I for not firing her before now!"

"Okay, Ri. Relax. What's going on? How can I help?"

"Unless you're an expert in time travel, you can't! I *have* to be at a showing in Midtown in fifteen minutes. Fifteen minutes!" she shouts with a hysterical cackle. "Superman himself could swoop down and pick me up, and I'm *still* never going to make it there in time."

She takes off, and I head back to the side of the bed to slide my boxer briefs on. Something about chasing her around the room with my dick flopping every which way seems less than ideal. I'll run a lot faster if it's not dragging the ground, you know. Or something like that.

Maria's the roadrunner, and I'm the coyote, only my plans for when I catch her don't involve any sort of anvils.

She scoots from the closet to the bathroom, and the sink runs and quits almost manically as she brushes her teeth. I listen for a sign that she's reaching the end of her truncated getting-ready routine, and I finally get it when she flips off the lights of the bathroom and heads for the hallway at a run.

I grab her by the hand as she passes, pulling her to a gentle stop and spinning her to face me. She's already shaking her head, convinced she doesn't have enough time for even a simple exchange, but I know better.

This may be about a scheduled appointment, but it's also a convenient excuse to avoid what happened last night. To shelve any embarrassment and uncertainty right next to the insecurities that'll allow them to fester. I can't let that happen. I won't.

"Remy, I'm late. I have to get Izzy and get to Midtown and—"

I pull her hand with a jerk, forcing her body into mine on a fall. She gasps at the unexpected change of direction, and I don't waste an opportunity with her open mouth. Soft and slow and sweet, I press my lips to hers, winding my tongue around the tip of hers and sinking my hands into the soft tresses of her hair. She feels so fucking good, so fucking memorable, I really have to challenge my self-control.

You cannot take her back to bed right now, you cannot take her back to bed right now.

I can feel her eyelashes flutter against mine in a soft whisper of surrender, and I deepen the kiss to ensure the enemy of doubt falls completely.

Her hands clasp at the flesh at my hips, the tips of her fingernails biting deliciously.

When I eventually pull away, her eyes are much, much lazier, and her heart is cracked back open. I slide right inside as quickly as I can.

"I'll get Izzy from Winnie. You go to your appointment, do what you have to do, and we'll meet up again when you're done for the day."

"What? No? Surely you have something to do? You know, for yourself, I mean."

"It's Saturday, babe. Markets are closed." I smile and shake my head. "And there's nothing better than spending the day with Iz while you get your shit done."

She wants to give in, but she can't do it just yet. "Are you sure?"

I, on the other hand, have no problem helping her get there. I place a smacking kiss to her lips. "Positive."

"Okay…but only, if you're, like, sure, *sure*," she says then, a loaded meaning slithering under the innocent surface.

"I'm sure," I affirm, hoping she can feel the unspoken words of my answer too.

I've made a lot of questionable decisions in my forty-four years on this earth, but making love to Maria last night and, even more than that, inserting myself into her and Izzy's lives like I have sure as fuck isn't one of them.

Hell, call me a selfish bastard, but I still don't even regret waking her up at three a.m. because I couldn't not be inside her again.

"Let me know when you're done, and I'll meet you, okay?"

"I have a few showings after this one."

"No problem. Just let me know when you're done, Ri. No rush. No big deal. Izzy and I will be fine."

She nods and then, finally, hesitantly, leans forward to press her lips to mine. "Thank you. I'll call you as soon as I'm done. *Oh!* And let me know if Winnie had any trouble with Izzy last night."

"You got it." I smile at Maria, holding open the front door as she rushes away, and watch her as she goes.

It's not a bad view. Her ass is perfect, and her hair shines even in the dim hallway light.

But I'm starting to realize the view that is her coming toward me is a fuck of a lot better.

THIRTY-FOUR

Remy

The air is warm and inviting this morning as I make my way from the subway station to my sister's brownstone two blocks away. I can feel the flicker of the sun's rays filtering through the still leafy trees along the sidewalk, and I turn my face up into them at every opening I get. The leaves are turning now and will be dropping soon, but for just a sliver of a moment, New York is blended with the perfect mix of summer and fall.

"Just can't get enough," I mumble to myself, swaying side to side to the Depeche Mode song playing in my ears.

I'm a walking cliché of bouncy steps and singing to myself, and I'm not even ashamed of it. Last night with Maria was incredible.

It was familiar and reminiscent of our days together as teenagers, but so far exceeding anything we even dreamed of back then that I'm not even sure I knew it existed.

When I round the corner on my sister's block to the sight of Wes closing the front door behind himself and bleeping the locks on his car at the curb, I pull my earbuds from my ears and call out loudly.

"Yo, Lancaster!"

His head jerks up at the sound of my voice, and then his gaze finds its way to the source. I smile hugely, and he does the same in return, his hand going to his chest and crisscrossing over it. "What have you got there, cowboy? An empty baby carrier?"

I shrug. "Can't put the baby in it until I pick her up from your wife, and wearing it is better than carrying it."

He chuckles with a shake of his head as I come to a stop directly in front of him.

"What are you still doing home, dude?" I ask. "Isn't this the busy season in your line of work? I thought the Mavs had a home game tomorrow."

"They do. But Nick came to pick Lex up for the weekend, and I wanted to have breakfast with her before she went."

Despite my suspicions over this rich fucker at the beginning of my sister's relationship with him, I'm happy to have him around. He's been a good husband to Win and an even better dad to Lexi, even if I did think he was a prick with ulterior motives in the early days.

I still don't completely trust that shitbrick Nick Raines, but that's probably because I dried too many tears my sister cried over him when he left her and Lex to fend for themselves.

For all intents and purposes, since he moved back to New York and shacked up with my ex-fiancée, he's been nothing but a doting father. The fuckface.

"I have to tell you, when Thatch first started texting me a whole bunch of bullshit about you taking over for Zach Galifianakis in *The Hangover 4*, I thought he'd accidentally gotten into Cassie's pot stash or something. But yesterday's dinner, and now, this look…" He lifts his eyebrows with a chuckle. "I'm seeing it."

"Thatch has been texting you about me?"

"You *and* Izzy." Wes laughs. "And yes, he's been texting me and pretty much everyone else in Manhattan, I'm sure. You can't tell me that after all these years of knowing him, you'd expect anything else after you showed up at his office with a baby strapped to your boobs."

My sigh is exasperated amusement. "Great."

"Look at it this way, dude, he's officially enrolled you in his contest for DILF of the Year. Last I heard, you were a contender, too. Though, don't get your hopes up. He names himself the winner every fucking year."

"What? You're full of shit," I snap, and Wes laughs again, turning to open his door and toss his briefcase in the passenger seat of his sporty little BMW two-seater.

"Dude, do you even know Thatch at all? How is any of this a surprise?"

I shake my head. "I guess I've just never been the one in his sights before."

Wes reaches out and claps me on the shoulder with a wink. "Welcome to the fold, brother."

I give him a salute and a wave as he rounds the trunk to the driver's side and climbs inside, firing up the engine.

I jog up the steps to his house as he pulls away and lift my hand to ring the bell before thinking better of it—if Izzy is sleeping, I don't want to wake her, and a lot of times, she dozes off after her first morning bottle.

Moving my knuckles to the wood surface of their door, I knock instead, pulling my phone out of my pocket and scrolling through it just in case I've missed any messages from Maria while I wait.

There's nothing from her, but there is a new message from Cleo, much to my chagrin.

C: You know what they say? Diving is a leap of faith, and gravity will be there to finish the job. I hope you'll enjoy the fall, my dear.

What the hell?

Me: Cleo, hun, you gotta cut the shit. You know the rules.

Her answer is immediate…almost as though she already knew what I was going to say.

C: When it comes to love, there are no rules. You know that better than most. But I'll take my leave for now, my love. Reach out when you need me.

I know what she's trying to do, but I refuse to acknowledge it. Instead, I scoff, laugh a little, and shove my phone back into my pocket, just as Winnie answers the door with a big smile on her face.

"Heeeyyy there, Rem," Winnie singsongs. My baby sister is brilliant and vibrant and loving and kind and a whole list of incredible things. What she isn't, unfortunately, is subtle in any way, shape, or form.

"Hi, Winnie," I greet, keeping my voice neutral in a way that I know for a fact gets her goat. "How was Izzy last night?"

"She was great. No problem whatsoever."

"Fantastic. Thanks again for keeping her."

"And where is the lovely *Maria*? Did you guys have a *good* night last night?" she asks, her voice making it apparent she is desperate to be in the know. She is practically bursting from the inside, waiting for me to give her any kind of idea of how things went.

"She had a few showings this morning, so Izzy will be hanging with me for the day," I tell her, bypassing the question she wants me to answer the most on purpose.

"Remy, seriously?" She stomps her foot impatiently, almost making me laugh. "Don't leave me hanging here! Did my tequila make the clothes fall off?"

"Win," I chastise, my voice low and authoritarian. The kind of thing only the oldest brother in the family can pull off. And even then, evidently, I can only pull it off a fraction of the time because Winnie is utterly unfazed.

"I'm sorry, but *no*." She holds up a defiant hand toward my face. "I donated to the cause. I took the morning off work. I spent all night thinking about it. I deserve confirmation."

"You spent all night thinking about Maria and me?" I tease with a shake of my head. "That's pretty sick, sis."

"Shut up. You're stalling. Tell me if it worked and she's madly in love with you or not."

"Win, that's not what the night was about. She just lost her sister and her brother-in-law, and she has no support system in place. I'm—"

"Blah, blah, blah, Rem. I *know* all of that. I know. And it's really freaking sad, okay? But you know there's another dimension to this. A happy dimension that I don't know about and want to know right now. It's written all over your damn face." She takes a deep breath. "Tell me what I don't know."

Tired of fighting it, I sigh heavily and stare directly into her eyes. It's not a confirmation, but at the same time, it is. Winnie knows me better than almost anyone in my family, and the look on my face doesn't go unnoticed.

Suddenly overcome by craziness, she jumps up and down with a squeal and claps her hands together in front of her. "Oh yay! I'm so excited! I've always liked her so much, and now I get to like her on another level. She's so cute with you, and the way she looks at you when you hold Izzy, and the way she got you a plate from the—"

I groan. "Winnie. Stop. Please. I'm begging you. It's new. It's all *very* new, and the last thing I need is the pressure of your visions for our life, okay?"

"But can I envision silently?" she whispers with her hands still clasped together like she's praying.

I scoff. "I wouldn't even dare to be foolish enough to think I could stop you."

She smiles, jumping up and down again and leaning forward to place a kiss on my cheek. "Thank you."

"Yeah, yeah."

She giggles as she retreats down the hall with a wave over her shoulder. "I'll go get Izzy."

I breathe in extraordinarily deeply, step inside the door and close it, and let my head sink back to the wall just inside. The truth is, I haven't stopped to think about much of anything since we left here last night. I've been going on instinct and feeling and gut.

I spent time with someone I enjoy. I took that enjoyment to the next level. And I comforted a woman I care about as she freaked out this morning.

I know that, eventually, all of that will have to come into much more vivid detail, but for now, I'm okay with miring myself in the haziness and enjoying it.

So much of my life is exact. Numbers, timing, consequences. I want just a moment to enjoy myself before reality comes crashing down.

My phone buzzes again in my pocket as I'm waiting for Winnie to return with Iz, and as much as I don't want to deal with yet another person giving me shit, I pull it out anyway. I'm shocked to find a message from my most taciturn brother.

Flynn: Winnie says you've got Izzy today. Daisy is busy with work, and I've got the boys. Baby playdate at the library downtown?

A baby fucking playdate? Add those to the list of words I never thought would come from Flynn.

And there's only one person besides Maria who knows what I'm up to today.

Winnie walks back down the hall with my girl in her arms, and it's all I can do not to yank Izzy from her hold and contact the authorities to come pick up the traitor. "What the hell, Win? Are you superhuman? How have you spread the news of me being with Izzy today so quickly?" I ask, holding the phone and message up as evidence.

She waves me off with her hand. "I sent one little group text. It's no big deal."

"Group text? As in, the *whole* group?" I question. Without delay, my phone starts having a technology seizure in my hand, text message notifications nearly blowing it up.

Jude: Just heard you're opening a day care, dude. Mind if I put Sophie's and my future child on the list now so I know we'll have a spot?

Ty: You should take Izzy to the Carlyle today. I hear they do a nice lunch spread.

Mom: I heard you're spending today with Izzy! Think I can get a few pictures to print out at Walgreens? I want to put her on the fridge!

I look up from my phone and into Winnie's unrepentant eyes without answering any of them. "If you weren't the mother of my favorite niece, I would kill you."

She cocks her head shamelessly. "Tell me, Rem. How's that cleaning going that I set up for you?"

"Hand over the baby, Winnie."

She pretends to pout, but she hands Izzy to me and places the diaper bag on my shoulder.

And when she sees I'm already on the move, she calls toward me, "Rem! Why are you leaving so soon? You don't want to hang out here with your favorite sister? Have a cup of tea? Chat about the weather?"

I hold up my middle finger over my shoulder as I jog down the stairs, spinning around to face her and strap Iz into the carrier when I get to the bottom.

"Thanks to you, we're a little busy today. Got a library playdate with Flynn and the boys to get to now."

Winnie grins and waves and then blows a kiss to Izzy. "Have fun."

I don't even bother waving before turning to head down the block and placing a kiss to the top of Izzy's sweet head. "I'm sorry I left you overnight with a crazy lady, baby."

Izzy kicks and squirms, and after I'm assured she's secure and comfortable in her spot in front of me, I pull out my phone one last time and commit to something that *has* to be out of another dimension.

A playdate. With Flynn. And three infants.

Me: We'll meet you at the library in 30. But I'm going to be really disappointed if they don't have snacks.

THIRTY-FIVE

Remy

Izzy and I turn up the block where the library is located, and she snorts a snot bubble right into my chest. I laugh, grabbing a tissue from my pocket and wiping at her teeny nose. "That's better, girlfriend. Can't be meeting up with Flynn and the boys with boogers on our face, can we?" I shake my head down at her. "No way."

She stares at me as I chat, and I smooth a hand over her fuzzy-haired head. When I look up to focus on the library, movement catches me off guard out of the corner of my eye.

After a double take, I realize it's Flynn, Ryder, and Roman, walking out of the Naked Turtle…a bar I haven't been inside in at least ten years.

"Did you really just come walking out of a bar with two babies in your arms?"

Flynn shrugs. "What's the big deal? They weren't drinking."

"Were you?"

"Sure."

My eyes widen slightly, but he qualifies his answer with a grin before they can pop out of my head.

"Green tea."

Bastard. I smirk. "Fatherhood has changed you, bro."

"I've always been the same. The babies just make it more obvious."

"How? What are they? Baby highlighters?"

He rolls his eyes. "They bring out basic emotions. Their primal needs and the unabashed way they ask for them enlighten your psyche to your own. It makes you hypersensitive to things you're normally not."

"I'm not even going to pretend I understand what you're talking about, which makes me think Lexi is the one who shared this information with you."

Flynn shrugs, completely unaffected. "She's a better source of information than just about anyone. And it doesn't really bother me if you're slow on the uptake." I swear, he's the least invested in other people's lives than anyone I've ever met. If it doesn't affect him directly, he is the definition of live and let live.

The two of us climb the steps to the library in tandem, and I can't help but muse on the fact that we're even in this situation. "I still can't believe I'm spending the day play-dating with you. Never fucking thought that would happen."

Flynn smirks. "I figured after Win sold you upriver with the group message, you were going to need a wingman and an out."

"I'll remember your kindness," I say with a chuckle, adjusting Izzy as I transition onto the flat platform at the top of the steps. There's a folding sign out front with teddy bears and balloons adorning it and overdramatic hands on a clock denoting that story time today will be taking place at 3:30 p.m. "Shit," I remark. "Did you know story time didn't start for another, like…" I glance at my watch. "Five and a half hours?"

Flynn shrugs.

"You didn't check the website or something?"

He grins. "Who do you think I am? Mary Poppins? The babies get bored staring at the walls in our apartment. Not doing that is about as far as I planned."

I roll my eyes and shake my head at Ryder and Roman. "Your daddy thinks he has to have a flying umbrella to find a schedule online, guys. I apologize for what that's going to mean for your future."

Ryder just grins, and Roman reaches out to tug on Flynn's shirt.

Flynn, not one to lie down and take any abuse, hits me right back. "That's rich coming from the guy who couldn't be more vague about his future if he tried. What exactly are you doing with Maria? The baby? Are you committed?"

I roll my eyes and groan. Even a little surprised that Flynn, of all people, is going there.

"You invited this, bro. You've only got yourself to blame."

"I don't know. I could blame you. Seeing as you knew my full fortune from Cleo and didn't bother to tell me."

Flynn's eyes widen ever so slightly with surprise. "I figured you wouldn't want to know."

"I mean, I get that in the beginning, but recently? With all of yours coming to fruition? Why the hell wouldn't you tell me?"

"Because I think it's bullshit. Whether the fortunes have come true or not, no man should have anyone involved in his destiny other than himself. You have to make your own choices, carve your own path. Not sit around waiting for some shit a lady with velvet curtains tells you is going to happen."

The thing I love about Flynn is that he doesn't even ask me how I knew there was more to my fortune. He's reliable with that kind of shit. He's the guy who waits for you to want to tell him, instead of pushing and prying like everyone else in our family.

"Well…" I pause and sigh. "Who is going to be in charge of our destiny today? Now that the library's not happening."

Flynn grins at my avoidance and points in the direction of Wall Street. "They're having some sort of fall carnival down there with all kinds of shit."

"Do they have stuff for infants?"

"Dude." Flynn laughs. "Does anywhere have stuff for infants? I'm sure it'll do."

He has a point. It's not like Izzy is going to be hopping on a Ferris wheel anytime soon. "All right. Let's do it."

Almost in tandem, the two of us pull our sunglasses from our heads and slide them down onto our eyes, jogging down the steps of the library again like some sort of scene out of *Ocean's 11*.

Watch out, George Clooney and Brad Pitt. A new duo is coming to town.

Though, this duo has three babies. One of whom is named Ryder and is now screeching like a banshee in Flynn's arms.

But still, come hell or high water, we're a-coming, babies in tow.

Upon arrival at the fall carnival, I can see that we've made an egregious error.

This is the kind of dog and pony show people plan to attend for nearly a month in advance, so that they can create a plot of attack and brief their kids on how many dollars they'll get to spend on games. There are rides and vendors and game booths and food trucks everywhere, and the smell of frying dough for funnel cakes hangs heavy in the air.

Instantly, something deep down, something from my childhood, is invigorated within me. It feels fun and exciting and like this carnival is just as much for me as it is for Izzy.

I glance to Flynn, scanning the environment with a twin on each hip, and realize it's not just me. He's feeling it too.

It's time to make this fall carnival our bitch.

Silent communication strikes true as we meet each other's gaze and nod. The Winslow Brothers are ready for anything.

Fully engaged with our environment, Flynn and I walk down the aisles between the booths, looking for something to catch our eyes. Children shout and people laugh all around us.

And Izzy, Roman, and Ryder pick up on our vibe and, instantly, become our ride-or-dies. They calmly let us get the lay of the carnival land without a peep of resistance.

Yeah. These babies get it.

"Balloon pop," I murmur, spotting a booth with brightly colored balloons and a patron throwing darts.

Flynn shakes his head in the negative, and the twins turn up their noses via annoyed whines.

Message received, fellas. That's not the one.

Cruising a little farther, we hang a left to the main aisle of the carnival. Dead ahead, a huge, rectangular ring toss booth sports hundreds of goldfish in adorned fishbowls spinning and swirling in the center. A dad is there, bright-white Reebok sneakers on his feet and a baby on his chest, and immediately, a feeling washes over me.

And I'm not the only one. Flynn jerks up his chin, remarking simply, "This is the one."

The twins perk up, their heads swinging in the direction of the booth and their sweet baby eyes going alert. Izzy nuzzles into my chest, playing it cool.

The dad makes a move to toss the ring at the center, missing completely and splashing it in the water. Frustrated, he tries again, landing it on the second to highest level of points.

Flynn and I glance to each other, and even with our sunglasses on, the mood is palpable.

It's on.

Forward and then into a divide, the two of us split the booth and circle it like a couple of sharks. The dad notices fairly quickly, and the corners of his eyes wrinkle up with the intensity of his squint.

His baby is asleep in the carrier at his chest, but almost as if he senses the change in his dad's intensity, he wakes up and scans the area for threats.

Ah, a worthy opponent. I lean down to whisper conspiratorially to Izzy. "We got a battle on our hands, Iz. But don't you worry. Uncle Flynn and I are going to take them down in the end. I promise."

Stalking and prowling around one another, the three of us move to different sides of the fish table and jerk our chins up at the attendant wearing a bright-red golf cap. It's clear he's a little intimidated by our friendly competition, so he does his best not to show favoritism, going to the other dad first simply because he's a returning customer.

"I'll take five more rings," the Reebok-wearer declares, raising his voice in a way I just know is done for Flynn's and my benefit.

When the attendee heads to Flynn, he jerks up his chin for the same, officially calling the other dad's bet.

Five rings, it is. May the best man-baby duo win.

Both Flynn and our new rival wait impatiently for me to get my weapons, their rings on the counter surface in front of them, their fingers wiggling for a quick draw—at least, figuratively.

Flynn's still got his arms full of babies, but I can tell by the way he's standing, he's ready to set one on the counter and rapid-fire toss when he needs to.

The attendant places my rings in front of me and scrambles out of the way, rushing to the end of the booth unoccupied by our standoff.

I glance from our opponent to Flynn and then down to Izzy, and then, after one last, final deep breath to prepare, I nod my okay.

A silent countdown commences, and as soon as three seconds are up, the three of us are tossing.

I hit with my first and miss with my second, and a bead of sweat builds on my brow at the fact that I'm now down by one. I grab the next ring and toss, cheering, "Yes!" in a burst of triumph that makes even Izzy throw up her arms when it lands on the most prized of targets in the center of them all.

Flynn points at me in that special way that says I'm the man and then scoops up his eight-month-old baby Roman before he can crawl right off the counter into the rocks.

The attendee works diligently to fill my bag with two fish while we toss the rest of our rings rather carelessly, and the other dad stares daggers into my soul.

I'm wearing my protector Izzy, though, and she shields me perfectly from any of his rage.

His baby fusses slightly at his chest, so he pulls a binky out of his fanny-pack pocket and plops it in his son's mouth expertly. It's pretty incredible how good his aim is, considering he hasn't taken his eyes off me, and I have to give him credit.

I dip my chin, and his eyes narrow. *Okay, then. Not open to friendliness yet, I see.* Losing so quickly and after having far more practice than Flynn and I is a hard pill to swallow, so I'll allow it.

My phone buzzes in my pocket, so I pull it out to read it quickly.

Maria: How's it going? Is Izzy okay?

I smile.

Me: Oh, it's going fantastic. Izzy and I are champions.

Maria: Okayyy... I don't understand what that means, so I'm just going to tell myself it means you're good. LOL. I have to run into a showing right now, and then right into another, but I'll let you know when I'm done.

Me: No worries. Take your time.

We've got shit to do anyway.

I take the two bagged fish from the attendant and round the booth to Flynn, who jerks up his chin in congratulations. I grin like the victor I am. "It was all Izzy, dude. She gave me the perfect center of gravity."

"Fuck," Flynn replies with a smirk. "That must be why I didn't get it. I'm used to holding two, and I only had one."

"For sure. Your equilibrium was all off." I nod fervently. "Where to next?" I ask, subtly checking to see if the other dad is still mentally spearing me. He's moved on to feeding his kid a bottle, but I can tell he's lingering on purpose—giving his best impression of an undercover agent, casing our whereabouts.

"I think I saw one of those spinning hang bars across from where we turned. Want to give that a go?"

I nod my agreement. Izzy's going to make it easy for me with this one too. She practically weighs nothing still.

Flynn readjusts his sunglasses after Ryder tries to grab them off his face, and then we're off again, headed in the direction of the hanging challenge.

I glance back briefly when we make it down from the booth a little, and I spot the Reebok dad following closely.

I nudge Flynn with a soft elbow. "Got a bogey on our six, dude. Looks like Reebok wants to dance again."

"Well, then, Goose. I guess it's time to hit the brakes, see if he'll fly on by."

There's nothing I love more than a *Top Gun* reference. Plus, there's probably nothing dad-lier that Flynn or I could have done in that moment. Still, I don't think this is a bait and switch situation. I think, if we're going to really win this epic battle, we're going to have to meet the challenge head on.

I shake my head. "Nope. I think we have to see this through to the end. Let's just win."

Flynn smirks. "Roger that."

We stop at the booth, set up with the hanging bar and a two-minute clock display. It looks simple enough, but I know there's not a chance in hell so many people have trouble for no reason.

The trick here isn't to get cocky.

"This one's all you," Flynn defers, lifting each of the boys about six inches higher to make his reasoning evident. With two arms full and muscles that must be burning to hell and back after carrying them all day, he's not our best chance anyway, so I don't fight it.

It's up to Izzy and me, and we can handle it, I'm sure.

Brazenly, Reebok dad stops at the booth behind us, without even bothering to feign interest in something else.

This, I'd say, is a declaration of war.

I turn to Flynn and hold out the bag of fish, to which he laughs directly in my face. "You're joking, right?" he questions, lifting up both twins a little higher.

"Why the hell didn't you bring a stroller?"

"Because I didn't need one."

Great. I sigh, and then gently set the fish bags on the ground.

Stepping up to the booth and paying my fee, I tighten Izzy's carrier straps and check to make sure her head is good and secure. Her eyes flutter, and I know immediately that she's giving me a wink.

She's confident in me, and I'm confident in her. Together, we can handle anything.

Assured she's comfortable and ready for action, I climb onto the foot pegs on the bottom sides of the bar structure and reach up to take it into my hands as gently as possible.

It's simple at first, hanging calmly as the clock starts to click. Flynn shifts Roman in his left arm and then boosts Ryder farther onto his hip on the right.

The boys giggle and squeal and try like hell to make Flynn release them so they can crawl on the ground, but he's stalwart, a true warrior, and keeps them locked up tight so he can remain my support.

I don't know what it is, but my arms start to feel some kind of sympathy pains or something because when the clock rounds its way into the second minute, I begin to feel the burn. My palms are also starting to get sweaty against the sun-warmed metal bar, and Reebok gets a twinkle in his eye at the signs of my weakness.

Dammit.

The bar starts to spin as I try to double over my grip, and the stress on my shoulders as it gets looser and looser is too much to handle.

I have to give in, putting my feet back to the pegs and climbing down, defeated. I couldn't risk it, though, knowing an uncontrolled fall from the bar would be way too jarring for a baby as young as Iz.

Flynn pats me on the shoulder in consolation, and I hang my head with a shake. "I'm sorry, Iz," I whisper down at her sweet face. "I know I'm letting the team down."

But I swear, she tries to crack her first smile at me.

"Thanks, babe," I tell her, grateful for the support.

Subtlety gone, Flynn and I plant ourselves there as Reebok pays his money and tries his hand. I widen my stance and put my hands to my hips, and Flynn boosts the boys higher so they can get a better view. The fish can hang out on the ground a little longer.

"No way this guy is going to do this, right?" I remark under my breath, to which Flynn replies with a snort that says, *no fucking way.*

I nod, confidence renewed. *We got this.*

Reebok climbs the pegs and grabs the bar, his cargo shorts billowing in the wind. The clock starts its count, and the longer it goes, the sicker to my stomach I start to feel.

He's got a smirk on his face and a glimmer in his eye, and his baby boy is staring me down in a way that screams *I know something you don't.*

Flynn shifts next to me as we approach the last fifteen seconds of his count, and even without him saying anything, I know he's feeling the nerves too.

This fucker is about to tie this shit up. I can hardly believe it.

The buzzer sounds, and the dad climbs down and picks up his baby's arm to high-five it. The attendant presents him with a big, stuffed bear, and Flynn groans, ending the sound with the words, "Fuck me."

I nod. Tell me about it.

Steely-eyed and more determined than ever, I scoop up the fish, and we turn from the booth and head down the road to the main stage. We need something we know we can win. Something that's a shoo-in. We need a tiebreaker and a clincher in one, and as soon as I spot the banner draped across the top of the performance platform, I know exactly what it is.

"Flynn, look." I point. "Over there."

He follows the line of my finger and then looks back to me, perplexed. "A hot dog eating contest?"

"It's the perfect way to put this competition to rest."

Flynn scoffs. "If you're the one doing it, maybe. I suffer from far too much indigestion. Dais'll kill me if I come home all fucked up."

I frown. "Well, shit. I was planning on meeting Maria for dinner later, too. I can't eat, like, fifty hot dogs."

Right then, as if he's been flying below the radar, Reebok appears directly in front of us, meeting our eyes over his shoulder as he adds his name to the hot dog eating sign-up list.

"Fuck, Flynn," I mutter under my breath at the sight. "He's throwing down the gauntlet. What are we going to do?"

"I'll tell you what we're going to do," he says simply, shifting Roman to his shoulders, pulling out his phone, and typing resolutely. "We're going to call in some goddamn reinforcements. There's a reason Wendy Winslow had so many fucking kids, and we're about to use it."

"You're texting Jude?" I ask, instantly understanding where he's going with this.

"Has he ever turned down a bet? Or lost a challenge, for that matter?"

Exactly. "He's the home run we need."

A few seconds later, Flynn smiles, holding up the phone with Jude's response for me to see.

Jude: Say no more. I'll be there in ten, ready to swallow some meat sticks.

I laugh. "I've never been surer of two things. One, our brother is deeply disturbed. And two, we got this in the bag."

Flynn nods. "Have to take the good with the bad."

"The highs with the lows."

"The outsourcing with the circumstances."

"The win with the Jude."

Flynn jerks up his chin. "And we can just chill with our babies."

His casual comment makes me still, but it's not long before I start again. Izzy may not be mine biologically, but technically, she's not Maria's either.

And I've never seen two people love a little girl as much as we do.

Maybe, just maybe, these stupid little details don't matter. At least, not to me.

Now, I just have to figure out if they matter to Maria.

THIRTY-SIX

Maria

I look at the last message I received from Remy to double-check that I'm at the right place.

It's safe to say, after waking up a little hungover, the adrenaline that came with the realization of what last night entailed and dealing with Claudia's inability to schedule showings at the correct time, I could've easily gotten my wires crossed.

Remy: Meet us at the Capital Grille around 6. We'll be coming from Wall Street Station.

With one glance at the sign on the restaurant in front of me, I verify that I am correct.

And a quick peek at my watch later, I realize I'm on time too.

I peer in the direction Remy said he'd be coming from, and I'm finding strangely that, while I enjoy the freedom to do what I need to do without Izzy, I miss her immensely in the time away. I want a snuggle and a sniff of her fresh baby scent and the feel of her warm skin as she nuzzles under my chin.

I miss my girl.

It's an oddly comforting reminder of my sister and everything she was, and the reason it's odd is because it doesn't make me feel sad. It makes me feel hope and connection and love and…lucky.

I could have lost Isabella and Oliver and had nothing of them in return. Instead, I was given the extraordinary gift of having a piece of each of them with me all day, every day.

When I was pregnant, I never would have imagined I'd feel this way this soon.

That I'd be able to feel joy and positivity when I looked into Izzy's eyes. But the truth is, she's the life I didn't know I was missing. She's breathed a new dimension into me.

I scour the sidewalk again, looking for a glimpse of Remy's dark hair and Izzy's tiny head, but it's crowded and cramped with business-pantsuit-wearing commuters, scuttling home or to their final meeting of the day. I don't know why there are so many corporate minions running around on a Saturday, but it doesn't matter.

In the distance, though, a balloon in the shape of a butterfly catches my attention. It bounces in the wind, rocketing from one side of the sidewalk to the other on a long, pink-ribboned tail. It looks so out of place with the straitlaced pedestrians below it, and without conscious decision, I feel my lips tip up in delight.

It's only when the crowd in front of the balloon clears enough to reveal the holder—Remy, of all people—that my smile turns into a guffaw.

Oh, what the heck?

With Izzy in the carrier on his chest, he's holding the string of the balloon and a bag with a goldfish in one hand, and a huge stuffed animal in the other. Painted animals cover one of his cheeks, and he's wearing a smile the size of Texas.

What in the land of holy water is going on here?

His face lights up even further as he spots me standing in front of the Capital Grille, and he lifts the arm with the fish and balloons to wave.

I shake my head in laughter as he approaches, hardly able to come up with words.

Remy comes to a stop in front of me, and he shifts his body so I can peek at Izzy inside the baby carrier, her little self still too small to be front-facing just yet, and that's when I see the baby-sized sunglasses on her teeny, currently sleeping face.

He waves Izzy's tiny hand at me. "Hi, Mommy."

The moniker is new, one I haven't really used myself for fear that it'll drum up some sort of impostor syndrome, but I'm pleasantly surprised to find out it feels *good*. She might not be mine biologically, but she's mine in the sense that she has my whole heart.

Our relationship is complicated—but that doesn't mean it's not special. And I'm working on finding a way to be okay with that.

"My God, Remy!" I say now that I've had a chance to take full inventory of their display. It's not one fish, it's two, the animals on Remy's cheek are glitter butterflies, and Izzy's fingernails are painted with a clear-coated bright-pink sparkle polish.

He laughs, completely unfazed by both the ridiculousness of their appearance and my reaction to it. "We had a good day."

"Where did you go? A carnival?"

He smiles and nods. "Yeah, actually. Downtown. They were having a big street-fair-style party, and Flynn and I decided to give it a shot when we had a scheduling issue with story time at the library."

"Scheduling issue?"

"Flynn forgot to check if they have one."

I grin.

"Couldn't help but think a carnival might be more fun than story time anyway—sensory-wise, at this age, I mean—and well…when we do something, we do it big."

"Remy, you're holding fish. That's not big. That's gargantuan," I tease him out of pure joy. "Not sure if you realize, but Izzy girl here isn't going to provide an ounce of assistance in keeping them alive."

"Eh," he says, waving me off. "Fish are easy and take up no space. It's about the only pet you can get in Manhattan without typing up a fifteen-page manual of logistics for your landlord. And if it's a problem at your place, I can take them to mine. No big deal."

"They're…fine," I find myself saying, not wanting to be a wet blanket. "I just wasn't expecting your day with Izzy to end with new aquatic friends." I glance at his handsome face covered in glitter and reach up to touch it softly. "This is a bit of a surprise too."

He smiles again, this time unabashedly. I can't help but melt into it, right there on the busy sidewalk. "I didn't want to do Izzy's without knowing yet if her skin gets irritated easily, so we settled on a little bit of baby-safe nail polish."

"Please tell me Flynn has glitter butterflies on his face too."

Big, silent, mysterious Flynn with face paint. I swear I'd pay money to see that.

"Nope." His face breaks with humor. "He got glitter monster trucks to match the twins."

I cackle. I can't help it. "Wow. Big day for the Winslow Brothers' Daddy Day Care, huh?"

A quick, unexpected pang of weirdness hits me at the idea of calling Remy a daddy in this scenario. The truth is, I don't know what he is. Or what we are, for that matter. We had sex last night—twice—after drinking an entire bottle of tequila, and he practically lives for taking care of Izzy and me, but beyond that, I have zero clue. Hell, I haven't even been to his apartment yet.

"Oh, Ri, you have no idea. We got into this battle with another dad until Jude scorched him in the hot dog eating contest." He waves with one hand in front of him. "It's a long story that I'll have to tell you later, but I'll be damned if the dude didn't end up shaking our hands in the end."

Remy is still laughing when I come back from my momentary lapse with reality, me having only half heard his story with something about hot dogs and Jude, and he's started to move us toward the front door of the restaurant with a fish-filled hand to the small of my back and the other still holding Izzy's hand in the carrier at his chest *and* the ribbons of the balloons.

"Flynn went buck wild, to be honest. I think he partied harder with the twins today than he did at any of the Winslow bachelor parties."

I shake my head to clear it, realizing I'm missing some pretty important shit. I should be laughing at the mental image of Flynn "partying hard" with a group of infants.

Still, as Remy holds the door and smiles at the hostess like the proud head of a young family, I can't stop my thoughts from swirling entirely.

This thing we're doing…it's already complicated. And quite frankly, I'm starting to rely on it pretty freaking heavily.

Remy's help is central to my schedule these days, and I don't know what I'm going to do if bringing sex into it is the thing that turns it all on its head.

Like, incredible, had-forgotten-it-existed kind of orgasmic sex. But still. I've grown to need him in lots of ways. His friendship. His support. His selfless help.

And I can't decide if it makes me selfish that I honestly don't know what I'd do without him at this point.

Remy looks back with crinkled eyebrows as the hostess grabs our menus and heads in the direction of a table. "You coming, Ri?" he asks, suspicion of my distance lurking right under the surface of his friendly face.

I smile then, taking his outstretched hand and walking to our table in the back of the restaurant. I'm not confident that I have any of the answers I'm looking for, and I'm even less sure I'll get them.

But Remy's warm hand and smile are like gifts from heaven above, making my chest feel full and free at the same time. I'm not about to let myself fuck that up right now. No way.

When we sit down at the table, I open my menu dutifully, ready to pick out my meal and keep my mouth shut like a good little girl.

Remy chats amiably with both me and the baby, and I smile and nod back when I can manage.

But for as much as I stare at the menu and the man and the baby and try to remind myself that only a twisted individual would jeopardize this moment with thoughts, all I can see is the image of Remy on top of me, his cock between my legs and my heart beating out of my chest. Even while the waiter comes to take our order—and after—all I can see is a physically, *intimately* connected Remy and me.

I mean, the man is hot. The sex was hot. I don't have a clue on earth how

I'm going to continue on like nothing ever happened. I just wish that didn't seem like the only option here.

Mouth with a mind of its own, I blurt. Just word vomit all over the table and Remy and every carefully placed plan I've just come up with. He's even in the middle of talking about something else entirely, but my nerves don't care. They can't wait.

"Maybe we can—"

"Maybe we should talk about the fact that we had sex last night."

Remy instantly jumps from his position and reaches forward to cover Izzy's ears. "Ixnay on the ex-say. There's a baby here."

I roll my eyes. "You know she can't understand you, right? She has no idea what sex means. She doesn't even really know what words mean, Rem."

"Actually, there are several studies on the psychology of influence at an early age and promiscuity. They can be directly tied to low self-worth and impulsivity."

"Influence of having a conversation in front of a baby can do all that? Where on earth did you hear that?"

"A very reputable source."

I crook an eyebrow, and he chuckles.

"Okay, it was Lexi. But I'm telling you, if that kid said it, it's true."

"I just feel like we need to talk about it," I state without wavering. "And while I know Lexi is brilliant beyond her years, Izzy isn't going to understand a single word that's being said right now. Like, not at all." I pointedly nod down at the still-sleeping baby attached to his chest.

But he just takes it all in stride. Easy peasy, relaxed as can be. "Don't worry, we'll talk about it."

"We will?"

"Definitely."

"Remy—"

"Ri, I promise you, we'll talk about it. I would *love* to talk about it, in fact. There are so many things I could discuss in relation to this topic. But let's do it later, okay? Right now, let's just have dinner."

"I just don't want things to be—"

"They're not," he cuts me off to comfort.

I shake my head. "You don't even know what I was going to say."

"I can think of three options, and all of them have the same answer. We will talk later. Hash out the game footage. Really go through the whole thing."

My head jerks back. "Whoa, whoa, I'm not saying I want to—"

"Oh, we're going to," he promises lightly. "We're going to get into it. Just not *here*, you know?"

I sigh and then, finally, nod my agreement. He's right, after all. It's not like I'd feel comfortable having the kind of conversation we really need to have smack-dab in the middle of a busy Manhattan restaurant.

"Now, tell me how your showings went today," he says, and it's the opening that's needed to move our conversation away from the s-e-x subject.

I tell him about Conrad Blakely, even the whole story about Claudia telling him I had diarrhea last night, and by the time our food comes to the table, we're back to our usual fun banter that's been there since the very beginning of when Remy and Maria were even a thing.

But just before I'm about to cut into my chicken, I can't help but notice that Remy's rice looks an awful lot like mashed potatoes. For some reason, though, Remy doesn't say anything, smiling down at his plate instead and then turning to look at Izzy at his chest.

"Um, excuse me, sorry," I say to get the waiter's attention as he moves to head back toward the kitchen. "I don't want to be a bother, but his mashed potatoes were supposed to be rice."

The busy waiter glances back at Remy's plate and seemingly sees it for the first time. I'm sure he's dead on his feet.

"Oh no," he agrees then. "You're right. I'm so sorry."

I shake my head. "No, don't apologize! We can see you're slammed. But if you don't mind switching it out when you get a chance, we'd really appreciate it."

"Of course!" he says, jumping forward and scooping up Remy's plate. "I'll be right back with it." I make a mental note to give him a bigger tip, just to make up for him having to run back and forth an extra time.

But when he steps away with the plate, Remy is looking at me with an intensity I can't exactly place. "What? What is it?"

"You didn't have to do that. I would have eaten the potatoes."

"I know you would have. But you deserve to eat what you want."

"Are you taking care of me, Maria Baros?"

I blush a little, but then I straighten my spine. The truth is the truth. There's no avoiding it. "I'm trying to."

"Why?"

"Because you're sure as hell taking care of me and Iz." My own words make me smile. "The least I can do is return the favor every once in a while."

But truth be told, with a glitter-cheeked, baby-wearing Remy staring back at me with the sweetest of gazes, I'm starting to think I'll never be able to keep up.

THIRTY-SEVEN

Maria

As I round the bed to my nightstand to grab my nighttime moisturizer, the sight of Remy's clean boxer briefs on the bed catches my attention.

He's in the shower now, and the white noise of the water and steam from the small crack in the door send my mind racing with visualizations.

He's naked, in my bathroom, right now, and I'm not doing anything about it. Izzy is sound asleep, exhausted from her day in the city, so I don't even have that as an excuse, but I can't get myself to stop thinking long enough to enjoy the moment.

It's big—this thing that's going on here. Momentous, even. And without taking any time to process it or talk it out, I'm afraid Remy is missing that. I mean, after dinner, he ran to his place to grab some stuff and came back *here*, to my place, to stay the night again.

There's a whole boatload of things happening around us, and we're going to have to face them head on at some point…*right?*

Shaking my head, I grab the moisturizer jar from my nightstand and head across the room toward my door, bound for the living room, but the sound of Remy's phone buzzing on the bedside table makes me pause.

I shouldn't look. I know I shouldn't. It's an invasion of privacy and beyond none of my business. But it's also going on nearly eleven p.m., and the devil on my shoulder likes to think she knows what that means.

Listening briefly to the sound of the shower still going, I tiptoe over to his nightstand and pause, hovering there above the now dark-screened phone.

Don't do it, Maria. Don't do it, don't do—

Bing.

Just like that, another message rolls in, lighting up the screen and stacking itself on top of the other notification. The sender of both of them? A single letter. "C."

I run away from the phone like it's the freaking sun and if I stare at it too long I'll go blind, and I don't slow down until I'm in the living room, plopped on the couch and breathing heavily from the small bout of exercise.

Why, why, why did I do that to myself?

Sometimes it's genuinely better not to know. Plus, now I feel all clammy and my heart is racing, and it's all because of something I know *nothing* about. Sure, the letter C does happen to be the first letter of his ex-fiancée's name, but it's the first letter of a lot of things, for Pete's sake. It could be his…cook. Or cleaner. Or counselor. Or courier. His fucking chemist, I don't know. But it could be a lot of things, and as an over forty-year-old woman, I *refuse* to let myself spiral out of control over something that's most likely nothing.

Over something that's not necessarily my business either. Remy is an adult man, and despite my momentary lapse in judgment, I'm an adult woman who understands that I'm privy to whatever information he wants me to be privy to.

Not a teenage girl who is doing weird shit to try to avoid her insecurities.

Irritated with myself, I open my jar of moisturizer and do both my hands and feet.

I even get up to check on our new aquatic roomies that are currently swimming around in the fishbowl Remy and I picked up on our way home from dinner. Both goldfish appear content in their little home, and I drop a few pellets of food into the water.

But eventually, I know I need to face what I'm currently avoiding and make a resolution with myself.

I'm going to confront my feelings and questions and insecurities head on. Sex isn't something to be avoided—*especially not when it's as good as the sex with Remy.*

Standing from the couch in one smooth motion, I pad my way back to the bedroom at a walk. I am calm. I am collected. I am a cucumber. *I might as well be the C on his phone at this point.*

My sister's picture in the hallway stops me briefly, and it's eerily like she's watching me. Her smile is knowing, and her eyes are alight. She wants me to know she's proud of me. I can't describe exactly how I know, but I can feel it.

My nose stings, and I swallow hard. Sometimes it's overbearing how much I miss her. With a shake of my head and a whispered *I love you*, I continue down the hall to my bedroom and push gently on the half-closed door.

Remy is out of the shower now, sitting bare-chested in bed, and his black reader glasses are perched on his nose as he scrolls through his phone. His head comes up at the sound of the door, but as soon as he sees me, he puts the phone on the bedside table and pats the spot on the bed next to him with a smile. "Come join me."

I cross the room, stripping off my robe to reveal a simple silk slip nightie and climb into bed next to him. Remy watches me, but the part of me that's still freaking out about all of this shit doesn't dare let me look at him. Instead, I turn into an outright coward, reaching for my lamp and clicking it off, and shortly after, he does the same.

The darkness and silence are so potent, I only make it a second and a half before reaching back to my lamp and clicking it back on.

Remy is staring right at me, a half smirk on his handsome face when I turn around. "Yes?" he prompts, his deep, rich voice going up an octave at the end. It's the lilt of teasing, but I don't have the cool, calm cucumber thing going on anymore. Suddenly, I am a spicy pepper, and I need to know what's going on *right now.*

"Rem, we had sex last night."

"We did. Two glorious times, in fact."

I wait for him to say more, but when he doesn't, I'm left to put it all out there myself.

"And…well, I can't go to sleep until I know what to do with that—where to file it in my emotional cabinet."

"How about you file it in the folder titled *First of many?*"

"What?"

"We had sex last night, Ria. Fucking great, incredible, sexy sex. And I think, in my very professional personal opinion, that we should do it again. Right now, preferably."

I furrow my brow. "Remy, be serious."

"Maria, I've never been more serious about anything in my life."

Hold the phone. "Wait…what? You want to do it again? Right now?"

"Right now. Only this time, I'd like you to be on top again…but with the lights on so I can see every fucking beautiful inch of you while you're riding my cock."

"Remy!"

His eyes smirk back at me, amused by my shock. "Hey, I thought this was open sharing time. Just putting it all out there on the table, you know."

"You don't think this is a little too complicated?"

"Sex?" He winks. "Nah. I think I can figure it out."

"*Rem.* You know what I mean."

"Why do we have to think about it so hard, Ri? Can't we just enjoy each other? Don't you think we both deserve that just a little bit?"

Just enjoy each other? I stare at my fingers that are now toying with the comforter, my mind trying to understand if I should feel as excited as I'm currently feeling over that prospect. "It was good," I admit quietly, my eyes slowly peering back up at him.

"Good? Excuse me?" Remy questions with distaste and a shake of his head. "It was great. Fucking incredible."

"Yeah," I say, relenting with a little giggle. "That too."

Remy climbs across the bed then, stopping only when his chest is pressed firmly against my own. He's on top of me, and his eyes are intense. I remember looking at them like this in high school and wondering if they had special powers. They trap you in their swirling blue graces and beg of you to let your guard down.

Without fail, for me anyway, it always seems to work.

There's nothing like the confident stare of Remy Winslow to convince you you're safe. Nothing.

He sinks his hands into the hair at the sides of my head, and before I know it, we're kissing. Just like this morning. Smooth and slow and sure of ourselves. Our tongues are familiar enough with each other to hit all the right notes without any awkward bumbles, and Remy's fingertips on my scalp are enough to lull me right into readiness.

I separate my thighs and pull them up onto his hips, squeezing and rubbing as my arousal tightens in my stomach. One of Remy's hands leaves my hair to grab the flesh of my thigh, and a moan I'm not expecting slides up my throat and straight into his mouth.

"Ditto, babe," he murmurs in response, the curve of his cheeks as he smiles taking my own with it.

God, this feels good.

Remy skates his other hand down the line of my body, stopping at my hip, and then in one smooth move, he rolls us over, placing me on top.

Without the cloak of darkness or inhibition-releasing tequila, I feel a tiny bit more vulnerable up here, but with the way Remy is looking at me, I know the insecurity won't last long.

He has a way of making me feel like the only woman on the planet. Like my existence is exactly what he asked for when he put in an application for a woman. There's not a lot of room for uncertainty when a man like Remy looks at you like that.

Soft and sure, he lifts at the hem of my nightie, sliding it up my skin with gentle pressure from his hands until my whole body is bared, my heavy breasts swaying above his face. Up and over my head, he removes the fabric entirely and tosses it to the floor beside the bed.

His smile is bright and unchecked as he surveys me, once again placing a hand on the faint tiger stripes across my stomach.

"Fucking beautiful," he whispers and then reaches up to pull my head down to meet his own.

Our lips crash, and our previously soft kiss turns hungry and wanton. Both of us are more than ready—I can feel the hard pulse of his cock underneath me, and I'm practically soaking him through my lace panties.

"Remy," I say, the desperation in my whisper plain to my own ears.

"I know," he responds with a half-tortured laugh. "We should have lost the underwear sooner."

I giggle—I can't help it—but Remy, he gets down to work. Adjusting me up and off, he strips off his boxer briefs, rolls me to my back to pull off my panties, and then lifts me back on top, all in under ten seconds.

I'm breathing heavily, and I didn't even do anything.

Remy slides on a condom. Where it came from, I don't know. But as much as I'd love to feel him directly against me, it's necessary. I'm in no way prepared to have unprotected sex, no matter how good I know it'd feel. I appreciate him doing the legwork to make sure we're covered.

I shift my knees in the bed and lift myself taller, taking hold of his cock with my hand and guiding it inside myself. Remy laughs the kind of sexy laugh that could make me come on the spot. Head back, eyes half closed, his perfect teeth biting deliciously into his lip.

He's so sexy, I can hardly believe it.

"Ri, that might be the hottest thing I've ever witnessed in my life. If you didn't feel so good around me, I'd make you take my cock back out just so you could put it in again."

I blush a little, but mostly, I just feel empowered. If grabbing him and putting him inside me is that much of a turn-on for him, I'm excited about what else I might be able to do.

Lifting up quickly and then sliding down slowly, I take him by surprise. His eyes widen, and his pupils dilate to fill the extra space.

"God, Ria. Fuck."

The sound of him coming unraveled might be the most invigorating thing I've ever experienced. His praise is like a drug, drawing me to chase another hit like an addict.

I lift up again and spread my thighs wider so I can accommodate all of him inside me as I move up and down his length three more times.

He groans, his eyes roll back, and I feel another high.

Up and down, I lift my hips, squeezing my Kegel muscles with each stroke until he's breathing so heavily, I can hear each and every intake of air.

I lean down more, my breasts brushing across his face with each stroke of his cock, and he licks and nips at them gently.

He practically growls as he grips my ass and pushes himself even deeper. The stretch I feel is so deliciously intense that I'm panting and desperate to keep matching him stroke for stroke, to keep pushing his cock as deep inside me as it can go.

Remy has taken over all of my senses now, and the only thing I'm missing is the feel of his tongue on mine.

On pure, raw need, I lean forward until we're chest-to-chest and press my mouth to his. We're totally connected in every way, and our kisses become greedy, breathy movements between moans.

"Fuck, Ria. It's so fucking good. It's always so fucking good."

A moan bubbles up from my lungs as he continues to drive into me, each thrust of his big cock guiding me closer and closer to the edge.

Remy is loud now, but so am I, my lips knocking against his as I push myself onto him with force. Down, down, down, I bounce, gasping at the end of every stroke.

I'm practically wailing, I'm so overcome, but Remy is too, his hands clutching at the sides of my head and holding my mouth to his own.

We kiss and taste and lick and nip, and just when I think I'm going to die from the excruciating pace, I fall over the cliff of pleasure, landing in a pool of utter satisfaction when Remy tumbles right with me.

"Fuck, fuck, fuck," he groans directly into my mouth, his hand clenching at the back of my head so hard it flirts the line of pain.

And yet, it feels good. So, *so* good.

It's dangerous and daring, just like everything I know I'm risking by taking this chance with Remy.

I just have to hope I can stay on the pleasure side of the line—enjoy the fun, the companionship, the help, the laughs, and the sex without letting myself do something stupid like falling completely head over heels in love and subjecting myself to the possibility of a world of hurt.

I stare into Remy's blue eyes as they study me. A soft, gratified smile plays at his lips, and the instant contentment I feel makes me bury my face into his chest on a whisper of a sigh and nearly pass out.

Good luck resisting the L-word, Ria. You might already be too late.

THE PAST

THE REAL L-O-V-E

Twenty-Six and a Half Years Ago...

Sophomore year, Friday afternoon in December

Maria

I am officially a free woman.

Well, free from midterms, that is. As of thirty minutes ago, I turned in my last exam to Mr. Parton, my chemistry teacher. *Thank everything!*

The excitement of Christmas break sits before me as I step off the subway. My house is only a short block away, but the chilly December air warrants me to button up my navy-blue pea coat as I walk up the steps that lead to the sidewalk.

No homework. No exams. No waking up early, I mentally list off the positives of winter break. *More time with Remy. Christmas morning with my mom and Isabella. Christmas dinner with the wild Winslows.*

My head is basically in the clouds as I maneuver through the busy pedestrian traffic that's mixed with locals taking a lunch break and tourists exploring the city while it's all dressed up for the holidays.

Once I'm in my building, the aroma of cookies hits me right in the face.

They smell absolutely delicious, but since there's no way that's coming from *my* apartment—with my mom at work, Isabella should be the only one home, and she's strictly forbidden from using any major appliances while she is— I'll just have to taste them in my dreams.

Isabella wasn't too thrilled over the prospect of being alone at all, actually, but with her winter break starting two days before mine, we didn't really have many other options. I assured her my midterm wouldn't take long, and our mom made sure Cindy, our kind next-door neighbor, would be home in case she needed anything, but she has to be getting hungry with the smell of chocolate chips in the air.

I climb the final staircase to our floor and unlock and shove open the door quickly, closing out the blizzard-like cold of winter behind me as fast as I can.

"Isabella," I call out as I remove my jacket and toss my purse, keys, and backpack down in the catchall area of our entryway. "Isabella!" I shout for her again, only this time, my voice is much louder.

"In the kitchen, Ri!"

Wait, the kitchen? Please tell me she hasn't decided to try her hand at baking and rebelling against authority.

Isabella might be nearing twelve now, but she's liable to burn down our whole building with how easily she gets distracted. She's unbelievably book smart, but when it comes to common-sense life stuff, she has the attention span of a squirrel.

Quickly, I slip off my brown boots and pad down the hallway, my sights set on the kitchen and a hopefully empty oven.

But what I find there is not at all what I expect. The oven isn't empty, and neither is a single square inch of the counter.

"My God," I whisper into the untidy space and the sight of Isabella, Remy, and Winnie baking in holiday-themed aprons. "What on earth is going on here?" I ask, my eyes scanning the current state of the kitchen. It's an absolute mess—sprinkles, icing, bowls, and all sorts of baking utensils and ingredients are everywhere.

Dreaded thoughts of cleanup disappear in a *poof!* of air, though, as soon as I look back to them. Their smiles could fill a cruise ship, they're so big.

"Maria! You're home! Look! We're baking cookies!" Winnie exclaims proudly, and Isabella lifts a cookie in the shape of a snowman to prove the point.

"You *have* to try our snowman sugar cookies, Ri. You'll love 'em."

"Hey, babe. How did the big chem midterm go?" Remy asks, his smile taking on a more knowing edge as he scrubs his hands down the front of his apron and closes the distance between us.

"Good, I think… But I thought I wasn't going to see you until tonight?" I question, and he shrugs.

"I figured since I didn't have any exams today and I knew your mom was at work and you would be busy until noonish with your midterm, Winnie and I could come over and keep Isabella company until you were done."

It sounds like such a simple thing, him baking cookies with our sisters, but it's not.

Remy could've slept in today or hung out with some of his buddies or done pretty much anything he wanted, but he decided to entertain our sisters. Entertain *my* sister, so she wouldn't have to be alone.

He could've chosen to do a hundred different things, but he chose to be *here*.

"I love you," I blurt out, the words shooting past my lips before I can even think about it, and his smile migrates up his face until it's inside his eyes.

"I love you too, Ria."

This doesn't even come close to the first time we've exchanged *I love yous*, but in this moment, it's like I can actually *feel* it more than I've ever felt it before.

Flutters of the Bible quote that starts with "Love is patient, love is kind" whisper through my mind, but I can't remember how the rest goes.

But it doesn't matter.

Because right now, I know love is Remy baking cookies in the kitchen with our sisters. It's Remy making sure Isabella was okay while I was at my midterm without my even having to ask him.

It's all of the things he does and all of the things he makes me feel.

Love is *this*.

"Ugh! Remy, I need help!" Winnie announces, and she scrunches up her face in disgust when the cookie she's holding slips from her hand and falls icing-first onto the table. "Oh no!"

"Looks like I better get back to baking duty." Remy sighs, but he also laughs. And then he presses one soft peck of his lips to mine and pulls me into a quick hug before releasing me to go help his sister.

I just stand there, watching the boy I met over a year and a half ago, the one who looks more like a full-fledged man each day, knowing I am really, truly, deeply in love with him.

I love Remington Winslow. Period but, hopefully, not end of story.

Fingers and toes and everything crossed.

THIRTY-EIGHT

Friday, November 8th

Remy

It's Friday night, and I'm not out at a damn club or at some bar grabbing a drink with one of my buddies or brothers. I'm not even sitting in my home office, alone, overworking myself despite the fact that the markets won't open for another forty-eight hours.

I'm at home with Maria and Izzy and Lexi and two goldfish that have somehow managed to survive four weeks of life with us, despite the fact that both Maria and I often forget about them.

And I'm actually fucking happy.

Man, life sure has changed. *In the best way possible.*

Maria moves in the kitchen, pulling plates down from the cabinets and setting them on the counter with silverware. Spaghetti sauce bubbles in a pan to her right, and the garlic bread baking in the oven fills the kitchen with an irresistible aroma.

I glance back at her occasionally, just to be sure she doesn't need any assistance, and help Izzy pretend to fly. Three months old now, she's gaining an incredible amount of head and neck control with every day that passes. Her first real smile, her first tiny giggle, Izzy girl is hitting a lot of milestones these days, and flying through the sky has become one of her favorite games.

Izzy laughs, coos, and her eyes move to where my niece sits on the couch beside us.

"Hey, cute girl," Lexi says, smiling as she reaches forward to poke a finger at Izzy's hand in the hope that she'll grab it. "Who's a cute girl?" She attempts again, but Izzy just grins, too busy watching Lex's mouth move to notice her finger.

My niece loves babies, and as luck would have it, babies love her. *Especially* Izzy.

Lex will forever be the first person to get a real, true, authentic smile to crest Izzy's lips. It occurred about two weeks ago and made me feel like I'd grown an extra damn heart. Maria had cried. Then she'd laughed. Then she'd cried a little more.

And since Izzy has enough awareness to notice who she's with, and she most definitely *loves* when Lexi is around, Maria and I have taken to having Lex over as much as we can these days.

"Hey, Ri, how'd your showing with the Tomlinsons go today?" I ask toward the kitchen. She's been worried about working with the Tomlinsons for a week now, with the missus, in particular, having quite the reputation for being hard to please.

"Better than I expected, thankfully. They didn't like the apartment, but they're open to looking in Nolita."

"That's great news, babe. You have so much more inventory there."

"I know, right?" she replies and flashes a relieved grin at me from the kitchen. "I obviously pushed in that direction a little bit, but honestly, the area is a great fit for them. Daniel is showing them a couple of places tomorrow while I'm with the Blakelys, but I spent two hours with him today going over all the particulars of Mrs. Tomlinson's quirks. I think he can handle it."

"Definitely. There's no way you can do it all. That's why you have other agents on your team. And Tonya, too. So you can delegate."

Tonya is Maria's newest assistant and has been working for the company for a few weeks now. Claudia, while horrible at her job, is still on the team because Isabella's soft spot for her is apparently still living and thriving within Maria. But Tonya is proving to be a huge asset, oftentimes ensuring that Claudia doesn't fuck shit up.

"You have to admit, I'm getting better at the whole delegating thing."

"That you are. I about passed out last weekend when you agreed to take the day off *and* let Winnie keep Izzy for us."

Maria laughs, and Lexi waggles her eyebrows. She's no stranger to our teasing at this point.

"Are you spending the night again, Lexi Lou?" Maria asks casually. The sound of water whooshing into the sink as she drains the pasta is my cue to get my ass into the kitchen.

I hand the baby to Lexi, who shifts back into the couch and holds her carefully while she answers, "Yes. But only if you pick the movie. Uncle Remy has bad cinematic taste."

"Brooo," I groan, grabbing Lexi by the shoulder and giving her a tiny shake that makes her smile. "You really gonna do me like that?"

She shrugs, ruthless as always. "You made us watch *Glitter* last time."

"It's Mariah! You can't be mad at Mariah!" I defend.

Maria doesn't even bother to hide her laughs in the kitchen.

I roll my eyes and groan, pretending to be put out by their criticism. "Fine. What film will the two of you be selecting tonight, then? Huh? Prove your superiority."

With her free arm, Lexi carefully grabs the remote from the cushion next to her and pulls up Amazon Prime. An endless bounty of options fills the screen, and she starts scrolling to find the best one.

I make my way into the kitchen and start stirring the sauce while Maria puts the noodles back into the hot pot. Once we mix them both together tag-team-style, I head over to the oven to remove the garlic bread.

"If Lex is staying, that means one of us is going to have to run her Uptown in the morning. I think I can do it if my first showing is where I think it is, I just have to check the schedule," Maria chirps, running down a plan.

"No need, babe. Tomorrow's Saturday, remember?"

Maria lets out a little chortle, letting her head drop back. "Holy shit, how did I completely lose track of the days this week?"

I pull her into the side of my body for a shoulder squeeze and a hug. "Because you're incredibly busy being Superwoman. But I've got the kids." I raise my voice and project toward the living room on purpose so that Lexi will hear the next part. "I may even take the girls to breakfast at Lex's favorite brunch spot."

"Bunrise?" Lexi practically yells, her head whipping over her shoulder to look back at us. The name is a little cutesy if you ask me, but that's New York for you.

"Can I take your shout as enthusiasm? Is that a yes vote for brunch?"

"Yes!" Lex hoots. "You're the best, Uncle Remy!"

In an instant, her words switch my focus, and I grab my phone out of my pocket to fire off a high-priority text.

"What exactly are you doing?" Maria asks as my fingers move swiftly across the screen.

"You think I'm going to let her declare me the best uncle and not text that to my brothers?" I scoff. "No way. I have to let them know I'm atop the podium."

Maria rolls her eyes, but she does it with a grin. "You're children, all of you."

I don't deny it. Instead, I hit send.

Me: Sorry to have to break it to you losers, but I've been crowned favorite uncle…again. I know it's tough for all of you, losing so much, but you have to be getting used to it at this point, right? I mean, it's basically expected.

Ty: Like fuck, you are. Rachel and I babysat for Ryder and Roman two nights last weekend AND took Lex to the Mavericks game on Sunday. We're totally winning.

Jude: Everyone knows I'm the fun uncle. Everyone.

Me: Sorry, nope. We're having spaghetti tonight, AND I'm taking Lex to brunch at Bunrise tomorrow morning.

Flynn: The evidence is clear in this case. Remy wins.

Ty: That means you lose too, jackhole.

Flynn: I'm not competing with any of you fuckers. Lex and I have a relation-ship that's in a category of its own.

Ignoring the rest of their bullshit banter now that I've been declared the distinguished winner, I set our group chat on Do Not Disturb and tuck my phone back into my pocket, just as Maria is putting the garlic bread and spa-ghetti in serving dishes.

Shit. Looks like I missed most of the work.

"I'll set the table," I offer, leaning forward to press a kiss to Maria's cheek. She hums an *uh-huh,* her eyes sparkling with amusement.

"No more bragging tonight—until later," I whisper in her ear. "But I'll earn it, I promise."

I discreetly squeeze her ass for good measure, earning a little squeal of shock, and get to work on setting the table. Once all of the plates and silverware and napkins are in place and the chairs are moved so we're all facing toward the TV, Lex shouts her victory from the living room.

"Found it!"

"You found one? But is it a *good* one?" I tease, knowing full well I'll enjoy the experience of watching a movie with my girls whether I like the movie or not.

"*Hidden Figures,*" she replies simply, stating only the title of the movie before clicking the description on the screen and reading it aloud to us. "An incred-ible and inspiring untold true story about three women at NASA who were instrumental in one of history's greatest operations."

"Oooh!" Maria crows from the kitchen, picking up the dish of spaghetti, a hot pad, and the basket of garlic bread all at once to come to the table. "That sounds good, Lexi Lou. Go ahead and get it started."

"I'll come get Iz," I add, rounding the table to do just that so that Lexi can come sit down.

Once a happy Izzy is buckled into the bouncer seat we always keep by us during dinner, I give her one last tickle and set the mobile overhang and vibrations in motion. One squeeze to Maria's hip and I pull out the chair beside her. She takes a seat with a grateful smile and then promptly starts dishing the food onto all our plates.

Lexi's first, then mine, then her own. Like always, she makes sure to take care of us.

As the movie starts and we dive into the food, I can't help but notice the immediate similarities between one of the main women, Katherine, and our Lexi.

"She's smart like you, Lex," I remark, making her mouth curve up in a bashful smile. It's a special expression, one I've come to cherish from her over the years. It's not big and bright and toothy—it's shy and intentional. It's a tiny sliver of her golden light, escaping the secret place she keeps it, for all to see.

It also reminds me that I haven't told her parents she's staying the night, and I grab my phone to do it before I forget. "Just going to tell Winnie and Wes that she's staying," I explain to Maria.

She nods appreciatively, remarking, "Good idea. Don't want them thinking we stole their kid."

I smirk and hit send on a text to Wes and Winnie.

Me: Lex is going to stay the night here…if that works for you guys.

I quickly look up to see if Maria can see my phone from where she's sitting, and when I note that her eyes are riveted to the TV, I shoot off another text. Mind you, it's slightly in code, but I'm confident they'll understand.

Me: PS: I can drop the packages off at mom's house tomorrow. Both of them. After brunch.

Starting tomorrow, Wendy Winslow will be hosting a girls-only slumber party. Well, girls only, plus Howard.

It originally started out as her watching Izzy because I have a big surprise planned for Maria, but once Lex found out her favorite tiny human was going to be with her grandmother for five days straight, she all but begged Winnie to join in on the fun this weekend.

Winnie: Oh yeah, THE PACKAGES… So glad you can do that. *wink wink* And it works out perfectly for tonight since we're running behind at the stadium.

Me: You realize the whole *wink wink* is a real tip-off, right?

Winnie: I have no idea what you're talking about *wink wink*

Wes: Thanks for doing that, man. *wink wink*

Winnie: Yeah, thanks, Rem. *wink wink*

Smartasses.

Wes: PS: Word on the street is that you're currently in first place for DILF of the Year.

Me: What? Thatch still has me in that fucking contest?

Winnie: HAHAHAHAHAHAHAHAHA

My sister is clearly getting far too much amusement out of this.

Wes: It's Thatch. Don't even bother trying to stop it, bro. Your effort would be wasted. But I have to say, he's never let anyone sit in first place for this long. You should feel special, dude.

Oh yeah, so fucking special.

Switching message threads, I move over to Thatch's—previously filled with crap about investments—and address the issue at hand.

Me: What's this shit I hear about DILF of the Year?

Thatch: You're winning, dude! Complete underdog situation if you ask me, considering you haven't even signed any adoption papers yet!

Me: I would like to rescind my entry.

Thatch: Sorry, darling. Once the contest begins, you can't pull out.

Me: But I never fucking entered the contest in the first place.

Thatch: Unfortunately, the rules of the contest are set in stone, and just between us, the dude who runs it is a real stickler about them.

Me: BUT IT'S YOU.

Thatch: Like I said, rules are rules.

Me: I forfeit.

Thatch: Uh-oh. Trouble in Full House paradise? Tell me you're not done with the hot single mom already?

Me: There's no trouble. I just don't want to be a clown in your circus.

Thatch: Wait…what do you mean by clown? If you tell me you're dressing up as a clown for your baby, I've underestimated you.

Me: I swear, sometimes I feel like I'm on drugs talking to you.

Knowing full well this conversation is heading nowhere fast, I lock the screen of my phone on an exasperated sigh and set it on the kitchen table beside my plate.

Maria looks over at me, her pretty brown eyes searching mine. "Everything okay over there?"

"Just talking to a lunatic," I mutter, but when she tilts her head to the side, I elaborate a little more. "Thatcher Kelly."

Instantly, her eyes stretch with understanding, but also, the hint of a smile follows. She doesn't even need to respond. Doesn't even need to acknowledge that she knows who I'm talking about.

Last week, she had the pleasure of meeting Thatch while we were dropping Lexi off at Wes and Winnie's. It was a brief introduction, but it doesn't take much for a guy like that to leave an impression.

I nod at her, my eyes saying, *You have no idea.*

"Are you guys having, like, telepathic sex or something?" Lexi asks so suddenly and matter-of-factly that it catches both Maria and me off guard. We spiral into a simultaneous coughing and choking fit, and I start slapping at Maria's back swiftly. She then does the same for me as I try to catch my breath.

THE REDO | 333

"What on earth? Telepathic sex?" I ask when I can finally speak. "Where did you even hear about that?"

"Online."

"Maybe I should text your mom to update your protection settings," I mutter under my breath.

Lexi is unfazed. "This fortune lady Cleo says that two people whose chakras are aligned can have telepathic sex."

All of a sudden, I'm choking again, this time for more than just the fact that I had to hear my niece repeat the word sex. "I'm sorry, what did you say? Who says that?"

"Cleo. She has a huge online blog about parallel dimensions and fate signals."

Cleo?

Suddenly, my head feels like it's a fucking top and is seconds away from spinning off my damn neck as Lexi prattles on.

"One of the main things she does is channel love chakras. She says love is a lava flow just waiting to overtake all of us. But it's not about finding it, it's about being ready for it. Oftentimes, it's been right in front of us all along."

I feel sweat bead on my forehead as I become paranoid that Cleo is somehow sending me messages without using the phone now, channeling the power of my extraordinary niece instead, just to send me her vague shit about love.

But Lexi puts that insanity out of my mind when she utilizes my phone to pull up a video. "This is her. Cleo."

Like a fool, I watch the brief clip. The woman is talking to a crowd of people and is the very opposite of the Cleo I know. She's far too fucking commercial, if I'm being honest, and I'm both relieved and confused as hell.

Looks like C's texts are starting to get under your skin there, buddy. Maybe making you look a little deeper into your current man-of-the-house situation?

I kind of want to punch myself in the face.

Cleo's texts aren't doing jack shit to me. I know what I'm doing with Maria, and I don't need some coo-coo-ca-choo fortune-teller causing confusion where there most certainly doesn't need to be confusion.

The obnoxious voice in my head whispers, *Are you sure about that?* But I shake it off.

Yes, Maria and I haven't exactly defined anything, but we've been enjoying each other's company, enjoying Izzy, living our lives together without putting pressure on ourselves to label it.

What we have is good. What we have is right. Nothing can change that.

I, Remington Winslow, know exactly what the fuck I'm doing here.

Right?

THIRTY-NINE

Saturday, November 9th

Maria

The morning sun is peeking through the curtains of my walk-in closet as I attempt to fold the basket of clean laundry that's been sitting in here for the past two days. Just fitting in a few mundane chores, if you will, before Remy and Izzy and Lexi wake up and all of the responsibilities of the day get ahead of me.

How is it possible for one little person to create so much dang laundry? I think to myself as I stack Izzy's onesies in a pile on the floor.

But before I can shift them over to her dedicated hamper so I can put them in her nursery, my attention is pulled by a soft but sleepy whisper behind me.

"Hi, Maria. Is Izzy up yet?"

I look over my shoulder to see Lexi standing in the doorway in her pajamas, her blond hair still an adorable mess from just waking up.

"She's still sleeping," I explain. "But you're up pretty early, sweetheart. Did you sleep okay?"

"I'm always up this early." She shrugs and shuffles her slipper-covered feet farther into my closet to sit down on the cozy chaise sofa Remy put in here a couple of weeks ago in the name of making it easier for me to juggle Izzy while I'm trying to get ready for work.

But she only stays seated for about two minutes before she's up and perusing the contents of my closet. First, my shoes, then my dresses, and when she reaches a row of button-down dress shirts, she pauses to look at me. "You have a big closet. And *a lot* of clothes."

"That I do." A soft laugh jumps from my lips. "I guess you could say shopping is a bit of a hobby of mine." Or at least, it *was*. I haven't had much shopping time since Izzy made her big debut.

And having a massive walk-in closet was a must when I'd saved enough money to buy my own apartment. A girl needs a giant place to fit all of her retail therapy.

"Shopping can be a hobby?" Lex asks, and I nod with big, sure-as-hell eyes.

"Oh yeah, honey. Shopping can definitely be a hobby."

"Then, shopping is one of my mom's hobbies, too."

I grin. "Does she have a closet like mine?"

"Yep." Her fingers skim across the shelves that hold my accessories—belts, necklaces, bracelets, earrings, and purses. "I'm beginning to see the appeal of fashion," she adds, her voice so prudent for a girl her age that it makes me smile.

Man, I love this kid.

"I take it you didn't see the appeal before?"

"Nope." She shakes her head. "I thought it was dumb that Mom would want to spend so much money on something to wear."

"And now what do you think?"

She considers my question for a long minute, her brow furrowing as she comes to a conclusion. "I think fashion, for a lot of people, is a healthy expression of their personality."

"I think that's a brilliant insight, Lex. One I would definitely agree with."

"Is that what fashion is for you?" she asks, and I walk over to where she stands, her fingers busy exploring my necklaces and bracelets.

When I spot one particular necklace, a colorful Chanel choker that my sister Isabella used to wear every day until she gave it to me a few years ago for my birthday, something inside me makes me pick it up. And the urge to see it on her is too real to deny.

"Fashion is a few things for me," I tell Lexi as I lift the choker over her head and place it gently around her neck. "It's important for my job, so I can showcase myself as a professional, successful real estate agent. It allows me to express my personality, like you said." With my fingers, I secure the clasp. "And it makes me feel confident, too."

"Clothes can make you feel confident?" she asks, and I gently turn her around by the shoulders so she can see herself in the mirror.

"Clothes, fashion, accessories like this Chanel right here—" I wink "—can definitely make you feel confident. I've found that if I'm wearing something that makes me feel good, it can ensure I'm going to have a fantastic day."

Lexi reaches up to run her fingers across the colorful metal letters C-H-A-N-E-L, and I meet her reflection in the mirror with a smile.

"I think this necklace looks fantastic on you. Do you like it?"

"It's really pretty, Maria." She nods, and the shy smile that covers her face makes my heart expand inside my chest.

I quietly observe the way Lexi's eyes stay glued to the necklace. It's as if she's entranced by the way she looks in the mirror now. She doesn't just like it; she *loves* it, and the confirmation of that fact is written all over her pretty face.

"You know what? I think you should keep it."

Lex's eyes jerk to mine. "But it's yours…"

"It *was* mine," I correct her. "But now, it belongs with you."

Lexi glances at her reflection in the mirror again, and the smile on her face makes nostalgia flutter inside my belly. Every day, she's growing closer to becoming a teenage girl, and seeing the changes within her remind me so much of how I got to watch little Winnie Winslow grow up right before my very eyes.

If only Isabella could see what her old childhood friend is up to now. If only she could see that her daughter and Winnie's daughter are the best of buds.

"You know, a very long time ago, my sister Isabella gave me this as a birthday present," I add quietly. "And I know she'd be over the moon to see it on you. To know that it's yours now."

"My mom told me that she used to be friends with your sister and that she was really funny."

"Isabella loved your mom, and yes, she was hilarious." I nod. "My sister was sweet and kind and just…wonderful. Anyone who met her loved her."

"Is it hard to talk about her?"

"I think the scariest thing for me, when it comes to my sister, is forgetting things about her. I don't ever want to forget how special she was," I answer as honestly as I can. "But all thanks to you, for giving me the opportunity to talk about her right now, I'm remembering all of my favorite things about her, and *that* is making my heart smile."

Without responding with words, Lexi surprises the hell out of me by turning around and wrapping her arms around my waist and hugging me tightly.

And it's almost uncanny how much this hug was exactly what I needed and how Lexi, one of the least outwardly affectionate children I've met, knew just how to give it to me.

Thank you, sweet girl.

Just after our hug comes to an end and Lexi is busy looking at herself in my mirror some more, I hear the soft sounds of Izzy beginning to wake up in her crib. She's recently started this thing where she doesn't start crying at first, but more, yelling for us. It's basically baby babble for "Hey, I'm awake! Come get me!"

"I think I hear Izzy," Lexi updates, and I nod in amusement.

"Yep. That definitely sounds like her. What do you say we go get her out of her crib and you can feed her a bottle while I start getting ready for work?"

"Should we get Uncle Remy up, too?"

"How about we let him sleep a little longer?" I offer a secret smile and drop my voice to a whisper. "I think he's still taking it hard that he's so horrible at picking out good movies for movie night."

"Okay." She giggles at that.

Once we both manage to quietly get out of the master bedroom without waking Remy and then into Izzy's nursery, we're greeted with a big baby smile.

While I'm changing a wiggly Izzy's diaper, Lex stands beside her, trying to keep her entertained with silly faces. Izzy practically squeals, she loves it so much.

"Maria, I think you should marry my uncle Remy," Lexi says out of the damn blue, practically shocking me into a seizure.

"Uh…w-what?"

She lets Izzy hold on to her finger and makes another silly face at my girl, but eventually, she repeats her words. "I think you and my uncle Remy should get married."

I don't really know what to say to that, but thankfully, Lexi moves on quickly and becomes fully invested in making Izzy giggle some more.

But *I* haven't moved on.

I haven't moved on at all.

In fact, I'm right back in my teenage shoes, dreaming of a life with Remington Winslow and wondering if it's all going to slip through my fingers.

THE PAST

YOU'RE GOING TO MARRY HIM SOMEDAY

Twenty-Six Years Ago…

Sophomore year, early May

Maria

I finish writing the letters R-E-M-Y on the big poster board on my floor and stand back to see if they're centered below Remy's senior picture.

I think? I *hope?*

"Whatcha doing?" My sister's voice fills my ears, and I glance over my shoulder to see her standing in the doorway of my bedroom.

"Making a poster."

She walks into my room and stands right beside me, staring down at the poster board by my feet. "Is that for Remy?"

"Well…I really hope it is, or else I've put the wrong name and picture on some other dude's poster." I grin over at her, and she playfully shoves at my shoulder. "It's a poster for Remy's senior night next weekend, actually. Every senior gets one."

"What's senior night?"

"It's a party for all the seniors to celebrate graduating high school."

She moves over to my desk, sits down in the chair, and starts doodling on one of my notepads. "When is Remy's graduation again?"

"First week in June."

"That's so soon!" She drops the pen from her hand, and her eyes morph into saucers. "I can't believe Remy is going to be moving off to college! Like, you're still going to be in high school, but he's going to be in freaking college, Ri! What do you think that's going to be like?"

Gah. Hard. Really, really hard.

"Um…I don't know," I mutter and try to busy myself with adding a little confetti pizzaz to Rem's poster.

Honestly, even though I've tried to carefully broach the subject, we've yet to *really* talk about the fact that he's not going to be staying local. And anytime I bring up that soon-to-be reality, Remy tends to change the subject entirely.

"How old do you need to be to get married?"

"Excuse me?" That startles a laugh from my throat. "Is there something you need to tell me? Don't you think you're a little young for you and Brandon to be thinking about marriage?"

"Get real, sis. I broke up with Brandon two weeks ago." Isabella rolls her eyes. "And I wasn't talking about me. I was talking about you and Remy. I think that's what you guys should do."

"Remy and I should do what?"

"Get married! Duh!"

I turn to look at her. "You do realize I'm only sixteen, right? That's a bit young to be getting married. Or even thinking about getting married."

"Yeah, but you're going to end up marrying him someday anyway. Why not just do it now?"

"Because I'm sixteen and still have my whole life ahead of me." I narrow my eyes suspiciously. "You trying to get me out of the house just so you can take over my bedroom or something?"

"No…" She pauses and then adds, "But you bring up a really good point."

I pick up a pillow and throw it at her head. "Jerk!"

She laughs and tosses it back at me before shuffling back out of my room, but not before shouting over her shoulder, "I still think you guys should get married!"

She's crazy, obviously, but man, my mind can't stop replaying her words.

You're going to end up marrying him someday anyway.

My heart wants to jump on the bandwagon and agree with her, but my mind is *way* too logical for that.

I may be young, but I'm not naïve. Most high school relationships don't last. Especially when one-half of the relationship will be in high school for two more years, while the other half is college-bound.

And with the way Remy has been avoiding the whole conversation revolving around him going off to college and where that leaves us, I can't help but wonder if it's for reasons I might find hard to hear.

Reasons that might break your heart.

FORTY

Remy

When I step into the bathroom, I'm pleasantly surprised to find Maria standing in front of the mirror, putting on lipstick. Her long brown hair hangs down past her shoulders, and her body is dressed to impress in the kind of silk blouse and tight pencil skirt that makes her ass look juicy as hell.

Damn, she's sexy.

I step over to my gorgeous woman at the sink, stand directly behind her, and wrap my arms around her waist. "Mornin', babe. I had a feeling you'd be in here getting ready."

"Good morning, sleepyhead."

I squeeze her hips. "Are the girls awake yet?"

"Lexi just finished feeding Izzy her bottle and is currently entertaining her in the living room."

"You should've woken me up. I would've handled them while you got ready."

"Why?" she questions and meets my reflection in the mirror. "You looked peaceful, and Lex and I had it covered."

"What time do you need to be at your first showing?"

"In about forty minutes," she updates and uses a brush to make the apples of her cheeks pink. "There's fresh coffee in the kitchen, by the way. Just made a pot about ten minutes ago."

I know I should leave her to whatever it is women need to do to get ready, but man, *her ass, in this skirt,* is nearly too much for my mind to stay on task.

Before I know it, I'm sliding both of my big hands away from her hips and straight onto the perfect, rounded, curvy ass of hers that makes my brain short-circuit and my dick take far too much notice.

"Remy," she says, her voice a warning. An amused warning, mind you.

"What?" I feign innocence but still keep my grip. "I'm just smoothing out a few wrinkles."

"Off the skirt I just ironed?"

"Irons are tricky things, babe." I shrug. "Sometimes they miss a few spots."

She snorts, and I squeeze my big hands into her curvy flesh some more.

"Remy!" She's laughing now.

"Just a few pieces of lint, babe." Still squeezing. "I think I got it…" I pause, staring down at her ass like I'm just trying to help her out. "Oh…wait…just a few more pieces of lint," I add, squeezing a little harder this time.

That's her cue to turn around and playfully slap me away, but she's no match for my speed because I have her in my arms and her breasts pressed tight to my chest in two seconds flat.

Her lips are just a hint away from mine, and I stare at them, silently wondering if she'll be pissed if I kiss the hell out of her and risk messing up her makeup.

Fuck it. Let her be mad.

I fall victim to the urge, pressing my mouth to hers, and coaxing her lips open with my tongue. She's an easy sell, giving in to the moment, and I slide my hands back to her ass and pull her body as close to mine as I can.

My dick is hard now, and my mind is already visualizing one hundred different scenarios that end with her panties around her ankles and me inside her.

It takes all my willpower to remind myself she has important places to be and not to follow through with any of it.

"Fuck." On a sigh, I slow our kiss to a stop, give her lips one more gentle press, and release her from my hold.

Maria blinks several times, her mind trying to come back down to planet earth, and I have to adjust my cock in my boxer briefs on a groan.

"You're kind of a bastard, you know that?" Her voice is teasing as she meets my eyes in the reflection in the mirror.

It's then I notice that her lipstick is smeared to shit on both of our faces.

"I don't think this is my color, babe," I respond, pretending to examine my face in the mirror and frowning a little. "I think I'm more of a coral, you know?"

"You're such a pain in my ass sometimes!" She slaps my chest on a laugh and then proceeds to grab a tissue to fix her face and mine.

"I won't deny that, but I think the big question here is…am I going to get a rain check on what we just started?" I ask, my hands coming together in front of my chest like I'm praying.

"We didn't start anything. *You* started it."

"Very true," I agree. "But you still didn't answer my question."

She lets out an exasperated sigh, but when I lean forward to press my lips to her neck, whispering the words, "Please, Ria?" against her skin, a little moan escapes her throat.

I smile. I can't help it.

We're definitely cashing in on that rain check later. In fact, starting this evening, we're going to have the opportunity to cash in on lots of rain checks, days' worth of them.

The realization makes me press one final kiss to her skin and step away from her. "How about I let you finish getting ready for work and I go check on the girls?"

"You know, crazily enough, I think that's a good idea," Maria comments with a roll of her pretty brown eyes. "Plus, I'm sure Lexi is nearly bursting with excitement for brunch at Bunrise."

"You're probably right," I agree, reaching out to squeeze her ass one more time for good measure.

And then I head out of the bathroom and toward the living room where my other two favorite girls are located.

Today is going to be a good fucking day.

Bunrise is a staple in this city, and it should be no surprise that it's packed to the gills. I'm talking a two-hour wait outside, and every table inside filled with patrons laughing and chatting over pancakes and mimosas and their signature sunny-side up egg, bacon, and cheese on a home-baked bun.

Thankfully, Maria is a thoughtful genius who called ahead and reserved a table for us with the hostess—a single mom in need of an apartment at a fair price whom Maria just happened to make things happen for a couple of years ago—while she was headed toward her first showing of the day, and the three of us were whisked right to an open table the second we stepped inside the doors.

Before our food arrived, I sent Maria a message thanking her for saving my ass and telling her I owed her for ensuring I didn't have to wait to be seated for two damn hours while trying to keep Lexi and Izzy entertained.

Obviously, she's just now had the time to respond.

Maria: You're welcome. And don't worry, I can think of several ways for you to repay me.

I smirk down at my phone.

Me: Oh, don't worry, babe. I already have plans for how I'm going to repay you.

Maria: I am ALL ears. Do tell, and don't leave a single detail out.

Me: It's a surprise.

A surprise bigger than she could ever expect and one that was set in motion way before today.

Maria: Ugh. Can you at least give me a hint? Like, is it an s-e-x kind of surprise?

Me: Nope.

Maria: No s-e-x?

Pfft. Yeah, right. There's definitely s-e-x involved in this surprise. A lot of it, if it's up to me.

Me: No hint.

Maria: You know this is going to drive me crazy for the rest of the day, right?

Me: Oh, I'm aware.

Maria: I can practically see you smiling through the damn phone.

Me: ;) See you after work, babe.

*Maria: *rolls eyes**

"Are you texting, Maria?" Lexi asks just before shoving a bite of her favorite French toast into her mouth. *Sarabeth's Flat and Fluffy French Toast*, to be specific. The owners named it after their daughter since it's her favorite dish.

"Yes, Ms. Nosy. I was."

Lex is unbothered by the nickname and shoves another bite of French toast into her mouth.

From her spot in my lap, Izzy watches on with big, intrigued eyes and reaches out to shakily bang her hands on the table. The motion practically knocks my coffee into my egg, bacon, and cheese sandwich, and a laugh jumps from my throat as I juggle her away from causing a disaster.

"I think she wants a bite of my French toast," Lex says through a giggle and prolongs poor Izzy's misery by shoving another big bite into her mouth. Powdered sugar covers her lips in the most adorable way, and it's then that I notice a necklace around her petite neck.

A fucking Chanel necklace, mind you.

"What's that, Lex?"

"What's what?"

"The necklace," I say and nod toward it.

She glances down and shrugs. "Maria gave it to me."

"Maria gave you a Chanel necklace?"

What the hell?

"That's what I said. Are you having trouble hearing?"

I'll be honest, this is the first time I've ever seen Lexi wear a necklace, or any jewelry for that matter, and I'm surprised it took me this long to notice it.

"When did you start liking jewelry, Lex?"

"I'm getting close to my teenage years, Uncle Remy. It's normal for girls my age to begin exploring fashion."

Her teenage years. Fucking hell.

"Oh, so it's not just jewelry, but fashion?" I feign a dramatic sigh. "This is becoming too much for your Uncle Rem. Soon you're going to be telling me you have a boyfriend."

"I do have a boyfriend."

Brakes squeal to a stop inside my head. "What?"

"His name is Connor," Lex updates like it's no big thing. "He's on my Mathletes team."

But it *is* a big thing. A very big thing, in my opinion.

"And how long have you had this boyfriend?"

"We've only been going out for about a month, but that's pretty long, considering the standard for any middle school relationship is roughly two weeks."

"Going out? Where exactly do you go?"

"We don't go anywhere."

What?

"What does that even mean?" I question. "How are you 'going out' but you don't go anywhere?"

Lexi rolls her eyes like I'm the biggest bore on the planet. "It's just an expression kids use, Uncle Remy. It's another way to say he's my boyfriend and I'm his girlfriend."

His girlfriend? Lexi is some kid's girlfriend? Who is this little prick?

"And this Connor, is he a nice kid?"

Lexi shrugs. "He can compute complex physics equations in his head, Uncle Rem."

"So, you just like him because he's good at math?"

Okay. Okay. Maybe I can handle this...

"And he's cute."

Never fucking mind.

My niece thinks a boy is cute? Suddenly, my mind wants to start replaying the conversation I had with her at that Mavericks game back in October, when she was noticing the players' asses.

"Does Wes know about this?"

"Yeah."

"And he's okay with it?"

"Yeah. My mom and Nick and Charlotte are too."

I'm about ten seconds away from asking her a thousand questions. What's Connor's last name? How old is he? Where does this little asshole live?

But Izzy starts to get antsy in my lap, her little fists banging against the table, and I decide to save those questions for another time and just focus on not having a heart attack over the news of Lexi's fucking boyfriend.

A boyfriend.

My little Lexi has a damn boyfriend. *You couldn't possibly also be freaking out because your preteen niece has managed to declare her intentions before you, could you?*

I give Izzy her pacifier and adjust her in my lap so that she's cradled close to my chest and try to finish up the rest of my eggs and bacon, shutting out stupid head-voices altogether.

I'm going to ignore a lot of things if I'm going to get through the rest of this meal without freaking out completely. I mean, I knew my little Lexi Lou would eventually start having boyfriends and shit, but I was thinking more like eighteen, twenty-one, *thirty-five.*

Not this damn soon. Not to a smart little science-y prick named Connor. I mean, *Connor?* That name just spells fucking trouble.

"Uncle Remy?"

"Yeah, Lex?"

Please don't tell me you're engaged. I'll die right here, I swear.

"Is Maria your girlfriend?"

Fucking hell, so much for ignoring that internal voice, bro. Sounds like it's external now.

"Uh…" I pause, completely unsure of what to answer—which, I'll admit, doesn't make me feel good.

I mean, what is Maria to me? The word girlfriend doesn't even come close to showcasing what I feel for her. It's a pathetic fucking word to describe the role she plays in my life, but declaring her as—

"I think you should marry her and make her your wife." She chews. "That way, Maria will be my real Aunt Maria."

And there it is. The consequences of my actions.

Just because I've been enjoying what Maria and I have been doing over the past few months without putting labels on it doesn't mean I'm the only one affected by what's growing between us.

There are two specific someones being affected, actually, and they're sitting right at this table with me.

I need to start figuring my shit out and quick. Maria deserves more than a helpful guy with the ability to walk away anytime he wants. With everything she is and has been through? She's earned a hell of a lot more.

Good thing you're about to have five days alone with her to start figuring it out...

FORTY-ONE

Remy

I'm shocked when my sister is the one who answers my mom's front door.

"Mommy!" Lex exclaims and steps forward to wrap her arms around Winnie's waist.

"Hi, sweetie!"

"What are you doing here, Win?"

"I missed my girl," she explains, giving Lexi a quick but tight hug. "So, I figured I'd stop over here for a bit and spend some time with her before I have to go back to the stadium."

"Where's Mom?"

"She ran out to get some groceries. Left right after you texted her to tell her you and the girls were on your way. Should be back soon," she continues to update as we step inside my mom's duplex.

Instantly, my sister's eyes go to Izzy, who is currently sitting cozy in the baby carrier around my chest.

Technically, she's a little young by her age to be front-facing, but by weight and with her pediatrician's approval after seeing how much neck strength she has, we've graduated her to being able to see the world in front of us, instead of stuck staring at our shirts.

"Well, hello there, my little honeybee. I've missed your cute face."

Izzy squeals and kicks her legs a bit, and Winnie smiles like she's smitten. Lex joins in on the fun, and it doesn't take long before she wins a few belly laughs from the baby on my chest.

"I swear, that is the best sound in the world," Winnie muses and turns her attention back to me. "Everything go okay last night?"

"Of course it did. Lex is the best. And word on the street is that I'm also the best uncle."

"The game that will never end." Winnie snorts and looks at Lexi. "Did you have fun? Did Uncle Remy behave himself too?"

"Tons of fun. We watched a movie last night, and Maria gave me this," Lexi announces, showing off the Chanel necklace I still can't believe Maria gave to her.

My sister's eyes grow big as she reaches out to touch the letters that read C-H-A-N-E-L. "Maria gave you this necklace?"

"Yep." Lex nods proudly. "Isn't it pretty? It was Maria's sister's necklace."

That catches both Winnie's and my attention.

"This was Isabella's?" I ask, and Lexi nods like it's no big thing.

"Yep."

But to me, it is a big thing. It's huge. Both Winnie and I can feel it; I can tell by the gentle sheen I see in her eyes and the sting I feel in mine.

I can't even begin to imagine how big of a deal—the depth of what Maria must feel for Lexi—this had to be.

"I'm going to put my stuff upstairs in Grandma's guest room," Lexi announces and wraps her arms around my waist to give me a quick hug. "Thanks for the sleepover and brunch, Uncle Rem. I had fun."

"I had fun with you too, kiddo."

"Uncle Rem, kiddo isn't really a good nickname for me anymore," she says matter-of-factly. "Just Lex or Lexi is best."

"Oh, that's right, you're basically a full-fledged woman now who wears Chanel and has a boyfriend named Connor." I eye my sister pointedly. "How could I forget?"

But Lex is already done with the small talk in the foyer. Her overnight bag in her hand, she runs up the stairs without another word.

"I take it she told you about the boyfriend?"

"Yep," I answer and tilt my head to the side. "Which means you have some explaining to do."

"What do you mean?"

"Why is she allowed to have a boyfriend?"

Winnie bursts into laughter. "Oh, c'mon, Rem. I'm not going to ban Lexi from having a boyfriend. You're being overprotective."

"I'm realistic."

"You realize all they do is say they're boyfriend and girlfriend and send each other text messages about astrophysical engineering, right? It's harmless."

"What the fuck? They're *texting* each other?"

Winnie laughs. "Man. Men are so hilarious." Without anything more, she smiles as she pulls Izzy out of her baby carrier, not even bothering to ask for permission. I unstrap it from my chest and lay it down in case she needs it.

"I'm serious, Win. This is too much."

"Oh, I know you're serious. But you're also nuts."

"I'm not nuts—"

"Don't you have somewhere to be?" she questions, cutting me off at the knees. "Pretty sure you have a big trip to get ready for…"

I sigh and point one index finger toward her. "This conversation isn't over."

"Oh, I realize that." She grins and kisses the top of Izzy's head. "But if you don't mind, I'm going to spend some time with Lex and this little sweetie right here before Grandma gets back and becomes a baby hog. So, you can go ahead and move your ass out the door."

"You're kicking me out?"

"It's for your own good, Rem. Time is a-ticking, and even though Wes set up the private flight for you, pilots like to leave on time."

I hate when my smartass baby sister is right, but...she's right. I still have to get Maria and myself packed before she gets home from her last showing. Truthfully, we'll only have about an hour to get to the airport once her workday is done.

"Go enjoy yourself," she adds over her shoulder. "Enjoy tropical bliss with Maria. You both deserve it. I know from experience that the Bahamas are gorgeous this time of year. Perfect for photos by the beach and telling the woman you love that you love her and want to mar—"

"Oh shit, look at the time. I better get going, sis."

"Uh-huh. Of course you do." She just sticks her tongue out at me and turns to take Izzy into my mom's living room. "Love you, big bro! Have fun!"

Is it just me, or is there a lot of pressure surrounding Maria's and my relationship these days?

Pressure rushes to fill holes, dude. Maybe this is a sign telling you to use Maria to fill yours.

After I dropped the girls off at my mom's, I grabbed a fresh bouquet of flowers at the market up the corner from Maria's place before heading there to get us packed. Lord knows if I'd let Maria pack her own suitcase, she'd end up bringing half her damn closet, and I know for a fact she's not going to need a lot of clothes.

Besides the guest of honor getting home, we're all set to be Bahamas-bound.

I hear Maria's key jiggle in the lock and hurriedly grab the bouquet of flowers from the coffee table and stand up to greet her. But when the door opens, her phone is pressed to her ear as she juggles her purse and leather briefcase. "Claudia, I know you hate contacting mortgage brokers," she says through a sigh and heads into the kitchen, completely oblivious to my presence in the living room. "But that's the next step in this process and kind of, if you'll excuse my language, your fucking job."

She paces the hardwood floor, and I already know why. Claudia is the worst assistant on the planet. She's disorganized, forgetful, and is shit at reading people. Truthfully, I'm wondering why Maria isn't having Tonya deal with whatever it is she's trying to get Claudia to do.

"Yes, it is Saturday," Maria answers and puts the phone on speaker while she grabs a bottle of water from the fridge. "But all it's going to take is some phone calls, Claudia. I'm not asking you to go to the mortgage broker's house for cocktails."

"But I have yoga at four," Claudia whines, and it sounds like she's chewing gum between words. "And then I'm supposed to do champagne dinner with the girls."

Maria lets her head fall back on a quiet groan.

"Can't it wait until Monday?"

"The goal of you reaching out to them today is so that, on Monday, they start the week focused on our client."

"So, like, I don't need to actually talk to anyone?"

Maria sighs. "No, that's not the goal. The goal is to talk to Hank, our client's mortgage broker, and find out what in the hell is going on with the underwriters."

"Who are the underwriters again?" she questions. "They sound scary."

"The people who approve the loan, Claudia."

"Oh." More gum chewing.

More sighing from Maria.

I just stand in the kitchen holding the bouquet of white lilies in my hands, trying to figure out when I need to step into this conversation and discreetly remind Claudia of the plan I discussed with her weeks ago.

The plan that included me surprising Maria with a tropical getaway for just the two of us that includes zero work.

I guess it's a good thing that I also managed to rope Tonya into the big surprise. Surely she'll be able to keep Claudia on task between her yoga and boozy dinners.

"So, I just, like, need to call them, right?"

"Yep," Maria responds, popping the p in frustration. "You call Hank and remind him that we're waiting on the underwriters to approve the final conditions the Langleys sent over on Thursday."

"Ohhhhh-kay. Whatever you say, boss."

Once Maria ends the call, most of her hope and all of her patience gone, she turns around to find me standing in the kitchen and nearly jumps out of her skin. "Oh my God, Rem!" One petite hand goes to her chest. "You scared the crap out of me!"

"Sorry," I say through a smile. "But I didn't want to interrupt the important meeting of the minds."

"Oh yeah." She snorts and drops her hand back to her side. "Some meeting of the minds."

"I take it Claudia is still being Claudia."

She nods, and then she moves her eyes down to the flowers in my hand. "Flowers?"

"For you." I grin and hold them out toward her. The way her face lights up makes my heart feel like it's playing bumper cars with my lungs.

"That was so sweet, Rem," she says and steps forward to press a gentle kiss to my lips. "Thank you."

But when she starts to step away, I wrap my hands around her waist, smooshing the flowers between our chests, and deepen the kiss. Maria giggles, but eventually, she falls into the rhythm and kisses me back with the same fervor.

Once I feel like she's good and relaxed, I step back and prepare to reveal my big surprise. "So…I have some news."

"Yeah?" Maria starts to turn around and put the flowers in a vase, but she stops with her hand in midair, seeking out a vase from the cabinet. "Wait… where's my Izzy girl, by the way? Taking a nap?"

"Actually, she's at my mom's house."

"What?" She tilts her head to the side. "Why?"

"Because of the surprise."

A cheeky smile crests her mouth. "And do I need to be naked right now for this surprise?"

"Already loving where your head's at, but…you're going to have to stay dressed for our flight. The FAA strongly enforces clothing for at least takeoff and landing."

"Our flight?"

"I'm taking you somewhere, and I've already made all the appropriate arrangements. My mom will keep Izzy. The cleaner is going to check on the fish. Claudia has been made aware," I start to explain, but when she looks terrified, I add, "And Tonya is also aware. Which, I have a feeling, Tonya will be the one making sure Daniel and Brenda are holding down the fort while you're gone."

"Wait…you're not joking," she comments and sets the flowers down on the counter.

"Nope. This is the real deal, babe." I step forward to wrap my arms around her waist again. "You and I are going to enjoy a little getaway for a few days."

My words give her pause. "And Izzy is going to stay with your mom the entire time?"

I nod. "She is."

Maria digs her teeth into her bottom lip. It's the look of a woman who is at war with herself. The look of a mother who is trying to decide whether she can be okay with leaving her baby in someone else's care for a few days.

"You deserve this, Maria," I reassure her. "You deserve to enjoy a few days in the Bahamas."

"Wait…you're taking me to the Bahamas?"

I nod.

"The *Bahamas*. Right now?"

"Is that okay with you?"

"Um…*yes*," she says, and her beaming smile shows she's finally come to terms with the truth that she *does* deserve this, with a little help from the vision of conch, aqua water, and white sand dancing through her head. "Holy hell! You're insane, but yeah, okay! Count me in! Let's go relax in the Bahamas!" she squeals and jumps into my arms.

"And have sex, too. Lots of sex," I add and punctuate that statement by squeezing her ass. "Lots and lots *and lots* of sex."

She giggles. "How long have you had this planned, crazy man?"

"For about two weeks now."

"You've hidden this from me for two whole weeks?" she questions, shocked I've managed to pull this off without her knowing.

"Let me tell you, it was no easy feat." I wink. "But we only have about an hour to get to the airport, so you're going to have to move your sexy ass. Our bags are packed. All you need to do is change into whatever you feel like wearing for our flight."

She doesn't hesitate to jump into action.

"I can't believe we're going to the Bahamas. Right now! For the first time in my life, I'm happy I didn't ruin a surprise!" Maria dances down the hallway, and I stand there, watching her, smiling like a loon—*smiling like a man who's* in love.

FORTY-TWO

Maria

"You seriously got us a private jet," I repeat what I've said at least ten times since we arrived at Teterboro Airport and didn't have to go through security or deal with any of the other annoying shit that comes with flying commercial.

Rem just smiles, having tired slightly from answering the same question three or four times ago, and continues the process of putting our carry-on bags in the fancy little closet in the front.

I walk around the cabin, taking in the luxury cream leather seating, the champagne on ice, the charcuterie display of fruits and nuts and cheese and crackers and meats. I even check out the back area where a bedroom with pretty white linens and a bathroom with an actual shower reside.

I've never flown private. Not once in my entire life.

My sister Isabella, on the other hand? Well, she loved flying private. She and Oliver flew private often, and now I'm understanding why.

"Champagne?" a flight attendant with red hair and a name tag that reads Susan asks with a friendly smile. She holds out a glass, and I take it...because apparently that's what you do on private jets. You drink fancy champagne.

"Thank you."

"Mr. and Mrs. Winslow, if you want to start getting in your seats, we'll be taking off shortly."

Mr. and Mrs. Winslow? I probably shouldn't like the way that sounds so much.

"Uh...I'm not—" I start to stay, but Remy cuts me off by pulling me down onto his lap. Champagne sloshes out of my glass, and I squeal.

"Rem!"

He just laughs like a man without a fucking care in the world, and damn, I love the sound of it.

"You know what I think?" he asks quietly into my ear, and I turn my head to meet his eyes. "I think I'm going to find a way to keep us fused together for this entire trip."

"Did you recently buy stock in super glue?"

"Not that kind of fused, babe," he comments and presses a kiss to the shell of my ear. "My cock inside you at all times kind of fused."

Oh boy.

"You trying to con me into a Mile High Club situation?" I question with a quirk of my brow, but he just shakes his head.

"Mile High Club initiation usually involves bathrooms, and that's not our style right now."

"We're too good for the giant bathroom on this jet?"

"Not too good." He shakes his head again. "Too dirty."

Wait…what?

I start to open my mouth to request that he elaborate on that statement, but he distracts me completely by grabbing a blanket from the back of the leather chair beside us and placing it over our legs.

And then he slides his hand up my bare thigh, under my dress, and his pesky fingers proceed to slide my panties to the side. His finger is inside me before I can even realize what's happening.

I clench around him—the feel too shocking and too good at the same time— and search his eyes. "*Remy*," I whisper. "What are you doing?"

"Just keeping you warm, Ria. Just keeping you warm." His smile is salacious, and it makes me clench again. His finger does a little twirl, and his thumb finds my clit, gently circling the sensitive bud with expert precision.

Well, *hell.* Now I know what Reese Witherspoon felt like on that roller coaster with Mark Wahlberg and, more than that, why that movie made such a huge impression on me and every other girl I knew.

Damn, this feels good.

My thighs start to shake, and my head falls back onto his shoulder, and Remy just sits there, smirking like the devil.

When Susan, the flight attendant, walks down the aisle, I start to try to find a way to get off Remy's lap without flashing her my goods, but he keeps me firmly in place with his free hand on my thigh. The other hand…well, it's *still* touching me. Working me over. Making me feel fucking crazy.

But Susan doesn't say anything. Instead, she walks right past us and toward the front of the plane until I can't see her anymore.

The pilot makes a quick announcement that we're ready for takeoff.

But other than that, we're left to our own devices. No demands for me to get out of Remy's lap. Just left *alone*…with Remy's finger inside me.

"Fuck, you're wet," he whispers harshly into my ear. "It's making me so hard."

A whimper escapes my throat, and he just keeps *working me over*. His finger moves in and out of me, his thumb circles my clit, and his free hand is inside my dress, grabbing at my breasts.

"Fuck, Ria. I have to be inside you."

"Are we allowed t-to go into the bedroom du-during takeoff?"

"Oh, we don't need the bedroom. We're fine right here."

My eyes go wide, but he just flashes a confident-as-hell smile at me. His eyes, though, well, they're fucking determined. Heated. And it's not long before he pulls his cock out of his jeans and spreads my thighs over his lap enough to slide inside me. Somehow, managing all of it with the blanket still concealing what we're doing.

Remy is inside me.

While we're taking off.

"Fuck. You're heaven," he groans into my ear and slides my hair over my shoulder as his lips and tongue and teeth nip and kiss at the skin of my neck.

The plane jolts into action, picking up speed as it heads down the runway, but I'm hardly aware.

How could I be, though? The hottest man on the planet has his cock inside me.

Remy thrusts deeper, and it takes every ounce of strength I have not to moan so loud it'll alert our flight attendant.

A little bit of turbulence jostles the plane, and Remy groans hoarsely into my ear as he grips my thighs and pushes himself to the hilt. One hand finds my clit again, rubbing smooth circles around the sensitive bud, while he continues to drive into me. He builds up a deliciously deep, persistent rhythm that makes my nipples hard and my mind all scrambly.

"You're going to come on my cock," he whispers directly into my ear, his warm breath brushing against my neck and causing goose bumps to roll up my spine. "And then, I'm going to fill you up with my come. Because that's where it belongs, Maria. Inside your perfect cunt."

Holy hell.

I swallow my moan *and* silently praise myself for starting birth control a month ago.

Sex with Remy is amazing, but sex with Remy bare inside me? It's…nirvana.

"I'm so close," I pant through the building pressure inside my body.

"Good girl." His voice is all raspy and his cock is deep, and I feel like I'm only being held together by a single tiny thread.

Remy has no mercy. In between thrusts, he whispers hotly into my ear, "Come.

For.

Me.

Maria."

I'm done. Burned fucking toast. Pushed over the edge and into the kind of pleasure that I swear holds the answers to world peace.

My climax crashes into nerve endings I didn't even know I had, and I have to dig my teeth into my bottom lip so I don't scream. Over and over again, waves of pleasure roll through my body, and Remy just keeps on fucking me while I try to keep some semblance of control over my volume.

But his hard cock *keeps hitting* all the right spots, while his thumb on my clit prolongs my orgasm.

It feels so good it's almost painful.

And when Remy hits his peak, he keeps his word. He grips my thighs, pushes himself as deep as he can go, and fills me up with his come.

If this is what he has in store for this trip, count me the hell in.

"So much for the FAA, huh?" I ask when I finally have enough breath back to speak.

Remy laughs, a sly smile making me tingle all the way to my toes again. "Technically, we're still wearing clothes."

I snort, but he shakes his head and grabs me by the chin, commanding my attention entirely.

"We're in the air now, Ria. All bets are off."

Oh boy. I think I'm in trouble.

FORTY-THREE

Monday, November 11th

Remy

This is my second morning waking up in tropical paradise, and I would've much preferred to stay in bed with a naked Maria wrapped around my body like a second skin.

But since it's Monday morning, the damn market has forced my hand.

I know I told Maria this was a no-work vacation, but yeah, even on a trip, I still have to put in some hours. And, truthfully, it's *she* who needs the rest and relaxation. I just need alone time with her. Lots of naked, sex-filled alone time, to be specific.

Thankfully, the Bahamas is on East Coast time and didn't require me to get up before six.

Just as the sun was starting to show its face on the horizon, I slipped out of bed, made some coffee, and took my laptop out onto the terrace of the private beach house an investment client of mine let me utilize for Maria's big getaway surprise.

It's a beauty of a property, nearly six thousand square feet of modern luxury and overlooking the clear blue waters of the Atlantic. The instant Maria stepped inside this place, she pretty much lost her Realtor mind.

Thankfully, the promise of spending another day on the beach with my woman in a bikini has proven to keep me efficient. And even though it's only a little after eight and the market still has another hour before its official open, I've managed to make most of the investment moves I'd planned for my clients.

Secured a few options, sold a few short-term stocks, and shifted some important money to ride the wave of quarterly earnings reports.

All in all, it's a good start to the day.

My cell rings, and I see *Incoming Call Thatch* on the screen. I groan, but I also pick it up by the second ring for fear it could still manage to wake up Maria.

"If you're calling me about your fucking DILF contest, I'm hanging up," I say, bypassing a greeting completely, and his booming voice is quick with a comeback.

"Oh, c'mon, Remy. You should be proud for coming in second place."

"So, the contest is over?" Thank fuck.

"Not yet, but your attitude about the contest really lost you some points the other day. A true DILF is motherfluffing proud of his DILFdom."

"You need your head checked."

He just laughs me off like he's not the craziest motherfucker on this call. "Anyhoo, you got any room in your schedule for ol' Thatcher today? Come by my office around ten?"

"I can't. I'm not in New York."

"Where the fuck are you?"

"On vacation. Bahamas."

"You're in the Bahamas?" he questions and then quickly adds, "Ohhhh…wait a minute! You took your sexy *mamacita* for a little tropical getaway, didn't you?"

I laugh. "I did bring Maria, yes."

"Hmmm…well, that's interesting, Rem. So, let me get this straight… You're basically living together. You love her kid. And you're taking her on tropical getaways. I can't be sure, but it's almost like you're in a committed relationship…"

While I can't necessarily disagree with him, I'm not going to encourage a dive into my love life with Thatcher Kelly before I've even straightened shit out inside my own head.

"You have concerns about your portfolio that you can't figure out for yourself?" I ask, hitting him where it hurts in an attempt to refocus the call.

The bastard cackles. "Look at you, trying to dodge the truth."

"Good talk, Thatch. I'll see you later."

"Hold up, sweetheart," he chimes in before I can hang up. "At least tell me what your game plan is with Cron stock. Hold or sell?"

"My game plan is done. I already put in to sell an hour ago."

"Without fluffing telling me?"

A throat clearing behind me grabs my attention, and I glance over my shoulder to find Maria standing on the terrace…completely *naked*.

Fuck me.

"Uh…excuse me, sir? Are you on a work call?" she asks quietly with narrowed eyes and a determined hand to her hip.

I shrug one shoulder. "Maybe?"

"*Maybe?* What the fuck does that mean?" Thatch demands into my ear.

"You said no work calls," Maria adds, still standing there gloriously naked and eyeing me with a pointed stare.

I literally can't take my eyes off her. Not her full breasts or rounded hips or tanned thighs. She looks like a fucking goddess standing there with the Caribbean sun shining down on her. Like God himself created her as the example of true, undeniable beauty.

"Yo, Rem? You still there, brother? Or did you fall into the fucking ocean?" Thatch is still in my ear. I sigh.

"The ocean is looking pretty inviting," I say, looking at the waves of one Maria Baros.

I crook a finger at her. "Come here," I mouth, but she doesn't move, simply tilting her head to the side. "Come here," I say quietly this time.

"Come where?" Thatch asks, and I ignore him, setting my phone down on the table and setting it to speaker.

Slowly, Maria sashays her sexy self over to me, and I don't hesitate to scoot my chair back from the table and tug her down onto my lap.

She fights the urge to giggle, and her eyes go wide as she tries to convey to me that my phone isn't muted, but when I wrap my mouth around her nipple and suck, a tiny little moan spills from her throat.

"Remy," she whispers directly into my ear. "What are you doing?"

"Enjoying our vacation," I whisper back. "Enjoying *you*."

"Joying-You? What does that even mean, Rem?" Thatch's voice booms from the speaker of my phone. "Is that some kind of new age tech stock I don't know about? What's the ticker?"

"Give me a sec, man. Internet is slow."

"That's fucking lame," he comments, but I ignore him and move my mouth to Maria's other nipple.

She squirms her hips in my lap, and it makes my cock throb in anticipation.

"Fuck. I need to be inside you," I whisper hotly into her ear. "Right now."

"Remy," she mouths, eyes wide and head nodding toward the phone I've pretty much forgotten all about.

But I'm already busy adjusting her body so that she's facing away from me, her thighs draped over my legs. And then I'm pulling myself out of my boxer briefs and savoring the feel of me filling her pussy with my cock.

Yessss. This is exactly what I needed.

Her head falls back onto my shoulder, and her breasts push out in a way that makes it impossible for me not to take both of them into my hands.

"Rem?" Thatch is still there, but who the fuck cares when Maria is wet and warm and perfectly wrapped around my cock.

She glances over her shoulder with wide, persistent, you-are-crazy eyes, but when I thrust inside her once, twice, three, four…ten times, those eyes turn hooded and glazed over, and her breaths turn to soft pants.

"Rem, seriously, man? What the fuck are you doing over there?"

Having sex with the most beautiful woman on the fucking planet.

Maria doesn't hesitate to do the honors of reaching out and ending the call before the persistent bastard can say anything else.

And then she surprises the hell out of me by standing up, turning around, and straddling her thighs over my lap.

Slowly, oh so fucking slowly, she slides herself back down on my length, and it's my turn for my head to fall back from the amazing feel of her wrapped around me.

"You said no work," she says, grabbing my chin and forcing me to meet her eyes.

"Technically, I was only working while you were sleeping. And then I was working while I was fucking you. So, I'd say I was just multitasking."

"Oh, that's how you look at it?" she questions, and I reach out to grab both of her breasts in my big, greedy hands again.

"Uh-huh."

"So, I can take work calls too?"

"Only if my cock is inside you."

She giggles, but then when I grip her hips and start up a rhythm, those giggles turn to moans at a rapid pace.

And it's not long before my beautiful Maria is coming hard on my cock and I'm pushed to the hilt, filling her up.

Fuck. I never want to stop doing this with her.

FORTY-FOUR

Tuesday, November 12th

Maria

I am dressed and ready for Remy's and my dinner out at a fancy restaurant that's apparently a twenty-minute drive from the private beach house he rented for us in the Bahamas.

That's right. I'm in the freaking *Bahamas*, and I'm about to go on a real, actual date with no work calls or showings or the responsibilities that come with being a mom.

Honestly, I can't remember the last time I traveled somewhere for fun. It feels like it's been years. Even before I got pregnant with Izzy, I always stayed too busy with work to do anything besides, well, work.

Because you've been a workaholic for the past two decades.

It's kind of sad how I've just let my life pass me by because I've been too focused on my career. Obviously, I love what I've achieved, I'm proud of what I've achieved, but I realize now more than ever that work shouldn't define my life.

And I have my sweet little Izzy to thank for that. She's shown me there's more to life than hitting career goals.

Remy's shown you that, too.

"Maria, the car will be here in about four minutes!" Remy calls out from somewhere in the living room, and I quickly toss my lipstick and compact into my purse.

"Okay! But I want to call and check on Izzy before we go!" I answer back as I head out of the bathroom and down the hallway.

But when I reach the living room, I find Remy sitting on one of the big white sofas with his phone held up toward his face. He grins at me and turns the screen so that I can see his mom's smiling face with a sleeping Izzy in her arms.

Aw, my sweet baby.

My heart expands and wants to crack in half at the same time.

"Izzy is an angel. I'm keeping her forever," Wendy says, and I don't hesitate to take the phone from Remy's hands.

"Is she doing okay? Eating and sleeping like she should? What about diaper rash? Have you—"

"Maria, she's doing fantastic." Remy's mom cuts me off with a soft whisper and a knowing look in her eyes. "She's eating well, sleeping around seven hours a night, and hasn't had any issues with diaper rash or gas."

"I miss her," I whisper, watching the way her little eyelids flutter in her baby dreams. "Goodness, is it normal to feel like half your heart is missing?"

"The first time I left all five of my kids with their aunt Paula and uncle Brad so I could enjoy a girls' weekend, I sobbed for hours in my hotel room."

"Okay, so I'm not crazy, then?" A self-deprecating laugh jumps from my lips. "This is normal that I feel like I'm a bad mom for loving that Rem surprised me with this trip? But knowing that, while loving it, I've left my baby behind?"

"You're not crazy. And you're a good momma." Wendy pointedly meets my eyes. "You're in the Bahamas, refilling your cup, enjoying a little relaxation, and that will only make you a *better* momma for Izzy when you get back. Self-care is one of the most important but often forgotten things with motherhood. It's as if we'd rather run ourselves into the ground for our kids than take some time for ourselves."

Her words hit the nail on the head.

"You're saying all the things I needed to hear right now."

"All the things you *deserved* to hear."

"Thank you," I whisper, and Remy comes up behind me to wrap his arms around my waist. We're both on the screen now, looking at his mom as she holds a still-sleeping Izzy in her arms.

"Thanks for taking care of our girl, Mom."

"That's what grandmas are for," she says through a smile. "Now, go enjoy yourselves. I'll text you some picture updates tomorrow."

At first, I don't balk at Wendy calling herself Izzy's grandma, but once we're off the phone, it won't stop rolling around inside my brain. *Is she Izzy's grandma?*

Izzy *does* have living grandparents—Oliver's parents—whom I still make a point to FaceTime fairly often so they can see Izzy. I even plan to visit them when I feel like Izzy is old enough to travel that far, but their health and international location make it impossible for them to be the kind of grandparents that are active in her life.

But Wendy? She's very much become an active member in Izzy's life.

So…is she Izzy's grandma, then?

To truly answer that question, I'd have to know the answer to a much bigger question—*what are Remy and I?*—and I find myself quickly shoving it aside and trying to focus on the whole point of this vacation.

We're here to have fun. To enjoy ourselves. To just…be in the moment.

But isn't that what you've been saying you've been doing this whole time? Even before this trip?

"You ready to go enjoy some dinner, babe?" Remy asks, distracting my attention, and I turn to find him shoving his phone and wallet into the pocket of his linen pants.

I swallow down my doubts and nod. "Uh-huh."

"Good." He closes the distance between us, wraps his strong arms around me, and kisses me with a deep, exploratory kiss that fogs my brain in the best kind of way.

And by the time a honk alerts us that our car has arrived, I'm half aroused and solely focused on enjoying a date night with Remy.

Damn, he's sexy, I think to myself as I watch the way his tight ass moves in his linen pants as he walks toward the front door.

And I just keep gawking at him, thinking about how I'm in the Bahamas with the sexiest man on the planet and the urge to say "Fuck the dinner" and rip his clothes off right now is becoming stronger by the minute.

When he notices that I'm not following behind, he glances over his shoulder with a curious raise of his brows. "You coming, babe?"

My dirty mind takes his words a little *too* literally, and I get an idea.

Yes. Fun. Just focus on the fun.

"I forgot to put on perfume! Be right back!" I half lie and hurry back into the bathroom.

Now, I *do* spray a little of my favorite Chanel No. 5 on my wrists, but I also reach up beneath my dress and slide my panties down my legs and…*leave them off for good.*

And then I give myself one final look in the mirror.

Hair? Check.

Makeup? Check.

Cute beachy dress and heels? Check.

No underwear? Check. Check. Check.

If this trip is about fun, then I'm ready to have some fun. The rest, I can deal with when we get back home…*right?*

I take a sip of my wine, set my napkin in my lap, and look around the restaurant Remy chose for the night. Dune is located inside one of Nassau's fanciest hotels. The vibe is expensive and cozy, with white tablecloths and dim lighting and candles creating mesmerizing shadows around the room. And the floor-to-ceiling windows that surround the intimate space provide a gorgeous view of the ocean.

Not to mention, the food here is supposed to be phenomenal. And after our friendly server Eduardo talked me into ordering their most popular dish—the porcini-crusted salmon—I'm curious to find out if it lives up to the hype.

"You doing okay, babe?" Remy reaches out and grabs my hand, smiling across the table at me.

"Of course." I tilt my head to the side in confusion. "Why wouldn't I be doing okay?"

"I know it's not easy leaving Izzy for this long," he says with a little frown. "Hell, I find myself having a hard time with it often."

"Really?"

"Yeah." He nods, and a humble laugh leaves his lips. "I don't know what it is about little girls, but they have a way of wrapping me around their tiny fingers. I remember feeling the same way about Lexi at times when she was just a baby. Though, with Izzy, it feels way more intense. Maybe I've gotten soft in my old age." He mocks himself, and I silently wonder if there's more he's not saying.

But I don't harp on it. Instead, I keep the mood light.

"And just think, now Lexi is almost a teenager with a boyfriend."

He grimaces. "Don't remind me."

I can't hide the smile on my lips.

"It's not funny, Ria."

"Oh, but it *is* funny," I tell him and squeeze his hand. "But it's funny in an adorable way because you're really sweet with her. And Lexi just adores you. In her eyes, the sun basically rises and sets from your ass."

"And what about in your eyes?"

I quirk a skeptical eyebrow. "You fishing for compliments, Rem?"

"From you? I'm always fishing for whatever I can get. Compliments. Smiles. Your laughter." He drops his voice, "My mouth on your pussy. *You coming on my cock.*"

Um…*yes, please.*

The fact that I'm not wearing any panties becomes a stark and heady realization. Of their own accord, my hips fidget in my seat.

"Although, I'm hoping—" he waggles his brows at me "—those last two are something we can explore after we get back from dinner tonight."

Looks like I'm not the only one with dirty thoughts tonight.

Game on.

"Remy?"

"Yeah, babe?"

"I have a little bit of a secret to confess."

His eyebrows pull together. "A secret?"

"Uh-huh." I nod, but before I tell him, I scoot my seat closer to his, and I don't stop until we're side by side and I'm positive the tablecloth is going to keep my *secret* under wraps from the rest of the restaurant patrons.

Remy watches me the entire time while simultaneously searching my eyes in bewilderment.

"So…my secret," I whisper toward him and reach up onto the table to grab his hand.

"Yeah. Your secret. Not going to lie, Ria, it's starting to feel a little serious."

"Oh, it *is* serious. *Top secret* kind of serious."

He smirks. "And I really hope you're going to tell me it soon."

"Remy, I forgot my panties."

He chokes on his tongue. "I'm sorry, what?"

But I don't repeat myself. Instead, I grab his hand and put it underneath the tablecloth until it rests on my thigh. And then I glide that hand of his under my dress until his fingers are brushing against me, touching me, *right there*, where I'm as bare as the day I was born.

"Fuck me," he mutters, and his eyes lock with mine. "You weren't kidding."

I shake my head. "And, actually, I have another secret I want to tell you."

He swallows. "Damn, Ria. If it's as good as the last one, I can't be held liable for what I do."

"The first time you came over to my apartment to help me with Izzy. Remember that?"

"The day I took you to Jacob's Pickles?"

"Yeah. That's the one."

He's utterly confused now, silently wondering how I've gone from showing him I've made my underwear disappear to talking about a day I was barely hanging on by a thread.

While I take his index finger and slide it inside me, I lean forward until my lips are right beside his ear. "When I took a shower that day, I touched myself. Just like this. I got myself off. While thinking about you."

"Eduardo! Check, please!"

⌒⌒⌒

We didn't eat dinner. Barely touched our glasses of wine. But somehow, Remy managed to get us back to our private beach house in thirty minutes flat.

And let me tell you, the whole ride back was a true lesson in self-restraint. For the entire drive, he wouldn't stop touching me. Wouldn't remove his finger from inside me.

It was the sweetest fucking torture I've ever experienced in my life.

The second the driver pulled up to our rental, I hopped out of the cab and headed straight for the bedroom, leaving Remy to handle paying the fare. Now, I'm completely naked and not-so-patiently waiting for him to come find me on the bed.

And it doesn't take him long to step past the threshold of the bedroom door.

The instant he spots me, his eyes flash with the kind of heat that promises pleasure.

"Oh, Maria." He tsks his tongue. "I'm getting the sense that you're wanting to be bad tonight."

Yes. Yes, I do.

He stands at the foot of the bed now and crosses his arms over his chest, his gaze raking along my naked body. "Is that what you want? To be a bad girl tonight?"

I swallow. Nod.

"Then, get on all fours," he demands.

Oh boy.

I don't hesitate to follow through. Onto my belly, I push myself up onto my hands and knees, my ass pointed toward the head of the bed and my face toward Remy.

Like he's the lion and I'm his prey, he stalks around me, moving from one side of the bed to the other. It's intense and hot, and the vulnerability and rawness of my position make a throbbing ache form between my thighs.

And then his hands are on me, his fingers gentle whispers across my skin. First, up my legs and then over my ass, and they don't stop until they're at the nape of my neck. He grips my hair and tugs back with a gentle but firm pull. "I think since you didn't eat dinner, I should feed you. What do you think, Maria? Are you hungry for my cock?"

Oh, holy shit.

"Because I can tell you," he continues, "my cock is ready for you. Those little secrets of yours have kept me hard since the instant they left your dirty little mouth."

He moves to the edge of the bed, positioning his body right in front of my face. His hands undo the button on his pants, and then he's pulling himself out, proving that his words aren't bullshit. Proving that he's hard...so incredibly hard that his cock looks almost angry. The head is swollen and pink, and his length is so rigid it's just jutting out from his body.

I feel wild. Crazy. And it's everything I want. Everything I wanted to happen when I decided to remove my panties before we left the house. Tonight, I want to see Remy lose control. I want us both to let go completely and just give in to pleasure, in to dirty fucking desire.

"Feed me," I whisper toward him, my lashes fluttering as I look up and into his eyes. "Please?"

"Fuck me," he mutters, but he also steps closer to the bed, grips himself in his hand, and slowly slides his cock into my now-open mouth.

He is thick and hard and perfect, and I take as much of him as I can. He tastes and feels like silk and velvet and *Remy*, and I flick my tongue up and down his length as I suck him back toward my throat.

A growl escapes his lips when he sees that he's too big for me to take him entirely into my mouth, and I have to squeeze my thighs together to try to ease the building ache that's growing within me.

It's erotic, *hedonism on ecstasy*, and it's something I don't think I'll ever forget for the rest of my life. I swear, I'll be fantasizing about this when I'm ninety-five and getting ready to take my last breath.

Normally, Remy is always so careful with me. It's fucking invigorating to see him lose control like this. It makes me feel crazy with power and confidence because I am the one who's doing this to him. I'm the one who can make him feel like this.

His hips jerk forward when I suck him as deep as I can go.

"Fuck me, Maria, you're so good at this," he says through a groan and reaches down to grip the strands of hair at my neck. He tugs on them again, gently forcing my head back so that my eyes meet his and only the tip of his cock remains in my mouth.

"You're fucking perfect," he whispers toward me, and his jaw clenches with strained arousal. "But now, I need to make you come with my cock."

I moan.

He doesn't waste any time climbing onto the bed. Once he's directly behind me, Remy drives himself inside me in one strong thrust. And then he fucks me like we're animals. Like he can't get enough of me.

I can relate, though, because I feel the same exact way. My hips move back and forth erratically, trying to match him thrust for thrust. And he feels so deep, but at the same time, not deep enough. And I feel so full, but at the same time, I just want more.

More and more and more of whatever he has to give.

More and more and more of him.

More and more and more of us together.

To the point that I don't know if I'll ever have enough.

FORTY-FIVE

Wednesday, November 13th

Remy

Stretched out on a beach lounger beside me and wearing only a little white bikini that showcases all of her curves in the sexiest way, Maria lies on her belly, her eyes closed behind her fancy sunglasses and her mouth etched into a soft smile as she savors the sun on her skin.

Today is our last official day in the Bahamas. Tomorrow, we'll be leaving our little paradise and heading back home. Heading back to our girl. I'm a little sad, but mostly, I'm relieved. Time away from Izzy is starting to wear on me. And I know for a fact, Maria feels the same.

After I take a drink from the bottle of water beside my chair, I let my head relax back into my lounger and just shut my eyes, letting the sounds of the waves soothe me.

At one point, I think I even doze off for a bit, but Maria's voice urges my eyes to open again.

"You're going to burn," she says, and I see that she's now standing up from her chair, sunscreen already in her hands.

"I'm fine, babe."

"Um, *no*. You're not. You're already getting red." She scoffs, but when I give her a look, she adds on a laugh, "Relax, buddy. This will only take a minute. Just close your eyes and keep doing what you're doing. Act like I don't even exist."

Ha. Like I could ever pretend Maria doesn't exist. Hell, most of the time, I'm busy trying to make sure she's always everywhere I am.

She grins at me from behind her sunglasses and pointedly squirts sunscreen into her hands and proceeds to rub it into my chest and shoulders.

And I just sit there, watching her from behind my Ray-Bans, thinking about how much this woman means to me, the way she affects me, and all the things she does for me.

Even with all the shit she has going on in her life, all the responsibilities that come with being a mom to Izzy and running a business by herself, she still finds time to take care of me. Even if it's little shit like this, right now, putting sunscreen on me so I don't burn.

Our relationship isn't one-sided. I give and Maria gives. We take care of each other. We take care of Izzy. And we have fun together. So much fucking fun.

And the sex, well, it's exciting and multifaceted. It's sweet and powerful like the first time, and it's dirty and wild like last night.

It's just…all the fucking things, Maria and I.

It's love, you bastard. It's fucking love, and you know it.

"Babe, I think you got a text," Maria says, and I look up to realize she's already finished with my sunscreen and is now back to lying on her chair.

With her head still resting on her lounger, she holds my phone out toward me, and I take it from her hand, looking down to find a new notification on the screen from **C**.

When I glance back at Maria, I see that she's already back to her lazy snooze in the sun, and I find myself opening the message to read it.

C: *Tell me, Remington, how does it feel to be in love again?*

And for the first time in I don't know how long, I actually text her back.

Me: *Like coming home.*

FORTY-SIX

Friday, November 15th

Maria

"Maria? Earth to Maria?"

I look up from my laptop to find Tonya standing there, staring at me with a curious look on her face.

"You were, like, a million miles away, huh?"

I smile, embarrassed. "I guess I'm still in vacation mode."

It's only been a day since Remy and I got back from the Bahamas, and I'll be honest, the last thing I felt like doing was coming into the office this afternoon. The only thing that made me feel better about it was that I basically spent the whole night cuddling Izzy and kissing her sweet little face off.

And since Remy and I were able to tag team our schedules today, I didn't come into the office until he was done with his work stuff, so that Izzy could stay with him while I touch base with my staff and try to catch up on everything I've missed while we were gone.

"It's fine." Tonya grins. "And I just wanted to let you know all the contracts on the Nolita penthouse for the Tomlinsons have been signed, and the closing is set for three weeks from Friday."

"Perfect. Thanks, Tonya." Somehow, during my getaway, Daniel managed to find a place Mrs. Tomlinson loved enough to put in an offer. It's honestly a joy to see him thriving in his position within my company and a relief for me, too.

She starts to head for the door but pauses and flashes a wink in my direction. "By the way, I'd still be in vacation mode too, if I got to take trips with that sweet, handsome-as-hell man of yours."

And then she's back out of my office and heading toward her desk. Completely unaware of the word bomb she just dropped at my feet.

Man of yours.

I don't know what it is about those three words, but they urge a twinge in my chest. They make my head turn all weird and uncomfortable.

I mean, I'd love to say that Remy *is* my man, but truthfully, I have no idea what we are.

Like…at all.

You'd think, when two people who spend as much time as we have together, who are basically sharing their lives with each other at this point, we'd have at least talked about what it is we're even doing by now.

But we haven't.

Maybe there's a reason it's never been discussed…

I try like hell to shake off the doubts that come with that line of thinking, but it feels like it takes a Herculean effort. I mean, Remy isn't exactly Mr. Long-Term Relationship. Hell, he's had exactly *zero* long-term relationships since his failed wedding all those years ago.

Not to mention, he's told me what he thinks about marriage and settling down.

A big, fat *No* was his exact response.

Instantly, my head and heart start to war with each other. On the one hand, my heart is all *You love him. You've always loved him.* But my brain? Well, she is being incredibly cautious…and skeptical. *All you've been doing is playing house for the past couple of months with exactly no guarantee of a commitment.*

Is that what we're doing? Playing house?

My chest grows tight at the thought, and I can't stop myself from thinking about Izzy. Especially the *consequences* of something like that for Izzy.

This is a little girl who lost her parents before she was even born. It doesn't seem fair to put her in a situation where she gets attached to a father figure who inevitably won't stick around.

Actually, it feels pretty fucking cruel.

Surely that's not what Remy would do, though, right? I mean, he's a good man. A kind man who has done nothing but be there for me during the most difficult time of my life.

I don't know why my head is a clusterfuck of landmines, but I decide now isn't the time to ruminate on all this shit. If anything, I just need to have a conversation with Remy. An actual conversation where we discuss what it is we're doing, and no matter how scary it might feel, that conversation needs to occur sooner rather than later. That's for damn sure.

Eventually, I convince myself to focus on the last few items on today's to-do list, but I only manage two more priority tasks before my cell starts vibrating like crazy on my desk.

I pick it up to find several missed text messages in a group chat with Winnie, Sophie, Daisy, and Rachel.

Winnie: Dinner tonight at my house. 7:30 p.m. Can anyone bring dessert?

Rachel: Oh girl, like you even have to ask. I've got the dessert.

Sophie: LOL. The perks of being related to a bakery owner.

Rachel: Damn straight. My sis and Lou will hook us up with all the goods.

Daisy: I'm a fan of this plan. The twins will undoubtedly be fans too.

Winnie: Oh, and tonight we need to start figuring out holiday plans for Thanksgiving and Christmas.

Sophie: Good thinking.

Rachel: Ty keeps saying he wants to spend Christmas at the lake house this year.

The lake house? Man, that brings back memories. It's been years since I've been to Remy's Uncle Brad and Aunt Paula's lake house, but I spent many summer weekends and holidays there in my teen years.

Winnie: Ty wants to spend Christmas at the lake house every year because he's obsessed with Aunt Paula's cinnamon rolls.

Rachel: Lol. He might've mentioned that.

Sophie: Even though Jude would hate to see me defend Ty in any way, he's not wrong. The lake house is pretty much the perfect place to spend Christmas.

Rachel: Don't worry, your secret is safe with me, Soph. ;)

Sophie: LOL. That's greatly appreciated.

Winnie: Okay. Then, I guess we can assign Ty the task of convincing Uncle Brad it's a good idea to host all of us.

Rachel: I'll let the Professor know about his new assignment.

Winnie: Perfect. Hey, Maria, by the way, is it bad that I've already started my Christmas shopping for Izzy?

Sophie: Oh my God, SAME! I found the cutest outfit when Jude and I were at the mall the other day. Girl baby clothes are addictively adorable.

Me: I swear, you guys are going to spoil her rotten.

Winnie: Damn straight we are. That's what aunts are for. You guys are coming to dinner tonight, right? And my little Izzy?

That's what aunts are for. Obviously, that innocent comment does nothing for my current mental state. I force myself to respond, though, letting her know we'll all be there.

But when the conversation moves to Rachel and Ty's wedding plans, I have to set my phone down. Not because I don't love talking with them, but because it makes me feel like an outsider. Like I shouldn't even be involved.

This conversation has Remy's sister, two of his sisters-in-law, and one soon-to-be sister-in-law, and they're talking about family holidays and buying Izzy gifts and planning Ty and Rachel's wedding, and I just can't stop wondering… Where do I even fit in this equation?

Well, you are completely and emotionally invested in Remy and want forever with him…

I can't deny that I want to be with him. I love waking up to him in my bed in the morning and seeing his face when I get home from work at night. I love how he is with Izzy. I love having him present in her life. I love having his support.

I just…love him. I am in love with him.

But I don't know what he wants.

I know he feels deeply for me, but I don't know if Remy Winslow can ever allow himself to go all in with a woman again. I never like to hold people's pasts against them, but the reality is, his track record after his ex Charlotte called off their wedding isn't exactly good.

And there're times I just feel like he's not opening himself up completely to me.

I think about the mysterious texts from "C" he still gets.

Or the fact that, after all this time, we've never once stayed at his place. I've literally never been to his apartment, and that feels like a giant red fucking flag. Like, what woman would just go along with something like that?

And what could all of that really mean in terms of where Remy's head is at when it comes to us?

You need to figure that shit out and quick, because it's not just your heart at risk. It's Izzy's, too.

Shit. The mere idea of putting Izzy through something like that makes me feel beyond terrible. I mean, I'm a grown woman. I've been through breakups and relationships ending, but Izzy is an innocent child. She doesn't deserve to be a casualty because I was being stupid.

She doesn't deserve to one day feel like a father figure walked out of her life because her mom was too naïve and too much of a coward to face reality.

I mean, does Remy want forever with us, or he is just playing house?

And perhaps more importantly, if he's just playing house, with no plans for a future, where would that leave Izzy and me when he decides he's done?

FORTY-SEVEN

Maria

Winnie's dining room is bustling with the entire Winslow gang. Even Uncle Brad and Aunt Paula have joined in tonight's dinner.

Everyone is gathered around a spread of lasagna and garlic bread and salad, eating to their hearts' content while the room bounces with laughter and chatter.

"Okay, we need to figure out what we're doing for the holidays," Winnie announces, taking her fork and tapping it against her wineglass. "We can do Thanksgiving here."

"Aunt Paula, we should do Christmas at the lake house!" Ty shouts around a mouthful of pasta. "The ladies assigned me to the task of convincing you of that, by the way. So, consider this me, convincing you."

"Real smooth." Rachel slaps him on the back of the head with a sigh.

"You're such an idiot," Winnie mutters, but Paula is already smiling.

"Christmas at the lake house with everyone sounds like a wonderful plan to me," she says, and her husband Brad grins and squeezes her shoulders.

"Only if you promise to make those cinnamon rolls." He winks. "You know how much I like your buns, sweetie pie."

Wendy and Howard snicker. Half the room groans. And Paula blushes and smacks her husband on the chest.

"Oh my gosh, Brad, you're a dirty bird!"

But Brad just keeps it up. "Oh, but baby, you know you have the best buns."

"Can we keep this conversation moving along?" Jude chimes in. "Or else Uncle Brad is going to make shit weird."

"Don't be such a prude, Jude," Brad retorts, and Ty snorts.

"Yeah, Jude. Don't be such a fucking prude."

"Language!" Wendy exclaims with a roll of her eyes, and Howard chuckles softly beside her.

The whole table erupts into more laughter and chatter, and it takes Wes standing up from his seat to let out a high-pitched wolf whistle to shut everyone up.

Once all eyes are on him, he sits back down and mutters, "The floor is yours again, Win."

"Thank you, honey," she states and eyes everyone at the table, especially Brad, Jude, and Ty, before going back to figuring out family holiday plans.

The conversation moves along pretty steadily after that. Thanksgiving will be at Wes and Winnie's, and for Christmas, everyone will go to the lake house and spend both Christmas Eve and Christmas Day there.

And I just mostly try to ignore the discussion by busying myself with Izzy. Of course, she's being an absolute angel right now, sleeping through all the commotion. No crying, no fussing…just sleeping. Which means I'm basically just staring down at the bouncer chair Winnie bought for her that sits between Rem and me with nothing to do.

But hell, I still can't shake the feeling that I'm an outsider in all of this. I'm not technically a part of this family. And at the core of it all, that's a big problem for me when I now know in my heart that I want to *be* a part of a family. I want to settle down with someone. I want to get married and be someone's wife. *Be Remy's wife.*

"What do you think, Maria?" Rem asks, and I look up to find him looking at me. Actually, everyone at the table is looking at me.

"What do I think about what?"

"Thanksgiving at Winnie's and Christmas at the lake house?" he questions. "Can we make it work?"

Can *we.*

As in, me and him.

I don't know why, but it just…sets me off. Like, how in the hell am I supposed to know? We haven't even had an actual discussion about what we're even fucking doing here. How in the hell can I commit to holiday plans with a family I don't even know if I'm a part of?

"Um…I'm not sure," I answer, trying like hell to find a delicate way to extricate myself from this conversation so we can have a normal discussion about it later…you know…when we're not surrounded by his family.

"You're not sure?" he repeats on a soft laugh and wraps his arm around my shoulders. "Babe, surely you can get the time off work, right? Shift some showings and listing appointments around to make it work in the name of being with family at Christmas. I mean, it'd be great to bring Izzy to the lake house this winter."

"I don't know, Rem. I'll have to check my schedule."

"Ri, you're being weird. Are you okay?" he asks, furrowing his brow and unintentionally hanging me out to dry in front of everyone.

I feel pushed into a corner, like the whole damn room might as well be closing in on me.

"Yeah, I'm fine."

He searches my eyes, and whatever he finds certainly doesn't encourage him to move along from the awkwardness. "Well, we can at least commit to Thanksgiving, right?"

"Rem, I really don't want to talk about this right now."

Please stop pushing me. Please, please, please.

"Talk about what? Thanksgiving?" he questions, and it is my official undoing. The match to my flame.

"Everything," I blurt out in a rush and push myself back from the table with two firm hands. "Everything. Thanksgiving. Christmas. Making future plans when I don't even know what the hell we're doing here. I don't even know what we are, Remy!"

"Oh shit," someone in the room mutters, but Rem is too focused on me to even notice.

"What?" he questions, and he leans his body away from mine. "You're questioning *us?* That's what this is all about?"

Normally, I wouldn't answer that question, or maybe I'd ask him to step out of the damn dining room to discuss it privately, but it's like I've reached a breaking point. I'm so done with carrying around all this stress and uncertainty that I can't think about anything besides getting it off my chest.

"Oh, c'mon, Rem," I retort. "You have to realize that we haven't established anything about our relationship. Or if we even *have* a relationship. *Let's just enjoy ourselves and not worry about the rest, Maria. Can't we do that?*" I taunt in his voice, and Winnie's eyes widen to the size of saucers. Even Ty's and Jude's mouths look like they've been permanently sewn shut.

"We're together all the time, Maria." Remy looks at me like I've slapped him. "We just went on a trip together. I don't know how much more obvious it could be."

"Do you realize that I've never even been to your apartment?"

"That's because all of Izzy's stuff is at your place! I always thought it was just easier that way. If you want to go to my apartment, then we can go to my apartment. I don't give a shit where we go."

He's getting frustrated now, but yeah, join the club. One by one, the people behind him start to file out of the room as quickly as they can manage. Winnie is the only one brave enough to come get Izzy, but to be honest, Remy and I are so entrenched in our shitfest, we barely even notice.

"It's not about that, Rem. It's about the fact that it feels a lot like we've been playing house, but we've never had a serious conversation about what we're really doing. And it's becoming too much. Izzy is so attached to you.

And I feel guilty for allowing that when I don't even know if we have a future."

"What the fuck, Maria?" he nearly shouts and stands up from his chair.

The dining room is empty save for us, in the middle of it, shouting at each other. *Way to ruin a family dinner.*

"Remy, now isn't the time for us to have this discussion."

"Oh, but it is. You've started it, Ri, and now we're going to finish it."

"No, we're *not.*" I stand up from my chair. "I'm going to take Izzy home. You stay here and enjoy the rest of dinner with your family."

"They're your family, too, you know."

Knowing anything else I say will just set him off, I simply walk toward the dining room doors to leave. If I want time, I should have time, dammit.

But when I turn the knob, the door doesn't budge.

What the hell?

I tug on the door some more, hoping to jiggle it free, but it's not moving.

What the fuck? Did those Winslow fuckers lock us in here together?

"I can't believe you're all of a sudden questioning all this," Remy continues on a tirade. "That's so fucked up."

"How is that fucked up?" I turn back toward him, irritation guiding my movements. "I'm pretty sure any woman in my situation would start questioning shit. Especially when there's a child involved."

"A child whom I've done nothing but love and take care of."

"You're right, you have. You've been amazing to Izzy, Rem. And to me too. More than amazing, actually. But at this point, I have to ask myself, what are we even doing? Is there even a future? In one year, are you still going to be around? What about two or three? Or *ten?* And if not, what will that do to Izzy?"

What would that do to you?

The mere idea of it all, of Remy just up and leaving us, well, it feels almost as painful as the day I found out my sister wasn't coming home.

It feels like losing a piece of myself. Like losing my person. My family.

"I've lost enough," I find myself whispering raggedly. "I can't lose another person I love. And for as long as things continue on like they are, without definition or labels, I can't know that I won't. *And that's fucking scary.*"

FORTY-EIGHT

Remy

I watch Maria's eyes fill with tears. She quickly turns back toward the door and tugs on it some more, apparently unable to open the damn thing.

But it's hard for me to focus on that because I feel like she just tore my heart out of my chest.

She just acted like it was possible for me to walk away from her and Izzy. Like one day, I'll just decide that I'm done with them and simply leave them behind.

I am not my father, and I am most definitely not that guy.

She's banging her fists on the door now. "Can someone open this? It's locked!"

"I know it's locked." Jude's voice echoes from the other side of the wall.

"Jude, unlock it, please," Maria begs, and her voice is shaky with unshed tears. "I need to go."

"No." My sister is now chiming in. "You need to stay and talk it out."

"Winnie?" Maria lets her forehead fall to the door with a soft thud. "What the hell? I need to make sure Izzy is okay."

"She's good, hun. Still sleeping. My mom has her."

Maria turns back to me. "You do realize your family locked us in here, right?"

I nod. "I do."

"Okay…but how are we supposed to get out of here?"

"We'll let you out once you two talk it out!" Jude is back. "Not sure if you realize this, Maria, but you and my brother belong together!"

His words unleash something inside her, causing a flood of tears to roll down her cheeks.

It's heartbreaking, to be honest. To see her like this, knowing that I play a part in why she's upset. It reminds me so much of the day that I've come to regret more than anything in my life.

The day I watched Maria cry just like this…and then let her walk away.

THE PAST

THE END OF IT ALL

Twenty-Six Years Ago

Late Summer, after senior year

Remy

Nerves fill my chest, and Maria sits beside me, at one of our favorite spots in Central Park. She fidgets with her jean shorts, and I try to gain the strength to have a conversation with her that I know is going to be hard.

In less than a week, I'm going to be heading off for college, and Maria will be here, finishing her last two years of high school.

I love this girl like crazy, I really do, but I don't think staying together is the right thing. She should enjoy her last two years of high school, and I should have the freedom to enjoy being in college.

We shouldn't be stressed over a long-distance relationship right now.

We should just be living our lives. Having fun. Enjoying being young while we can.

"Do you want to grab dinner aft—" she starts to say just as I finally find the courage to tell her. As a result, we pretty much talk over each other.

"We need to talk, babe."

Her eyes jerk to mine, but I repeat myself, just to ensure she hears me.

"We need to talk, babe."

She doesn't say anything at first, instead searching my gaze. Eventually, she looks out toward the park and nods. "Yeah, I guess we do, huh? You're leaving soon, and we need to figure out where we go from here."

"Yeah," I say, nodding even though she isn't looking at me. "I don't want to break up, but I don't see how we're going to be able to stay together."

She grimaces, her eyes fixated on her shoes. "You don't think we can manage long-distance," she says, her voice tinged with sadness.

Fuck. This is hard. Harder than I thought it would be.

"I…I don't think that would be good for either one of us, you know?"

She looks up at me, and one tear slips from her lid and down her cheek.

I feel like the biggest bastard on the planet.

"Fuck, babe. I'm sorry. I hate this. I hate—"

"It's okay." She shakes her head and sniffles. "I understand. You deserve to start college with a clean slate. A new beginning without anything holding you back."

I don't know what to say to that, but Maria doesn't give me any time to figure it out. She stands up from the park bench and leans down to press a soft kiss to my cheek. Her *last* kiss to my cheek. "Goodbye, Remington Winslow."

Fucking hell. This isn't how this was supposed to go. This isn't how it was supposed to *feel*—like I've intentionally put myself in a meat grinder.

"Maria, I don't want it to end like this between us," I start to say, but she shakes her head and pulls up to stand straight.

"Nothing else needs to be said, okay? I understand. You're moving on, and one day, so will I." Her eyes shine with more emotion, but she doesn't linger after that. With a flick of her hair and a turn of her toe, all I'm left with is the sight of her walking away.

I pull my Walkman from my pocket and put my headphones on in an effort to drown out the feeling of sitting on this bench all alone.

I expect it to make me feel better, to help me find the reasoning in my decision and settle into the consequences. But when the opening lyrics of "Someone Like You" start to fill my ears, I find myself thinking, *I hope, one day, I'll find someone like Maria again.*

FORTY-NINE

Still Friday, November 15th

Remy

I was such a fucking idiot back then.

An eighteen-year-old prick who broke up with Maria because he was going off to college. Because he wanted freedom. Wanted tail. Wanted to play the fucking field. A dumb little shit who had his priorities all fucked up.

But I know better now.

I know what my priorities are, and I know exactly what the woman standing in front of me means.

"Maria." I try to get her attention, try to get her to turn around and look at me. "Can you just hear what I have to say about us? About our future?"

"Remy, I really just want to go," Maria whispers back, and when she turns around to look at me, a fresh sheen of tears makes her eyes shine beneath the dining room lights. "I just want to get Izzy and go."

It breaks my heart.

"And you want me to stay here?"

She averts her eyes and nods.

"Well, that plan doesn't work for me, Ria," I tell her, anger and frustration and adrenaline and even fear starting to pump through my veins. I *refuse* to let her walk away from me this time. "It's actually a really horrible plan."

When she doesn't respond, still won't look at me, I keep going.

"When we broke up all those years ago, I remember thinking to myself, I hope I meet someone like Maria again. And I might've been a fucking fool back then, but I'm not a fool now. I don't want someone like you, Maria. I want *you*. Just *you*."

She looks up to meet my eyes, and I step toward her.

"I love you. I've always loved you, Maria. But somehow, ever since we got stuck in an elevator…twice…I've fallen deeper in love with you each day that we've spent together. When I see our future, I see you and me and Izzy. I see more sleepless nights with a fussy baby and busy days with a wild toddler and silly arguments over what movie we're going to watch when Lexi stays the night. For the past fifteen years of my life, I've been closed off. I haven't wanted a relationship with anyone. But that's not who I am when I'm with you. I want commitment with you. I need it. This has never been about playing fucking house, Maria. This has been about a man falling in love with a woman and wanting to spend his life with her. This is about me finding my family in you and Izzy."

I'm nearly angry that she couldn't see any of this, but at the same time, I can understand why she all of a sudden got cold feet and found herself questioning shit.

"Do you want to know what I really think this is?" I ask and pull the ring box I've been carrying around with me since I bought it in a jewelry shop the evening before we left the Bahamas. Three hours after I told Cleo that being in love with Maria felt like coming home.

I set it on the table and look at her. "That's what I think this is. *Forever*. Me and you, getting married and spending the rest of our lives together. You are the only woman who makes me want to be a better man. Who makes me want to settle down and get married. Who makes me need all of the things I never thought I needed. You're it for me, Maria."

Tears stream down her cheeks, and she stares at the box on the table.

"I want that too," she says, her tone just barely a whisper and her voice shaking with emotion. "I want that too, Rem. All of it. With you."

In an instant, I close the distance between us and pull her into my arms and kiss her like my life depends on it. Because it does. She is my fucking life.

Her tears are salty against my tongue, but her mouth is just as hungry, just as desperate as mine. And the kiss feels like the only thing I'll ever need for the rest of my life. I could live off this kiss. No water. No food. No sleep. Just Maria and her perfect lips against mine.

"I'm sorry," she whispers through a stuttered breath and leans back to meet my eyes. "I just…I don't know…I got scared. The idea of you not wanting what I want felt like a knife to my chest. I didn't know if I'd survive it, and I just—"

I cut her off with another kiss.

"I love you, Maria," I say against her lips and feel each word more than I have ever felt them for anyone. "Never for one second doubt that."

"I love you too."

"Thank fuck for that," I mutter, and she giggles against my mouth. "By the way, you're not getting that ring right now."

She leans back to search my eyes.

"I'm going to propose to you, but not here. Not like this."

"You've got big plans, Rem?"

I wink. "Something like that."

She kisses me hard, and I don't hesitate to pull her tighter to my chest, to the point that her legs are wrapped around my waist and my fingers are sliding through her hair.

Maria. My Maria. She is *my* real-life Maria in that Brooks & Dunn song. My gypsy lady, my miracle worker, the one woman who can set my soul free and on fire at the same time.

Eventually though, it's apparent that we may be the only ones in the room, but we're not the only ones in this house.

"Can…uh…we come in now and finish dinner?" someone asks from outside the door, and we both pause to look at each other.

Maria giggles. I grin. But before either one of us can answer, the dining room doors are swinging open and my whole damn family is standing there, big-ass grins on every single one of their faces. Winnie's even holding Izzy up in our direction to make it look like she's looking on with the rest of them.

"Fucking finally!" Jude shouts at the top of his lungs, but this time, my mom doesn't bitch at his language choice.

Instead, she chimes in with an emotional, "I couldn't agree more!"

She heads straight for us then, wrapping both Maria and me up in a hug. "Finally. *Finally*, you two realize what I've known all these years. You belong together."

"Oh, c'mon, Wendy!" Ty calls out. "You weren't the only one who knew!"

"Yeah, Mom!" Jude agrees. "Pretty sure we were all aware. A fucking blind man could've seen it coming since the moment Remy turned into a sap over Maria in high school!"

I wish I could tell them they're all full of crap, but I'd be a liar. Deep down, back then, I knew Maria and I belonged together. And even though it's taken me far too long to get my shit together and realize it, I'm here now. With her.

Forever.

FIFTY

Saturday, November 16th

Remy

"Oh my God," Maria comments on a laugh when she realizes where I've taken her. "You're finally taking me to your apartment."

Izzy coos from her carrier that's currently secured on Maria's chest, even kicking her short legs a little.

"You did say you've never been in my apartment, so…" I grin over at her, knowing full well she doesn't know the half of why I brought her here.

Maria just smiles, and I wrap my arm around her shoulders as we step inside my building and head toward the elevator. I discreetly wink at Dan the Maintenance Guy as I pass him in the lobby.

"I can't deny that I'm incredibly curious what the inside of your place looks like."

"What do you think it'll look like?" I ask and usher her and Izzy onto the elevator.

"Honestly? I'm not sure," she answers with a grin just as the doors close. "I can imagine you have quite the office with lots of screens because you're the king of investments, but the rest?" She taps her chin thoughtfully. "I can't quite decide, but if I had to take a guess, I'd say you're working with mostly neutral tones and a minimalist approach."

"Minimalist approach?"

"Yeah." She shrugs. "A less is more vibe. I know you don't like clutter."

She's not wrong. I absolutely loathe clutter.

But now isn't the time to talk about furniture and shit. Now is the time for something way more important.

The *most* important.

Abruptly, the elevator comes to a halting stop between the fifth and sixth floors, and Maria furrows her brow. "What the hell?"

Me, on the other hand, I'm silently cheering Dan the Maintenance Guy and jack-of-all-trades for being on his A game today.

Maria steps forward to tap the button to my floor again, but when nothing happens, she turns to look at me. "Uh…Rem? Are we seriously stuck in an elevator again?"

"It looks that way, babe."

She searches my eyes. "Why are you so calm about this?"

Izzy giggles for some strange reason, and it makes me smile.

"Izzy seems calm?" I offer, and Maria groans and starts pushing all the buttons like a maniac.

"Remy! We are stuck in the elevator with our baby! This is not good!"

Truthfully, I'm not that calm. I'm more the complete opposite of calm. The inside of my body feels like it's vibrating with the kind of energy and emotion I can't put into words.

"I mean, in a funny way, babe, this is kind of par for the course for us, you know?" I respond with a shrug. "I think I've gotten used to it."

"Used to being stuck in an elevator? That's deranged. No one should feel okay with being in an elevator cart that's hovering hundreds of feet above the ground."

We're not exactly hundreds of feet. I mean, I told Dan to stop us at the third floor, but that's probably beside the point when you're concerned you're trapped in an elevator for the third fucking time.

Maria tries the red emergency phone, but it doesn't do shit because I made sure it wouldn't. Because we're not trapped at all. This, right here, was by choice. This is me taking my own fate into my hands. It's me taking *our* future into my hands.

It's now or never, dude.

"Maybe I also planned it?"

"What?" She spins around on her heels to look at me, and the way Izzy is flashing a drool-filled smile my way gives me all the courage I need to continue.

"You know, inside this very elevator, is when I realized that I was in love with you." I start to put it all out there for her. To lay my heart on the line and let her know my truth. "It's when I realized that I'd *always* been in love with you. Watching you tackle giving birth in an elevator was the most badass, incredible, life-changing thing I've ever witnessed." I reach out to take both of her hands in mine, and Izzy even tries to join in, placing one of her tiny hands on Maria's wrist. "You were so strong, Ria. So fucking strong. And so goddamn beautiful."

She searches my eyes, and I don't miss the way a sheen of tears covers hers.

"I love you, Maria Carmen Baros, and I'm asking you for one more redo. One *final* redo. But this time, I want it to last forever." I kneel down on one knee, staring up at her as I pull the ring box out of my pocket. And this time, I open it. "Will you marry me?"

My woman doesn't waste any time with giving me her answer.

"Yes," she whispers, staring deep into my eyes.

And after I slide the ring down her left ring finger, I lean forward and carefully wrap my arms around both of my girls, planting kisses on both of their perfect faces.

Izzy squeals and Maria giggles through her tears, and I feel like I'm the luckiest man who has ever lived.

But that's probably because with Maria by my side, promising to spend the rest of forever with me, I am.

EPILOGUE

Six Months Later…

Saturday, May 16th

Maria

My phone vibrates from my nightstand, and I groggily pick it up to check the screen.

Remy: How are you feeling, babe? You think we need to cancel dinner tonight?

Knowing full well what he has planned for tonight's big family dinner, there is no way we're going to cancel. I'll carry a Ziploc vomit bag around with me if I have to.

Thankfully, my nap did help.

Me: Nope. I'm feeling a lot better. You and Izzy on your way home?

This afternoon, Remy met up with Flynn and the twins for story time at the library. Frankly, the two of them have been making it a monthly thing these days.

And while I would've loved to join in on the fun, especially since seeing Flynn wrangle his one-year-old boys is a riot, I woke up with a migraine that felt like a semitruck had parked itself in my skull, *and* I had the horrible pleasure of throwing up a couple of times. I even had to get Daniel to take over the one and only showing I had this morning.

Remy: Actually, there's a kids' fair in Midtown, so we're going to hang out here for a bit.

Me: That sounds like trouble. And for the love of God, we don't need any more goldfish.

Last time Remy and Flynn went to a carnival, he came back with goldfish that we ended up giving to Lexi when she noticed we weren't taking care of them to the proper standards. I always thought that if the fish was alive, you were doing it right, but now I know better. The water needs a certain temperature and pH level and all sorts of things Lexi is a whole lot better equipped to give. Mind you, Winnie wasn't that thrilled.

Remy: So, let's say I happen to accidentally win some goldfish and I'm forced to bring them home, what kind of trouble will that bring me?

Me: The bad kind of trouble.

Remy: Like, hot and dirty bad?

Me: REMY. NO GOLDFISH.

Remy: And bunny rabbits? How do you feel about them?

Me: REMY. NO ANIMALS OF ANY KIND.

Remy: Love you, Ria.

I roll my eyes at him. And then I tell him exactly that.

Me: I love you too *rolls eyes*

Remy: *smiles at you even though you're rolling your eyes at me because I love you even when you're rolling your eyes at me*

Me: LOL. Go run Daddy Day Care, crazy man. I'll see you when you get home.

My husband is insane. I swear. But hell if he doesn't make me laugh out loud.

And yes, that's right, *my husband*. As of four months ago, I am officially Remy's wife. Though, considering we got married on a whim without telling anyone, our family is still a little pissed off at us.

It was one Sunday afternoon when Lexi had stayed with us the night before, and Remy just looked at me while we were sitting on the couch watching Lexi play with Izzy and said, "Let's get married today."

So, we did. With Izzy as my Daughter of Honor and Lexi as Remy's Best

Niece, we said "I do" at the courthouse. Just me, Remy, Izzy, and Lexi in attendance.

Normally, you can't get married at the courthouse on a Sunday, but it definitely helped that Remy does investments for the mayor *and* could also guarantee Mavericks' fifty-yard-line game tickets to the justice of the peace who ended up coming in on his day off.

It might seem crazy to have done it that way, but with Ty and Rachel's wedding on the horizon, we didn't know when we'd get to do it the big way, and we didn't want to wait.

And I still think it was the best idea we've ever had.

When I realize it's nearing noon, I decide to get my ass out of bed and take a shower so I can start preparing the food for tonight. Ever since Remy and I decided to sell our apartments and buy a brownstone not far from Winnie and Wes, we've been alternating playing hostess.

And tonight, Winslow Family Dinner will be at our house.

The instant I crawl out of bed, I don't miss the way I ache from between my legs—courtesy of the hot sex Remy and I had at three in the morning last night. I also don't miss that my breasts feel sore and my lower back has decided to let me know I'm forty-three now.

Being middle-aged is a real bitch.

I tiptoe into our master bathroom and make quick work of a shower.

Once I'm out, dried off, and standing in front of the sink to brush my teeth, my eyes catch sight of the two rings on my left ring finger.

I'm married. To Remy Winslow.

My smile grows bigger, but also, surprisingly, tears start to fill my eyes.

Damn, we've come a long way, he and I. We've both been through incredibly hard times. And somehow, we found our way back to each other.

Thank everything.

The stupid tears are now streaming down my cheeks.

Sheesh. I'm emotional these days.

I almost want to laugh at how ridiculous I've been lately, but when I lean down to spit the toothpaste into the sink and accidentally bump my boobs against the counter, the responding shooting pain from my nipples stops me dead in my tracks.

Damn, those suckers are sensitive today.

I stare at my naked breasts in the mirror.

And a bit on the big side too…

My brain takes inventory of my current state—emotional, sensitive boobs, migraines, lower back pain—and I drop my toothbrush onto the counter.

No way, right? No fucking way.

I mean, I'm forty-three. There's no way I'm pregnant.

I look at my boobs again in the mirror, and when I notice that my nipples are red as fucking roses, I decide it probably wouldn't be a bad idea to just make sure that I'm not pregnant.

Obviously, I'm not. I mean, that would be crazy. But I'll just grab a test at the grocery store while I'm out getting stuff for dinner tonight.

Yeah. That's exactly what I'll do.

Just in case.

<hr />

Maria

An hour later, I'm surrounded by six pregnancy tests, all out of their boxes, and all freshly peed on by yours truly.

I don't know what made me take six of these fuckers, but here we are.

I set my phone timer to the recommended five minutes and head back into the kitchen to start cutting up some fruit and vegetables while I wait on the confirmation that I'm not pregnant.

And I almost want to laugh at myself that I'm even taking these tests. I mean, if anything, I'm probably nearing freaking menopause, not another round of motherhood.

My phone's alarm goes off, and I wash my hands in the sink before heading back into our bathroom to check the results. You know, the ones that are going to say, *You're not pregnant, you're just a little crazy.*

I grab the first one off the counter and look down at it—**Pregnant.**

What the…?

Instantly, I start picking up the other five sticks.

Pregnant.

Pregnant.

Pregnant.

Pregnant.

Pregnant.

Holy shit! I'm not in menopause! I'm with child!

I stare at myself in the reflection of the mirror, and I look exactly how a forty-three-year-old woman with a nine-month-old baby who just found out she's pregnant would look. Absolutely freaked out.

How am I pregnant? I'm on birth control!

"Oh, c'mon, Maria. You're old enough to know that birth control isn't pregnancy-proof. Only abstinence is," I muse, now talking to myself. "And since your husband is crazy hot and you just looooove having sex with him, abstaining is out of the question for you."

Remy and I are going to have a baby.

Izzy is going to have a little sister or little brother.

Holy fucking shit.

Wide-eyed, I stare at myself in the mirror, trying to figure out how I'm going to manage making dinner for the entire Winslow gang now.

And when should I tell Remy? Before or after dinner tonight?

Instantly, I'm reminded of the big surprise he's planned for his brothers.

"After," I tell myself. "Yeah, definitely after. And looks like we're all going to be eating pizza tonight."

Let's hope the mysterious "C" likes pepperoni.

<hr />

Remy

I press a kiss to Maria's cheek, snag a whining Izzy off her hip, and head into the dining room, where the rest of our family is seated and ready to dive into dinner.

After she dealt with a migraine all morning, I'm glad my wife decided not to slave over a hot oven and went with ordering pizza instead.

And by the looks of my brothers' plates, stacked up like they're heathens, it's safe to say no one minds that tonight's meal was catered by the little pizzeria up the street.

Izzy whines in my arms, her little legs kicking against my hip while she tries her best to escape my hold so she can try her hand at crawling around the room.

At nine months old, my girl likes to be on the move.

"Izzy girl!" Lexi calls for her, and thankfully, Izzy spots her right away.

Seated by her high chair, her favorite cousin Lexi is waving at her, and Izzy immediately holds out her hands, letting me know exactly where she wants to go.

And I don't hesitate to set her down, strap her in, and put a few small pieces of watermelon on her tray while Lexi keeps her entertained.

I glance at the screen of my phone, wondering where in the hell my guest of honor is, but there are no missed notifications. *What the hell?*

I would've thought she would've been here by now. Surely she isn't going to stand me up, right?

From across the room, I watch as my beautiful wife takes a seat, her skin glowing with the kind of beauty that always seems to hit me square in the chest, and I decide to sit down beside her and enjoy the meal.

If she shows, she shows. If she doesn't, well—

The doorbell rings, and three knocks sound right after it.

Fucking yes!

Maria looks over at me with a secret smile, and I hop out of my chair to go answer the door.

"Who else is coming?" I hear Jude asking behind me, and I'm practically bouncing on my fucking feet over how excited I am for him to see the answer to that question.

And when I swing open the door, I am not disappointed. There stands Cleo, with a smile on her lips.

"The feeling is mutual, Remington," she says by way of greeting, and I laugh.

"C'mon in, Cleo. It's time to get the band back together like you've wanted for so long."

Her eyes are amused, but she follows my lead, down our entry hallway and into the dining room.

Maria is the first to notice her, and since she is well aware of the whole backstory when it comes to Cleo, she has to bite her lip to fight the urge to burst into laughter.

And then, the dominoes start to fall.

Ty's eyes take up his whole face. "What the fuck?"

Jude looks up, and his jaw practically hits the table. "Holy shit."

And then Flynn, last but not least, unleashes a cackling burst of laughter that has him slapping his hand on the table. *Flynn.* The quietest brother of them all.

"Everyone," I begin the introductions. "This is my friend Cleo. Actually, she's friends with Ty and Jude and Flynn, too. And she was kind enough to agree to join us tonight for a little reunion of sorts."

"It is my pleasure," Cleo says, and I don't miss the way she smiles at my two youngest brothers who are still trying to pick their jaws up off the floor.

"Any friend of Remy's is a friend of ours," Uncle Brad announces. "But if you don't mind my asking, how exactly do you know our boys?"

Jude chokes on his own saliva.

"Many, many years ago, she was our fortune-teller," I explain, and Cleo grins over at me. "The night of my non-wedding's bachelor party."

"What?" Uncle Brad looks around the room. "Who goes to a fortune-teller at a bachelor party?"

"It was Jude's idea!" Ty chimes in.

"Wait…are you a…?"

"No, Brad. I am not a stripper," Cleo answers before he finishes his question, her mouth turning up into an entertained smile.

"What the hell? What idiot planned that for a bachelor party?"

"Uncle Brad, we went to a strip club first, then the fortune-teller," Jude mutters. "Fuck."

I don't miss that Flynn is now eyeing me with amused curiosity, his brain calculating how current events came to be.

"I've been handling her investments," I tell him, and he shakes his head on a laugh.

"You're screwing with me."

"No." I grin. "For the last fourteen years, actually."

"You've been handling her investments for fourteen fucking years, and you never told us?!" Ty shouts. "What the hell?"

"Ty!" My mother is quick to chastise. "We have a guest!"

I'm loving this all too much, I know I am. But after all the shit I've put up with from my brothers over the years, it feels outrageously fun to be the one pulling a stunt.

Maria eventually steps in, introducing Cleo to each member of our family by name and then offering her a seat at the table.

Of course, Cleo takes it all in stride and sits down, her eyes very much enjoying the show around her.

"You like word games, Cleo?" Howard asks, his favorite party trick always holstered and at the ready, and she nods.

"Love word games, my dear."

"Okay, I'm going to give you a word—" he starts to tell her, and she stops him midsentence.

"I know the rules, my dear. Go ahead with your first word."

He furrows his brow, a little creeped out by the whole thing, but does what Howard is so good at doing and just goes with it. "Surprise?"

"Pregnancy."

From beside me, Maria starts coughing into her hand, damn near choking on food or something. "You okay, babe?" I ask her, and she nods erratically, reaching for her water glass to take a sip.

"Fine. I'm fine."

But when I look across the table and meet Cleo's eyes, I don't miss the fact that she's staring directly at me. And she's smiling, like she knows something I don't know.

Then she winks at my wife, and a chill runs up my damn spine.

I look at Maria, and Maria looks at me. She sucks in a breath that makes her face swell up.

"Babe?"

"I'm pregnant!" she blurts out in a rush, her puffed cheeks caving without much fight. "I just took a test today and I was going to tell you after everyone left, but this is too much. I'm pregnant, Remy. With a baby. Our baby. We're going to have another baby."

The room around us erupts into chatter and questions like *"Maria's pregnant?"* and *"Oh, holy shit!"* and *"Oh my goodness, another baby!"* but I do my best to slice through the mental chaos.

This is big news—huge. And my chest feels like it's going to rupture, it's so full.

"You're pregnant?" I ask her, and she nods as tears begin to form in her pretty eyes.

"We're going to have a baby, Rem."

We're going to have a baby.

Immediately, I'm on my feet, pulling Maria out of her chair and up into my arms. With my hands on either side of her face, I stare deep into her eyes and declare three words with every fiber of my being. "I love you."

"I love you too," she whispers back. "I know this is a pretty big deal and crazy unexpected… but…are you okay with this?"

"Am I okay with this?" I repeat. "Ria, I feel like the luckiest son of bitch in the world right now. We're going to have a baby." I reach down and gently touch her stomach. "*Our* baby is growing inside you. Right now."

She nods again, and a few tears streak down her cheeks.

And I can't stop myself from leaning forward to kiss her.

The room explodes into cheering, confusion forgotten and joy taking over, everyone in our family very much in attendance for the moment, but I don't mind. If anything, it feels right.

After everyone stands up to give us hugs and congratulations, somehow, we all manage to sit back down and start digging back into the food. Even in times of celebration, the Winslows know not to let yum-yums go to waste.

But Cleo has other plans.

"I want to thank you all for letting me be here tonight," she announces to everyone in the room. "This has been a real joy. So many faces I know and so many faces I'm glad I've finally gotten to meet. And I'm just overwhelmed by your love and your elation, and I can't wait to see you all expand it with more Winslows soon."

"What? More *Winslows*? As in, plural?" Ty questions and looks at Maria with wide eyes. "Wait…is she—"

"Not twins, my dear," Cleo answers with a taunting cluck and wag of her finger. "Sweet Maria isn't the only one in the room with child."

"I'm sorry…what?" Jude blinks several times, dropping his fork with a clang.

Ty can't stop blinking as he looks around the room.

And with Roman and Ryder crawling all over him like a fucking jungle gym, Flynn looks like he's about to have a heart attack.

Maria isn't the only one who's pregnant?

Holy shit.

"Who is it?" Jude shouts, barely able to stop himself from shooting through the ceiling.

Cleo tuts with a shake of her red-tipped finger. "Now that, my dear, is not my news to reveal. Carrying a child, forming a new life—it's serious, personal

THE END

Did you really think we'd leaving you hanging on a cliffhanger like that?

HA. No freaking way.

We have EVEN MORE Winslow Brothers' fun for you in an *exclusive* Extended Epilogue.

And, we can't deny, you're going to love every second of it.

Download THE REDO'S EXTENDED EPILOGUE at https://dl.bookfunnel.com/f4mow65p91

It's completely FREE and not-to-be missed!

Plus, you're probably dying to find out who else is pregnant, right?

Trust us, you have no idea what you're about to get into, but it's in the very best way. ;) ;)

⌇

Completely new to the Winslow Brothers?

Grab *The Bet* to read all about how Jude and Sophie fell madly in love. Trust us, you won't regret it.

Keep scrolling to read an excerpt if you need a little more convincing!

⌇

BEEN THERE, DONE THAT TO ALL OF THE ABOVE?

Never fear, we have a list of nearly FORTY other titles to keep you busy for as long as your little reading heart desires! Check them out at our website: *www.authormaxmonroe.com*

COMPLETELY NEW TO MAX MONROE AND DON'T KNOW WHERE TO START?

Check out our Suggested Reading Order on our website!
www.authormaxmonroe.com/max-monroe-suggested-reading-order

WHAT'S NEXT FROM MAX MONROE?

Stay up-to-date with our characters and our upcoming releases by signing up for our newsletter on our website: *www.authormaxmonroe.com/newsletter*!

You may live to regret much, but we promise it won't be subscribing to our newsletter.

Seriously, we make it fun! Character conversations about royal babies, parenting woes, embarrassing moments, and shitty horoscopes are just the beginning! If you're already signed up, consider sending us a message to tell us how much you love us. We really like that. ;)

Follow us online:

Facebook: www.facebook.com/authormaxmonroe

Reader Group: www.facebook.com/groups/1561640154166388

Twitter: www.twitter.com/authormaxmonroe

Instagram: www.instagram.com/authormaxmonroe

TikTok: /vm.tiktok.com/ZMe1jv5kQ

Goodreads: https://goo.gl/8VUIz2

ACKNOWLEDGMENTS

First of all, THANK YOU for reading. That goes for anyone who has bought a copy, read an ARC, helped us beta, edited, or found time in their busy schedule just to make sure we stayed on track. Thank you for supporting us, for talking about our books, and for just being so unbelievably loving and supportive of our characters. You've made this our MOST favorite adventure thus far.

THANK YOU to each other. Monroe is thanking Max. Max is thanking Monroe. Yes. We know. We're like a broken record at this point, but we can't help ourselves. We simply *love* writing books together.

THANK YOU, Lisa, for being an editing Queen (please, don't edit the Q to lowercase because you very much deserve the capital) whom we can't live without. We love you to infinity and beyond.

THANK YOU, Stacey, for making the insides of our books always look so pretty! We adore you!

THANK YOU, Peter (aka Banana), for rocking our covers and making ALL the Winslow brothers look sexy AF.

THANK YOU, John, for rolling with the punches we're constantly throwing your way!

THANK YOU to every blogger and influencer who has read, reviewed, posted, shared, and supported us. Your enthusiasm, support, and hard work do not go unnoticed. We love youuuuuuuuuuuuu!

THANK YOU to the people who love us—our family. You are our biggest supporters and motivators. We couldn't do this without you. And we know we just took a vacation, but how about another one? Remy Winslow's book was *looooooooong*. We feel like we need another break. LOL.

THANK YOU to our Awesome ARC-ers. We love and appreciate you guys so much.

THANK YOU to our Camp Love Yourself friends! We love you. You always find a way to make us smile and laugh every single freaking day. You're the best.

As always, all our love.

XOXO,

Max & Monroe